Strindberg's Ghost Sonata and Other Uncollected Tales

Publisher's Acknowledgements

Immanion Press would like to thank Jeremy Brett and his staff, at the Cushing Memorial Library & Archives, Texas A&M University, for providing scanned archive copies of the stories in this book, which made its compilation so much easier. Thanks also to Allison Rich, who administers Tanith Lee's online bibliography 'Daughter of the Night', for her assistance in sourcing the stories and proof-reading the finished book.

Strindberg's Ghost Sonata and Other Uncollected Tales

Tanith Lee

IMMANION
PRESS
Stafford England

Cover Art by John Kaiine
Cover Design by Danielle Lainton
Interior layout by Storm Constantine

Set in Garamond

ISBN 978-1-912815-00-5

IP0151

Author Site:
Daughter of the Night: An Annotated Tanith Lee Bibliography:
http://www.daughterofthenight.com/

Facebook Page for Tanith Lee's readers: Paradys Forum - Daughter of the Night - Tanith Lee

An Immanion Press Edition
http://www.immanion–press.com
info@immanion–press.com

Contents

Fantastic Worlds and Secret Histories

An Introduction by Storm Constantine

Tanith Lee, one of the UK's most talented authors of genre fiction, wrote prodigiously – stories flowed from her as if from an unending, magical stream. She ceased writing only a couple of weeks before her death in May 2015. Over her career, she contributed stories across all genres to anthologies with prestigious editors, released through big publishers, and to well-known genre magazines. But she was also keen to support independent, small press publishers, even if the books and magazines her tales appeared in might only have had small print runs, with little publicity – and, in some cases, little remuneration.

Tanith's stories have been collected in volume form steadily over the years, so that her work is preserved for new generations of readers, but still some remain uncollected. A few tales appeared in such obscure publications they might have been read only by a tiny fraction of the author's loyal readers.

This book collects twenty stories that have not yet appeared in books devoted solely to Tanith's short fiction, and while no publisher can ever again produce a book of freshly-written Tanith tales, some of the pieces in this book will undoubtedly be new to many readers. We're also very pleased to include a story that has never been published before – 'Iron City', which was written in 1987, at the time when Tanith first met her future husband, John Kaiine. Another story, 'The Origin of Snow' appeared only on the author's now defunct web site in 2002.

The stories in this collection are fantasy, rather than horror or science fiction, although 'Elvenbrood' can be termed 'dark fantasy', since it takes place in the 'real world'. Certain stories are both fantasy *and* horror – Tanith enjoyed playing with genres. The collection also includes two stories set in The Flat Earth – among the most popular of the worlds Tanith created.

'Strindberg's Ghost Sonata', the title piece of this collection, was written for *The Ghost Quartet*, edited by Marvin Kaye and published by TOR in 2008. This book contained only four novellas, each of them a ghost story. Tanith's tale is set in an alternate Russia and derives from the 'literature of theatre'. It was inspired by a short play of the Swedish playwright, August Strindberg (1849-1912). The original 'Ghost Sonata' is a surrealistic work, centring upon an apartment building in Stockholm. A young student becomes obsessed with this building, curious about its inhabitants, and eventually manages to inveigle his way inside. Here, far from the idealised view he had of who might live within, he finds a grotesque nightmare – ghosts walk in daylight, a lovely woman is transformed into a mummy and kept in a cupboard, and a bizarre family of strangers conduct peculiar, twisted lives within the building. Tanith clearly saw great potential in creating an adaptation of this work – or at least writing a story inspired by it. As in the original play, the protagonist is a student, who in this rendition is lured into the apartment block rather than being desperate to seek entrance. The inhabitants seem only to want to lavish care upon him, but they hide a secret. 'Strindberg's Ghost Sonata' is a disturbing, atmospheric tale – in which greed and cruelty are disguised as love and longing.

The stories in this book fall broadly into three categories: alternate histories, fairy tales and fantastical worlds, and I'll say a little about each of them, beginning with the tales set in vivid alternate versions of ancient cultures.

'Ceres Passing' is inspired by the myth of Persephone, (the personification of spring), who was the daughter of the Greek crop goddess, Ceres. Persephone was abducted by Hades, the lord of Underworld, and condemned to spend six months of the year there, the dark months of autumn and winter. Her mother never stopped searching for her, wandering the land with a band of weeping women. In this story, a young girl's song attracts the attention of the grieving goddess.

'Persian Eyes' is a horror-fantasy story set in Ancient Rome. A mysterious slave girl is passed from family to family, because none are prepared to keep her. Misfortune follows her or perhaps *is* her.

In 'The Three Brides of Hamid-Dar', set in an alternate Ancient Arabia, a lame street beggar, who is handsome and sought after clandestinely by rich ladies, accepts what he thinks is the usual kind of invitation to a woman's chamber. Except in this case he finds himself plunged into a nightmarish adventure within the desert, confronting three horrific creatures who comprise the Brides of the title.

Some of the stories in this book are fairy-tales, clearly inspired by traditional tales, but spiced with Tanith's ingenuity and rich imagination. While 'Among the Leaves so Green' is set in what appears to be a fantasy world based upon the landscapes of Europe, the author revealed her inspirations alongside the story in its initial publication in *The Green Man: Tales from the Mythic Forest* (2002) "The inspiration came from a long-standing interest in Dionysus who, in ancient Greece, was most decidedly one of the gods of the Wild Wood. Often misunderstood, Dionysus is far more than a wine deity. He is the Breaker of Chains, who rescues not only the flesh but the heart and spirit from too much of worldly regulations and duties. He is a god of joy and freedom. Any uncultivated, tangled, and primal woodland is very much his domain. As for the sisters and their background, they arrived at once and took over. One of the reasons I like writing such a lot: it's always fascinating to see new places and meet new people!"

In 'Elvenbrood', a tale exploring the myth of fairy abduction, a family move to a rural town and here encounter the capricious spirits of the land. As author notes in *The Faery Reel: Tales from the Mystic Forest* (2004), the book in which the story was published, Tanith reveals: "I first had the idea for this story when I was seventeen. It seemed to me that all the wild land in England was being taken over by Man. And so, just like foxes, frogs and owls, the fairy-kind might end up living very close – even in our own fields and gardens. The Elvenbrood themselves appeared mentally before me and have stayed in my mind, therefore, for almost forty years."

'Felidis' features a young man who encounters a strange woman living in the woods – seen as a witch by the local population, but also as a 'cat woman'. Radlo is entranced by Felidis and is compelled to penetrate her secrets.

'Goldenhair' is set in a medieval world, in which an arrogant Lord is forced to confront his cruelty and lust, haunted and tormented by a creature that might be a snake or an animated plait of woman's hair.

The remaining stories are set in fantastical worlds – often inspired by ancient cultures of our own world, but occasionally featuring entirely new landscapes. 'Beauty is the Beast' explores the fine line between good and evil and how much perception shapes our opinions of them.

In 'Cold Spell' a witch challenges the King of Winter to end his icy hold over her country. In order to succeed, she must also outwit Death.

'In the Balance' centres around magical initiation, and the young magician faced with a test of life or death. But the test is not as it seems.

'Iron City', the only previously unpublished story in this collection is a steampunk tale that is more like social commentary than fantastical horror, although it is in places horrific. A serial killer is on the loose, prowling through the dark underworld of a dark, twisted vision of Victorian London.

'The Origin of Snow' and 'The Pain of Glass' are both set in The Flat Earth mythos. In the first story, the demon prince Azhrarn travels to Upperearth to discover the truth behind a prophecy he's overheard concerning the advent of a new god, while in 'The Pain of Glass' a vulture witch compels a merchant to gather a peculiar sand from the desert known as 'Vast Harsh'. The haunted artefact his glass-maker brother-in-law crafts from this sand is destined to change the future of kings.

'Question a Stone' continues a theme Tanith first visited in 'The Woman in Scarlet', a much-anthologised story, first published in *Realms of Fantasy* in 2000. In both stories, the swords wielded by heroes are magically-wrought and possess their own living spirits. While in 'The Woman in Scarlet' the female spirit of the sword betrays the man who wields her, in this story, the spirits occupying the swords of two men, doomed by circumstance to fight to the death, decide how this story must end. The swords have their own desires. In *The Feathered Edge: Tales of Magic, Love and Daring*, in which the story was first published, Tanith explained: "My husband suggested this idea – not the first time he's done that! He also, having heard its description, named the inn. The two swordsmen and the swords themselves quickly made themselves known, including the backgrounds to the secret inner lives."

In 'A Tower of Arkrondurl', a magician seeks to subdue the spirit of a wicked sorcerer, who is allegedly unkillable. How to kill the dead? Especially when they pose a threat to all the world. Only the most imaginative plan will solve the problem.

The heroes of 'Two Lions, a Witch and a War-Robe' must also use cunning and ingenuity to overcome the impossible tasks they are set, under the duress of magic, in order to free the kingdom from a curse. Assistance comes to them in a most unusual and unexpected form.

The last tale in the book 'The Woman' is perhaps the darkest and the most poignant. A young man, Leopard, sees The Woman, a fabled female of his city. To see her is to fall hopelessly in love with her. He is compelled to undergo the trials to win her favour, and perhaps a permanent partnership, but over recent years hundreds of young men have died trying. Who and *what* is The Woman, and how does she wield such power? The answer is not what you might expect.

The book also includes two vignettes. In 'Last Drink Bird Head', a condemned man must choose his last meal. He asks for cheese and the drink Bird Head, which no one has heard of. A woman who loves him resolves to find this mysterious beverage. The vignette was written for a charity publication, called Ministry of Whimsy, in 2009. 'Herowhine' appeared in Anduril magazine in 1979, musing upon what a heroine's true nature might be.

The full publishing history of the stories can be found at the end of the book.

Begin your journey into new realms. Step now into an eerie alternate Russia of ages past, and the bizarre secrets that hide within the walls of a tenement called Perfection…

Strindberg's Ghost Sonata

Sonata: A composition for one instrument or two...
usually in several movements...
Oxford Concise English Dictionary

The Student

ONE

It was Christmas, and he was dying.

Blya Sovinen lay on the ice of the embankment. Above him, the grim stone statues of warriors, and – far below – the partly frozen belt of the River Vlova.

All around, others were occupied as he was, with death. Men, and several women, stretched out or seated quite decorously under the plinths of the damnable statues.

The night was freezingly cold. A white night of winter – the pale blue sky, bright as an early dusk, this effect caused by the icebergs floating offshore to the north and west. The moon hit them, and cast an umbrella of light back into the ether. But light scarcely mattered. It was so cold in the city, they said, fires froze in braziers. Oh yes, it was a night to die.

He himself was spread under the statue of Kurlinsay, the ancient king who had saved the city from invaders many centuries ago. Blya, when he had first looked up, had seen the icicles depending from Kurlinsay's upraised spear and gauntlet. But that had been, surely, three hours before. Blya had heard the bells from the Gethsameen sound three times.

How long it took to die, he thought drearily. Even so long to lose consciousness. Others had been luckier. Their faces for an hour back were blue and empty already.

Something pressed like wetness against Blya's cheek and eyelid. It was unwelcome, intrusive, and too alien even for the infernal night.

His eyes flew open.

Warm light scalded down.

He felt blinded and scorched, and writhed in an agony of rage and distress, his mittened hands pressed to his eyes. Generally the police did not intrude on the process of departure…

And a voice: "No, friend, we are not *police*. No, no. Let me look at you."

"Let me alone!" Blya howled. But *his* voice was little more than a croak.

Then, a woman's tone, soft as a feather, whispered by his ear. "Ssh, baby. There. Look, Oska – *he can be the one.*"

In a torpid horror, like that caused by some paralysing drug, Blya found himself staring into the face of the young woman who bent over him. She was smiling with a sort of joy. The man was only a shadow behind her, though he too had sounded quite young. Something clinked against Blya's clenched teeth.

"Drink, dear friend. It's only vodash. It will do you good."

"Let me – be."

"Never, friend."

What were they? Were they insane? Or – had he passed un-knowing into some limbo actually policed by demons?

Despite himself, a trickle of the fiery, water-coloured alcohol ran into Blya's mouth. He swallowed it. Rather than cough or choke he lapsed back on the ground, feeling the base of the hero's plinth grinding into his cap, his hair, his skull. He was crying. *They* took no notice.

They were devils with gentle hands. They drew him up, there among the other wreckage, the drunks with ice forming on their beards, the ice-white mother and her azure baby, she who alone watched with dying and contemptuous eyes.

"This way, friend. Not too far. Take some more vodash. That's it. This is Zophi. All's well, now."

This city he had known for two years flowed by in a dream. The route was easy and familiar. They guided him – half carrying him like a large toy – off the Heroic Vlova Bridge. Then along North Vista, one of the city's wider avenues. Blya's feet trailed in the road, in snow that was slushy where the braziers burned, (no, not all frozen after all), and slick as vitreous between. Torches like torn banners up on their poles. By the great houses, set back from the street, bloomed ranks of lamps. They soon passed the Cathedral-Church of the Gethsameen, whose opened doors gave on a golden cave. He had the impression of priests processing round and round, bearing the icons of saints in scarlet.

"Holy Mother, I was resigned to Hell. Why didn't you let me die?"

"What's he saying, Zophi?"

"Some foolish thing. Hush, baby. We'll soon be home."

Off the North Vista lay the city domicile of the old Tzaers, called the White Palace. Behind wrought-iron gates, garlanded with fir boughs and silver ribbon, was the little ice-lake. In the midst of this stood the palace, made also to resemble ice, in milk- glass and marble. It had been hollowed to a skeleton by its festive lights. Carriages were parked all along the lake shore, and on the causeway lanterns moved to and fro.

"Or is this Hell?"

"Ssh."

Blya fainted – why not long before – at the turning into Weavers Alley. He knew no more until he woke in the house. *Their* house. A tenement called *Perfection*.

TWO

Blya lay in a stupor for a long while, dimly aware only of warmth, which at first nearly hurt him, then made him burn with fever. Some strange part of himself monitored all this pedantically: He even experienced visions or hallucinations – perhaps fever dreams – of talking with professors at the University, who demanded a firm analysis of his condition from him, and chided him when apparently they thought his opinions too sketchy.

He had studied at the University for one year and eleven months before utter penury drove him out on the streets. He could by then no longer afford books or writing materials, was cast from his lodging on Smite Street, and sold his only coat for a loaf of bread. Most of the bread was stolen from him anyway by militant beggars in the Narzret District. (He had been significantly robbed before. To that their attack was minor.) Hunger stopped his concentration in the classes. One tutor, the always-angry Polinov, struck Blya on the side of the head as he sat drooping from famine on the bench. "Wake up, Sovinen! You're not here to sleep but to learn the greatness of this world." He had been too fuddled to reply. In his twenty-first year, Blya anyway would never have struck back at Polinov, an old man; a wonderful teacher with a heart of granite, and wit only for his subject.

Now Polinov, in Blya's dream, did not hit out; he only declared in ringing tones: "Wait until she sees him." And the other students laughed; only Blya did not know what Polinov meant.

External to his fever-exercised brain, Blya Sovinen was thin as a rail, pale as ashes, but beautiful to behold. Even his sufferings had not yet cancelled this beauty, for he was young, and, in the past, had not been badly nourished or cared for. Jet black curls poured about his face on the pillow. Black brows and lashes indelibly marked his eyes which, when they occasionally undid themselves, were the light blue-green of a spring river of the Stepi. His body, despite being so thin, was well made and strong enough, though slender in natural build. His hands were those of a musician or scholar.

"He's like the picture of a young saint," Timara exclaimed to Zophi, leaning over the delirious man. "Santus Yivan – or the Angel Mihaly..."

All of the girls and women, one by one or in groups, came to flutter or mutter over him. The men of the tenement – called Perfection in the days of the Tzaers – also came to view. They were generally more judgmental.

"Oska – is he good enough? Yes, handsome – exceedingly – but will he *do*?"

Or, more sternly, and not using a pet name, "*Ossif* – will he even *live*?"

Perhaps all this visitor activity was what infused Blya's fever with scenes of interrogation. Perhaps not. Coming back to life when he had been so near the threshold was very difficult – worse in fact, because he was young and not unvigorous. His body pulled one way like a cart horse, his inclination, long ago disgusted by the world's vicious surprises, the other.

But life won.

As a rule, given the right conditions, it does. In one form or another...

At last Blya woke up fully, dazed and cool, his limbs like boneless lead, and saw a crowd of his saviours gathered there, looking at him like an audience.

It had been only two days and nights since his abduction from the Heroic Vlova Bridge. Since *then*, spooning soup between his lips, or water, or Vodash the Water of the Grain, they had become, all these people, nearly his parents.

He stared back at them in the candlelight, through the haze of the rich warmth of the stovepipe that angled up like a white worm in the corner.

"What is this place?"

They told him, almost in unison, like a speaking choir: "The Perfection Tenement."

"On Copper Walk," added one of the older men.

"Why am I here?"

"We brought you here."

Blya's eyes, not dazzled but foolishly clear from recovery, roamed over them. Some were young, and a few quite elderly. A little huddle of old women over there, grannies in head dresses from thirty years before, and two old men, one with a triangular popular guitar across his back.

But a girl came forward, not more than sixteen, a pretty, happy-looking girl, carrying broth in a cup.

"I'm Mariasha – and you are Blachi!"

The pet name for 'Blya'. "How do you know my name?"

"Oh, we asked you. And you said."

Probably it was true. In the delirium the professors had asked his name from him, over and over.

Now they propped him high on pillows. He found he could just manage the broth with both hands. It was good, and had meat-juice in it, even wine, he thought.

Yet they were not wealthy. And this was a tenement, some ancient mansion now carved up into apartments for the working-class. They had put Blya into one of the nicest rooms, a chamber where a pipe ran from the main stove below. They gave him broth and wine. They gazed at him with a sort of *joy*.

Were they crazy? Perhaps some mad sect dedicated to the Virgin, to Christ or some saint?

It was the season of Christmas, the Twenty Days of Light. Maybe they always went out at this time and rescued some poor unfortunate. A charitable act.

No sooner did the broth land in his guts, than sleep put its heavy soft hands down on him.

Someone took the cup.

Laughing quietly, congratulating him and each other, all the people were ambling from the room. Mariasha murmured, "Sleep well, dearest."

He had no choice, the body again making its demands over heart and intellect. Blya slept.

It was morning when he woke again.

Outside, and through the house, he could hear human noises—arguments and calls, children crying or shouting, the clank of pans, feet running up and down stone stairs.

The air in the warm room smelled of flowers.

Blya saw that a pot of lush blue hyacinths had been placed on a small table across from the bed. Their scent was intense, nearly alcoholic. How had anyone grown this plant in winter? Perhaps, having a powerful stove, it had been possible to force the blooms…

He was not sure he really liked the perfume. It reminded him of something read in the previous months, read in another language, and finally watched on stage in his own. A peculiar and haunting work that, although it stirred now along the backrooms of his mind, was so muddied by other associations, he repressed it like a scream. He thought very clearly, however: *A collection of persons trapped like suicidal spider-flies in a sticky and deserved web of their own making – which also snares evil things and innocent things, randomly perhaps, and without pity.*

Then the door opened, and in came a huge woman, fat and majestic, who paused to look Blya over, with, curiously, both approval and *dis*approval.

"Here *he* is," she said.

Where else was he supposed to be?

Behind her stood a youngish boy holding up the gurgling urn of a self-bubble. The aroma of black tea conquered the scent of the hyacinths.

"There now," said the woman. She loomed over Blya as he struggled to sit up. "I am Olcha, the house mother of the Perfection tenement. My word is law here." She seemed quite playful. Playful as a cat is likely to be with a newly-caught mouse. Cruelty and opulence coexisted with great smugness in her round red face.

The tea was served him, and a cherry conserve, and a piece of dark bread only just cooling from the oven. Blya stared at the bread. The urge to weep stumbled behind his eyes and throat.

"Yes, this is for you, handsome little goblin. Eat up and get strong."

Blya held the bread against his lips, kissing, not biting.

But the house-mother of Perfection swung off round the room, and with an awesome whisk of her fat arm, raised a cover from a rotund copper bath. "Koresh there will bring the hot water, soap, razor and towels. The bath will do you good, wash the last poisons

18

of the fever from you, make you wholesome and pleasant."

Blya thought of the house-mother of his own previous wretched tenement near the Smitings. She had been bleak and indifferent to all her charges, letting the house self-bubble go cold, refusing to see to rats or to keep other unwanted visitors out – nor did she like to let wanted ones in. Only those able to bribe her got any service from her, and any who reported her to the landlord she herself then accused of horrible crimes, and so had them thrown out.

"Why?" Blya said, as jolly Olcha pirouetted like a padded, aproned elephant through the room.

"*Why*? To make you fit for society."

"Why this kindness, Mother?"

"Oh, we are very kind here," she threateningly said.

He had the sudden, unassailable notion they would feed him up, wash and groom him, in order to cook and devour him on Christmas Night.

He smiled at this sadly. At least it made some sense to him. Altruism always had its price. He had never met disinterested generosity in his life, save from his father and mother in boyhood. But even they had wanted him ultimately to bribe them, with unqualified affectionate respect, and by ceaselessly studying and passing examinations, and so becoming a scholar of whom they could boast.

Reassured by the macabre idea of providing a good dinner for the house, Blya began to eat the bread and drink the sweetened tea. Presently when the boy – Koresh – came back with hot water, Blya took a bath.

Clean clothes, a shirt and trousers, a jacket, even a waistcoat of old, darned silk, a scarf, a new cap, undergarments of once excellent material—all these were laid on the bed by Koresh. *Of course*, Blya thought dreamily, intoxicated by warmth, tea, and hyacinths, *when they put me in the oven, they'll redeem these clothes. That's all right then.*

But also he thought, *If I grow well, then I'll see the true danger and madness of all this. I'm not sane yet myself, but presumably it will come. God help me, then.*

The Days of Light, the twenty days of Christmas, moved four steps further along the calendar of the city.

Blya Sovinen grew stronger. He got up and wandered about his allotted apartment and then, partly driven out by the scent of the hyacinths, about the tenement. He found cramped seeping passageways, stairs, side chambers and cupboards, and abrupt open rooms of great size, usually untenanted but always full of objects – elder caskets and chests, chairs and cabinets green with mildew, emptied wine crates, heaps of fusty curtains, and so on. Cornices traced the upper reaches of these areas, and whorls of carved leaves and roses indicated where once, years back, chandeliers had hung glittering with crystal and flame.

The *shut* rooms, the cells of the people who lived in Perfection, he did not naturally attempt to enter. But sometimes doors stood wide open, and seeing him the inhabitants always called out some greeting, bleary or cheery, depending on their condition. Some insisted he visit them. They played cards and often sang, if the old man with the guitar was present. Every one of them seemed to know who Blya Sovinen was, and that he was new among them, and extremely welcome.

Surely, for so many people, he would furnish only a small meal, a slice or so of meat?

There were also grand bathrooms in the house, three of them, with marble tubs. Two latrines existed, perched out sidelong from the walls about cesspit tubes that ran down into the paving of the yard to the sump. On the roof, looking east towards the Vlova, a single gargoyle reared, a sort of dragon, but its head was off, and snow had swamped it.

The snow had fallen again while Blya lay unconscious. The city was muffled in a thick white counterpane, from which black smokes rose to an ivory sky. At night the sky was silver, and slits of windows shone dull red and amber, but the bells blasted the atmosphere with ringing accolades to the forthcoming birth of the Christ.

In the evenings a bell rang also in the tenement. Koresh rang it for the house-mother. They all trooped, all the tenants who wanted and had paid, to a communal supper in one of the big old ballrooms on the second floor. Cauldrons of cabbage and onion soup, pancakes and flat black loaves of bread, dishes of sausages made in the Bocsash District, and once a pink salmon caught between the city and the port, and *once* beaming drops like static golden tears – kaviah. Fruit sometimes appeared also, persimmons and apples and bitter black slahs to be eaten with goat cheese and crystallized honey. Vodash constantly passed about the table, and on the third night, an iron-tasting yellow wine in a gigantic bottle large as a two-year-old child and known as a Bible.

What luxury, in this house named Perfection.

Blya assumed a cellar still existed here, overlooked from the days of the Tzaers. He reasoned the house-mother Olcha had valuable connections with grocers, butchers, and fishermen. But doubtless too they had saved for the season. The mystery in it all was only his inclusion.

As when passing apartments, in some of which twelve people resided, he was always made welcome at the feast — in fact boisterously *dragged* down to the dining hall if he was shy, as on the first night he had been. "Payment? What nonsense. You're our guest, Blachi."

Everyone spoke to him as if they had known him for years, needed therefore to ask him nothing beyond what he wanted for his comfort — loved him and valued him. It was so bizarre he had given over questioning it. Either they were deranged or he had died, and entered a curious half-Heaven or luxurious demi-Hell. They even brought him books, when naively he mentioned his lack of them, and sheets of paper and ink, pen, and pencil. They all knew his name.

Conversely he knew nothing about any of them, not even properly remembering half their names. And though they told *him* at once anything *he* asked (aside from why they valued him: "Blachi, you're too modest — why should we *not* value you?"), the ninety or a hundred persons in Perfection had so many complex and varied histories, that he could not individually retain them, or barely. They became for him an entity. It was twenty-seven years of age, or fifty or nineteen, or eighty-two, had worked on the tramlines at Ursusk, fallen through ice at the White Palace lake and been saved, or fought in the Rebellious War, eaten a bear for a bet, and borne sixteen children, fifteen of them now dead, and the sixteenth a rich kept woman on the West Vista.

Occasionally he caught odd snatches of their own conversations. Many of them seemed to be waiting for a visitor — a female in each case — wives, daughters, sisters, he deduced.

Blya's awareness staggered among informations. But they all knew who *he* was. All of them looked at him with affirming affection.

At night he went to bed in the stovepipe room with the hyacinths on the table. Their odour slid him in moments to dense, drugged slumber.

But as he grew stronger, (four days and nights, then six), Blya came doggedly back towards his sanity, all the saneness a volatile young man of imagination and sorrow could possess.

Until then he had not attempted to leave the tenement. That morning he did.

Timara and Mariasha came up to him among the hanging washing in the yard.

"I must tell you a story, Blachi."

Back into the house, with velvet hands they led him.

"This was once a magician's house!"

"Have you heard, Blachi, of Nezchai?"

Blya nodded. He had *read* of Nezchai, an alchemist said to be of part-Mongol extraction, and comparable in some ways, perhaps, to the mighty sorcerer Volkh – who had been not only an exponent of the magic arts, but a shape changer and werewolf. Volkh was still said to have defended the city of Keev against Infidel invasion, rather as Kurlinsay had defended this one.

Nezchai too had been able to take on the form of a wolf. But in those days – three hundred years ago – wild beasts had often ambled the streets of this metropolis, which was then built more of wood, while the vast River Vlova was straddled only by a wooden bridge, which several times burned.

"However," Blya said, consideringly, "I never heard Nezchai kept a house here."

"One of many," said Mariasha.

They had led him up to the attics of the tenement. Even here a few persons made their home. But all were away working, like bees. The last coil of the stovepipe ended in the upper wall. Socks, mittens and coats hung steaming in the heat, giving off the smell of wet wool. Outside the narrow windows lay the landscape of the snow, only here and there a whitened tower or tall roof rising above it.

Mariasha and Timara sat on a carpet near the pipe. He sat with them, not knowing what else to do.

"The house was different then. It was built of wood, but the centre was a stone tower. Part of the tower still lingers in a central wall, and part of the roof of the tower still hangs above this attic. That's why we brought you up here, isn't it, Masha?" Beyond the grimy window glass, thin snow was falling again. Blya watched it, hypnotised.

He thought, *I can't escape them. Someone will always prevent my leaving. Till they're done with me.*

Taking it in turns, sometimes speaking excitedly, or else dramatically, the two young women told him of Nezchai.

It seemed there had been groves or a wood in this area then, and the house stood alone, clear of the original walls of the wooden city, though later urbanity drew in on it. Wolves wintered in the trees, and on white nights Nezchai became a wolf himself, pale as frost, and joined them.

"Sometimes he *mated* with one of the females."

"But she never bore a cub. He was a man, after all."

Miles off from the wooden city was the great port that the Petran Tzaers had built on the northwest coast. The port and the city were linked by the great loop of the River Vlova, and down the river from the sea, even in winter when ice formed at the edges of the water, came ships with slaves to man the sewers of the city, cut logs, and work at the urban building, or other tasks.

"One afternoon," said Mariasha, "the low winter sun was setting lower yet, and the sky was clear, a luminous grey-lavender, with high translucent, cream-coloured clouds lit up by the sunset dripping back on coastal ice-floes…"

Blya stared over at her. Was she quoting from some book? "And Nezchai was walking, as a man, in his black furs above the bank, along the ancient road where now North Vista runs."

"He saw her on a ship."

"Saw whom?" Blya heard himself blurt, like an infant eager for the story. Why had he done this?

"Ah. He saw a woman," said Timara, smiling mysteriously, "so beautiful, even though she stood there among the filthy, ragged, weeping slaves…"

"So *beautiful* that he, the mighty Nezchai, felt his belly light with desire and his heart sag with melting pity," whispered Masha.

How thickly the snow descended now. Blya could not take his eyes from it. And yet, against its twirling patterns, which made the attic space seem to be flying always upward – imagination placed the picture of the wintry river, the antique ship, the girl gleaming there like a diamond.

Such was Nezchai that he spoke a word, and the moving vessel instantly stopped still as if turned to marble.

Only the people on her could move.

The slave-gangs cried and moaned, and the master of the ship rushed up on deck. He spotted the sorcerer at once, positioned on the shore, black in his coats as ebony, and the rings of power flashing on his fingers.

"How have I offended you?" screamed the ship's master and all the sailors, and as many of the slaves as knew the language of the city, and grasped what they were in the presence of, plummeted on their knees howling in fear. But the girl stayed motionless, her eyes cast down now, her hair, which was itself black as a raven's back, mantling her round.

Nezchai only walked down the bank, the ground itself making for him a special track, and when he reached the ice below the bank, a raft of it carried him carefully out to the ship.

I will have her, said Nezchai.

She is only a slave, Lord Magician. She comes from the savage forests to the east, where humans exist disgustingly, like animals.

Nezchai said nothing. He folded his arms.

The master shouted to a pair of his sailors to let her down over the side, onto the ice.

When this happened, the young woman raised her eyes again to the sorcerer. They were dark blue, the shade of Baltic corundum.

She was dressed in rags and dirt like all the rest of the captives. But when her feet reached the ice she said quietly, in a stumbling and heavily accented way, (yet even so her voice like sweet music), *Don't remove me from my people.*

Nezchai took her hand and the bloodied cord that bound her wrists dropped in the river.

You have no people, he said. *There are none to match you. You shall be mine always. My treasure.*

I have been raped and whipped and starved, she answered, without any emotion.

What is any of that to me? Nothing can flaw your perfection. I doubt you are even a human thing, after all.

No, I am not, she replied, *while I live.*

On the soft whirling of the snowflakes, Blya saw her image standing there. Her exquisite face was turned towards him, not to the magician. Her indigo eyes were fixed on his.

Blya's head nodded abruptly, as if he had dozed asleep. The shock – it did shock him – propelled him to his feet.

Some curious spell had been shattered. In bewilderment he saw that Mariasha and Timara were only taking down, in business-like fashion, the dried socks and other garments from the strings across the beams. The two girls were laughing and ordinary.

He gaped at them, unsatisfied, knowing, *without* knowing either how – or what – they had nevertheless cast some skein around him, cerebral, perhaps psychic. A web.

"What became of her, then?"

They turned and smiled on him.

"Oh, if you drop off to sleep, so bored with our storytelling..."

"Why should we bother to tell you more, my darling?"

Blya Sovinen had never shown violence to any man in his life, let alone a woman. But he strode across the attic and both girls, to his consternation, burst giggling and squeaking away from him, as if all of it were a rather chancy game, but one which all three of them knew well.

"*Now* he wants to hear the rest!"

"*Now* he is interested!"

Blya stopped. He felt dizzy. He put his hand on the wall and said nothing.

Then Masha stole up and laid her head against his arm. "*She* came to live in the house. With wicked and indefatigable Nezchai. *Here*. At least, on this spot, before his house was destroyed by evil spirits and flew away in bits through the air, leaving only the tower, which then mostly collapsed. This – our mansion – was built on the site of Nezchai's, two hundred years after. But he was gone by then, down to Hell, they say, for all his terrible deeds."

"So did she too die?"

"Yes, but long, long before," said Timara, also stealing up to his other side. "She was only mortal, despite what she said. Only a short while did she stay as his possession before she died. She was yet quite young. About your age of twenty years."

"Of what..." he hesitated, "...of what then did she die?"

Mariasha spoke: "Of beauty. It was too great for her to bear in her fleshly form."

But Timara murmured, "She died as we all do. It isn't *death* that kills us. It's life that does us in."

Blya sat in his room until the irritating, irresistible bell began to ring for supper and many fists beat on his door, and then a herd of them came in to take him to dine, his parental stranger-friends from the tenement.

His eyes had been wet with tears.

He had kept thinking of it, this girl who died of beauty or of life. What had been her name?

Fool. It was a story.

THREE

He understood by the eighth day that truly they would never let him leave. He had gone out to the yard two or three times, but someone always appeared and led him off somewhere, even to the house-mother's kitchen, where they sat him by the larger self-bubble, and he watched Koresh and a thin girl scrubbing plates and pots. Once Blya had even sought one of the two yard latrines, and hidden there, looking out through the tiny eyelet in the door to see when the area might be vacant. At first there were endless arrivals and departures – people going to their work, or to shop for provisions. Others wanted the conveniences, and one man, old Zergoi, rattled on the door, calling cheerily, "Are you ill, child?"

"No," Blya replied sheepishly, "just a touch of the winter trouble."

Later, when the yard had been utterly depopulated and no one was either at a window above, or loitering in the wide doorway, Blya darted out and hurried towards the yard gate. The instant he reached it Staivn and Ossif appeared from the snowy walls beyond, carrying between them several huge logs in a sling. "Give us a hand, Blachi."

Had they lain in wait?

Blya said, "I wanted to go to the market."

"Oh, why do that? Koresh or Mother can get you anything you want. That way you won't have to pay for it, either."

Helping swing the heavy fire-logs in along the tenement corridor, Blya said very bleakly, "You won't allow me to leave the house."

"Decidedly not," said Ossif, surprising Blya by such frankness.

"*Why* not?"

"Because we love you. You're dear to us."

"*Why?*"

"Don't stall with those logs – you're worse than a bad donkey, Blachi."

Staivn said, "Has no one ever loved you, Blya, that you can't accept this gift? Are you so unlikeable? We've never found you so."

"Am I your prisoner?" Blya said, as they heaved the logs into the store beside the colossal white stove.

Staivn laughed. "We're all prisoners of something. It could be worse, couldn't it? The prisoners of the ancient Tzaers used to rot in green dungeons, gnawed by rats. The present authorities use similar methods. Much nicer to be the prisoner of your friends."

The tenth night of the Days of Light was Christ's Eve, the Night of the Dead. Blya, on the eighth day, conceived a different plan. For surely some of the people in the house would go out to visit a local graveyard, to put paper flowers, cakes, and vodash on the graves in respect. He might be able, under cover of this, to slip away.

Trying to prompt some of them to suggest or intimate the intention of honouring this custom, Blya wandered again about the tenement. (In his room, the pot of hyacinths had achieved a thick threnody of perfume, somewhere between the delicious and the decaying. It was impossible to sit there long, and at night when he slept, he felt the fleshy blooms striking like blue velvet hammers in his brain. He woke always with a headache that dispersed only once he was elsewhere in the house.)

He believed he was quite sane now.

The notion he was to be a Christ's Eve dinner for the tenement's citizens had left him. Whatever this was, it must be far worse.

He climbed the long shallow flights of stone stairs up to the attics, passing as he did so girls with baskets of washing, Yori the cobbler stitching shoes in the room he shared with five others, and then Zergoi, playing the triangular guitar, leaning on a banister.

All greeted Blya, none detained or coerced him. None spoke of going out to honour the dead on the Tenth Night.

Blya thought, *Perhaps, from the attic roof there is a way down to the street, unseen and unexpected…*

As he came up onto the last flight, which was narrower and the steps wooden, an alien sound went through the air.

What was it?

It was like a guitar string snapping – or a pane of thinnest ice cracking right across, with a high, dull, metallic yap.

Blya paused.

Above, the landing was shadowy, for the windows up here were small and caked with dirt inside and snow out.

He had thought this part of the premises uninhabited by day – his main reason for finally roaming up to it. The denizens of the attics worked all of them from dawn to twilight at various manufactories and mills to the east of the city over the river. Some worked through portions of the darkness too, creeping back at midnight like mice, drunk with exhaustion and vodash – yet on such nights they slept lower in the house, to save themselves the stairs.

But now, after all, a figure was there, standing above Blya on the landing.

The weird breaking note quivered again, plucking at Blya's nerves.

Miles below he had heard all this beneath the murmur of Zergoi's guitar, yet now even this seemed to be fading away, not as if the recital ended, more as if the lower house were metaphysically detaching itself from the upper.

A deep silence enfolded the attic region. And she came out along the landing and stepped onto the stairway. She moved as if rather unsure of the stairs, as if she were not yet *used* to stairs, having lived all her brief young life on flat surfaces, with the only tall things being trees or mountains she did not think to climb.

Her hair was unbound, and so long it drew around her slender shape a thick black pencilling, almost, he thought, to her knees. She was pale as an ermine, and her eyes were lowered. In her left hand she carried a little dish and seemed to be studying it with her cast-down gaze.

Blya stood back against the bannister to let her pass.

She descended towards him, step by slow, graceful, cautious step. At the last moment, as she trod down onto the stair he too occupied, her face tilted up. She stopped quite still, looking at him. Her eyes were an extraordinary dark blue, like polished coals made into mirrors. Her loveliness was dreadful. It was unbearable.

As if she knew, her eyes flooded with tears of shame. She glanced away from Blya, who stood there speechless, not four feet from her, unable himself to move. In a blank despair, a sort of horror, he watched her further descend the wooden steps.

She had given off no human warmth; the skirt of her dress, brushing by him, had been insubstantial.

At the bottom of the stair, in the split second before she turned the corner, she vanished.

There could be no doubt she did this. You could not tell yourself you had imagined it. One breath she had been there, then she had exhaled herself back into some dusk otherness, with the smooth down stroke of a soundless sigh.

That eighth night all of them, *all*, crammed into the ballroom for the evening feast. Even the poorest members of the tenement, though obviously they could have paid nothing into the communal purse. Or perhaps they had—what could Blya know for sure? Blya looked at them, this hundred or more, this entity and mass.

Elderly road-sweepers rubbed shoulders with clerks and neat seamstresses. The lamplighter from the northwest streets sat beside a plump whore, chatting, doubtless each knowing the other from their dissimilar street-walking. Combined now with the refined attention of some was the coarse pathos and uncouthness of others, slurping wine from saucers, taking off boots and cutting their toenails and flicking the debris behind the stove, chuckling that the house-mother paid no heed, or else lachrymose as another large wine-Bible lumbered with the vodash down the long tables.

They all, whatever their calling or condition, seemed delighted with each other, and the world.

The big room had been decked too with boughs of fir. Silver-papered nuts hung from candle branches now each with two or three candles burning in them, some tied with bright red crepe to prophecy the sacrifice of the Christ. Yet this was the eighth night still, the celebration two nights early . . . were they then celebrating some other thing, special to the house, though now incorporated with Christmas?

As the first Bible flagged, another one appeared.

No one chided Blya for his set, brooding face. Rather they kept toasting him. All of them used his name, or the pet name 'Blachi' he had not heard since he had been a child with his parents.

He sat between Ossif and Zergoi, who filled his glass with the wine, and then, when the food began to come, ladled off cuts of salt beef, sour cream and dumplings onto his platter.

What have they done? How is it possible?

"Cheer up, sweet prince," said Ossif at last.

"Let him alone. He's our blessing," amended Zergoi.

From her large chair among the benches, the house-mother rose. She raised her goblet. "We salute the night!"

They clambered to their feet and roared and drained their glasses or mugs.

Only Blya Sovinen remained seated.

Then, when they all sat down, he got up and walked along by the table to stand next to the mother, Olcha. She looked up at him, her face already dewed with sweat from the hearty meal. "Yes, handsome goblin, how can I assist you?"

Blya turned his own face away. Disgust stifled his thoughts. He did not know what could be said and grasped none of it. As he strode out of the ballroom, Mariasha dashed up from her place and ran after him. She caught up to him in the passageway. "Blachi – Blya – come back! Share our happiness."

"There's no happiness."

It was dark in the passage; the flaming light of the dining room excluded by the corridor's coiling progress. They might be standing inside a worm, its inner walls dripping moisture, echoing stupidly with far-off laughter and cries from hidden outer places.

"Blya, there *is* happiness and joy. Oh, you've made us so happy. And don't you think we *deserve* a little happiness in our poor lives?"

"No. None of us," he whispered, "*none* of us do."

"But Blya, how can you think *she* could be content to live always in *oblivion*. Isn't it better to bring her back to us? We're like her family, Blya. Since I was a child, I've known her, *seen* her. *Felt* her go by me. Sometimes she speaks. Can you imagine that? Her voice is just like in the story, accented and hesitating, and full of a pure music."

"She's dead. She died three centuries ago."

"Yes, of course. In a way. But we – and those before us – and now *you* – give her life."

"It's unholy. Worse than that, intellectually wrong. And how can I have given her life?" But as he said this, Blya blindly guessed the truth of her words, and his heart sank like a stone into a frozen river.

"Sometimes she fades away. Three hundred years – it's been such a time for her. After she died, mighty Nezchai couldn't bear to lose her beauty. At first he embalmed her dead body by his arts…"

"Horrible!"

"But the finished body was hard as alabaster, and the face had no personality. The eyes – shut. It gave him little pleasure and eventually he put it away in a vault where, they say, in the end… the rats…"

"Christ – Christ – don't tell me anymore…"

"Then naturally I won't. But this I *will* tell you. He had to have her still. And though he could not restore her flesh – by his power he brought her back to him. His magic was so strong – it outlasted even Nezchai. And now, whenever it seems she flags, *we* bring her back. It happened when I was a baby. She faded then. Like a lamp sinking for lack of oil. The whole house was full of fear and crying. But they found a young woman that time in the city, and Orena came here, and *she* was summoned back by this new young life – Orena's youth and vitality and good looks. Blya, that is what guides her here. Like a traveller to a beacon – like a moth to a flame. And love. Love most of all. *New* love. Do you see? She becomes accustomed to us, to Orena, too, as to others in the past. And so, again we must wake up the fire. And you – *you* love her? Yes, you must, or how else have you brought her into the house again? Even when you were hearing the story, you fell in love with her then. We hadn't seen her, any of us, for a month – it was like a year to us. The tenement is named for her, I suppose you realised. Perfection. *Hers*."

Blya's ears were singing and drumming at the loud angry stamping of his heart. He leaned on the moist wall, dimly aware that others had now followed them out and filled up the worm of the passage, like shit, he thought, gathering in a cloaca.

Nevertheless, his mouth formed words he could not resist.

"What's her name?"

"She? Oh, she's always called The Swan. For her grace and paleness, her long throat. Nezchai called her that. Decades after he was dead and all the first house blown to bits and carried off by demons, *she* was seen here, wandering among the huts that people lived in on the waste ground. All loved her, Blachi. How could anyone not love her? Not want to *keep* her. She is *ours*. We must have something beautiful in our lives. We must have something."

"She isn't your – possession."

"No. Our treasure. As she was Nezchai's. Our secret, too. None of us would betray it, even under torture And nor could you."

"I," he said bitterly. "*I*. Your insect."

"Only *love* her, Blachi. Keep her alive. It's so simple."

"*She's a ghost*. She is a ghost and you shut her out of Heaven."

"Oh, and is there a Heaven, Blya Sovinen?" Mariasha's voice was tired and flinty. "How can we know? We're only shown this harsh world, and then an open grave. If she's able, through Nezchai's possessive sorcery, to evade *that*, why shouldn't we help and have her? Like – like a hyacinth in winter, when no flowers grow."

Blya raised his eyes. At the twist of the passage, just before it bulged back into the ballroom and the feast, balked the fat house-mother, smiling. She held a slice of beef in her hand. She spoke across the rest, who respectfully listened. "Evil, not beauty, killed The Swan. But it was *love* trapped her here. Love, Blya Sovinen, however selfish, warped and lunatic, however soft, kindly and adoring, is always stronger than evil. And therefore, far more terrible. "Lifting her hand, the Mother crammed all the meat into her mouth and ate it in one gulp.

FOUR

The ninth and tenth day he lay on his bed in the hyacinth smoke, (which now smelled to him of burning houses and dead rats coated with scented blue powder).

He refused to go about the house.

But oh, he heard all the others coming and going, and now and then, perhaps deliberately vocalised outside his door: "I have *seen* her!"

"She has returned."

"More lovely than ever."

"Last night I met her in the annexe by the fourth cupboard, and she said quietly, *It is night now*."

He was reminded of reported visitations of the Virgin, said to have occurred in the Narzret District a year before. She had reappeared at some sacred spot. This washerwoman or that drunk had seen her. A two-month wonder.

But this, in the tenement, would not end so swiftly.

Blya asked himself what he had done and been made party to. And also he prayed, as – for five years – he had never done.

"Oh God. Correct this error. You supposedly see even the sparrow's fall. Each of us is numbered upon the eternal nacre of your carapace, like stars upon the endless skies."

But once Blya Sovinen, then sixteen years of age, had heard a priest say, "God will always listen, but rarely will He answer."

Besides, it was no use.

Food and drink were put outside the door. Whenever he went to collect it, (despising his own hunger), no one was ever there. Only the beehive hum of the house explained to him it still intransigently existed. His prison. And once he had chewed a crust, drunk down the tea or alcohol, Blya slept, and dreamed of The Swan. She walked slowly towards him, in an antique gown of hyacinth blue, holding her little white dish in which something golden seemed to lie. And in his dream, he always went to her. He took hold of her. Nor did she vanish then. She laid her perfect head on his shoulder, her hair glimmering over them both like black rain or a river. He *felt* her body on his, her *warmth*.

He loved her. As Masha had said, how could he not?

What had she been to be so beautiful? It was her beauty which had trapped her, for it was her beauty which caused this vampiric love from all who were able to recognise her, regardless of their gender or sexual inclination.

No wonder she had begged the magus to leave her with her own people on the slave ship. *They* apparently had *not* been able to see her properly. Not to see she was a piece cut from Heaven, a treasure on earth never to be let go.

Other dreams came.

He married her in the Cathedral-Church of the Gethsameen, he and she crowned with willow and gold wire. He made love to her on a huge white bed, never quite seeing all her loveliness un-concealed, never quite reaching the climax of lust, detained by her serene sad face upon the pillows, void as a fallen star.

When the tenth night came, Christ's Eve, the Night of the Dead, he had forgotten all about his former plan to slip away.

Zophi, Masha, Timara and Staivn entered, having barely rapped on the door.

They behaved as if this had all been agreed between him and themselves, a pre-arranged treat, for which he had omitted to be ready out of playfulness.

"Look! There's the hot water. Shave quickly, Blachi."

"Here's a greatcoat. It was one of Yori's son's coats – but he's rich and away in Archaroy – it will fit you."

"Now, the comb for your hair. Such tangled locks."

They laughed and bounded round him.

He let them make him do things. It was all nonsensical. Listlessly, he said, "Are we to go out then?"

"Up to the roof, dearest Blachi."

Zophi and Masha told him how, since it was the Night of the Dead, plenty of people from the tenement, who had no urge to visit anyone in the city graveyards, would climb out on the house roof to hear the bells from the Gethsameen and other churches, and to watch the processions of lights.

"Have you ever seen the candles and torches from high up?"

Dully, Blya answered he had not.

Last Christmas, on this night, as he remembered, he had still not been badly off, and had got drunk at a cheap restaurant on East Vista, with two or three other students from the University. He then went to bed with a wild blonde girl. In the morning – Christmas Day – he had sat alone in his lodging, his aching head anointed with oil of rosemary and lavender, working at his studies. In the evening he wrote a dutiful letter to his mother and father. (This year he had had some superstitious plan of writing them another, by now post-mortem, letter, and carrying it on this very night to the graveyard of the Santa Ukatrin. Here he would have pinned it up on a post already thick with other such communications to the dead. But that wish had been mere self-indulgent folly. What would he even have said to them, now they were dead, and everything had changed? That he was a fool, and deserved nothing better than a death on the Heroic Bridge?)

But as for last year's Night of the Dead, he had a memory only of the lamps and lights streaming up and down beyond the restaurant windows, as he sat over salt fish, pickles, and black vodash. And there had been lights under the window, too, where he had gone with the blonde.

How wonderful she had been, that girl. Alluring enough, with slanting Eastern eyes, but freckled and with big ugly feet. So divinely human. Flawed – like an emerald.

"There we are now. He's quite ready."

In another place and time, Blya recalled he had loved the blonde for her imperfection. And though next day he had forgotten her until now, *now* he wanted her back. Conversely, he had never wanted to reclaim his parents, even when dead. They withered, like their last gifts, from the vine of his life, as dead things must...

"There we are now," said Timara again. "Now we've tidied him, what a charming young being he is. No wonder..."

"No wonder," glowed Zophi, "he proved quite irresistible..."

Staivn had wiped and folded up the razor.

I should, Blya Sovinen thought. *But I should – what?*

All up the stone stairs, moving among the throng of the others, toting their bottles of drink, their cakes, and their own candles as yet unlit. All the way up the wood stairs to the attics. He was sick with dread that suddenly, as before, she would be there in front of him, in front of them all. The Swan.

But she did not – *manifest.*

Had they been mistaken? Had he? Some strange mesmeric communal hallucination brought on by their determined greed?

In the attics, among new, down-hanging forests of steamy socks, stockings and shirts, Mariasha gently blindfolded him. *They know, even now, if I could I'd escape them…*

But Zophi said, "It's not just you, Blachi. Lots of us can't bear to look when we're on the roof stair, it's so dangerous, more a ladder – but safe enough if the surefooted ones guide you."

A madhouse. Climbing ladders blindfolded or with eyes squeezed shut. Like life. Or death.

They guided him up the stair, which was indeed a sort of ladder, and also so meanly made that with every step, two-thirds of each foot poked back off the tread. You must go on tiptoe, and not breathe. He counted fifteen of these stairs, then he was assisted out into the clear crystal ice-breath of the night. The blindfold was drawn off. He stood up. Sections of the city lay spread below, from Copper Street to North Vista. Startlingly near, the Vlova snaked in a sugared rope, beyond darker walls from which some of the snow had dropped away. (The river was partly frozen solid, it would seem, though the muscular current would keep a central channel free.) A galaxy of veiled windows, street-lamps and torches dotting like amber and garnet beads the better thoroughfares, did not rival the glittering ice-quills of the stars above, where some enormous diamond bowl might have been shattered in the air. *Numbered… like stars upon the endless skies…*

Blya drew breath. The cold stung his lips, flayed his lungs. The night itself was clean.

He looked over the parapet. The rail was neither very sturdy nor raised much higher than his knees, yet every one of them crowded all about, sometimes even slipping on the surface of the roof, which

35

was flat here. Over the pyramid of a Dutch gable, the dragon gargoyle craned headlessly from the snow.

Copper Street, directly below, was formless, these slums darker than the places nearer the Vista.

Staivn and Ossif had produced pocket watches.

"In one moment only – the bells."

And abruptly then all the churches across the city woke to their midnight tumult, clanging and ringing together and out of tune, one colossal bellow of bronze and iron.

At once the processions began everywhere below.

"Do you see, Blya?" asked the soft voice of Mariasha at his side.

Out of a thousand, thousand houses, tenements, huts, down steps, cobbled hillocks and stairs, over bridges; lamps and lanterns, torches, candles, tapers – the torrents of the lights came pouring.

Like golden threads running on some vast unfathomable machine of great magnificence, some clockwork device perhaps inside the brain of God. Together and away, around, beneath, above. Every street and alley, valley and rise of the city, fluttering as if on fire, weaving woof and weft to make some garment of flame, or coin some new serpentine currency for the use of angels.

"See how beautiful it is, Blya," said Masha's low voice, muffled a little by the bells and by her fur hood.

And Blya saw the beauty of the streams of fire, webbing and threading back and forth.

Yes, after all, beauty was easy enough to fashion. Men created it, he had once thought, from a memory of the ethereal world beyond the earth, to which, once liberated, they could go back...

"Why do they do this thing?" Mariasha now murmured, her voice lower yet and remote too, and strange. "When I see it, I ask then, why?"

"To honour Christ," he said, unthinking, hypnotised by the threading fire as before by the falling snow.

"Who is Christ?"

Blya turned.

All the others had drawn off to the edges of the flat roof. They were motionless, hands clasped, some of them, as if in prayer or supplication. Their faces were stamped with all the expressions known to mankind in transports of enlightenment. But Blya did not even glance at their faces.

It was not Mariasha beside him.

The Swan stood there.

Her eyes were wide as his. *His* eyes seemed to stretch his bones, like two open mouths that tried to roar or scream.

Yet he heard himself say coldly, "Did the enchanter never tell you of Christ? Nezchai lived in Christian times. Did *no one* ever say?"

"Perhaps they have said," she replied. Her voice was sweet. Like music.

Blya stepped back from the apparition called The Swan. He went quickly over the roof, over to the opening. He nearly ran, and mostly slid, down the uncanny ladder-stair, landing in the attics, catching at and pulling loose the woollen stockings and shirts, like hollow feet and torsos of the truly dead.

FIVE

The house-mother Olcha was positioned between Blya Sovinen and the door of his room. Her fat bulk that had, he surmised, nothing *yielding* about it, blocked his way, a fearful *military* bolster.

"Let me by."

"Ah, clever goblin. Not only handsome but wise."

"*Let me…*"

"To catch her interest, our white Swan. Then to fly away. What can she do but pursue you, Blya of the curly hair? Honey to her you are, honey that makes even a butterfly stick."

"*God help me!*" he shouted.

The words hit the ceiling of the passage.

She was not discomposed – or at least, seemed not to be.

Her voice was like that of a human wolf.

"Once I was the bait for her, Blya Sovinen. *I.* Yes – this bulbous slab of meat. Once I was slim and charming as you, my baby. Years back – ten, fifteen years. I was Orena then – what? They *told* you? Pretty Orena from the sinks of the city, still good enough to offer to our Swan. Didn't you think, *thoughtful* little *boy*, that 'Olcha' is the familiar version of Orena?"

Blya put his face to the wall. "What am I to do?"

"You spineless, shell-less crab – what can any of us *do*? Your best. That's what you must do. What more is plausible?" She stood back in a barrage of skirts and malignity that long ago – just conceivably – had been lissom and hopeful and not unkind.

"There's your door. Go in. Go in, shell-less crab, and *hide* under your stone. "

Marvelling in a wintry horror, he went by her and through the undone door.

The room was solid with the putrefaction of the dying hyacinths, which seemed to have cast a web all about from wall to wall, as the pure processional lights of the Night of the Dead had webbed and woven the city. They had been benign. This, poisonous.

He slammed the door, crossed to the pot of flowers, lifted it to smash it, pointlessly, on the floor. Remembered the theatrical drama he had read and witnessed, it seemed so long, long ago… the other web *it* described, which had formed of small-minded, awful wickedness, remorselessly trapping not only the cruel, the stupid and the unjust to punish them, but also the only innocent, and the supernaturally evil.

Then the pot fell from his hands, smashing as he had thought he meant it to.

The Swan was in the corner, quite near the pipe of the stove. She still carried her little dish, with something gold shining in it. Her sorrowful eyes met his. To be so beautiful – it must be for her as if, he thought, she had been drenched in vitriol…

He crunched over the broken pot, the flowers, and reached her and said, "I am irredeemably in love with you. It's too late. Everything is over." And this was like what had happened to him before, after the play.

But The Swan put out her right hand and touched his face. He could not feel it. Of course not. She was a ghost.

The Swan

ONE

As soon as the sun gained its nadir, the trees of the forest became animals and spirits. It was possible, even in daylight, however, to see what kind of creature each might really be, and so be extra wary of it.

For example, the thin high pine in whose serrated trunk might clearly be spotted the snake-head and folded wings of a dragon. Or the little birch in the glade, damaged by recent lightning, and so beheaded of its bare winter crown, that even so resembled the clawed hand which, after dark, it became, rummaging along the ground, scratching and snuffling after unwary beasts and men.

Thirteen years old, the child had been numbered as a woman for three years. But also she, too, was not quite human. Her mother had conceived her, as sometimes happened, while the male partner was away at a long summer river fishing. Many of the men went to the fishings. They lifted whole colonies of blue sturgeon and black salmon from the waters and salted them for winter provisions. Several men came back, too, and found their women carrying progeny that could hardly be theirs. Some killed their mates as faithless. Others shrugged, carefully marking the stay-at-home man who had probably sired the baby, to see if his genetic virtues were worth raising in the home hut. Now and then a wife went straight to her house-bonder on his return. This the child-woman's mother had done.

It seemed the bond wife had been out tending a village cornfield in the clearing, with other women. But she was overtaken by an unusual sleepiness and had, in the late afternoon, lain down between the standing stalks. She woke alone and alarmed as the last glow guttered through the trees. Worse, standing up, the woman found a wetness between her legs and on her skirt, not blood. In the crimson shadows, plainly showing among the young cornstalks, were uncouth footprints, webbed, like those of some water bird or – more likely – demon, coming toward her and going away. Sensibly the woman rushed at once to her nearby village and brought back everyone she could to witness these prints. They were quite obvious still in the twilight, though by morning they had faded.

The woman told her returned house-bond humbly that he might

kill her if he had to, but he had still better wait till the child was birthed. Otherwise the demon might be angry at the waste of its seed.

Later a travelling priest, one of the Volkheshy, tramped through the village. He bent to tap the woman's distended belly and told them all she would bear a magical child; on no account must she or it be slaughtered. In the future it might prove significant.

The Volkheshy were feared and respected. They alone could wander about the Lesha, the Great Forest, free from danger through their knowledge of gods and powers of sorcery.

When the child was born and began to grow, it was seen anyway that it was a very bizarre thing, slender and proportionate, a female, but not made like the usual villager of either sex, who was stocky and grew low to the ground, mid-dark of skin and hair. The demon's get had a white skin and hair black as the black feathers of certain birds. Her eyes were of a colour seen only in the sky of high summer nights, when the sun did not quite sink – or on winter nights, when the ice floes to the far north threw back moonlight on the earth's ceiling. None of this was believed to be attractive in her. But certainly it confirmed her mother had not lied.

Now the girl ran through the trees in order to escape impending tree elementals let loose at sundown. She understood besides if she met her true father, the water demon – who undoubtedly lived in the swamp an hour's journey off – he would at the least push her over and do to her the self-same thing he had done to her mother. At *worst*, he would abduct her. She would be sunk in the mud and thick green swamp water. Here she would live in captive misery, or else simply drown.

The anomaly of her position had always been totally commonplace to her: to be unhuman yet bound by human laws of obedience, superstition, and survival.

It did not, any of it, seem strange to her. She never questioned. None in the village did. They made offerings to sky, lightning, wind and fire, to the Lesha, to the earth – the last, holding clods of soil in their hands, eating them even, for emphasis.

That her human foster father had already routinely forced her, and thereafter carnally used her on countless occasions, never mentally jarred against the to-be-avoided rape by the *demon* father. (Nor the fact that, during visits from her two uncles, hunters of prowess who always brought gifts of bear and squirrel meat, grey cat or wolf pelts, she was loaned to either or both of them like a warm blanket.) Such duties befell all daughters among the huts. Nothing in her was ever uneasy with her *mortal* life. She did not ache or pray for change. Only her given name sometimes troubled her. In the ancient tongue of the Lesha it meant White-Feather-Black-Feather-Sky-Blue. But generally she was called a name to do with her blood-father's webbed feet.

She reached the hut that night unscathed. It was just twilight. The single space was full of turgid murk, and on the open hearth rested a black bronze cauldron, full of ingredients such as dried meat, cow's milk, wild civia, grass. Three crocks stood about, with liquid fat burning a low, yellow flame. By this obfuscation everyone had learnt long ago to see.

Webbed had gathered roots and berries in the forest. Now her mother rose and tipped the leather bag out on the floor, searching through the haul, clucking and clicking over it.

No one else was there yet. Webbed sat down to clean off roots with a flint.

"Something comes," said the mother, presently. Webbed looked at her. "Old Woman say so. Bad. This night, all we go out."

"Out," repeated Webbed.

She knew what her mother referred to – not the threatening idea of the *coming* something, but the grim, tiring ritual that must be enacted if the Old Woman decreed. It had been performed twice before in Webbed's lifetime. Once she had been only six: too young to attend. She had seen her mother steal from the hut, and her elder sister, then not house-bonded elsewhere. Her foster father had turned on his side, feigning sleep. Men were not permitted to attend this semi-religious, magical act. The second time Webbed was eleven, and she too had had to go out. She was still a virgin then, which made her extra valuable at the rite, though why she never knew. Nor did she puzzle over it. Now her value that way was over.

"Hush," said her mother. Not because Webbed had spoken. *Hush* too was ritual. It meant, *Say nothing.*

The human father, who had been herding animals, then drinking khoumis with other men, did not arrive home until another hour had passed.

They ate some food. One of the village cows had been

slaughtered, and a slab of meat was added, by the man, to the brew in the cauldron. This obviously did not cook enough to be tender. The father was strengthened by the bits of half-raw meat and mounted the mother in their corner of the hut. She showed pleasure, naturally. It was a sign of his favour to take her, when he had a youngish daughter still to hand.

With the ritual in the offing, really it was fruitless to sleep. But Webbed was worn out from her berry-gatherings in the forest, which had started just after dawn. Therefore, she did sleep, until her mother roughly yanked her arm. Then, without a pause, Webbed got up, retied her hair by its scrap of dried gut, and followed the older woman from the hut. (As she did so, in the night-low ebb of the hearth, she saw her father turn hastily again on his side, not to see.)

Even late summer here was cool by night, for the sun by this time of year was all down. Outside the huts, under the still palish northern sky, the gathered women were like bears or cats or deer themselves, closed in their skin and fur garments.

The Old Woman led the procession from the village, towards the furthest of the field-clearings. The trek took half an hour. All the forest was by now full of phantom animals and elementals, but the Old Woman, waving her stick topped by a wolf skull, brushed them off. She was the daughter of one of the Volkheshy, and so she had this talent. Also she could foretell, which was the reason she had ordered them out tonight.

"Something coming," muttered Webbed's half-sister.

"What is?" another young woman asked.

"She not say."

A fact. The Old Woman had not.

In the chosen field she called a halt. It was an eerie spot, under the wide sky but with the soaring black trees ringing it round, full of unseen eyes watching, and vaguely heard demon-mouths whispering.

The corn had failed in this field. Which was why the Old Woman had brought them here.

She went about the women, young and old, tapping some of them with her wolf stick.

At length she selected three, an elderly widow, a young mother, and a girl of twelve.

They all knew what must be done, apart from the twelve-year-old, who became frightened, rolling her eyes when she, along with the widow and mother, was tied by a tough rope of bog-grass to a hefty rock lying partially embedded in the blighted field.

The other women quickly assembled to beat these three 'draught-beasts' with twigs and pine-switches, shouting loudly they must pull the plough. The young girl began to cry. But she strained as the others did to hoist the rock from the ground. Eventually it came out. Then the three women were made to drag it round the entire circumference of the field, the rest running along with them, still calling and shouting, casting down pebbles they had picked up on the way, or tiny skulls of birds or rats, in the uneven track – the furrow – the rock randomly made.

When the circuit was complete, the Old Woman went forward and yelled at the field: "Evil that threatens be closed in as this blight is by the furrow of the plough. May the sun burn you up as this field is burnt. May the lightning strike you. Mother Earth swallow you in her moist black mouth. "

The other women shouted some of the words too, even the elderly widow, who was exhausted, and the sobbing girl.

Webbed also shouted the words. She did not think about it. Such things were needful, happened. She felt only a faint anxiety about creatures in the woods, and her own overbearing tiredness.

A silence dropped from the sky when the shouts were done.

Drained, they stood gazing at the Old Woman. But she only spat on the ground, then turning, raised her staff and shook it again, glaring at the ring of forest to the west.

Usually she was able to dispel elementals quickly. But now her caws and shakings went on.

The other women, Webbed too, becoming perturbed, looked where their witch did.

A weird flutter of brownish-reddish light was leaping towards them through the trees.

Only the youngest two or three women shrieked. The oldest, she who had ploughed, groaned and said, "Not tree-things. Is torches…"

They had one moment more to be perplexed, even reassured. No man of the villages would dare come after them at such a time. This guarding spell was female, taught only to girl children by the earth herself.

The moment passed.

Out of the trees ran big, bear-like forms, men after all in thick, shining furs, the torchlight lashing bright above and around them. Many waved sticks, not capped like the Old Woman's with a skull, but which instead suddenly let out sharp farting cracks of sparks and thin smoke.

Astonished, the women saw Old Woman spin around. It must be some new magic to disperse these monstrous intruding strangers... But no. No, it was not magic, or if it was, an unrecognisable one. For the Old Woman spun and fell and lay prone on the field, one foot in the rock-furrow, and a rivulet of blood, very dark but unmistakable, crawled out from under her body.

The new running men, who had no fear of women's rituals, waved their guns, those sticks which spat fire and pellets of maiming or death. Most of the villagers had heard of these, dimly. Few had ever seen – or seen and lived to recount it.

The women dropped back together in a huddle; defensive, pointless, instinctual. Webbed found herself back to back with her own mother, who craned her neck to mumble the reminder in Webbed's ear: "Remember. Your father was demon."

A parting gift. Next second the mother, too, was felled, clubbed on the head and brained because she had tried to claw. She was too old anyway for the slave-takers with guns, who wanted only the youngest women and men from the forests, for the hard labour in their port and city.

Webbed saw her mother trodden on, along with the widow who had helped haul the plough to prevent all this. Then a huge stinking hand covered her own nose and mouth. She was lifted, only half conscious, up into the bear's embrace. In another language she had not yet learned, the slaver laughingly said, "This one's a find. I stake first claim to her. Maybe I'll wed her even, if she washes up nicely."

He did not keep her in the end. He raped her for a dozen nights and afternoons in the travelling bivouac of the slave camp, then lost her at cards to another man, who in turn gave her in exchange for some other woman they had found, who had coppery hair.

In reality, Webbed could not be anything but a slave. Though it was a shame, several of them had said it, that the lucrative days of sending pleasure-slaves to the Tzaers, and other princes of the cities, were gone. In a Christian era, such a habit was out of favour. Conversely, she was too good for the harsh work the rest must endure. Perhaps some fancy brothel might like her and pay a fine price. To this end, several of them took it on themselves to teach her proper speech, whipping her when she was slow and stupid, as mostly they found she was. The whippings only scarred her back a little. Not enough to spoil her for future use. Some fine fellows even liked such scars, they had heard.

What Webbed learned, along with the beginnings of their civilised tongue, was that what physically they did to her – therefore what her father and others had done – was neither a formality nor an acceptable act. Indeed, neither the sexual intrusions *or* the starvings and beatings for punishment. They told her this, although by an obtuse means. The punishments, they explained to her carefully, *were* punishments, things she would only have to suffer if she failed their expectations of her – *not* necessary customs of a family or group. As for the rapes, they would have to go to a priest to confess this use of her as a sin, a bad and vicious error *they* made, being too weak to resist. They discussed the confessions sometimes, and the grim penances they dreaded – kneeling on stone floors, praying, in cold chapels, the giving up of meat, vodash and wine.

That they thought her *tempting*, physically appealing, even beautiful, filled Webbed with utmost horror. Not because of the resulting assaults – which even if she had learned they were sins, she still put up with almost unthinkingly, as always – but because she thought these new men must be degenerate and insane to be attracted by her.

How could they want her? She was not like proper women in appearance. Her father and uncles had made do with her because they had nothing young that was better. If her sister had still been in the hut, she doubted they would have bothered with Webbed. And even these slave-takers, though taller and less gross in their looks than any villager, were still identifiable to her as human men. That was, debased, mentally limited, unwholesome in smell and action. Made of clay, in fact, as mankind must be, unless, like herself, formed by demons.

In the camp, she stayed, whenever possible, among her own people. But as most of her village had by then been split up with other slaver parties, those taken from other Lesha villages now predominated. These did not know her and shunned her for her peculiarities. This was as it must be. Humbly, she crouched at the edges of their lives, forlornly consoled by sane ostracisation.

But confusion clouded her days. It was worse than ill-treatment, to which she was accustomed. Worse even in some ways than her bewilderment at exile.

However, when they emerged from the forests at last, going up river firstly, on rafts and cranky boats, blind terror seized Webbed, as it did most of her compatriots.

The earth had become a sort of Hell. It was enormous. Its horizons stretched to unguessable limits, where, to the absolute despair of the forest people, it tumbled away into plains of sky slung with colossal mountains of cloud – which often seemed about to crash down on the land. Some of them had even done so in the past. They were visible far off, clouds that no longer moved, being broken from their fall. (The slavers, who had come across this sort of agoraphobia before, mocked the villagers, saying, Yes, yes, those mountains over there had certainly once been clouds, shot down by guns. Then they would threaten to fire at the real clouds. The threat would induce compliance, when needed.)

Rapids also smashed the passage of the river and frightened the slaves with their turmoil. Here boats and rafts were dragged ashore. This river was not as yet the mighty Vlova, but a mere eel which would, only finally, gush into it. Nevertheless, to the forest people, it was terrible, and must, like any water, be full of spirits and monsters, waiting to drown and devour.

Long months they had been on the journey. There were many stops. Other peoples began then to be seen, at fairs, in villages and towns along the river's course. When Webbed and her remaining group of slaves ultimately found themselves sailing slowly down the winter Vlova, further education took place. All knew they had entered a world of devils, taller and finer made, alien – for the earth had not constructed them.

But the slaves were quite numbed by then. Their rudimentary minds had been slapped into utter vacuity.

Therefore, though the vast Vlova appalled them, its southeast-north flowing loop miles wide beyond the port and paved with white winter ice, the black inner channel concealing malignity, they barely responded. The most refined cruelty could not perhaps have done this. It was too much ordinary experience which had shattered their souls.

An evening came, luminous, full of the danger of the low-flying clouds. Out of the landscape rose another landscape.

It was a city. They did not see this. Instead it must be another crashed cloud, fixed in unlikely shapes of stone and wood – presumably a cloud's original material. Here the demon-people had come to live in an enormous band, and had lit fires in the air, on poles. The sun set across the river like a scarlet mask. On a bank, black on the sun fall and the snow, one more black-furred alien stood, surveying the ship.

How had he been, Nezchai, able to see her such a way off in the middle of the crowded ship and the snow-flounced river? Well, he was a sorcerer. Besides, he owned a very ornate spyglass of faceted topaz.

TWO

Nezchai the sorcerer lived in a mansion built of foreign Javan wood, hard and black as vitreous. The manse was itself formed round the spine of a high, and slightly leaning, tower, a shaft of slated granite pierced with windows only at its top. By night, most of these might shine out. Sometimes the colours changed, yellow to rose, or to purple.

Inside it was a draughty wind-groaning house, with earth or stone floors, empty of almost everything but ancient books on shelves or stands, stone tables and wooden stools, carved chairs with cushions of ruined velvet, chests, vials and jars, bottles and crystals. Precious gems glinted and smouldered everywhere. An owl, or maybe a pair of them, had a roost in the tower-top, but also flew about inside the mansion, catching mice as a cat would, then letting loose agglomerated cones of condensed fur and tiny bones. The flights of these owls, or owl, seemed inexorably gliding and silent as time.

There was one human servant. He *was* human, squat and obese, swarthy of skin. Yet by now Webbed was wary of him, for she saw he was afraid of her in an unknown, sophisticated way: similar to, though not as magnified as, his fear of his master.

Other servants also plied the house of the magician. They were invisible and did things which distressed but did not shock her, for she had grown up in a forest similarly populated by elementals. Often objects would drift through the air, or be hurled. Things broke. Others did not. Book pages were turned. Or else different books, coiled up in linen jackets, sprang off, or hung down from the stands, or over the stairways. There were noises and voices, too. Just like the Lesha.

Strange reflected glimmers came and went on the ceilings – perhaps cast up from the river, though surely it was too far off.

"You will sleep in here," Nezchai told her, speaking clearly so she could follow. "Five hours each night. That is enough."

The room was narrow, and the bed, for a bed it was, also narrow. It sloped curiously, the head much higher than the foot. There were coverlets of fur and quilts stitched with worn antique pictures in bursting gold and silver thread. Seed pearls scattered the icy stony floor. The only two fireplaces were on the lower storey, in the wall. The human servant kept these flashing with fire, and sometimes threw in unguents that produced a glamorous smell. But Webbed's bedchamber was cold. Nor did she employ it properly to begin with. She took the covers from the bed and slept in the corner, rolled in them like a scroll in its linen case. One of the invisible servants must have reported this. Nezchai told her she must sleep in the bed. He picked her up and placed her on it, in the proposed position. After that she slept on the bed.

He seldom touched her. He had not raped her. Nor did he punish or strike her.

She did not mind the food, the haunches of deer broiled in the fireplaces, the goose stews, the pickled cabbage and plums, and hot bread.

"You must eat twice a day. I will show you how much. There is water to drink every day. It's clean, from the well in the grove. Drink wine in the evening from this beaker. It belonged to an Egyptian queen and is made from a single emerald. Two helpings, out of that jug."

He told her she must walk about the mansion all day, except after meals, when she must sit as still as she was able for one hour, which the spirit-servants (whom he named Striyi) would measure for her. They did this by delicately chiming a little bell hung from a beam at her sitting down, slamming a lid on a great urn of pickled fruits and cucumbers when the hour was accomplished.

Frequently she would be summoned into Nezchai's presence. The human servant was always the one to conduct her, though sometimes the spirits rolled about as he and she climbed the tower, nearly visible now and then on the stairs, like ribbons or balls of pale, tangled hairs.

The owl, or one of the owls, slept during the daylight hours. Once the low sun dropped from sight, the owl, or both owls, separately evolved, floating about the big tower-top room, skimming indecipherable gadgets and potions with raddled wicked feet.

Nezchai did not always look at her. But usually he did. He studied her. He *read* her, it seemed, like one more book. He felt her hair, now often washed with perfume, weighed her in an upright balance. And occasionally he looked into her eyes through a magnifying crystal, as he would examine a jewel.

Only twice did he require her to strip her clothing, the warm wool and furs he provided in winter, later the lighter garments put out for summer.

She was shocked the first time – not by the cold, for there was a brazier of charcoals burning in his alchemical laboratory – but at the infringement of her basic secrets. Her father and uncles had never made her bare any of her body, save for the essential part, and then they had not looked at it, only navigated an entry. The slave-takers *had* looked her over, but only in portions. One had wanted to see her breast, (one breast was enough), another her vagina, and so on.

This with the magician was plainly not a prelude, however, to sexual rape.

The very first time, he studied her for perhaps five hours, walking round her, seating himself, drinking wine or water, gazing. He took notes, writing in dark ink and eccentric characters, on a tablet of goatskin, then goose skin fixed with ambergris.

All this while Webbed stared into nothingness, shrivelling, deranged with a voiceless revulsion – and – what could it be? – *anger*? She had seen the rage of others, but did she know what *her* anger was?

The human servant did not intrude. A Stri kept the brazier active and hot.

After he was done with her, she hid herself until the following day in a cupboard in her room, where only marks in the dust showed where things might once have been stored. She stood among these phantoms and wept, as she had not done since earliest childhood.

He was teaching her words by then, for he read *to* her endlessly. Although she hardly ever knew what any of the matter of these readings comprised, sentences, phrases, solitary monosyllables had begun to take root in her. She was learning expressively to vocalise. She now spoke to herself, fumbling not in the forest jargon, but in the allegorical syntax of the sorcerer... *Shameful gold, debased metal like a moon, fire to water that changes into a shell...*

The second time he told her to remove her garments came years later. That summer evening she tore them off and threw them down.

"Yes," was all he said. Then, "You haven't changed your plumage, my Swan. Still white, still perfect. The same weight and almost the same age. How *will* you age, I wonder? Is it possible you even can?"

Swan was his name for her, from the beginning. She had absorbed the name gradually, like the other words.

Swan thought, *Acid to volcanic flame. Night is falling in crow wings.*

He only watched her nakedness, during that second perusal, for one quarter of an hour. By then she could judge time quite ably in the new way, from the water-clocks dripping all over the house, or the clockwork icon of gold and chrysoprase he kept in his tower, where an eye of rubicelle moved round and round a white owl face marked with numbers – which she had come to be able, also, to read. Though she could not count higher than twelve.

Of all humanity, Nezchai was to her the apogee of otherness. (As indeed he was to humans, who thought him actually *abhuman* – worse than the forest people had ever thought Swan, in fact.)

There was something direly significant in this. She had never fitted among humanity. Now, in the globe of human sorcerousness that was Nezchai's world, she felt her chastisement for having ever been born.

During summers, the mansion sweated and was hot. The walls smelled of the river down the long slope, and of struck tinder, the flint rasping on the tinderbox.

The odour of the volumes and scrolls also increased in summer. It drifted like pollen. Flowers and berries exploded on the banks of the Vlova, visible from windows, and in the groves beyond the house colour was rife where, in winter, lay only monochrome, and wolves perambulated like silver cogs in some other faunal clockwork. She had no urge to pluck a berry, let alone a flower. Besides, it was presumably forbidden.

In the house, anyway, bizarre flowers grew. They were brought to Nezchai, like the jewels and books and other curios, from everywhere on earth. She had thought he lied when he spoke to her or read of other countries of the earth – that he made them up to amuse himself. (Nezchai had told her some god had done precisely that, moving over nothingness, and talking lands and creatures into being.) One blue flower came from a situation he named *Holland*. The perfume was very strong. It looked like a sculpture of wax rather than a flower.

Ships moved along the river. The moon rose and sank. The sun crossed the vast sky (which, sheltered in the house, she was growing to accept) or balanced on the sky's high summer border, never quite disappearing, but dull as her mother's battered bronze cauldron.

Having no true life, Swan, who had been Webbed, began to form inadvertently another life, *not* true, but accessible and functioning.

Even so, meaningless.

It hooked itself, like owl claws, on language, words and concepts – which doubtless she did not understand, yet which, for herself, she formulated to strange (applicable?) meanings.

As in: "Going to the river, the man cast down a net in which came up a pike of solid gold, decorated all over with precious stones." This, to Swan, (or Webbed) transformed to a miniature event, a miniscule golden fish that swam in a dish, a sort of pool of the river where the men had fished in the forest. With this image, despite the views of the wide Vlova and the statically-reeling city, she was content. But no – *not* content. Such pictures were like the cupboard in which she had taken refuge. A small retreat from chaos, refuge from the inimical. (For she *was* human, whatever she might think. That very process of denial and miniaturisation was the one by which all mankind, even the maguses, retained their wits: shrinking eternity to the stars of the sky, and God to a wise elder man who sat there, and life to a single spurt from womb to grave.)

The Swan swam through the years in the sparkling, darkling sobriety of Nezchai's mansion, remembering how he rode to meet her on a piece of ice, the ship stopped dead in the river.

In sleep, summer and winter, spring and autumn, she dreamed only of her mother's hut with the smutty hearth. Even of her father's nasty fumblings. Even the drunken uncles reeking of khoumis fermented from the wild horse-deer of a neighbouring village. Sometimes she heard her mother mumbling, "Your father was demon." It had been a gift, that final announcement. Knowing *herself*, the webbed Swan managed to persist in limbo.

Language grew in her like plants, but otherwise she was silt and the slush of forgotten ice. Bread was never enough to live on, though no one, not even the Christian atheist Nezchai, had told her who might have suggested this. Not bread alone. You could not flourish on that. Nor on words, unless they sprang from a Word. *The* Word. No. She could not live.

THREE

Swan dreamed a new dream. She had been called up to the magician's chamber in the tower. When she had entered, he told her, for the third time, to take off her clothes.

Six years had passed by now. Among the forest clans she would have been long wife-bonded to a man. She would be growing old, like her mother. Here that had not happened. One more discrepancy.

Even so, she did begin to feel age. Wandering up and down the enormous mansion, even allowed, since the fourth year, into the single walled grove adjacent, or sitting in a chair while the invisible servants hurled things or fluttered the pages of his books, Swan became tired. She sat down and slept at hours not prescribed by Nezchai. Sometimes the Striyi servants, even the human man, played tricks and woke her – slamming the lids of jars and barrels, spilling water over her feet. But eventually they relented, or were bored with it, and left her alone.

It was during just such a nap that she dreamed of the magician's summons and his command that once more she strip.

"But I am old now," in the dream she said.

"Old? You're a maiden. You are a gem. Gems age in centuries but not appearance."

She did not, even in a dream, know quite why she would not do what he wished. Her reluctance was personal to herself, therefore irrelevant to her. But she could not, did not.

Then Nezchai crossed the room and put his hands on the ruby buttons of her collar. And in that instant, Swan felt herself turn into what he had told her of, a white and gleaming polished stone.

He started back. She had never seen him discomposed, let alone alarmed, before.

Inside her nacre armour she half smiled. She thought, *I can never be touched again.* This saddened and energised her. Autonomy, though random and not quite comprehended, was startlingly valuable.

When she woke, she lay on the tilted bed, where someone, probably the sorcerer, had placed her.

She was not, as in the dream, made of pearl. But she could barely move, nevertheless.

One moment she was freezing cold, the next very hot. It was as if the two great seasons of winter and summer rushed back and forth through her body, replacing each other every few minutes. Oddly, in this fashion, she was never too uncomfortable for too great a time. Between the dual states were intervals of relief and equilibrium, the cold growing warm, the heat cool. Spring? Autumn?

Nezchai stood at the bed-foot, reading over her some lesson or incantation.

The words for once were lost on her.

Then he put down the book.

"Have you drunk water outside the house?" he asked her quietly. He had forbidden her to do this. Of course, she had not. Only once had she disobeyed him – even in a dream.

"No."

"Has anything bitten or stung you?"

She pondered vaguely. In the forest of her childhood small animals and insects often did such a thing, yet here... After a while she recalled that a little black-green fly had settled on the back of her hand as she stood at a window of the mansion, looking at carts on the distant track by the Vlova. She had felt a sharp itching pain, as if a heated pin had been driven through her skin into the vein, and as she started the fly spun away on gilded wings.

She tried to tell Nezchai this but found the act of speaking very difficult. She mumbled, "I was made naked."

"That? That was long ago."

Presently he bent near, measuring her heartbeat, the rhythm and colour of her blood, staring into her eyes through a prism. He had always analysed her. She was not dismayed. She fell asleep.

When she woke the next time, she lay in a bath of liquid gold, up to her neck in it. She thought this was quite logical. She was changing into pearl and would need to be mounted in a golden boss, to hold her securely for his future scrutiny.

Still she was not distressed. She breathed slowly and heavily, and on the floor flowers in a pot gave off a blue marzipan of scent.

The sorcerer tried many methods to retain his treasure. A bath of mercuric silver when the gold failed, partial immersion in tar, and liquified pummice from the bowel of a volcano. Tiny bats bled her, and white maggots cleaned the wounds with their teeth. Needles of gold and steel were put through pinches of her skin at various points – the inner crook of the arm, an earlobe. Elixirs were mixed. She drank them awkwardly but always obediently. She had no interest in anything apart from the movement and patterns of light on her ceiling – the possible reflections off the river or the bank, or of lamps there after dark, or on the track below the groves, or fireflies crisscrossing the summer nights.

Her bodily functions were attended to by the invisible servants. These beings were quite gentle now, and unlike a human nurse, never impatient or enraged at the work. Having grown in the forest, she had never much cared anyway if another saw her urinate or crap; it had always been happening.

However, these functions ceased soon, as she put aside the chore of eating and drinking.

Swan was not restless. In the ripple of the ceiling she beheld people from her past, even enslaved villagers from the trip west and south.

One night she heard him raving in the room high above in his tower, something that had never happened, blaspheming some god she had not learned about or been properly aware of. Despite that, the *tone* of resentful blasphemy was unmistakable – she had heard it once or twice in the village. A man spitting at the sun, a woman cursing the demon that had broken her best pot. The man was struck by lightning a month later. The woman, though precautionally beaten, sickened and was good for very little.

Swan felt no unease for Nezchai. He was nothing to her, only a fact, like the immovable coming of day or night. Always alone, the tolerance of her village towards her had upheld her. But even this, of course, had emotionally not amounted to much. Lying on the bed, in the end, she stopped concocting nostalgia from the ceiling. Then she took an interest in the rippling for itself. Abstract and ever-altering, like the words Nezchai had read which she never really grasped, it absorbed her, teaching her a whole fresh library of concepts, feelings without any name – needing none.

She was evading Nezchai, slipping away through his clutching genius like water through the fingers of a boy. She was dying.

Then she was dead.

She never heard the raucous dumbness of his fury that night he lost her. Half the city claimed to have done so, and to have seen horrible waves of glare and shadow cast upward on the sky by his tantrum.

How long passed after? Accounts varied. A day, a year. Not long.

Why had he so uncontrollably wanted this trophy? His control elsewhere was phenomenal, legendary and feared. Nothing much was known of Nezchai's own youth. Maybe something then had left him prey to such avarice and villainy, this collector of books and gems.

For The Swan... as if in deep sleep, dreamless now, but following on some *magnificent* post-life dream instantly mislaid. Only its *sensation* lingering, already melting, gone. Hollow then, rushing through a nullity into a tiny keyhole of dull light that abruptly exploded. Like a golden fish landed on a rotten shore, slung down and forced to yield three alchemical secrets.

She found she stood in the world again, inside midnight and the flickering brazier red of Nezchai's tower, that stony, upright penis of his will.

And she could remember nothing of the place he had dragged her back from – less than nothing. Only the conviction that it had been full of things that, like the sublime awarenesses preceding death, were nameless and inexplicable.

But what ever had been? What had she ever *wished* to have explained?

She *did* know what he had done.

Nezchai had reclaimed not merely her phantom appearance, but her *true* ghost, the soul firmly meshed inside it. He had pulled her like thread through a needle's eye and glued her down again where he wanted.

Presently she noticed the magical symbols drawn on the floor.

He saw the frosts and blooms of the after world still littering her. On garments, and caught in her hair, as if she had been swept through a storm of butterflies or leaves.

But he only slammed shut his volume of spells, frowning with his triumph over every god who dared to exist.

For a few minutes he walked all round her, as he had done long ago. He ignored now the tinsels and ethereal cobwebs. Besides, they faded swiftly in the roar of reality. Then only she was there. But that was all he wanted.

"I have you back, my Swan. My jewel. Do you remember me, and where you are?"

She had not forgotten him. She had forgotten nothing worldly.

Perhaps in those moments, too, he thought he would outwit also his own death. Such things had been heard of among his kind. Perhaps, with the cranky sentiment of the cruel, he reckoned he had spared her something, and that, if he lived forever, she would have his eternal protection.

She was clothed in a perfect facsimile of her best garments. (The tactile original of the gown lay in a chest.)

He seized a broom of iron twigs and brushed the symbols off the floor.

Then she was free to move about as she wanted. Of course, all she did do was what he trained her to in life. She walked weightless to the door, and though not bothering to undo it, glided through and down the stairs.

In the mansion the invisible Striyi servants, still invisible, may have marvelled that now some of her abilities matched theirs. Certainly they no longer attempted tricks.

As for the human servant, he ran away. But first he burst into tears and kneeled down before her apparition. "Forgive – forgive – I am lost – shall burn in Hell – forgive me!"

The Swan glanced at him remotely. *No* one was preferable to her now. She was finally barred even from her longing for the society of proper humans.

He took her disconnection as a curse. He fled the house and hanged himself in a wood behind the Gethsameen. The priests buried him in unsanctified ground. He was a suicide and had been well known as Nezchai's minion.

FOUR

Did she mourn her loss of the other world? No. Did she pine? No. Was she ever anything save *there*? No.

Soulless in her phantasmal en-souled shape, The Swan drifted to and fro, a stray feather from the wing of an owl.

While he, like any cunning, clever, solipsistic child that gets its own way, spoiled, lost interest gradually.

Oh, he liked to see her. To meet her. To regard her. She was like all the trophies of his house.

He grew elderly, for now time was moving on, though it had seemed to pretend to hesitate, earlier on. Time discarded elements from itself – an owl, both owls, a wolf, a pack, a tree in the groves, the dark colour from a man's hair, the semi-tautness of middle-age from a man's face. The mansion was knee-deep in dusts of life, fallen pages, seed pearls, dropped hairs, desiccated thoughts.

But she did not alter. Could not.

Untouchable and untouching, wafted here and there, in and out.

Various persons on the road below saw her at high windows above the trees, a distanced figure still of discernible beauty, like some princess from an ancient tale. A handful saw her out on the bank, among the overgrowing groves. *Like a blue marsh flame,* they said.

Did she watch the building projects, the city massing and extending itself, like huge lungs inhaling, towers rising, churches, houses clustering close, the making of the great Vistas – the North one partly running below Nezchai's mansion, as if pushing it away.

No, she did not watch.

Sometimes he still called for her. She always did as she was bid.

"I saved you from a grave," said the man in the carved chair, whose hair was white string, his ringed fingers, despite all the potions, twisted by their crippled bones. "I shall not die," he assured her.

Did she ever speak?

Yes.

"Why does that ship sail by?" she asked the wind on the rivershore. "Why does that dog bark?" She knew the names of countless things. She did not know why she asked, even so, or even why she talked at all. Occasionally she spoke in the old way: "Stars drop deep in the river. A lion" (she did not know what lions were) "carries the spire of the sun on his back, whose rays change dew to opal."

Once in nine million heartbeats of a heart that no longer could

57

beat, a wisp stirred in her of memory unremembered. Then came a feeling of unpredicted sweet and shining *otherness*. The legacy of where she had been before he reclaimed her? Why not. Others know these moments, and they are not even ghosts.

And she was more than a ghost. She was a prisoner and a slave beyond all prisoners and slaves. An outcast from an unknown country.

Nezchai, in popular belief, was one hundred and twelve years of age when he perished.

Stories abounded as to why it came about. He had outstripped even his own villainy in some novel and outrageous sorcery. He had offended the Devil himself. Or offended so many various demons and sprites they banded together to overthrow him. Or else God, looking down, had simply said, "Is that wasp still crawling there?" And stamped on him.

It was near summer's end. The sky was extremely pale that night though the sun was fully down. It was pale like a plate of blue china from the East, and plaits of stars visible from horizon to horizon.

(In the making of the new great road, many of the trees had been chopped down, and parts of the bank levelled. All this had taken place only some three quarters of a mile beyond the slope where Nezchai's wooden house stood among its wolf-groves. Wolves no longer came there, had not done so for twenty years or more. Neither had the workmen paid much heed to the house, which looked only eccentric and ramshackle. They were miserable slaves, anyway, ignorant of cities. Only watchmen sometimes noted the lighted windows in the tower. But they wore their talismans and said their prayers. The metropolis had grown used to the sorcerer, perhaps judged him less.)

That night, too, there was a sense of impending storm. Not about the city, only in the vicinity of the house.

Old Nezchai had drunk deeply and become uncommonly boisterous, laughing and calling up illusions to perform acrobatics, and to dance.

Near midnight even so, he stiffly climbed the stair towards the tower-top, to spend time with his spell books.

On the way, the mage became aware that his rings struck sparks off the stone wall. A smell both pungent and metallic filled the tower.

Entering the room above, he flung a handful of powder on a tall lamp, that caused it to flare and lave the atmosphere with olibanos. The magician soon stood reading at a stand, often employing his emerald magnifying glass. But gradually he was conscious of non-corporeal comings and goings all around the space. It was as if half-visible patterns lifted in the plaster of the walls, or out of the floor, or off the shelves of phials and volumes, to swirl about. Tired eyes might miss-see in this way, but the eyes of Nezchai, though no longer as sharp as they had been, were never afflicted by such megrims. Magic was loose in the tower. A magic not of his making.

Even as he began to stare, a long, low hissing sound drove in through one of the windows. The shutter was leaning there on the wall, and it banged, and further showers of sparks flew up.

Nezchai went to the window. As he paced across the room, his very clothes, brushing the furniture, caused further sparkling pyrotechnics. Outside, above, the blue china sky was sullenly boiling. Vast clouds were running in across the river, resembling a high, abnormally sculpted, opaque fog. And in them wild twisting shapes and frills of white lightning. Elsewhere all about, the city lay becalmed. The approaching tempest was only here.

With the years of her captivity, The Swan had grown into her weariness and despair. But these negative states in themselves sometimes brought respite. For when unobserved, she would fade, literally, away. Then she sank into a kind of medium devoid of everything. It was a psychic grave. It was like sleep, but totally vacant, and granted her small tastes of peace. Forgetting it was not the state of death, she came to desire it very much.

When he summoned her, however, she had no choice but to return at once into both consciousness and appearance. So strong was the sorcery he had fashioned, so obdurate, it dwarfed even Nezchai himself. Flung from his brain like a knife, now it was an object of will in its own right.

Nezchai called his slave from her fading-place in order to protect her from what now encroached on the mansion. That was, in order to keep safe his property. For the same reason he sent the Striyi scurrying throughout the house to transport the most valuable items into the security of the tower. Nezchai had no doubts by now the onslaught of weather was unnatural and directed solely at him. He had no idea from whence it came. Who would dare? Not even the Tzaers bothered him. Rather, from time to time, they sent him little gifts. Whatever came, nevertheless, the tower, and everything in it, would withstand. It was built of mighty stones and shored up by occult craft. He was right, mostly, about the tower.

The Swan was aware of all the divergent currents as she rose along the stair, sometimes treading like a flesh-and-blood woman, sometimes levitating. That some of the whirling semi-visible entities were unfriendly she also sensed, though none showed any spite to her. They seemed actually indifferent to her.

At the instant she entered the tower room, all the windows blew inward together.

The Swan paused, impervious, in the inrushing gale of thin and thick glass. Murky vapours poured after. Yet the storm had no louder noise than a low grumbling.

Nezchai had scrambled up on a stone table. He made sweeping gestures to the night and shouted in his cracked flute of a voice. The floor was littered by books and vellum he had grabbed up, cast down, and now things were smashing on the shelves, and liquids and fires dripped and trickled.

The mansion shook.

With a series of terrible moans and grunts, pieces of its walls unlocked themselves from the central core, the tower.

A whirlwind filled the room, smoke, flame, glass, feathers, papers, liquids, broken wood, chips of stone, and Nezchai gave a loud bellow, like that of an animal felled with an axe. His powers were useless. His eyes were red, his blackened teeth bared, foam bubbling from his lips. There on the table, impotent at last, he shook his fists as the helpless did, and howled in a mania of rage and fear.

Then the whole wooden house disbanded and galloped upward, flying past the tower windows and its open doorway. Another list: long timbers and fireplaces, paving from the floors, panels and hangings, chests and chairs, cupboards without backs, or fronts, and all the jewels and bottles spangling and shattering like erupting stars. Even trees burst out of the courtyard and shot away Heavenward, fired from some sorcerous subterranean cannon.

The tower itself rocked, and with a ponderous booming slowness, half its length dissociated from the other. A fountain of flints and shards gushed down amid the ascending upward stampede of other stuffs. Nezchai tottered as the table also snapped in two. Wailing, he began to fall through the wound in the tower towards the earth. But next instant the huge fists of the storm had clasped him. *Up* then he, too, spiralled, kicking and shrieking, up and up in the flying debris of his mansion, until he grew tiny as a fly, and the clouded sky gulped him. Into some vortex he had been taken, and much of the wreckage with him. Although bits of it were still to be seen, roiling in the cloud, the lightnings smiting on them like swords. And with this cargo the storm gathered itself higher and higher, one huge fishing net, and rumbled away towards the west.

Final a-physical atomies, seen, unseen, semi-seen, followed it in an ultimate up-pouring. The invisible servants of the house went with them. They were glad, maybe, to have found a community at last.

Sighing, creaking, the night grew still. Its lid was all pale blue again, and the polished stars again gleamed out.

Ships rocking lightly at anchor, further along the river, revealed their ordinary pinpricks of lanterns. There was no evidence of disturbance or alarm. Dogs barked somewhere, and from a single church a single bell lamented some grief that had nothing to do with this.

In the dismembered tower, which had been swept clean of every other thing, only the ghost of The Swan remained.

FIVE

Did she have one minute, one hour, a night even, of belief his destruction might set her free? No. Any hope of it? No. She knew. The cage he had built for her would outlast the maker.

Though she was now unwatched and alone, able to fade to her resting nothingness, these escapes were no more available to her than sleep to a living thing. Had she been sheer ghost – a husk, an echo of life – she could probably have faded right away forever. But she was soul-trapped. He had bound her to the world, and her soul itself fettered her there. For where else did souls come, but to that same world, trapped by flesh and the chains of others?

Only death could let her go. But death had been outwitted. Perhaps Death had shrugged, not minding to lose one among so very many.

Mankind found her again quickly enough.

The first was a boy playing a pipe on the bank. He was off a ship. He saw her manifest, a blue flower among the trees above. He got up, bemused by her loveliness, and when she winked out like a blown flame, ran to the ship to tell them all.

They came and went, people.

Along this stretch of the river, and the North Vista, eventually grand palaces would rise, one with a man-made lake. A bridge would cross the Vlova, guarded by statues of heroes. Meanwhile huts and hovels went up among the last trees, were lived in, confiscated, felled, haphazardly rebuilt.

Foreign itinerants camped in the area of Nezchai's legendary mansion, using the bisected stone tower as shelter or else hauling slabs out of it for other purposes, so more of it crumbled down.

They, too, saw her.

The foul, stinking, butter-yellow candles of their scrabbling lives magnetised her, poor moth. It was not that she wished to be among them. It was the spell, always that. A sound – a cry – a call – the badly-played waver of a pipe. She had been propelled from her essential place by Nezchai's summons. Now by theirs.

The Swan did not question any of it. She never had.

But they, seeing her ghost, *they* haunted *her*. They were desperate always to look at her, watch her, *keep* her. They made her offerings, gross or full of pathos – a skinned hare, a silver ring...

Stay with us.

What beauty did they have in their wretched lives? None. They reached greedily for hers. A family treasure.

Like Nezchai, they encaged her.

She was *theirs*.

After unmeasured decades, the site was cleared. A fine house, the second mansion, was erected on the spot, among other such buildings, and the groves, what was left of them, were subsumed into a fashionable Italian garden. The stone tower was kept, augmented as a sort of inner chimney. A prince and his family settled in the house like fat, noisy birds, among a plethora of ill-used servants and slaves. If they had heard of the sorcerer Nezchai, they were too intelligent to believe he had been real. Or, if real, accomplished.

There had been a prolonged lacuna for The Swan. She had faded and rested some while. She was drawn from her peace this time in a quiet and hideous way, to burnished wooden floors and statues of Greek gods, a conservatory with trees like rhinoceros hide, stabbed at the top by dagged plumes.,

Life (the spell), had netted her once more.

She appeared first to a romantic son, a drunkard and idiot, who took his inebriated scribblings for fine verse, and had published the rubbish to some misguided acclaim. (It would be long after that truly vibrant and ideally glamorous life was thought necessary to draw her, a legitimate mistake made by those who reckoned themselves of little worth. It was new life, that was all. A new face.)

The drunk described her after as a blue crescent moon. But he had followed her through the house – it was late. "She had a small white dish, and in it a golden pike swimming. It was made of gold, I mean, set with precious jewels."

The drunkard-poet took the fish for her pet. It was not. It was her misplaced, vernacular, half alchemical symbol for her own condition. Dragged from liberty in limitless sea to be questioned, measured and admired.

The great innovative stove, a white iron monster, ornamented and painted in a barbaric style, sent its tentacle through the central house, passing along the route of the ancient tower. Stairs also ascended along a similar path. The stairs were the way she took, the poet's azure ghost.

But high above, near quarters where servants slept, she dissolved into thin air.

Somehow – the spell, also – they knew to title her The Swan.

So she remained with the family of nobles, drifting in and out of their rapid history, until there came a night of thunder and shouting. Red light of burning stained the river and along the snow. The Rebellious War had begun.

Her main manacle, the poet, shot himself in drunken terror. The rest escaped from the city and were cut down somewhere in the birch forests beyond. Released, The Swan sank to her rest.

Which was not long. The house was soon busy again, split into its rooms, *teeming* with people now, all aching for some beauty in their sordid and sorrowful existence.

This time a group of young women saw her first. Among them were the mothers of Zophi and Mariasha.

"She's like the Virgin!"

"Ssh. Don't blaspheme. But yes – beautiful… holy."

"So pure. She can never have…"

"No. She is the spirit of some chaste saint."

"Or a rich lady before…"

"Ssh. Don't talk of *them*, our oppressors. But yes, she has that look. Refined and pristine."

They came to see her, all of them. They came to keep her, all of them.

Their treasure.

Theirs.

The one thing that could not be rent from their struggle of living, that had nothing to do with it.

She faded to rest, but they rested in her.

Haunted.

And when she flagged, as now she did, worn out by their infatuated, ceaseless demands to see her, the cacophonous clamour of their delight, they, too, hauled her back, their golden fish, out of the ocean of nullity. They did it first accidentally, by bringing in a new and vivid person, a man or a woman. Then noticing it worked on her, the fresh life luring her. So then arrivals were primed by the story all had somehow learned of The Swan, from legend, or from the drunkard's scrawl. The arrivals duly fell in love with her, and so – back she came to one more rancid candle, one more music badly played.

Houses and alleys and slums and winding avenues now stood between the mansion on Copper Street and the river, with its fringe of palaces. What had seemed quite near was pushed far away.

From attics, unknowingly attracted there by the remnants of the tower, The Swan looked across at the Vlova. It ran like a platinum scar on the city's belly. But once more she never left the house. Human pressure was always on her. Even in her fading- place, even there, she sensed their dreams feel after her, stroke and pinch her to wake up and come back to them.

Nevertheless, flagging she was. Could it be possible at last, envampirised and drained utterly by the hunger of human things, even her *soul* could fade? Could die? Oh, how she longed for it. Drearily she sometimes spoke to the tenants of the house, sentences which to their ears had portent and profundity. But nothing had meaning for her but the idea of unravelling and peace: freedom.

Sometimes she even mentioned death. But they never understood. Her syntax still was not exactly theirs. In any case, how could such wonder wish to end? And how could such sweetness be anything but eternal. Like the wonder and sweetness of the Christ. She could not truly die. She could not leave them. For-never.

The Hyacinths

ONE

"Poor ghost," he said. He quoted inadvertently something he could not recall. But next he covered his face with his hands. She had told him all her history – either that, or he had read it from her phantom brain. Or – could it be? – imagined it only. No, it was true enough. What else. This despair.

The Swan had moved off again. She had sat down, as if she were able to sit, or needed to, in the mended chair across the room.

All over the floor, the broken pot and the broken hyacinths, their petalled tenements snapped, buds spilled like blue peas…

He was sorry.

He sat down also, on the side of the bed.

Naturally they had given him a room where the stovepipe ran. For the pipe partly adhered to the course of Nezchai's ancient tower. A magnet, for The Swan. (Perhaps iron filings were as unwilling as she, to be sucked into their magnetic lode-stone.)

Blya Sovinen thought, *what can I say to her? She doesn't want to hear how I, too, adore her, want to possess and keep her – worse than mere lust and sexual desire, this gnawing itch to coerce and cage. What can I say?*

"What may I call you?" he humbly asked.

At that she raised her eyes and stared at him.

Softly she said, "I had a name once."

"What? Tell me, do tell me…"

"Webby – Webbed. Web-Foot."

Blya caught his breath with revulsion. Perhaps she saw, or she did not.

She said, "There was another name, feathers and white and black and blue…"

He felt himself begin to cry for her, and was ashamed, and clenched the tears away behind his eyes.

On her lap, between her two quiescent hands, the little dish. In it the golden fish swam up and down, glittering with minute jewellery: the symbol of her worth and slavery.

"You are like a hyacinth," he said slowly. "Like a flower."

She looked up again at that, puzzled.

"The flower of night," she said remotely, "the giving way to the sun that rides on the back of white horses, and the lion bearing a diadem."

He said, "I can't think what I should call you. It's all quite wrong. What would you want to be called?"

She gazed at him. Suddenly, like a piercing ray of light through cloud, a peculiar intelligent exactness sharpened her face. "Nothing," she said.

Blya lowered his eyes. He knew not to look at her was not enough to release her, even temporally. His fascination, his love – if such it could be termed – bound her here, for now, for always.

After a while they – others – knocked loudly on the door.

He called out harshly, "I'm with *her*!"

Their noise fell off in murmurs. They were jealous. But then came the voice of Olcha who had been Orena, arch-envy incarnate, herding them off like naughty children. The "New One" must be given time to cement the spell.

The new one.

I, he thought. *I*.

The night was stretched over like a canopy. They sat, then lay beneath it. He had invited her to lie down on the bed. "I won't touch you – I *can't*, can I? Can't touch you? But rest here."

Patiently she did as he said. He understood she did not *rest* anywhere but in her fading-place. He wished he could release her to it, but even if he should doze, no doubt some part of him would act sentry, tying her in the room and the tenement. Anyway, he could not fall asleep. He lay studying her, her exquisite profile, her eyes turned to the ceiling. Did she see the curious, deceptive reflections rippling there still? The urge to ask her was very strong and he choked it down. She should not be asked a single thing. She had told all, or he had *absorbed* all, breathing it in like perfume from her phantasmal body and hair.

Hyacinths. But hyacinths that could not decay. Rats had eaten her embalmed corpse. He must not consider that, or he would surely go mad.

He stared on and on. He stared through her, though she was not at all transparent, and seemed real as any other element in the room, until or if he should try to make physical contact. Or she with him, as she had at first, when she put her hand upon him. Why had she done that? Did some remnant of compassion linger in her for her torturers, all these never-ending bands of slave-takers? *Don't ask. Let her be.*

No one else had tried to disturb him. Them.

Earlier there were riots of noise from below, their rejoicings, he thought. Later the inhabitants of the house went stumbling to their beds, singing, cheerily arguing, one vomiting on the stairway, chided and derided. Later again, quiet weighed down the tenement, heavy as lead. Outside, bells thinly gilded the night, far-spaced, it seemed to him. Tomorrow was Christmas Day. He thought the city saved itself now for all the great racket of the morning, all the shouting and ringing that betokened Christ's birth. Yet dawn did not arrive. Night went on and on. He had no watch – that, too, had been sold long since. Perhaps the night would never end.

She made no movement, did not speak. But in the faint illumination that somehow remained after the oil-lamp burned itself out, he could see her still, lying by him on the bed, her eyes closed now, as if she slept.

"Swan," he said, reluctant to use this label of a name, this title of her enslavement, "Swan, let me tell you my own story."

Astonishing him, for he had expected no visible reaction, the woman on the bed turned calmly on to her side. She put her slender left hand under her cheek and lay now looking directly into his face. This gesture was so human, it hurt him. It was as if she were his lover – or his wife – accustomed and fond, ready always to listen.

He told her, then, how he had come to be in that house, picked up off the bridge and used as bait for her.

"It was because of a previous night. The night I went, to see the play," Blya Sovinen said. "I'd been a student at the University less than two years, and had never heard anything from my parents, in return for my dutiful letters. But they had saved up money to send me for my education. Doubtless this was to serve their own ends, but I barely considered it at the time. It was what I was to do. And so my letters were full of my virtues, how hard I worked and how much I had already achieved. I must confess, I didn't love them, either of them. My father was a hot, fixed man who beat me often, *beating me into shape*, as he put it. And my mother was a cold woman who had no interest in me outside my possible skills. She was only happy in the little blind church, where she spent most of her time kneeling before the icons, more real to her than anything else. But, to come to the play in the city. That night I went to the play – I had just got on the street, rushing to the dilapidated theatre on Sunny Avenue – do you know the one? Oh – but you wouldn't know the one. A poor venue, with hard wooden benches like rails, or else one stood, but I had enough money, which I'd put by, to sit on a bench. This was a drama I especially wanted to see. A while before I'd read it, and in the original Scandinavian language. The play *haunted* me." Blya smiled, apologetic at the use of this word. "But on the street, as I went along, a man met me. He'd come all the distance from my village. It seemed my father and mother, who had never allowed me to love them, were dead from some illness of poverty and cold. And all the money they had accrued over many years, was put aside, as I'd done it for my theatre seat, for *me*. The messenger, an honest, savage man, a kind of ramshackle priest, had been entrusted to bring it to me. Which he duly did. There on that street he thrust it, sheaf on sheaf, into my hands that seemed to have lost all feeling. He said he was glad to be rid of it, the temptation had been enormous to thieve it, but he had triumphed. Huge pale bills they were, I remember still, written over and drawn with the heads of Tzaers, and of those who have replaced them. Never in all my life had I seen money quite of that form, and never so much. It was frankly meaningless to me – you will grasp that, I think. For money means nothing to you. But suppose I compare it to something you recognise? For example, the ability to be *free?* Yes. Yes, you know now what the money represented. But you see, I could not feel it. I stood on the cold ground, which I could experience bitterly through my threadbare boots, listening to the priest's story of death, and personal triumph over avarice. In the end I had the presence of mind to thank the man, whom I didn't know, though he claimed to be from my home village. I then made him a generous gift – I did all that as if I were some sort of machine. But at first he refused me, as if affronted. I had to insist, and then he took what I offered with a muttered curse. Only after this point I began to realise, rather vacantly, I could live well – in my own type of liberty from what I'd received. I might easily pay all my fees for the continuing period of my education. And besides, I might live in reasonable comfort – better, in fact, than on my father's former, intermittent hand-outs. Yet these things also meant at the hour absolutely nothing. However, I'm sure they would have come to do so. Because, without any sort of financial help from my father at all, I would soon become frankly destitute. Yet I wanted to get away from the proud messenger of death and riches. I did not have the gall to say to him I was hurrying to a theatre. Instead I announced I had a sick friend I must look after. To my credit, neither did I have the cheek to pretend I required time alone to grieve. After I left him, I glanced back once, and noticed he scurried into a tavern."

Blya said he ran then to the theatre. He found his place on a bench quite near the stage, and had no sooner sat down there, when two other late arrivals also hurried in and sat beside him. They were, he thought in the low light of the theatre, a mother and daughter, dark-skinned and good-looking, poorly dressed and wrapped in modest shawls. He made room for them a little. And suddenly a spasm of protectiveness for them veered through him. They seemed to huddle in against each other, and him, afraid to be in such a spot, afraid even of the play, for the playwright was sometimes reckoned scandalous, though of great talent.

"Don't worry, Mother," he whispered to the older woman, "I'll see no one insults you."

"Oh, you're a kind young man," she whispered back. "God will reward you."

"And God did reward me," Blya said, lying looking into the face of beauty, "for my foolishness and ignorance."

The play quickly absorbed all his concentration. It was a work of delicacy and grotesquery, mingled like swansdown and broken glass. One moment there was astonishment, then laughter, then marvel, then pity – then romance that drifted like a lovely scent to the acrid residue of an austere terror and a deep sorrow. The playwright had stipulated he preferred that no interval should be observed, but even so a slight one was inevitable. Such scenery as had been managed had to be rearranged. During these minutes, the younger of the two women seated by Blya, murmured that she felt unwell. Blya heard and looked about as both of them got to their feet. He asked if he could assist them in any way, but hoping, he afterwards acknowledged, they would refuse. He did not want to miss one iota of the play.

Refuse they did. The mother said lightly, "Oh, don't be concerned. She's subject to these fits. A turn in the air will put her right. Perhaps you would save our place if anyone tries to take it?" Blya said he would. They, very modestly, their heads bowed, slipped away. They were careful, he saw, to disturb no one.

"They did not return. But no one tried to steal their place. I admit I thought of them, once or twice, during the first dialogues of the new scene, but then I forgot. How callous I was – or am. I'd be the same now, perhaps. Or not. How can I tell? Besides, *now* I would have learnt a sort of lesson in such things."

Not until the play's end, when Blya stood up, intellectualy reeling, to wildly applaud, did he abruptly recollect his neighbours. Then he suffered a vague pang. Going out, he had a dismal idea he might find them in the snow, the girl prone, the mother bending over her, at her wit's end. But only his upright, hale, fellow theatregoers congested the outer thoroughfare. Neither woman or girl were anywhere to be seen.

"Maybe no one can believe this. Perhaps you, perhaps *you* of all persons, can credit me. I had also *forgotten* the money the angry priest gave me. It was so – unsuitable to my life, you see, as I had already lived it. And I'd crammed all the notes into the pocket of my coat. Like a fistful of rags. It was only when I put my hand in there to find a coin for a drink that instead... that instead I found nothing at all. And then I *did* remember. And then I stood astounded on the roadway, more crazed than when I had been given my father's fortune, with people jostling by me, and a carriage rushing along, striking sparks from the hoofs of the horses, the driver bellowing and swearing that I was in his way."

The modest women had competently robbed him, as the priest had not. Every note had been lifted (his own small stash of coins also), by the skill of the mother's almost fairy fingers. He had not felt anything of it, only her trusting warm closeness, and the chilly gap after she was gone. Probably they had seen him get the money in the first instance, and followed him, sliding into the theatre on some pretext. How cool she had been, to sit on there with him all through that initial scene, his life, as it were, in her pocket.

Blya and The Swan lay supine, looking at each other.

He said, "Because of that robbery of all my unlooked-for inheritance – which otherwise then, obviously dried up like a withered plant – I had nothing. I therefore struggled a while, selling what slight possessions I had. But soon enough I was ejected from my lodging and from the University. Do you know, I've often thought, my parents died when they did out of a sort of inertia. Their miserly tendencies had hastened their deaths certainly, but they had been miserly on my behalf. There's an extra parody to it, isn't there, that all their self-denial, meant to make of me such a supreme scholar, ended by rendering two thieves so happy? But really I believe they died simply because they thought I would no longer need them. Nor, despite any previous hope, they me."

Then Blya blushed. He had crassly spoken of the easy death of human things – to *her*.

But she did not seem to notice.

How lovely she was. What did anything else signify? He could lie forever by her, gazing on her. This was simple, too.

And nothing of any of it could matter to her.

Yet, her eyes were so luminous and holy.

"We are all," he said, "trapped and enslaved by the webs of others. And by the extravagant and stupid structures of events. If I had never gone to see that play, that work of genius and fire and fear – I shouldn't ever have ended up in penury, and so on the Heroic Vlova Bridge, and so – here, now. Did I say, the drama was by the writer Strindberg? It was called *The Ghost Sonata*."

Somewhere beyond the dark, yet low-lit cavern which contained them, another bell chimed over the river. Surely soon the dawn must break, the day of Christ's birth.

Abruptly Blya Sovinen sat up.

"Darling," he said. "Come with me now. Come back with me to the roof of the house."

Inevitably, he thought, she rose as he did. At the door, with a sombre tactfulness, he held it wide for her to pass. They went up the steps, he guiding her away from the pool of vomit, again as if it could mark or trouble her.

She made no sound, nor he. Behind other doors, drowsy mutterings and long, rattling snores, coughing and bed-shifting rolls, and bad dreams. Not a single waking note.

When they reached the attics, he entered first, now guiding her through the ironically ghostly stockings, beside all the sleepers there spread on mattresses, sighing and moaning in sleep.

They came to the hidden door behind a curtain, and the treacherous, ladder-like stair.

No one woke. He had known they would not. Some other sorcery was on the tenement, perhaps only that of tiredness, eating, and strong drink.

She – *blew* up the ladder. Thistledown, smoke rising. He was agile in only a mortal way. He closed the exit behind them.

TWO

How altered now, the city of the sleeping night.

Not a candle showing anywhere, only the isolated torches, dull as embers, and the greenish ebb of lanterns along some individual streets. Yet the snow itself was gleaming up, one entire white lamp, into the sky's indigo and star-streaked eye.

When she had finally met with people who themselves possessed great physical beauty, the indifference and apathy of The Swan were penetrated. For she saw they must be as she was, less than human. It had not happened often. In the household of the aristocrats there had been a kitchen girl of porcelain delicacy. And among the generation or so of tenants in the slum, once or twice, others shone out. One was an exceptional elderly man with long, silvered hair, and the features of a pagan god. But he died one evening. Another was an infant, a marvel, but *he* coarsened as he grew up. Both had disconcerted The Swan, for how could progression to proper humanness, let alone expiry, have happened? (Her own expiry she did not consider. She had not, anyway, been able to expire completely.) Orena was a member of this order, fair and blindingly pretty. But Orena became Olcha, waxing gross and amoeba-like, flowing over and absorbing the energies of any who approached too near.

Blya, though, had a beauty which inevitably struck and resonated on the awareness of The Swan. His beauty, in fact, was very much a male equivalent of her own – although neither understood this. Of them all, therefore, it stood to reason, the shackles he could lay on her were infinitely more mighty.

She had not fought against them. She never fought.

Yet as she heard him tell his short story, The Swan felt something move inside her, uneasy but almost sweet. Perhaps it was only the clank of the chains slithering to a more comfortable position. Blya, too, it was obvious to her, had been also demon-got, as had she. And like her he must have had to camouflage himself and take care to be tolerated among others. He, too, would have been always alone.

If her own story was precisely as Blya had read it from her, surely no one could be entirely certain. But the premise that a monster had sired her he, naturally, had never believed. More likely some oaf of another forest village had lain with the mother in the field. The woman then manufactured horrible webbed prints in the earth with a stone, to save herself a beating or worse. The slight science Blya knew informed him that two foul compounds, when mixed, could occasionally by some fluke produce a miracle – a flawless gem, an unusually coloured flower, a perfect child.

As they stood on the roof of the tenement together, The Swan looked closely at Blya Sovinen.

Her deductions had always been oblique. And now, too, they were quite strange. Bound by the chains he had refashioned, she did not guess, the ghost, that what currently held her so tight was neither coercion or compassion. Instead, she had begun to be in love with him. That was all it was. But she, so endlessly, greedily loved, did not know what love was. It filled her, and she could give it no name.

She watched his every movement, even the blinking of his eyes, the lashes rising and falling and rising. She *watched* him – as others watched *her*.

From her hand, the small dish with its golden, miniature pike, her symbol, had vanished.

If she had breathed, she would have held her breath, hanging on the turn of his head, the shape of his eyes when again they regarded her.

His story of himself had moved her to the quick, the soul. For they were of a kind, and she grasped his suffering better than her own.

What, what would he do now?

Blya Sovinen beckoned The Swan. They moved to the parapet, and then he stared down. The yard lay far below, packed with an ungiving snow, like adamant.

"Listen to me, my Swan. If human obsession traps you here – if *I* trap you here – I'll let you go."

In snow light, her face clear as ice – almost – *alert?* But she spoke. "How can you?" As a living woman might.

"Our boiling lives snare and bind you. All of them, but worse always, the *new one* – the fresh blood. This time, me. The enchanter's spell... *our* spell. Everyone wants to keep you, because you are beauty and *otherness*; you're the sudden fortune the thieves must never be allowed to steal. But they do. Oh, I bless those wretched women, since they sent me here. Let them become saints. All you've known, darling, my Swan, is to be gripped. But I – shall deliberately let you fall." Blya Sovinen's own face was filled with a radiance, as if the white flame of the snow had entered into him, or it was only the flame of madness, but a flame it was. "We hug life and you, we live for you and make you *suffer* this life, when you should be free of it. When you should be in Heaven." He put out his hand, and gently stroked her long dark hair, not feeling a strand of it, making no impression, as if he were the ghost, not she. "But I," he said, "I'll die for you. Watch, beloved. See how it's done…" And turning from her in one movement he leapt clear over the low parapet, his arms flung high, his face now tilted up exalting to the sky above, blind and insane with love, love's other side like the dark of the moon. Three heartbeats in the air, a bird in flight. Then the crash upon the iron earth. Everything of him broke apart at once – bones, body, blood. Carapace. Out of him the force of life erupted, cast back like a spray of unseen flowers and leaves.

Dead, he lay there on the yard. He had expected mere nothingness despite his words. For though he had been taught to believe in God, and in an after world, these hopes had died away like everything else, leaving only their disconsolate husks – to which, from sympathy, he showed respect. Dead then, Blya Sovinen. A shattered instrument, its music expelled. And she?

In the sky, wheeling, a slight snow purling past, soft and no longer cold. Below, the city, and the vast flexible river, broad-bordered with ice, and the ships at anchor strung with faint lamps, and the bells tinkling from the amber somnolence of the Gethsameen. And there in the east, a ribbon the colour of a ripe peach. Perhaps sunrise was still possible…

"How beautiful it is," she said.

"Are you here?" he said. "Am I?"

"When you fell – when you struck the ground – something hit me like one of my mother's blows – and then something else seized me," she said, "like two gigantic hands, and flung me outward. Am I the same as I was?"

"No, my love. Not at all. Am I?"

"No, my love," she said. "Not at all."

"There's no need," he said, "I think, no need to loiter here anymore. We have no names. We speak without language and exist without any form we have ever known, or if we know, then we had forgotten. And both of us – love?"

"We both of us love."

"Shall we then…?"

"Shall we," she said, "go there together?"

Above the river, something like two stars coming undone, spinning, flashing away into – into… And in the river, under the ice, the glint of rapid gold, some alchemy sinking, a coin or a fish. Or nothing. Nothing at all. Or perhaps…

"How bad the house feels," Olcha said. She stood in her nightgown, a faltering candle in her grasp, looking up the vault of stairs. "Empty," she said. To her horror she wept. All through the tenement they were waking and beginning to weep, sobbing and crying even in dreams. Zergoi cuddling his triangular guitar, Yori clutching a pair of shoes, Mariasha and Zophi and Timara running from room to room, Stavin smashing his pocket watch, as if to stop time, Koresh howling like a wolf, Ossif tearing at his hair. The world exploding apart and pieces flying upward in the storm. The mansion walls ran water as if it, too, lamented. The water soaked through the floors. It was the purging of a grief long withheld, from which few are exempt. At last, at last, it was mourning.

Among the Leaves So Green

"For I shall wed a fine young knight.
A handsome knight, quoth she…" sings Bergette as she throws open the wooden shutters.

Ghilane hears her, and knows this means trouble. Oh yes, despite the golden sun now falling in across the floor and bed like spilled honey.

Bergette is Ghilane's sister. Her half-sister. Their mother, the village's easy-woman, went with a woodcutter, and one year later there was Bergette. Then, two years after that, there was the *other* woodcutter. And then there was Ghilane. To the village, both girls are eyesores, the produce of sin. To Bergette, though, Ghilane is worse than that. Bergette was the first. Ghilane's an invader. From the beginning, Bergette has taken her revenge on Ghilane for being born, in one way or another. It used to be slaps and pinches and lies, and the stealing of food. Now it's often more rough – and more gloating – more inventive.

"Get up," says Bergette, turning and kicking at Ghilane. But Ghilane is already away and out of the bed.

They're lucky to have this straw bed up here. Their mother, because of her work, sleeps separately. (Last night the innkeeper was with her. They heard him scurrying off an hour ago, at cock-cry.) Unlike most of the village, neither girl is encouraged to get up too early. It might embarrass some retreating customer.

"And he will dress me in gowns of silk!" sings Bergette. She's sixteen, and black of hair, pale of skin. Ghilane, at fourteen, is the odd one, with her fair brown hair and light brown skin – where did she get those? Each has green eyes though, Ghilane's grape-green, Bergette's like the green of a snake's venom. Both would normally be married off by now, but that won't ever happen, seeing whose daughters they are.

Mother calls them in her demanding, unliking voice.

Bergette laughs, suddenly pushes Ghilane so she staggers, and goes down the ladder to the cottage's lower floor.

Before she follows, Ghilane glances out of the window at the village, an untidy smelly muddle of huts and lopsided houses with a grim stone church. Then she looks up the slope to the forest beyond. The forest which is so unsafe and uneasy, and for which the village is named. "Keep her away from me today," whispers Ghilane to the forest. "*Please.*"

They are sent on an errand the moment they've cooked and eaten the lumpy burnt pine-nut porridge.

"Go up to the Widow and get some eggs."

"No," says Bergette.

So Mother clouts Bergette across the face. And Bergette bursts into tears as hysterical and trouble-promising as her singing. What Mother does to her, she will later take out on Ghilane. There really is no escape now.

And why say no? They'll have to do it anyway, both of them.

The reason for the errand is threefold. 1) It gets them out of the house so that their mother can 'entertain', or just frowst about, more easily; 2) It gets them into the forest, which is dangerous – full of wolves, wild tusked pig, snakes, sudden traveller-gobbling bogs, and demons – and so is generally avoided by most of the village; besides, the Widow's shack is off the beaten track, so has yet more potential for getting them lost or in the way of a hungry large animal. The idea is, of course, though their mother would never admit this, to be permanently rid of them. 3) (Last and perhaps least), it must be the baker who's coming to visit today, because he likes eggs.

As they walk through the village, someone throws a stone. It hits Bergette, who turns, ready to kill, but no one is to be seen. Anyway, anyone could have thrown the stone. They all hate the easy-woman and her children – even the men hate them, this side of their house door.

The two girls both know too that a time will come when they won't be able themselves to put off their Turn, as Mother calls it. That is, when they take over Mother's job. Both Bergette and Ghilane choose to ignore this.

On the slope leading up through the coppice woods, into the main forest, Bergette sings again how the knight will court the lady.

Ghilane wants her to be silent so she can listen to the trees and everything that moves among them. But she has the sense not to ask Bergette to shut up.

The coppices are copper-red with buds and green with sap. But the forest, which is full of evergreens, is black and hardly ever loses its shadow. Pines and hemlocks, cedars and firs tower up, and holly trees still dappled with last winter's blood-showers of berries.

The sky is closed away.

Sun gone.

Bergette stops her singing.

"Now, you little pig…"

Ghilane is already running before the clawed hand sweeps her face. (Bergette, if she badly scratches her sister, can now blame it on the holly trees.)

But Ghilane runs fleet as a deer, ducking under the boughs, not stumbling on the great roots hooped up from the forest floor, where mushrooms sometimes grow or patches of briar and bladed grass. Bergette pounds after, not quite so clever at avoiding things.

It gets darker, and darker. The forest is a night-in-day, which now falls.

Oh, they're off the beaten track, well off now. Even the skinny path to the hen-keeping Widow's has been missed.

Ghilane thinks suddenly, madly, as she runs: *Why have I come this way…? I shouldn't have done that.* But where else could she go? It's instinct. She had seen, more than all the other times, near-murder stark in Bergette's white face, her viper-poison eyes, so, like the hunted stag, the ermine, the boar, Ghilane runs to her only hope of safety…

Which isn't safety. How can it be?

Not till she reaches the Tree does Ghilane stop, gasping, holding the stitch in her side.

Then, run out, she drops on her knees, bows her head, and waits for Bergette to come and beat her up among the leafy shadows.

The Tree is half an oak. Or rather it's two trees, a hornbeam *and* an oak, which have rooted so close they've grown together and become the Tree.

In all the forest-night of dark, these trees are green already with an early summer not much present in the rest of the woods. The leaves aren't full-blown, but they're still massed all over the two trees, frills of the oak, and the hand shapes of the hornbeam, with its strange yellow sprays like catkins hanging down. The Tree has been able, two in one, to pierce the roof of the forest. And down from there pours a fountain of green-gold sunlight, splashing and sparkling to the ground, where it breaks like scattered flames.

Slowly, despite everything, Ghilane looks up and watches the Tree. She takes in the coiling grapevine which will get purple grapes in fall-of-leaf, and the old honeycomb caught up between two boughs. She sees here, there, where a twist of ribbon has been tied on by others she's never met here. And on an apron-lap that opens from the trunks just at the right spot, offerings have been placed – some over-wintered apples, a crust of a fresh loaf.

All the birds that fly and bell about the forest visit the Tree, but they seldom disturb the offerings. Now they've gone quiet. It's as ominous as when Bergette stopped her song.

And then Bergette is *there*. With one hand she grabs Ghilane's hair and wrenches back her head, and Ghilane screws tight her eyes to save them...

And then, Bergette lets her go.

"What's this weird place?" asks Bergette.

Startled at the interruption to violence, "I don't know," lies Ghilane, who *knows*.

"It's a bad area. Trust you to drag us into it." And she cuffs Ghilane, but forgetfully now.

Bergette's eyes have gone to the altar in the Tree.

"Don't! Don't!" cries Ghilane, as Bergette fists up two of the apples that have been offered to the god of the forest, and begins to bite into them, first one, then the other.

But Bergette just grins, and goes on biting.

They don't often get an apple, or anything nice. Useless Mother has no garden plot, and those that do don't bother to bring anything like that when they 'visit'.

Ghilane stands up and waits for the god who is sometimes in the Tree to demonstrate his anger.

Why doesn't he do it?

Would Ghilane be glad if he struck Bergette? Oh yes, yes. But even so, Ghilane goes up to the Tree. She leans close as she's done before, and whispers, "Don't be angry. She's ignorant, that's all."

"Am I now?" Bergette pulls Ghilane away from the Tree and punches her just above the waist.

While Ghilane lies on the ground, trying to breathe again, Bergette slings the part-eaten apples hard against the Tree's trunk, so they squash.

"Filthy pagan thing!" screams Bergette at the Tree. "What's to be frightened of? What's to give things to? Nothing there."

Then she wheels round and runs off – terrified – into the forest.

Ghilane can't follow even if she'd like to. She isn't lost, anyway, she knows where she is. It's Bergette who is lost.

Ghilane finally gets up and goes back to the Tree.

She stands looking up and up into the cascade of green and gold. Then she touches the bark. "I'm sorry about that. Don't be angry." Then she takes the coin which Mother gave her for the eggs, and puts it down on the altar. "I know money doesn't mean anything to you, but it's all I've got to give." Why – why – does she do this? Ghilane herself isn't certain. Somehow she had a hideous picture of Bergette thrown into a prison for what she's done, and screaming – and despite everything, Ghilane can't stand it. That's just how she is – squeamish and over-imaginative – or compassionate.

The Tree rustles, a long sigh, as if it knows now Mother will also beat Ghilane for having 'dropped' the coin and failed to bring home the eggs. But of *course* the Tree knows. The god knows. The god and the Tree know everything.

The Christian priest in the church (who drinks too much beer) lectures them all on how they mustn't believe in *pagan* things, demons and spirits in the forest. The trees are only wood, the wolves are only wolves, and nothing else exists. However, he does tell them to believe in the Devil, who uses their superstition to entrap them. The Devil *is* in the forest, suggests the beery priest, and in their own wicked hearts.

Ghilane, on the other hand, who doesn't believe the Devil is particularly in the forest, believes that other things are.

Having nothing better to do now, she walks between the trees in the direction that will lead her over to the Widow's shack. Perhaps Bergette too may refind the path. And the Widow might let them have an egg for the baker anyway, without payment... She sometimes has in the past, when Bergette, who sets some store by money, has pocketed the coin.

The Widow is supposed, by some, to have been the wife of a (now dead) Crusader, who retired to the villages hereabouts for some unknown reason. A most unlikely story, but there is something peculiar about her.

She's old and bent, with gnarled brown hands, but she veils her face and hair over as they say women do in the heathen east. Sometimes you catch the flash of her narrow old eyes behind the veil, but not enough to see their colour. The rest of her features are invisible.

Her shack is tumbledown and not very clean, and cats live there in quantities, together with a vast, ivy-green toad. They cause each other no harm, strangely, the cats and the toad. Even the hens peck in and out, and sometimes birds from the forest, and the cats just yawn and go elsewhere to tear things apart.

Today, the Widow's out at the front, weeding her garden patch, where she cultivates wild cabbage, celeriac, and a walnut tree. Hens potter round her feet. There's no sign of Bergette.

The Widow straightens from her plants and stands staring at Ghilane through the veil.

"Good morning," says Ghilane. "Do you have any spare eggs?"

"Who bruised your ribs?" snaps out the old woman. How can she know? Perhaps the birds have told her.

"My sister."

"What else?" snaps the Widow.

"She stole the offering to the Tree." (And why say *that*?)

To Ghilane's surprise, the Widow laughs. She says, "No eggs. They haven't laid these past three days."

Ghilane turns to go, knowing now she'll be really thumped and belted, because there'll she be minus coin *and* eggs. The Widow says, "Come in the house."

Also oddly, Ghilane doesn't mind the Widow's shack. It smells of hens and cats (and toad?) but also of herbs and various medicines the Widow makes from nettles and similar things. Light streams in at a narrow window. They sit down on two stools.

"Have *you* made offerings at the Tree?" asks the Widow.

Ghilane hasn't lied to the Widow. Somehow she knows it wouldn't be much use. And the Widow anyway seems to know everything – all this is just a formality.

"Yes."

"What did you ask for in return?"

"Silly things. Not to be hit."

"Didn't work, did it?" says the Widow.

"No."

"But you go on thinking there's something in the Tree."

"Yes... I just think... he's too busy to take any notice of me. But I know – I know he's there."

"So it's a man?" slyly asks the Widow.

"Yes," says Ghilane. "But not a *man*." She goes red and looks away. "I saw him, once."

The Widow seems amused again. "What did you see?"

Ghilane blushes until she thinks her head will burst, but she says, anyway, "It was one early morning. Bergette scalded me, and I ran up there to the Tree, but when I got close, I waited, because there was a wild boar there. Only it wasn't goring at the trunk, just standing still. And then it walked off. And when it did – up in the leaves – sort of *under* the leaves..."

"Yes?"

"Him."

"What was he like, then?"

"Like..." Ghilane can't say, since she has so far nothing to compare him to. If she had, she'd say, "Like a young prince." Or maybe not. Finally she says, "He was handsome, and there were leaves and grapes in his hair, and his eyes were green, and then they were black. And then the wind moved the branches and he was gone."

"I'll tell you," says the old woman, "what you've been doing wrong at that Tree. You haven't been asking for enough."

"*Enough?* But..."

"Listen hard. I'll say it once. Don't ask him to let you off a slap, or make your bruise stop hurting. That's no use. Because if he does it, next minute you'll have another bruise and you'll be slapped again, won't you?"

Ghilane nods, watching the hens.

"So what would you really have, girl, from the god in the green Tree? Think. Think carefully. Then speak it out."

Ghilane shakes back her hair and stands up and raises her hands. "My life to be changed to something wonderful and new, something different – and far away from them all!"

"Be sure of it," says the Widow.

Ghilane is quite sure. She thinks, *she's a witch, I've always known...*

And then she sees straight through the Widow's veil, as if it isn't there.

Ghilane can't scream. She throws herself down on the floor, and the chickens cluck annoyedly. *They* don't worry about the presence

83

of a god who's been around forever and especially here since the Widow peacefully died at sunset, yesterday.

Bergette had blundered along until she tripped over a great root, and when she sat up, found she'd bruised her ribs and nearly knocked the breath out of herself.

She doesn't know where she is.

She begins to cry, blaming Ghilane for getting her deliberately lost. It's a trick Ghilane's thought up with Mother, who's always hated Bergette and secretly liked Ghilane because Ghilane is almost all one colour, honey brown, like a young tree. Bergette hates herself, too, and now she wants to kill someone or something, preferably Ghilane.

Then she looks up properly and the dark forest is all lit with the vividity of noon, the brilliant sunlight crashing down through all the black trees on top of Bergette.

Bergette considers. If the sun's up *there*, when half an hour ago it was over *there*, then that is the east, and she knows that the Widow's shack lies over that way.

In a minute or so, Bergette is limping on – she's hurt her foot too, in the fall. Birds sing, and she hates them and wants to wring their necks. She sees a spotted snake coiled high up, and curses it, and her snake-venom eyes become more venomous, so nasty in fact she can hardly see with them, and so it comes as no surprise when she at last looks round and finds she's now got into a clump of the darkest thickets, ringed by budding ash trees, which in turn seem ringed as if by a wall of thick, sable firs.

Bergette stops again. It was only noon just then, but suddenly she's cold. She shivers, and the firs do the same. As if something unseen is walking across the tops of them.

So Bergette says a prayer. But the prayer won't really come because it's all about being forgiven for her sins, and Bergette will be damned if she'll admit to having any of those right now.

It's all Ghilane's fault, this. Just let her wait…

Bravely, Bergette sings her song, a line or two:

"For I shall wed a bold young knight,
Come from the East, so fine and grave,
And he will dress me in ring of gold,
And I shall be his own true love.

Then he will take me for his bride
And I shall live well as a queen…"

(Bergette wants to stop singing now. Finds she can't.)

"And like the stars his armour all
Shines in among the leaves so green."

The forest is truly now black as night. Pitch black. A storm must have come up, covering the sky with cloud.

Bergette senses the approach of lightning, thunder – which never happen – but still she crouches down and starts to whimper. Until finally…

"I never meant to take your apples!" cries Bergette.

Too late?

There's someone coming out now from between the fir trees and the ash. Dark as the wood, as the sky. Black of eyes and hair and garments and – oh.

"Oh, it's you," croaks Bergette, as the old Widow-witch comes cranking up to her.

"And is it me?" says the Widow.

And then Bergette knows, with a gush of boiling fear that, no, it *isn't*.

"I never – I never never…"

"But you did."

"I was a fool."

"Yes, you were."

"Don't – don't – only say how I can put it right?"

"Is that all you'd ask for? Ask again."

In her panic, Bergette shrieks "Set me free! How can I be good when everything's so *bad*? Let my life be changed to something wonderful and new, something different – and far away from them all!" And knows she means this, though why she's said it would almost puzzle her, if she weren't so frightened.

"Where are those selfish beasts of girls?" shouts Mother, stamping about in her horrible dirty stinking house, that can't ever be called a home, even by the mice who have unrented rooms in the walls. (Let it be said here, not all easy women are as dreadful as Mother. No, she has developed a special talent for lousiness.)

However, the situation helps. The baker hasn't turned up.

Mother thinks, even so, *she* could have fancied an egg herself, couldn't she?

Those ungrateful parasites – those sluts – put them to work, that's what they needed. Why should she keep them in luxury – their own *bed* and all – she'd never wanted them.

It was the forest's fault. Those two handsome woodcutters. An evil place, the forest, everyone knew it, full of temptations and imps...

Of course, the woodcutters were both village men – another village, she didn't know where it was, they'd neither of them said. Yet, in the wood they hadn't either of them seemed like village oafs. They'd seemed witty and cultured. Especially the first one, Bergette's father. Well, Mother thought disgustedly, she'd almost been in love – twice! And so been careless. Twice.

Bang went the wind, blown down from the woods with its friend, the black sky. It would rain soon, and water would come through the roof.

Oh, she'd tan their hides, both of them, with the leather belt. When they got home.

And looking forward with slight anticipation to this treat – what Life does to Mother she's always ready, later, to take out on Ghilane and Bergette – Mother forgets something. Which is that it's now just possible her *other* (secret) wish – that of losing both daughters – may at last have come true.

When Ghilane wakes up, real night has come, prowling through the forest like a lynx, and she jumps to her feet in fear.

How could she have *slept* after what had happened? Oh, perhaps he made her sleep, the god. Lulled her asleep the way a supernatural being could. Or she'd simply fainted, from the shock. The last thing she remembers is how she stood there and said exactly what she wanted, although she can't actually remember *what* she said. Nor, come to that, what the god looked like...

Anyway. It was a dream. That must be it. She ran up here and found the poor old Widow had died (which is curious too, because Ghilane can't really remember this either, only that she knows about it). And then somehow the god was there, so she must have sat down exhausted among the chickens and dreamed all that about the god.

A shame. It had been a good dream. Alarming but also magical and – well, lovely.

Like the other dream she'd had once about seeing him in the Tree among the leaves.

Ghilane sits thinking about this, until some lights come wending along the path and stop at the door.

Then she glances up and sees ten old women, each one very much resembling the dead Widow, with their faces all veiled, and each one carrying a rush candle that burns with a bluish cat's-eye gleam.

This might be upsetting, but isn't really. The Widow was indeed part of a professional Witchery, and her sisters have felt her death and come to bury her in the proper, respectful witch fashion.

They therefore do so. Ghilane, who feels sorry about the old woman – though the witches assure Ghilane the Widow is happy, and even young again, now – `helps them. She holds candles, assists with spades, and also gathers in the chickens for the night.

"I'll live here now," says one old woman, who's exactly like the others. Ghilane really can't tell them apart.

Then three of them invite Ghilane to accompany them to their own house, which is apparently far across the forest. They seem to think Ghilane will have witch-power herself. "Something about you," they murmur, staring through and through her with their veiled eyes.

Ghilane knows, whatever else, she can't go home. She's not only not got coin or egg, she's 'dropped' her sister as well.

She feels mysteriously drawn to the three old women. She gives in.

They walk all night through the forest.

The trees look like bears in the dark, but the three old women don't seem bothered. The stars cast down their glitterings whenever there's a gap in the branches. Frogs creak from the quags. Once a wolf crosses their path. The old women greet the wolf and the wolf seems to nod, then trots on. A trick worth knowing, if nothing else. (As, come to that, is the trick of walking all day to get to the Widow's, and then all the way back without a real rest.)

Near dawn, they reach an edge of the forest which opens on a wide valley where a river runs. There's a great house down there, a timbered manor, set in walled gardens that have *flowers*.

The three witches blow out their rush candles, (which have

sorcerously lasted all this while), as the first pink tarnish of dawn begins in the east over the valley.

Then the witches draw off their veils and some threadbare mittens and their other dark clothes, and under them Ghilane s astonished to see three fine dresses trimmed with embroidery, and necklaces of gold and silver. But most astonished of all to find that, of the three old women, only one's at all *old*, with braided silver hair under a white hood. The other two are younger, one about the age of Ghilane's mother and the other only a few years older than Ghilane.

"There's our house," says the youngest witch. "Do you like it? You do? Then come live with us."

It seems that, like many Witcheries, the members range across all areas of society, from the highest to the most every day. They don't have any sense of class, however, as they mingle in the forest of the god, the rich women with the women who must pretend to sell eggs for their bread in case they're thought too clever.

And these three seem very much to want Ghilane to be part of their household – not, they explain, as servant or skivvy – but as another daughter.

They ask Ghilane nothing except would she like this?

She hesitates, of course, thinking this is too good to be true. Perhaps it's another dream. Perhaps they're lying and they will ill-treat her.

Then the sun comes up in the east, and Ghilane sees a man riding up the hill to meet the three ladies. He's the manor's lord, got up in his best and very polite to the witches, who are his mother, his wife, and his daughter. It's now fairly obvious, too, that Ghilane is also his daughter. His hair and skin are brown like hers. But none of the three witches appear dismayed. And he seems pleased to see her too.

Among the Witcheries, things are different.

So Ghilane accepts her wish come true, and goes down the hill with the ladies, and the lord who isn't a woodcutter, only made out he was long ago, when he was less just than now, and Mother less ugly and harsh.

And what is Ghilane going to, then? To worse unkindness from a jealous stepmother and even more furious half-sister? Judge from this:

Five years on, when Ghilane has been made the lord's legal

daughter and is gladsome, healthy, and very well-dressed, she is one day walking in the wood, having also become a full member of the Witchery by then. And she looks up and sees what she thinks is the god again, strolling through the wood. But it'll turn out this time it's only a man, though he is the son of that kingdom's king. So, being now a lady herself, there's nothing to stop Ghilane marrying him. Which she does. After all, it's what young women like Ghilane are meant to do.

Bergette, though.
Oh, Bergette.
Bergette the cruel, claws and fists and kicks and tricks. Bergette with the serpent-poison eyes. Who steals the coins, and steals too the offerings from the altar of a god, in a forest she knows – and she did – in her deepest heart, is the place of that god, or one of them. Stupidity added to viciousness, as so often happens.

Poor stupid, foul, disgusting Bergette, who ought, in the best tradition, to be punished for her endless crimes, just as Ghilane, who's really all right, has been rewarded for her kindness and clear vision.

Well, we've hurried here, you and I, haven't we, almost skipping over Ghilane's much-deserved and nice rest of her life. Sorry for that. But, you see – Bergette, awful Bergette – *she's* the special one.

Yes, didn't look like it, did it? All that underhand rottenness and that inability to see the forest glowing like a rising sun with the presence of the god...

Nevertheless...

When Bergette yelled what she really wanted, which was precisely the same (of course) as what Ghilane (and a great many people) really wanted, the most appalling thing in the world happened to her.

Up from the ground sprang vines and creepers and the very roots of the trees, and they caught her fast into themselves, they bound her tight and tighter than the tightest rope.

At first she screamed and fought. But it was no use at all. She couldn't move anymore, and then leaves had wound over her mouth and shut her up, too.

So then she hangs there, trapped in a spider web of forest. And the god's also still there, looking at her, the indescribable, beautiful god, but not like that, like a pillar of darkness having only eyes – yet eyes she can't *see*. The voice, though, that Bergette hears.

"Any are welcome," says the voice of the god, "to what lies on my altars, if they have need. The starving fox, the bird, the man, the woman. Any are welcome also to forget me and go instead to another Master, providing that lord is good. There is One. Most are staring in his face and missing him altogether. But you, Bergette, never know to do any of that. Therefore, since you are mine, I shall teach you."

That's what the god says to Bergette, and unlike her sister, she's going to remember it always.

It's the last thing she hears for a while, anyway.

Because next, the snaky creepers and other things are growing again, whirling around and around her, completely covering her, binding her over. Bergette shuts her eyes, thinking now she'll die, so she thinks she has.

And that way, she doesn't see, then, how a great tree is pushing up now out of all the other growth that wraps her, shutting her in like an upright wooden coffin of the finest oak.

Well, after all, that's quite a punishment, wouldn't you say?

In the forest, (across which Ghilane is busy becoming a lord's daughter), early summer ripens to fall. There are green beeches and red chestnuts among the pines and firs. Even the pines and firs are fringed with new green. Birds sing and then grow lazy. Hunting horns sound. Deer rush through and vanish like brown ghosts. Honey drips.

Imprisoned in her tree, Bergette isn't dead.

She's dreaming.

Oh, so many dreams.

First she sees her mother, as she once was, and here's another surprise – Mother is dancing with the witches. She was, then, one of the local Witchery! Mother was also good-looking then, with long, washed hair. Bergette in her dream watches sadly as Mother falls in love with the lord from the manor house, who's come to dance in the witch rituals, but in disguise. And then Bergette's dream takes her back three more years, and Mother is even younger, and falling in love for the first time – with this other one who is a lord, but said he was a woodcutter.

When Bergette in the dream sees this first woodcutter/lord, she sees who her father really is.

Then she realises he's telling her the story of her beginnings.

For Bergette's father, with his dark, long and curling hair, his eyes now vine-green and now grape-black, is the god-in-green, the Lord of the Wood, the Power of the forests.

Oh, he's much older than how he looks, older even than the oldest forest. Yet, though so old, always young. Yet, too… ancient, ancient and young both at once.

As soon as she grasps this, in her enchanted sleep, Bergette begins to trust him.

The stories go on as the dreams go on.

Bergette loves them. She loves being asleep and dreaming them. For the first time in a long while, she's happy.

Outside her strong fortress of bark, fall-of-leaf strips the woodland. The treacherous traveller-gobbling bogs groan with mud. Winter comes and colours everything dead white, but for the blackbirds feeding on the scarlet berries.

Bergette dreams on, seeing other times, other lands and worlds. Bergette is learning such a lot. It's like food and drink to her.

Outside, deer rub their horns on the trunk of the tree. Purple flowers open round its feet, and tawny colonies of mushrooms.

Then summer's back – though it's not the summer we expect, but another summer far off in the future, where now Bergette has come to be.

She opens her eyes.

It's a summer night and the forest smells of pine balsam and wild roses.

Bergette finds she's come out of the tree, she's passed right through its trunk.

For a time, she dances with her shadow – she still casts one, or thinks she does – on the moonlit grass between the trees.

Then a fox arrives, and later two wolves out courting. And an owl sits down in the tree.

Because they're not alarmed by Bergette, she sings them the song her mother had sung over her cradle. The old witch song about a knight from the East, and a lady, and the starry armour in the green leaves. She knows now who the knight is meant to be. It's Father, that's who the knight is.

After some hours, Bergette understands that she isn't as she was. She can, after all, walk into and out of trees – she's already tested this, walked back into her own and out again a couple of times. She looks into a forest pool and sees her long, grape-dark hair, and how her eyes are no longer the green of a snake's poison but of its gliding skin among the vine.

She dances with a wild cat, now.

She chases a marten up a spruce, and plays with it along the whippy boughs – fearless, of course, because even if she falls, it won't matter now; she can't be hurt anymore.

If she thinks about it, she supposes that yes, her life is changed, wonderful and new and different – and she's far away from them all.

But now, coming and going as she pleases in the forest, she notices the people who come there. Of these, few cut down trees. Most of the villages get their wood from the self-renewing coppices. But the villagers do gather a lot in the forest, fruits and berries, herbs and mushrooms, and reeds from the bogs. Sometimes, Bergette plays little tricks on these gatherers. Nothing terrible. She may move a basket, conceal a fallen glove, then put it back somewhere else, or tie the edge of a cloak to a bush. The people in the forest never see her, but they *sense* her, some of them anyway. Word gets round.

"Those imps are mucking about again in the forest."

"Stole my knife then stuck it in a clump of violets."

Sometimes too they accuse her of doing things she hasn't, but which someone *has* done... That is, someone of her *kind*.

Bergette knows there are others like herself among all the trees. Other brothers and sisters, the sons and daughters of Father. As yet, she only glimpses them – glimmering shadows, breezes blowing by. And for them, she thinks, so far she's the same – just a glimpse. Meetings will take time, but that's one thing she – they – have.

Meanwhile, Bergette begins to see, despite the games she plays, the people of the villages don't seem as wary of the forest as they did, despite what they may say. She becomes curious about this. One afternoon, when the heat runs over everything like slow water, Bergette wanders down to her own village, the place where she was born.

She's stunned.

It's not much like it was.

For one thing, it's ten times the size. The houses are better built too, and there are a lot of gardens. A few pigs wander up and down the streets, but they're fairly neat pigs.

In Mother's revolting house, there now lives a scholar. He has a housekeeper, and everything's immaculate (except the scholar, actually, who's an untidy old soul).

When Bergette gets up to the church, (walking all unseen, but sometimes sensed, among the market crowd), she stops, amazed. Because the church has turned into a plant, or vegetable. She can see this at once.

In the summer, the old stone sweats and has a colour like the Eastern mineral called jade. But more than this, the whole building has been *carved*. What carvings they are. Stone trees stride up the walls, inside and out, and in among the stone leaves are people of stone and little stone animals. And on the altar, where nothing much stood before, stands a beautiful calm Christ statue, crowned with thorns.

Bergette stays some while in the vegetable church, liking it. When the priest comes through, he's not the drunk one she remembers. He's fat and thoughtful, brown from the sun.

Bergette decides this religion too is, at its true heart, perfectly beautiful. It had only been spoilt a little by fools. The force of an ultimate God pours through the stones, as through the forest. And from this Ultimate spring all and everything, all trees, all carvings, all beasts and men. All gods.

Then Bergette sees, over by the wall, a young man is bending to work on the stone with a mallet and chisel. She knows he's the mason and the sculptor, one of many, maybe, who's carved the church into a sacred wood and shown true God on the altar. Bergette recalls what Father once said to her. She thinks that, though this aspect of God is perhaps the Other One he spoke of, Father too has a place inside the forest of stone.

She whispers in the mason's ear, and he hears her.

And under his cunning hands, the wall carving changes. It becomes a face masked in leaves and which is *speaking* leaves, smiling so they spill, the leaf-words, from its lips – the face of her father.

Then Bergette goes back into the forest, to live forever un-lonely, among her brother and sister trees.

Time goes on turning its pages of seasons and history.

One day, a princess comes riding into the May-green wood, which in her language they say is *blue* with leaves, because simply to say *green* doesn't describe such lushness.

The princess and her ladies discard the horses with their grooms and walk off into the depths of the forest.

After they find a place they think suits them, they begin to play like little girls with a gold-stitched ball, throwing it back and forth.

Bergette, sitting up in a cedar, looks over and sees – her *sister*, brown Ghilane, dancing there in a silk gown and rings of gold. A princess! When did *this* happen?

She isn't jealous, you understand; she doesn't hate Ghilane anymore. Why should she? Bergette's almost insanely happy, so there's no room in her anywhere for hate. Besides, she long ago forgave herself, and so forgave everyone else.

But Bergette is, well, fascinated. So she leans down and snatches the ball out of the Princess Ghilane's brown hands in the instant she throws it.

"It's gone into thin air!" cry the ladies, between thrill and unease. Everyone's always told them these woods are *weird*, which is why they like to go Maying here.

But the princess looks straight up into Bergette's face and seems to see her.

"Good morning," says the princess. "You must be the spirit of the tree. The Green Lady."

Bergette understands this; she can speak any language of the world now, just as she understands what the leaves themselves are saying. She smiles, but before she can reply, the princess offers her own name. "I am Princess Ghisella," says the princess.

Bergette remembers. Time isn't as it was, for her. She says, softly, "Not Ghilane."

"Ghilane? Let me think, that was my great-great-great-grandmother's name."

"Who's she talking to? She's gone off her head," mutter the ladies to each other, worried because, if she has, they'll almost definitely get the blame.

But the princess peers on into the tree at Bergette – whom she can apparently see because they're still dimly related.

"Can I have a wish?" asks the princess. Greedily.

Can I grant wishes?

Bergette wonders where her father is. She sometimes senses him passing in the forest, just as ordinary human things sense her. But she hasn't seen him for quite some time (centuries in fact). Somehow, that's never mattered. She has instead begun to meet – often by now

– with her own kind. Introductions come slowly here, because, once made, they'll last for millennia. She'd like to ask their advice, her kindred, but for once, all she hears is the whispering of the leaves.

So, "What do you want?" inquires Bergette uncertainly of the human princess.

Ghisella squares her jaw – something Ghilane never did.

"To be a queen, and the mother of a king."

Bergette thinks, (and this really is Bergette, thinking this), *what a shame.* And she hears herself say, "You won't get that. Why don't you ask for something important?"

But exactly then she sees Ghilane's great-great-great-granddaughter shaking her head angrily, frowning, glaring.

"It's disappeared! All a trick – how dare it? – doesn't it know who I *am*?!"

The ball thuds down on the ground.

But Bergette, who vanished to the princess when the princess became totally stupid, is now leaping laughing over the tops of the trees, and by her, taking her hands, are three or four just like her, their long hair full of leaves. And the whole forest seems to be laughing. And maybe even Ghilane, wherever she is by then, is laughing too.

Though obviously, years after, when poor silly Ghisella is the queen of a very large country, and her son the king-to-be, she thinks back smugly and says, "I asked this from a wood spirit, whom I charmed with my manner and grace." And everyone nods politely, though by now she's grown graceless and frowsty, like poor old Mother long ago.

Author's Note:
The inspiration came from a long-standing interest in Dionysus who, in ancient Greece, was most decidedly one of the gods of the Wild Wood. Often misunderstood, Dionysus is far more than a wine deity. He is the Breaker of Chains, who rescues not only the flesh but the heart and spirit from too much of worldly regulations and duties. He is a god of joy and freedom. Any uncultivated, tangled, and primal woodland is very much his domain.

As for the sisters and their background, they arrived at once and took over. One of the reasons I like writing such a lot: it's always fascinating to see new places and meet new people!

Beauty is the Beast

The land was in turmoil, and from the City of the Thousand Domes, the outlaws fled to the town of the Free North.

"How shall we be received?" they said to each other, as they rode wearily at sunset through a province of vines, and sighted such a town of fine old houses and leaning walls. In the yellow light, the world seemed peaceful. But they knew otherwise. "We bring them unrest and trouble. War – if they listen and come to our help."

But Northfree, by her very name, knew the state of the land, and how terror ruled southward, from the Capital. The town opened her gates and welcomed the outlaws, gave them food and wine, and lamps; let them shine and speak out from their broken hearts and blazing rage.

It was a fact, the City of the Thousand Domes had become in these years, *altered*. In the North they had heard of the riotous insanity. The citizens had thrown down the law and the religion. They lived now by vice and cruelty, and made a fetish of dirt, rags, ugliness, for they said all things were made equal, must therefore *be* equal, nothing better than another thing, but only as nature intended – though, in the way of the fetish, they occasionally drew attention to a deformity by ornamenting it in some curious manner. Ravens perched on the towers by day and rats ran like rivers in the streets by night, exalting in the carnage. For the new deity of the metropolis, whom they called The Reasonable, was a goddess of blood and demanded frequent sacrifice. All this, the outlaws reviewed for the town of Northfree, standing in the lamplit square. A vast crowd had gathered, the windows and balconies, the very roofs were filled by silent watches, listening. Even the stars looked down.

"For a year we struggled," said the spokesman of the outlaws. "By such legal means as are still recognised there, and also by schemes and plots, to bring back some sense, some justice to our heaven-cursed City. But we failed, and in fear of our lives at last, we fled." Then he covered his face with his hands and wept, and the crowd murmured.

Another spoke. He told how the City was now ruled by strange petty kings, who abused their power but refused power's name – being, of course, equal to everyone else. Evil madmen, magicians, who could ensorcel the creatures of the city, human and otherwise, bending men and women to their will, enlisting the terrifying rats as their minions, the ravens as their spies.

"To the unmerciful mercy of these monsters we were forced to leave our comrades, those imprisoned in the black dungeons on the river. They warned us to escape and will give their lives for ours."

And then the outlaws talked of raising armies here in the North, to march against the vicious rabble of the City, cast it and its masters down, and bring the reign of terror to an end. "Though they are magicians there, they are mortal. They can be killed."

The speakers enlarged upon particular tyrants, and though Northfree had heard of many of them, their names and deeds, the news had now a dreadful emphasis. Especially there was one, Chaquoh he was called, who was already well-known and infamous. It was said he wrote and uttered poison. Even to read a sentence he had penned could blind you. The malignity of his words slew, or sent mad. He stank of a terrible disease, which would long since have eaten him up, but that the disease of his *spite* was stronger. Or else it was the spite itself which furnished the disease – a parasite that thrived on him, but dared not finish him entirely.

A little before midnight, exhausted, the orators concluded. The crowd shouted instead. Hands were raised and vows sworn of loyalty and protection. The young men of the town sprang forward.

"We will be your army, and go with you, to blast this obscenity of a City from our country's earth. How shall we take it? Only tell us what to do."

Then there were fresh lamps lit, and bottles opened. The campaign began to be discussed.

It was only as faint colour started again to come in the sky that one of the outlaws – he who had wept – said to the townsman at his elbow, "Tell me, do you know the young woman who was standing, until a moment ago, up on that balcony there? At one point there was a tall man in white beside her, but he went away. She had only one old servant for company. But she was very remarkable."

"By your description, that is Maristarre," said the townsman.

"She will have grown tired and gone home to find rest, no doubt," said the outlaw, his thoughts straying somewhat from the honourable war, for she had been exceptionally beautiful, this Maristarre of Northfree. But then anger and pain and hope laid hold of him again, and he forgot her quite.

Maristarre of Northfree. It was true she was beautiful, with her whiteness like clear marble through which the light shines, her darkly polished hair, and darkly polished eyes that seemed always to see far off. There had been many offers, but she had not wished to leave her father, it would appear. Now she went home to one of the old houses of the town, and seating herself as the dawn bloomed, she wrote to him. "Forgive me," wrote Maristarre, "it has come to me what I must do. The young men will fight. They will form an army discernible from miles off, and all the power of the City will be turned against them. But I am one woman, and may pass unnoticed." (She was modest. At home, people turned always to look at her on the street. This very sunrise as she returned, a tall man in white had looked long after her, from the porch of a neighbouring church.]

It was also true that she was a visionary, this Maristarre. She did see far off. As the orators had poured forth their flaming passion, her spirit seemed to speak softly within her. She thought; *They would fight sorcerers. What if the sorcerers lie dead?* And she beheld Chaquoh the evil one, the Beast, perhaps mightiest of the great tyrant-masters of the City of the Thousand Domes. She saw his vileness conjured by the outcry of the outlaws. And herself also she saw. She, so purely fair, and he so hideous and steeped in venom. Opposites direly attracting. As if to a magnet she was drawn to this. All her years, where another might have looked into her mirror and grown proud, visionary Maristarre had simply been puzzled at herself. But now at once she understood. She was a clean bright sword, fashioned for one incredible stroke.

So in the earliest morning she left her father's house, and the town where she had lived all her life, and the province of vines. She found transport to a town farther south, and there transport to another more southerly. Until at length she boarded one of the rattling black chariots that hurled itself along the rutted roads to the City of the Thousand Domes.

She had dressed in plain slovenly garments, and her hair hung down to her waist, for so the women wore their hair in the Capital now, sometimes with a bloody flower tangled in it pinned through by a stiletto.

As the coach came near the City, Maristarre saw such things as these on the hills: burned fields, where corpses lay; trees with skulls tied in them by ribbons; tall garlanded gallows of ornate wrought-iron, with the hanged hanging. Once or twice a shepherdess drove her sheep across the road and the carriage halted. These girls carried pistols in their belts, and one a tall pike with a grinning painted mask fixed to the top. Their own faces were grinning and maleficent, and the sheep too were changed, scarlet or ochre in colour, with sharply pointed teeth. They did not bleat, but made a guttural sound, as if they were in the process of learning human speech, and half choked on it.

The sun had just gone down when they reached the City. Against a dying sky, Maristarre saw its thousand black domes, and all the points of light and rays of smoke that rose from its hell fires.

What a place was this, worse than any telling. But Maristarre was not dismayed. She knew her task, her destiny, her punishment even. She had accepted all, and had no need to be afraid.

At the gate of the City, men with broken teeth glared in, and bade her get out of the carriage. (One lacked an eye but wore a patch which read *Look! I have lost my eye!*, the words picked out in gems.)

"Your business, sister?" ('Sister, brother', these were the formal and only lawful modes of address in the Capital, where everyone-and-thing was equal.) These men were part of the city's Guard of Brotherhood, and they wore the blood-red insignia of The

Reasonable One.

"I am here," said Maristarre, calmly, "to join the glorious free women of the City."

The Guard approved of this. They were fascinated by beauty, too, provided it was natural; though generally they regarded it with suspicion.

"Your hands are smooth," one said to her, "there's no mark on you."

"I shall gain scars of honour, in the service of Chaquoh," said Maristarre. "I have come to offer him my whole self, for even in the nothing-town where I was born, his words ring like an alarm-bell. I am his slave. I will lie at his feet."

At this, the men toasted her in a deadly inky brandy they were prone to drink, and she was allowed to go on into the City. The name 'Chaquoh' would be a safe conduct. No one would touch her, if they thought her due to be his.

So she passed through the streets. In the narrower alleys, which she avoided, she heard the gutters chuckling and guessed what moved along them and how like a ruby it shone under the lamps. On the wide roads carriages whirled by, loud with drunken voices. The buildings, high-roofed and impressive always, were now much blemished from the fighting that had gone on in the City at the beginning of its alteration. Whole sections had been blasted from walls, and windows shattered, and all left gaping, so one could see in as if to a lighted picture. Quarrelling, debauche, and even manslaughter, these were the normal subject of everyone. Harlots went by, slender or bloated, feathers and knives in their nests of hair; and gangs of men, some of whom would have seized Maristarre, but she spoke the name of Chaquoh with such authority, they let her continue. Once, a hunchback questioned her. His humped shoulder was sprinkled with faceted jewels, though he wore foul rags. When she said she would serve Chaquoh, the hunchback laughed. He had served mighty brother Chaquoh too, he said.

On one street she came to a waxworks lit by torches, and doing fine business. The waxworks' specialty was to show life-like images of many persons who had been killed in the City, their faces having been modelled from death-masks obtained immediately after murder or execution. Several were victims of the goddess, The Reasonable One. Maristarre did not falter.

She reached a square where a forge was smoking up thick overcast and sparks. She told the blacksmith she wanted to buy from him a knife.

"See," he said, "look what I am melting down – a church bell and a holy cup to be cannon balls and swords. But here is a knife could disembowel a spider. This will do for you. Do you mean to slit the throat of some rival?"

"No," said Maristarre. "I intend to put the knife to the service of Chaquoh."

Then the blacksmith fawned on her and gave her the knife without taking any money for it.

Maristarre crossed the stone bridge over the City's river. All the statues on the bridge had been smashed and lay in piles of rubble, over which each traveller picked his way with difficulty. On days of festival, the bridges were almost impassable, due to the corpses heaped there. Down in the black river, fish sometimes leapt to the surface; corpse-fed and swollen, they had grown as large as dogs, and had luminous pale eyes. From the river, too, the prisons of the City rose up out of the water, and with narrow pale eyes, not unlike those of the unnatural fish, they scanned the dark as if searching for prey. But still Maristarre did not falter. Nor when, leaving the bridge, a tall man in white seemed to bar her way – but then he moved aside and was gone.

Having gained the other bank, she walked up a long and unlit lane, where the rats might be heard rustling and cheeping, and sometimes there came the flash of eager rat-eyes. But Maristarre had only to whisper the name: *Chaquoh*. She knew the rats would let her alone.

She had had no need to ask the way. The dwellings of all the magician-masters had been described in detail. She found the house of Chaquoh with no trouble.

It was tall, and leaned heavily on both its neighbours, which were ruined and empty, but for the scurrying, glittering rats. From colossal chimneys, grown by overuse seemingly too big for the building, vapours glided into the starless night. One window dully glowed, high up. There he would be, at his work. But even now Maristarre did not falter.

She knocked on the door; its knocker was a severed human hand, or so it looked—but made of white stone.

At the knock a hundred voices seemed to moan and cry. A rat, itself big as a spaniel, slid to her ankle, and the rat spoke to Maristarre, though its speech was awkward and impeded.

"Whatseek?" said the rat.

"Chaquoh, my brother."

"Whyseek?"

"To be Chaquoh's slave."

"Allusissame. Noslave."

"True, brother. But let Chaquoh correct me."

"Thenshall."

And the rat licked the door, which grated and drew open.

Beyond the doors, an empty vestibule, its corners filled by stacks of yellowing paper, and hung throughout by curtains of dust and webs. All these, and the paper stacks too, had been carefully spangled with gold-leaf, so no iota of the muck should be overlooked. On the long, crooked stairway, the broken tiles were rimmed by gold.

Maristarre went up the steps. On each landing there were doors, fast shut, though in some cases the wood was cracked, it was possible to see through – but only to darkness. Finally it seemed she had reached the attic of the house. Instead of a door, the stair opened directly on a cramped anteroom. Nothing was in it but a hard, wooden chair, and a lamp. A statue held this lamp, a statue of rusty iron in the shape of a snake with a woman's head and hands. "What do you require, sister?" asked the snake-statue.

"To see my brother, Chaquoh."

"Chaquoh is bathing. You must wait."

"Thank you, sister," said Maristarre. She sat on the hard chair and folded her hands. The knife nestled at her breast.

An hour passed. Out in the City of the Thousand Domes a bell struck for midnight, but the bell had a human voice, and every one of the twelve chimes was some ominous word. Maristarre caught such sounds as seemed to be *Pestilence, Despair, Hatred, Lies, Strangling* — and several others that do not look well written down. From the streets, too, came shrieks and growls, stupid laughter and wicked laughter, and now and then the noise of clashing swords, or shots.

Eventually Maristarre rose.

"What do you require, sister?" asked the statue-snake again.

"May I now go in to my brother, Chaquoh?"

The statue waited, then it said, "Yes, go in."

At this, a hole appeared in the wall, a jagged rent as if cannon-blast had passed through there, but every fissure was set with a pearl or a topaz. Beyond the fissure, a disheartening stair leading down and down, as the first stair had led up and up. But Maristarre took the stair, and went down it, into a vague luminous dark.

Far down at the stair's foot, she found herself above a great sewer full of murky fluid, which led away through channels on every side, apparently out into the City. A slight greenish slime on the water gleamed and illuminated the area.

There was a platform at the stair-bottom, jutting out on the water. Even as Maristarre stepped down on it, a creature appeared, swimming in from one of the outlets. It moved swiftly toward her, and suddenly, grasping the platform, its upper half emerged from the slime. Here was Chaquoh, it could be no other.

He was a man still, but barely. Now you could perceive the nature of his disease, his body scaled and plated—he was turning gradually and maybe less gradually with every hour, into a sort of alligator. Yet his hands and pale face, and his bright red eyes—these were like a rat's.

"You must pardon me, sister," he murmured to Maristarre, "but it is only here I can find comfort for my body."

His red-cold eyes stared at her, all over. He put one of his little rat paws on her foot. Maristarre did not falter. "Why," he hissed, "why, pretty sister, are you here?"

"I bring you the names of the traitors who recently escaped you," said Maristarre.

"Ah," said Chaquoh with a smile or grimace, "good news. Wait. My pen…" And he drew from behind one pointed ear a dagger-bladed quill whose long, long feather seemed to touch the very ceiling far overhead under the attic. "And ink…" At which he stabbed the pen into his arm, and as the swarthy blood spurted, he dipped the pen and wrote on the air – which sizzled – *The Names of Traitors*. "I promise you," he said, "they shall die in agony."

Then Maristarre leaned close and with her knife she struck Chaquoh through the throat, where he was not yet scaled, down into the heart. He gave a thin scream, more like a whistle. And then he dragged himself upward on the platform and dropped on his side. The blood from his death-wound was not of the shade of the other blood; it was black, and where it fell the platform smoked. "You have killed me," said Chaquoh.

"Yes," said Maristarre.

"Now," said Chaquoh, "you are indeed my slave." And then he died.

But Maristarre spurned his body and his words alike. She turned from him and stood composed to wait her punishment.

Very soon there began to be a screaming and shouting and roaring on all sides. The City felt his death. Things plunged in the sewer. The great black rats spilled round and stared at her. She thought she would be torn in pieces, and prepared herself to suffer it. But then men came, and women, rushing down the stair with torches in their hands, weeping and screeching. They took her by the arms.

They called her terrible things. "To the goddess!" they cried. "The goddess shall have you."

"I am the sacrifice," said Maristarre. "I have done what I came to do. The beast is dead."

But she was dragged away into streaming fire and darkness. Battered and bruised, spat on, beaten and enchained, cast into a dungeon blacker than moonless night, in the depths of the prison in the river.

Before dawn, a voice cried her sentence out of the black. As they had told her, she must meet the goddess.

But Maristarre's eyes looked far away. Her whiteness shone in the blackness. She said nothing. She had done what she had come to do.

They took her, the next sunset, to the temple where their

goddess was worshipped. It was an open amphitheatre, seating many thousands, and every seat filled. At its centre was a platform, and here rose two uprights of wood. They bound Maristarre between them so tightly she could not move. Then the Guard of Brotherhood, who had escorted her to the place, and bound her in it, hurried away to the edges of the arena. Drums began to beat and bugles to wail, and the multitude clapped and cawed, invoking The Reasonable One, entreating her to manifest and claim her due, this assassin of one of the City's holiest sons. The sky bled down and soon the night would come.

"How shall she know the goddess is near?" the guards had said, in grim banter, as they rode beside her chariot on the way.

"A shadow and a sound of wings," another answered.

"And then the sharp beak!"

All along the route, the people of the City had howled at Maristarre and cursed her and made gestures of rending her. But as she was to be given to the goddess, she escaped maiming. Others danced and sang about the vehicle, describing how it would be for her, to die, when the beak of the goddess slashed her apart. Children at the wayside ate sugar skulls. In some places, hawkers sold pigs' blood in which to dip various flowers, so they turned the proper tint.

But then, and now in the amphitheatre under the prescient sky, Maristarre showed no fear – and felt none? Between the upright stakes she stood in silence. Her eyes looked far away. *I am the clean sword, stained now by filthiness. Break me. I consent. Purity triumphs. The beast is dead. I am not their sacrifice. I die for the hope and beauty of the earth.*

Nevertheless, the far-seeing, far-off visionary eyes of Maristarre now glimpsed a man in the crowd, a tall man all in white, and she realised she had seen him twice, or maybe three times, before. Who could it be? Had he followed her all this way from the North? Some rescuer? No, such a rescue could not be possible.

And the last embers were crushed from the sun. The sky turned sable, a wind blew fiercely over the amphitheatre, shaking garments and hair, and rattling the chains that bound Maristarre.

"The goddess! The goddess arrives! The Reasonable!"

The crowd moaned and thundered. A shadow fell abysmal on

Maristarre and she heard a sound of wings…

Cold pain passed through her – but she recognised it was only the dash of the air, her chains falling away – she was in the sky, held firmly in the arms of a man, taller than any man she had ever seen, almost a giant, with a mane of pale hair flaming behind him, and vast white wings spread out, beating like the wings of a swan, as he bore her upward.

"Rescue, then?" questioned Maristarre.

"You may say so," he gently said to her.

"Where now?" said Maristarre. She did not speak of Northfree. He was the angel of death, and this she knew.

"You have seen a city of Hell-on-Earth," said the angel, as they spun higher and higher on his swan's wings, so high the sun was again visible far beneath, like a guttering lamp under their feet. "Now you must see another earthly city."

They made one enormous circle. The night revolved and was flung away like a stone; the sun, having fallen, blossomed once more.

There below, among the green lands of summer, lay a City of shining roofs and cupolas, with a silver river dividing it.

The angel spoke some sacred charm, and became a snow-white pigeon, and Maristarre a pearl-grey dove. They flew down into the shining City together, and in her visionary heart, her dove's heart, Beauty thought, *This is my doing. Good is victorious. This is how it will be.*

In the meadows girls picked flowers, and the sheep played, their wool ambered and pinkened by sunlight, their square little teeth harmlessly full of grass. Trees had paper rosettes tied on them; even the scarecrows were garlanded. The City gates stood wide, and the brave young men in their uniforms, with many honours pinned to them, saluted courteously whoever went in or out. All the women were lovely, and the men fine. Their faces were full of patience and optimism, and as they went about their work, or walked to and fro, they sang sweet or gallant songs. A woman passed with a load. A man hastened after her and aided her with it. A child fell down and a score of persons ran to console it. To a shop selling bread the hungry came, and received the hot loaves without a coin asked of them. A girl with a silver ring gave it gladly in barter for a daisy.

There had been some damage done to the buildings, it must have been in a fighting past unlike this harmonious present. Now the busy workmen patched the bricks, and where the workmen had not yet come, they had hung out wreaths and plants in pots and birds in cages and hand-switched banners, to soften any ugliness.

An image-maker's shop stood on a thoroughfare, where might be seen living celebrities and deceased. It was a popular place, each figure having been modelled from the life, even in some instances after death, that no falsehood might be told or injustice done the subject.

On the glistening river, the tranquil barges floated up and down. Lions of gold had been set on the bridges, from which the statues of oppressors had long since been removed. The golden lions reflected in the silver water. Each bore an inscription which said: "*Let us all be lions!*" But somewhere a bell had begun to dole with a melodious sadness.

Flying with the angel, Maristarre paused in the air, and looked down to see a massive procession winding along the river bank. Girls in white and solemn musicians, incense uncurling to the sky, and green branches strewn. And a lament was rising, and on every side men and women standing to watch and weep.

"Is it a funeral procession? Who has died?"

"One who loved us and cared for us…"

Then flying lower, Maristarre the dove beheld a chair borne high in the middle of the procession, and seated in it, seeming only to sleep, a man whose handsome face was darkened by nobility, sorrow and death.

In awe conceivably, certainly with attention, Maristarre followed the bier, and all its thousands of mourners.

As the procession flowed on, she saw one on whose humped shoulder the tears of another's compassion sparkled like jewels, and a one-eyed man, on whose bandage was written: *Gladly given for my country*. The roofs about were clustered with white pigeons; white hyacinths fell, dipped in wine. Children pressed white handkerchiefs to their lips, kissing the embroidered picture of the dead lamented one. Even the alley-rats, the knaves and thieves, stared after the cortege and wept. He forgave us. He knew poverty drove us on. He was our brother, and our master.

"*Chaquoh!*" they cried, and their tears ran like rivers to a sea of loss.

"*He?*" said Maristarre to the angel. "Have I misheard?"

"Even he," the angel said. "Remember, he wrote in his life's blood, without a qualm."

And presently, as the funeral wound away, Maristarre found herself standing again in the sky, above a scaffold. Her own body was being removed from it, taken away for burial.

"Their goddess, that they worship," said Maristarre.

"Again, you mistook the words you listened to," said the angel. "They called it, not Reason, but Razor. It is only a common axe, or very nearly."

Maristarre looked down and observed her body, and that it was no longer beautiful, or pristine, or whole, but ugly, crippled, the carcass of a frightful beast.

"Is this, then," said Maristarre, "the truth?"

"Each sees the truth is his own way. The City strives for one truth, which it believes to be as you have now had revealed to you. Those who oppose the City's values, or fear them, see everything as monstrous, and the architectural creation of monsters—as you have had it revealed to you formerly, and on which sight you have acted."

Maristarre looked behind her, and she saw a man approaching them over the sky. It was Chaquoh. He was neither handsome and noble, nor a scaled rat-alligator with red eyes. He was merely a man, worn out with labour and fury, with his own demons, and the world's. He glanced at Maristarre and passed her, walking on into the distance, which was not simply sky.

"It seems to me I must, in fact, follow and serve him. Is it so?" asked Maristarre.

"You took away his life."

"He erred in his life."

"His mistake. Yours is the robbery. Now you owe him the debt."

"Then I am to be his slave and he my master?"

"You have seen him as the City saw him, and yourself too,

through their eyes. Forget such terms as Master, Magician, Slave. Forget the masks men wear. Go now, and try to see the truth, which is never easy."

So Maristarre ceased gazing far off. She fixed her eyes on Chaquoh and she walked after him. And as she walked, she thought how he *had* written in his life's blood, and said – not "*They will die in agony*" – but: "*They or we will die in agony*". (How much had she misheard as well as mis-seen?)

Dimly behind her she fancied she detected now the shock of war, the North risen, the very shores of the planet, and the City rocking at the blast, blood and soot and violence: tears, courage, songs – till only the weeping of the rain could wash clean the thousand domes of it.

But how far away it seemed.

Ceres Passing

My mother, one of the King's twenty-six wives, was having her face creamed and massaged by a slave. It was messy, and boring to watch. Glittering insects buzzed in the colonnade. The nightly storm was crouching in the hills outside the city and everyone felt vaguely furious about something.

The slave batted ineffectually at the insects, cream slopped on the marble. I waited.

"Tonight," my mother remarked again.

She had remarked in the same way four or five times already. It was an annoying habit of hers. Everything distracted her, the flies, the slave, the storm, everything.

"Tonight?" I asked casually. It was useless to be more pressing.

My mother selected a small, inferior cake. (The best ones went to the Favourite Wives, of whom there were five. The Favourite Wives were also able to bum incense to keep the insects away.)

"Oh, how oppressive it is," said my mother, as if she had made a world-shattering discovery. She slapped the slave, who perhaps had got some cream in her eye. "Tonight, Angka," added my mother, "you are to dance in the Hall. There's someone your father wants to impress." Not impress too much, however, or it would have been the daughter of a more important wife.

"I see," I said.

"And you are not to be late again. Be there after the main courses of the feast. About the stuffed hedgehog, I should think."

The stuffed hedgehog was served, at Superior Feasts, after at least twenty dishes, but at Inferior Feasts it was twelve along. Presumably, as *I* was to dance, tonight the hedgehog would be number twelve.

I'm not a very good dancer and my father used me only on unimportant guests. They were always drunk by the moment of my arrival, so my wobbly twirls and limping efforts to resemble a "slender palm tree tossed by the wind" – as my teachers had it – were less noticeable. Perhaps they thought I was a wonderful dancer and it was the wine they had knocked back that made me look that way. Usually they were snoring by the end of my act.

"What would happen," I inquired, "if I didn't go?"

"Your father would whip you personally. You'd be scarred for life." She slapped the slave again absent-mindedly.

As I got up, the storm broke.

My mother screamed as great purple birds came squawking and flapping into the room, between the pillars. Rain exploded on the floor like broken glass, and the lightning gave a huge white wink.

"Ah!" screamed my mother. The birds rushed round us, and light furnishings crashed to the floor. It would really be quite simple to murder all of us, the two courtesy guards outside the door were so used to our continual commotions that they would never take any notice. Not that they would be at their posts, or that anyone would bother to murder us anyway. It's a marvellous status symbol to have a few murder attempts made on your life every month or so. The King's favourite Favourite Wife was always finding adders in her clothes chest or curses pinned to her bed curtains.

Birds zoomed over my head and tried to come out of the door with me, but I shut them in firmly with my mother.

In the corridor rain dappled the floor and my bare arms. Some of the tiny, furry pet animals that were everywhere in the palace sat in a puddle and gazed at me. There was no guard in sight.

As I crossed the dripping greens of the gardens lightning turned into a sizzling spear and shot downwards into the city. I was sure it had struck some historic old useless obelisk somewhere or other. This would mean rites and religious processions for the rest of the week, in hope that the gods would intercede with furious old useless ancestors demanding a new old useless obelisk we couldn't afford to put up.

My apartments, such as they are, lie at the dank bottom of the overgrown and gloomy Sun Garden, in a sort of pagoda, once the love-nook of some long-forgotten concubine. The garden leaned extra heavily on the pagoda tonight. Nevertheless, a flickering lamp welcomed me in at the porch. Inside, my elderly slave Talu was busy at her endless picking up after me, her arms full of shed clothes, her eyes full of horror at my rainy appearance.

"There's a hot bath prepared," she cried. "Into it you go at once."

Talu's only physical characteristic is her hair. It is made of iron and skewered in place by obsidian pins.

In herself, Talu has long since been trained to think of nothing but regular mealtimes, habits, baths, nourishing drinks, and so on. She therefore disapproved each time of my dancer duties, with all the frustrated anguish of the slave. She is nearly as powerless as I am.

I kicked off my sandals and dropped my clothes in the normal way as I went towards the bedchamber and bath. Talu came along behind, clucking and picking up. This was so much a ritual I did it now more to console her than anything; to my surprise, in past months, I'd become quite tidy when left to myself.

After the bath I dressed in an old silver thing and some jewellery Talu brought looking desperate to speak and my-lips-are-sealed. When she gave up on untangling my hair with the combs and brush, Talu went off and started taking down the storm amulets she hangs out every evening, in order to hang up the other lot to protect us through the night.

"Talu," I said, "do you know who my father's guest/guests is or are?" Once I'd said it, I couldn't think why I had. It could have no possible interest for me.

Talu sniffed, and said, "How should I know?"

But of course slaves know almost everything, and now it was to be a battle of wills, which poor Talu enjoyed so much, holding out, and finally giving in. So I had to go on.

"Oh, *you* know."

"I? A lowly drudge…?"

Et cetera.

The sunset had perished in the storm, and by now my father's dinner would be tackling course number eleven, (probably an unlucky warthog).   *

"…But perhaps I heard the under-scullion say something about a portent."

"What has a portent got to do with the guest/guests?" I said.

"It advised to be very *wary*," said Talu. "For here was One More Than She Seemed."

A single word stood out from this familiar type of injunction, which is of the sort the temples endlessly inflict on us. (Beware the failure of the evening storm, it may mean drought. Desist from wasting food, it may invoke famine. Regard the humble beggar in the refuse, he is more than he appears, for the gods now and then take human guise to test us.) The word that actually startled me was *She*.

"Do you mean the King's guest is a woman?"

Talu picked up a bracelet I had dropped to help her.

"What does a slave know?"

But now there was no more time to argue. I maliciously agreed of course, she could know nothing, and ran out.

In the wet haunted garden, glimmering with first night, statues and lurking ghouls with red greedy eyes cheeped as they came alive in among the orchids. Dilapidated ghosts clutched at me on the stair. "*Angka, stop and visit me!*" mooed the haunt on the thirty-first step – which may only be wind through a split column there, but then how has it learnt my name?

I thrust the door of the upper terrace shut behind me and was in the smart part of the palace. At once two guards leapt out and finding me, as ever, Princess Number Seventeen (unlike the haunt, hardly anyone else here has troubled to take my name), they flung open great portals with bronze fitments and I came into the Hall before the King.

As I'd thought, it had been warthog. Everyone was chewing with intent sullenness, or picking their teeth in obvious anxiety. Even as I entered, a cook did likewise, sweeping by me with a baked hedgehog on a platter for the high table. I felt a terrible sympathy for the hedgehog, which should have been out rattling along over some forest hillside. I had no strong emotion for any other one or thing in the Hall.

My mother was not present, along with the twenty other non-Favourite Wives, but The Five were much in evidence, vying with each other in apparel and pets. All had the most fantastic hairstyles – both Wives and pets; sometimes the pets were even part of the hairstyle.

The pillars in the Hall are painted with long green and scarlet stems and end in leaves of beaten copper against the roof. Otherwise the space was full of diners and dinner and wine jars, with slaves and escaped marmosets and hamsters scrambling in all directions.

My father sat in his ebony chair with the silver lions' feet. There was nothing remarkable about him. He was just another squat man with warthog-gravy in his beard.

Then I realised that there *was* something remarkable about him after all. He was extremely nervous. He was fidgeting and breathing fast, and his eyes were puffy and restless. I'd never seen him like that, although it was a mood he frequently brought on in others. I turned, to find out why.

In the guest's place, which normally is occupied only by men, sat a small bowed figure in mud-brown clothes. Although a dirty-looking veil concealed her hair, and most of her face, her hands were visible, and her feet were completely bare. Both hands and feet were sunburned the shade of mahogany. A trail of dusty hair came out of the veil and trickled along one shoulder. It looked the same colour as her skin. Her posture was that of an exhausted slave who has just been badly beaten.

Could this be *She*?

The hedgehog, meanwhile, was being greeted with gloomy cries of praise.

The King, my father, leaned an inch or two towards the slave-like woman and said, fawningly, "Lady, here's a great delicacy of my country. Will you taste some?"

It was then I noted, from the wreckage on the tables and floor (although the area before the woman was spotless, untouched), that about nineteen dishes had been served. This was a *Superior Feast*! And for — for *her*.

And then, then, then, she lifted her head, and she looked straight past the King, and along the Hall, and into my eyes. And I saw she was a queen. No. I saw she was a goddess.

It was terribly and terrifyingly apparent, once she revealed her face – her eyes. And equally terribly and terrifyingly easy to miss if she didn't. I thought excitedly: So it's true! All that nonsense with amulets, and that stuff the priests waffle on about. And, too, it isn't, because it's not the way they tell you.

When she looked at you, you saw she wasn't mahogany, but some new-minted material made on another world . . . the world of the gods. And her eyes were gold. But really she was impossible to describe. If you stare at the sun soon all you see is a dark blot. That's all that can be left from something so bright. Words aren't enough.

Presently she spoke, in a soft melodious voice that I knew could fill the city – perhaps the whole land, all lands – only she modulated it, just to fill the little space of the King's Hall, gently.

"King, won't your daughter dance for me?"

115

"Uh – *Lady* – of course! Haven't I called them all? Haven't the three best and the thirteen second-best daughters each danced, and each to complement a special dish?"

Her pure gold eyes were sad. They said, If only...

I'd disappointed her. It came to me dimly she'd been hoping I might be someone else... and incredibly, for half a second, she had seen a resemblance – but then it faded and I was only me.

I felt awful about dancing for her. It wasn't that I was frightened, for I wasn't in the least. But that was the kind of goddess she was. She scared someone like the King. He hadn't understood that you only had to accept what she was, that nothing you were could matter, that she was everything and all things, and all the numbing roaring Might of what she was passed over like a colossal shining cloud. It was that I felt awful about my dancing, which was so bad, and about which I hadn't troubled until now. But I'd have given anything to please her, to make her feel better for a solitary minute. And I looked a look at her, and the look said how sorry I was. And all at once – she laughed. She laughed out loud, and it was golden bells.

And something happened. There was music, but it wasn't the twanging and thumping of the King's musicians, although it must have been. She had done something to it.

I was dancing. Or, I was living something out – it was nothing I had ever felt before.

There was this dark forest, and in the forest a large clearing, a plain in the sunlight, and here I was weaving a garland. The sunlight poured round me and into me, and I was like the sunlight. There was a golden feel to being me. I couldn't have been ungraceful if I had tried. I ran liltingly to and fro, weaving the flowers which seemed only more alive after I picked them, until I saw a flower that was better than all the rest. It stretched out its silken wings, which were like the purple linings of a storm and edged with crimson-like fire. When I took hold of the flower it had a strength of its own and flirtatiously resisted me. But eventually I won. I uprooted it. The flower nestled against me and I danced with the flower, so glad to have it as it rested its head under my throat, and only at the last instant did I see it was really a snake of purple and fire – it reared back to bite at me as I stood in stony panic under the darkening sky. But before I could call my mother's name the earth opened under me, I was gone, into the darkest of all darks, under the ground.

When I had danced that I was still not frightened, only I felt a dreadful sorrow, something also I'd never known. I knew it was hers, the sorrow of the goddess, and that she searched for me over the earth. Her golden feet passed above my head, but all I could do was tap at the shell of the ground, and she never heard.

The music had stopped. I found I was sitting on the tiles in the middle of the King's Hall and there was absolute silence. I'd never heard it so quiet there.

The people were staring at me. Even the five Favourite Wives, (one with a small monkey plaited in her hair which was eating an orange fruit all over it), even they *stared*. And, with a flicker of pride, I thought maybe I could expect a couple of half-hearted assassination attempts in the next few days. I had danced not well, but amazingly. But it had only been because the goddess had given it to me to do. The point was, most of them were so stupid they could never grasp that; they would think it was me.

The goddess was standing, and she was crying. No, she was weeping, that's the word. Or even 'weeping' isn't. The tears fell from her eyes like falling stars. They left no moisture on her face. She made no noise.

She moved along the Hall as if no one else existed in it but she, and I. And when she came level with me, she looked at me. I wanted to touch her but, instead, she put her hand on my head. Her touch was all the best things, like warmth after cold, or cool water when you're thirsty. She said, "Only you, Angka, danced it as it should be danced."

And she was gone.

If she went out by the doors I don't know. I think probably she did, so as not to appal the banqueters more than she already had.

When I got up, the King was morosely cutting into the baked hedgehog, as if nothing had happened. And a piece of the monkey's orange had gone into the fifth Favourite's ear.

I too left, with the minimum of display as befitted my non-existent rank.

First thing in the morning there was a scene.

When Talu opened the door to her imperious Twenty-sixth-Wife-I-tell-you-I-am-important knock, my mother flounced into my bedchamber with her full panoply of two slaves.

"I have never," cawed my mother, "been so humiliated…"

"Oh, you have," I said, "lots of times."

"To make my daughter dance seventeenth and last," exclaimed my mother, "and so poorly I hear the guest left at once."

Something made me say, though I'd resolved all through my wakeful night not to, "She was a goddess, and could leave when she liked."

My mother glossed that over. "Get up at once. We must all go to the Main Temple this morning."

"Why?" I asked. I wondered if anyone other than a slave, or myself, would dare admit the truth now it was over.

But, "Lightning struck the obelisk of the Nine Thousandth Ancestor, and your father," said my mother, "is afraid we may have a plague if we don't offer something. I think it will be sheep," she appended fastidiously.

Outside the sun was burning a big hole in the sky; the only two things without a tarnish of dust. We trundled along the mud roads in our rusty chariot, under a slave-held sunshade. The slave, outside the shade, looked ready to faint, but the people who faint first are always the guard. Three went down as we arrived, flat on their faces. It always surprises me they don't break their noses when they do this. Perhaps they do.

"Hurry, we're late," hissed my mother, as if we mattered.

In the open square before the temple stood my father with the chief priest. Elsewhere were Wives, other priests droning, citizens with time to spare.

My mother and I arrived at our platform, more crowded than the King's and more out of sight.

Above the temple rose a rounded hill, clad with beehive-shaped tombs looking like lots of fat stone people come to stare. I thought of the goddess, and the daughter of the goddess, who was buried under the earth.

The guard carrying the banner fainted and was hastily replaced.

After the prayers the royal party, in which we were just included, went into the temple to watch the sheep being sacrificed, and then something quite weird happened. No sooner was the first sheep lifted to the altar than it gave a fierce bleat, leapt over my father's head and pelted for the exit, followed by its friends. Everybody scattered, as if they were being charged by lions or wild boar. The sheep sprinted out into the city and disappeared into the maze of alleys behind the temple.

Everyone was left looking more sheepish than the sheep had done. The escape was considered an ill-omen.

"Your father," said my mother, "will be most annoyed." She said this loudly, in case anyone might be listening who would immediately deduce that it was important to the King that the Twenty-sixth Wife foresaw he would be annoyed. I watched her admiringly.

I thought: *Suppose I had died, and vanished under the earth, what would my mother do? Would she wander all the lands like a beggar, weeping when she saw some girl who, for a fleeting moment, had a look of me?* But I knew perfectly well what my mother would and wouldn't do. She'd sob and scream and blame everyone, not excepting me, and soon she would forget me but for the odd mawkish minute that might be useful in engaging someone's sympathy for her.

There was no sacrifice that day. We went back to the palace.

The storm was late that evening, and some doom-sayers were out in the city claiming we were under a curse and now there would be a drought. Then the skies opened, and thunder, rain and lightning crashed down through the overgrown Sun Garden, hitting the pagoda roof like a gong.

Talu and I sat in the porch, preparing vegetables for our supper, watching the rain.

"Tell me about the goddess," I said.

"I? A mere sl..."

"Stop it, Talu," I snapped, exactly like my mother. "No one will talk about it. It's as if it didn't happen. And before it happened it was as if it wasn't going to. Only you told the truth."

Talu was flattered. Her iron hair quivered. So she recited to me what she knew.

"She's an elder goddess. Yes, she looks young enough, but she's centuries old. Her daughter she had by the god of the thunder, black-browed and golden-eyed... But then her daughter, tainted with the mortal world where she'd wandered about such a lot, she died. That's how it is with children. You let them go to play in the garden and something bad happens to them. They eat a poison apple, or a snake gets them."

"Talu."

"Well, some say it was a disease that killed her, or a snake's bite, or that a man, or even a god, carried her off. But she went away under the ground. And ever since, the goddess has searched for her over the earth, looking for the spot where she went down." Talu split a root with a nasty tactless crack. Then she paused, gazing away through the rain and trees. "But you see, she knows she'll find her again, one day, her girl. She'll come up through the black soil like the first flower of spring, like the green corn. So the goddess looks and looks. And now and then she sees a human girl who reminds her, and then the goddess weeps the stars. So they say."

I suddenly saw that Talu's eyes had tears in them. Unlike the flawless goddess she snuffled and wiped her nose with the back of her sleeve – not by any means the procedure with which she had indoctrinated me.

"I had a daughter," said Talu, "who died before she was a year old. Every mother fears that."

I thought of my mother in the room by the colonnade, eating cakes, batting her long-suffering slave with a fly-whisk.

I put my arm round Talu for three whole seconds. Then I kicked my sandals across the room so she could scold me and pick them up and went to tangle my hair for her.

Cold Spell

There came a time in the world when it was Winter all the year round. The lands were white as white mint candy from north to south, and from west to east they were white as congealed white wine. Where the seas had been, lay furrowed sheets like glass; only here and there were there channels of black water where the whales came up to breathe.

The great cities covered themselves with tiles like dragon-scales and found ways to keep warm by heating large furnaces in their cellars, and by focusing huge mirrors to refract down the rays of the feeble sun.

Meanwhile, in the villages, that had only poverty out of which to produce tiles and fires and mirrors, the people starved.

There lived a witch in the north. Her hair was the colour of yellow amber, and she wore it bound on her head in six thick burnished braids, secured by combs of green jasper, and over her shoulders was fastened a cloak of bearskin dyed scarlet, which the bear himself had left her on his death, since she had cast a spell for him once, when he was no more than a cub.

The witch would work magic for the villages round about, and tell fortunes with her cards, and the villagers would pay her. As the Winter grew more and more harsh and more and more permanent, however, no one could afford to pay a witch. Then she began to make magic without charging a penny for it. With her spells she contrived to get the poor houses as snug as she could. She magicked loose bricks back into walls and fallen chimneys back onto roofs. She cured the sick animals and the sick children, and brewed sorcerous broths, and said chants to deter the winds and the snows. But every year it became harder. The Winter was too adamant and cruel for just one village witch to keep it at bay, though she did her best. To be sure, she no longer told fortunes; what lay in the future was all too apparent.

She sold her combs of green jasper to travelling merchants from the cities, and next her scarlet bearskin, though it was of sentimental value. With the money she bought food for the villages, but soon the food was gone. Finally, the witch took down her yellow braids and cut off all her hair, leaving only an inch of it on her head, and she sold her hair to the merchants. After that, she could only sell her own person, and this, being a free soul, she could not bring herself to do.

Then Death began to visit.

First, he came and knocked on the doors of the houses where the elderly were dwelling; presently he took the animals from their pens, and the children from their cots. He would pass up and down the country in his inky cloak – even Death disliked the cold – and one night the witch felt him brush by her on a village street. She curtseyed and said:

"Lord Death, you come too often."

"Young lady," said Death, "I come only where the door is opened for me." And he showed her two babies curled up in his arm, looking fast asleep. "See how peacefully they rest. Their mother wept, but she was glad they should suffer no longer."

Then he went into a house and the witch followed him. Here a young woman lay on the bed.

"Come, daughter," said Death, "it is time to be going." And the woman smiled.

"Wait," said the witch. "Sister, tell this dark gentleman to be about his business."

"I am his business," said the woman. "And he is not dark to me, but a shining angel of light. I am that glad to leave my misery behind me. It is Winter I fear, not Death." And her spirit went to Death thankfully, and with a mocking bow to the witch, he strode away into the night.

"This will not do," said the witch. "Death knocks before his time and no one refuses him, for the Winter has made weaklings of all of us."

Then she pulled her cloak, which was made of coarse cloth now, closer about her and over her cropped head, and she sat thinking till the sun rose. And it seemed to her that she must find someone brave enough to fight the Winter and drive it back again to the grim lands it came from, and this someone must be a hero, such as antique stories mentioned, a tall strong man with armour of gold and sword of bronze.

Being a free soul, and a creature of impulse, the witch got up and went out into the dawn to search for one immediately.

The witch assumed that if there were heroes to be found, she would find them in the cities, and thus it was to the cities she journeyed.

Along the way, she infrequently met men, the hungry and the

sullen. Once, a pack of wolves hunted her, but she sent them away with a spell that made them see deer running.

It was a long road. When she came to the first city, her hair had already grown to her shoulders.

What a place it was. The roofs piled up against the leaden sky, crimson and gold; all the windows had coloured panes, and warm breezes blew about in the streets from the underground furnaces, and strange little stunted trees craned from pots along the pavement. Here and there men and women rode in carriages drawn by teams of tabby cats. The outer walls were of stone twenty feet thick.

The witch went to the market, and she put on a conjuring act. She plucked birds from thin air and changed a heap of hot-house apples into emeralds – it was all illusion, but she was applauded, and the people threw her coppers. The witch walked up and down the city, looking for a suitable hero. No one appeared tall or strong or daring enough. Inside the buildings were lamps that shone like the summer sun, and through the stained glass of the windows you could see no grey in the sky, because they altered everything to rose, lavender and green.

"You would never know there was a Winter at all," the witch said to a lady pruning a tiny oak tree in a vase.

"Winter?" squeaked the lady, giggling loudly. "What peculiar word is that? Why, we all know that it is forever Summer here."

Quite a crowd had collected to learn what the joke was.

The witch said quietly, "Outside the walls it is forever Winter. It will take a hero to drive this cold season away."

When the crowd heard, they shouted furiously. A captain of police in splendid uniform came up and seized the witch by the arm.

"You must not use foul language in this city," he said. "Naturally, some citizens are too innocent to know that the word you uttered is obscene. However, I cannot overlook such vileness."

And the witch was cast into prison for saying 'Winter' in a public place.

When night came, the city grew gaudier still, and it was not until the ashy sunrise that the witch ventured to unbar her cell by magic, and stole out into the streets, where a few drunkards were singing of the beautiful summer morning. Demonstrably, there were no heroes to be had here, and the witch left the city by the quickest route.

The next city she came to was altogether different.

It was built of crystal and alabaster and gave the impression of having been constructed of the snow and ice themselves. Although the furnaces heated the thoroughfares and houses, a chill blue light burned in the lamps. Strolling ladies dazzled in diamonds, gentlemen rode albino mammoths with trappings like icicles.

The witch went to a tavern and put on a conjuring act. She turned the wine three separate colours and feathers rained from the ceiling. After the applause and the coppers, she sat and watched the young men closely, but none was much like a hero. They played chess idly and smoked incense.

"This is a wintry city," said the witch to the bartender. "But I have been looking for a man valiant enough to drive the Winter away."

"Drive it away!" exclaimed the bartender in horror, dropping several frosty goblets. A crowd gathered instantly. "Why, who is so stupid they cannot see the perfection of Winter?"

"Yes, indeed," agreed the young men. "There is such delicacy and artistry in snow and ice, we welcome them. Thank heavens the ghastly brash Summer does not show his face around here anymore." And they yawned and wandered back to their chessboards and pipes.

The witch left the city before sunset.

After these adventures, the witch was an age on the road. Her hair had grown down to her waist on the day she came to an enormous wall and a pair of iron gates which was the entrance to the third city.

Inside was an awesome scene.

About the streets of grotesque dwellings stood groups of silent, black-clad people. The roads themselves ran up to a vast edifice of granite, and no sooner had the witch come in the gates, than a thunderous cannon went off amidst clouds of smoke. At this terrifying signal, the people began to climb the streets towards the ominous building, chanting dolorously.

Overhead, the sun-reflectors turned with a dim whining sound, and underfoot growled the furnaces, but there seemed little warmth in the black city. The witch accompanied the throng and found herself in a menacing temple. Here the multitude threw themselves on the ground in front of a colossal statue half hidden behind curtaining, while priests in black beat gongs.

Then the High Priest roared:

"O eternal master, pray hurt us as much as you have ever hurt us. Send the snow and the wind and the bitter weather. Pray destroy us if you wish, for we are your devoted slaves, and we give you homage."

The witch called to this priest, for she reverenced him not at all: "Who is this dreadful god you are worshipping?"

"Silence, blasphemer," said the priest, "and you shall gaze on the face of him we extol, none other than King Winter himself."

And he touched the curtain, which fell away.

What was revealed was unspeakably shocking. The statue was of a giant man; half his face was white, half black, his eyes – which had neither pupil nor iris – were red, and flickered with fires, and his hair of steel snakes writhed as if alive. In one hand he held a flail of iron, in the other hand, which was bloody, a doll resembling a dead child. At the sight of this vision most of the crowd buried their heads in their arms, and some fainted. Only the witch remained standing.

"Kneel and repent your pride," bellowed the priest. "Kneel before the lord of entire creation."

"I never will," said the witch, and she went right up to the statue. "Perhaps I am not strong enough to match you and perhaps I shall never find one who can, but neither will I call you lord." And the witch spat at the feet of the idol and went her way without another glance.

One dull noon, when the witch's hair had grown down as far as her ankles – long enough indeed to braid, if she had had combs to secure it – she heard a soft tinkling of bells.

Turning about, she noted a silver sled drawn by six white wolves, the leader of whom nodded and politely asked:

"Are you the young lady who has been inquiring after a hero sufficiently brave to fight Winter?"

"Most certainly I am," said the witch, who was not as tremendously surprised to come on a talking wolf as anyone else might be.

"Please to get into the sled," said the wolf.

This the witch did at once, and the wolves loped off, the bells on their harness singing.

Over the snow-fields and ice-meadows they went, under the

125

shadow of high mountains whose toothed crowns were gnawing the sky, across a coagulated indigo sea, where miles off the witch saw the blue seals sliding on the ice and the whales blowing water at the lemon sun. Eventually the sled drew up outside a big pale tent with platinum tassels, and inside sat a young man in a chair of white bone. His hair was black as night, but his eyes were blue as sapphire, and he bowed slightly when he saw the witch, stood up and bade her enter.

The witch was pleased to see him, for he looked strong and clever, and definitely of the material from which heroes are assembled. She was also aware of some bright armour on a peg, a helm of azure metal and a shining sword.

"Well," said the hero, beckoning her to a seat, "before we debate matters, maybe you will play a game of cards with me."

"Gladly," said the witch for, cards being part of her witch's craft, she had rather missed this aspect of her trade.

Soon a little table was set between them, and they began.

First they played two-handed whist and then they played quadrille, and after a while, euchre. The hero would win a game, but the witch would win the next; then the hero would win again, and then the witch again. Presently the sun was low, and they played cribbage and bezique, and when the dusk commenced, faro and fan-tan. And, for every game the hero won, the witch would beat him at the next.

When the glittering stars appeared, the hero lit the chandeliers in the roof of the tent and laid down a board of squares, and they played rouge et noir, with untold magics as the stakes. The hero won, and the witch won. As the moon was rising, their score was still equal.

"I see how it is between us," said the hero. "Neither can best the other, and neither win. Your luck is unusually good. We had better discuss terms."

"My terms are these," said the witch, "if you will challenge King Winter and drive him from the land, then I will work witchery for you for as long as you wish, and do anything in my power to make you happy."

"You are very generous, young lady," said the hero, "but I think you have been misled. As we played cards, now and then our hands have touched. Tell me, have you noticed nothing strange?"

"Your hands," said the witch, "are very cold."

"Draw a card from the pack," said the hero, gravely, "and you shall know me."

This the witch did, and the card she drew was the king of diamonds. That was how she discovered that it was Winter himself she had been sitting with all afternoon. "You are not as they say you are," remarked the witch.

"Few things are as white as they are painted," said Winter. "This much agreed, it seems to me we must compromise. Since you have been resolute, courageous and amusing enough to seek my destruction, I will listen to whatever you ask."

"I ask only that you be less harsh to men," said the witch.

"That I cannot help. It is my function and my destiny. I am as I am and have no choice. Cold all the way through. However, there is one thing will change me."

"And what is that?"

"You must kiss me, thrice, on the mouth."

"Is that then so hard to do?" asked the witch, for privately she thought him very handsome.

"You may find it is," admitted Winter.

Maybe the witch felt some foreboding, but she had spoken even to Death and not been afraid. She took Winter's face between her palms and kissed him three times on the lips.

At the first kiss, a little colour appeared in Winter's cheeks and the witch's cheeks became a little pale.

At the second kiss, the hands of Winter grew warmer, and the hands of the witch turned numb with cold.

At the third kiss, Winter smiled; outside there was a sharp yammer of ice cracking: the thaw had begun. A wind blew up from the south, and a mild rain scattered the earth. By midnight, the seas had started to groan and melt. The snow slid from the mountains, and at first light, the Spring had opened half of one green eye on the world she had not seen for a chiliad. Winter himself, with a mixed shout of annoyance and laughter, leapt on his sled. The white wolves dashed off to the north with him over the fast-dissolving pack-ice. The pallid tent blew away into the sky. Even the cards took flight.

Shortly, only a single item remained. An image made of glass, or was it solid rime? A pretty snow-woman. A witch, frozen by Winter's kiss.

What did she think? Perhaps she was too cold to think at all.

Perhaps not. Perhaps she thought: *What a fool I have been.* Perhaps, as with the jasper combs, the bearskin cloak, her hair, she thought: *it has not been wasted.*

As for Winter, he raced back to his old palace in the middle of northern nowhere, without properly understanding he had been routed, trying to pretend everything was normal. The snows had settled in drifts in the draughty halls, and the aurora borealis in the lamps burned low. He went upstairs and sat down to play at a piano with stalactites and stalagmites for keys. He was remembering the witch. Where he had made her cold, she had warmed him quite amazingly. His heart was almost human, and as he wished events had turned out differently, the piano became extremely loud.

Right through the spring, the witch stood petrified among the grass and the small flowers. The temperate weather was not enough to thaw her after the embrace of Winter himself.

One day, Death came by, black as a scowl. He glanced at the primroses and crocuses, and he murmured to them, "By Summer, you will have withered, and be growing in my kingdom." He tapped the glacial witch with his thumbnail, and he asked, "Yes?"

But there was no reply from within.

"Surely," said Death, "you do not wish to remain like this forever? What life do you have, young lady, frozen stiff as you are? The sophisticated and philosophical thing to do," added Death, "would be to renounce this shadow of your former self and come to me."

Still, there was no reply.

Death looked closely. He looked into the eyes of the witch and through her eyes, into her mind. Eyes and mind had not been frosted over, being too alert and too warm to freeze. When he stared, there came a flash inside them very like – Death arched his brows – scorn?

"Come now," said Death. "Do you suppose anyone else will bother with you? You have freed the earth of perpetual Winter, but does the earth thank you? Do the people run up and lay garlands at your feet and offer prayers for your recovery? No, indeed. As is generally the case, I am the only one with any time to spare for the sick, the only one who takes any sincere interest in them." And Death sighed heavily at his onerous task.

In the witch's mind, something laughed. Death ignored it.

"Consider what I have told you. Weigh the alternatives. You can enjoy a comfortable sojourn in my land, or a wretched eternity of this. Make your choice. I shall be back."

And Death strode off, whistling a dirge fortissimo.

But the sun shone, and the flowers faded and new flowers flourished, and soon he returned, this time with his black cloak over his arm, smartly dressed, and wearing a lot of rings. Behind him came a grave concert party, pale haggard minstrels with curious instruments; a mandolin made from a yellow skull and strung with human hair, hollow ivory tibias, a xylobone. This orchestra stationed itself before the witch and began to play bitter-sweet laments.

"There," said Death. "Listen to the pretty music. Think how the world will regret you at your passing. They will bring wreaths to your resting place, and weep and exclaim: 'If only we had shown more gratitude.' You, meanwhile, shall be my honoured guest. What do you say?"

Death looked into the witch's eyes. The witch's eyes said, "While there is hope there is life."

"Platitudes," said Death, offended. "Young lady, it is not usual, but since you are so ignorant of the joys of my domain, I will show them to you here and now."

Death's face darkened with concentration, and he made images enter the witch's brain. Thus, she saw her fourth city: Death's.

Very grand it was, like a huge graveyard where only kings were buried. The palaces were mausoleums of white marble, mantled with ivy and lichen, the streets were paved with tombstones. A river ran through the city, black as the black sky, afloat with funeral barges draped in black velvet. People rode solemnly in them or walked up and down the streets discoursing learnedly.

The primroses which had withered from the earth pushed between the tombstones, but they were pale as paper and had no scent. Even the nightingales did not sing on the steeples but chimed like small silver knells.

A woman who had died of starvation sat on the river bank. "How good it is not to be hungry," she said.

Two travellers, who had perished of frostbite, played bat and ball in a courtyard. "How good it is not to be cold," they cried, "and to have all our fingers."

A boy and a wolf were drinking wine in a cemetery garden. "I do apologise for eating you," said the wolf, who had been killed by hunters that afternoon.

"Please think no more of it," said the boy.

Then Death showed the witch a room of green ceramic, lit by a hundred tapers, with silver bier, and chairs.

"Accept this chamber as yours," said Death graciously. "Contemplate the peace and serenity you will know there."

In the mind of the witch something said: "It is very kind of you, Lord Death, and I am glad your kingdom is of benefit to those who are ready for it. But I am not ready, and while I believe in my life and my freedom – for I am a free soul – I never shall be ready."

"Damnation!" shouted Death, inappropriately, for he knew there was no such thing. And, scattering the musicians, he stalked away, only growling over his shoulder, "I shall be back."

Months later, the witch in her shell felt the faintest glimmer of sunlight break through to her. She observed, coming along the road from the south, a tall man in gold armour with a sword of bronze. This, she thought, is the hero I was after finding in the first place.

It was Summer. He peered at her sheepishly, embarrassed because he had been in hiding such a great while. As he passed, the witch felt a Summer heat like a fire, but even this was not enough to thaw her after Winter's embrace.

Needless to say, Death was close behind.

He was wearing a mask of bones to frighten her. He rapped on her glassy surface and demanded, "Are you ready now? Even the Summer has not done the trick. Do you suppose anything else can warm you?" Then he shivered and put on his cloak. "This is too much," said Death, as up the sunny slope came walking a snow-storm with Winter in the middle of it.

Winter stepped out. He looked twice as sheepish as Summer had done, and much angrier than Death.

"This living-death is mine," said Death at once, pointing to the witch.

"No, mine," said Winter furiously. "She is nearly ice, and the ice belongs to me."

"Nearly ice: nearly belongs to you. Nearly dead, and nearly belongs to me."

They darted ferocious glances at the witch, whose eyes said, "To neither. I belong only to myself."

Death said, "I have shown the young lady the wonders I am able to lay at her feet. You had better inform her of what you have to offer. Apart, of course, from a cold palace and a nice view of some glaciers."

Winter scowled. "Being of a friendly and generous nature," he shouted, "I am prepared to offer myself." Then, growing calmer, "Listen to me, girl. If you will come and live in the north lands with me, I will try to help you."

The witch could only answer with her eyes. Her eyes said, "How can I refuse to let you salve your conscience?" But there was a smile there too, and quite suddenly some of the ice that imprisoned her melted.

Death stroked his chin, musingly, having sensibly taken off his mask.

"Yours I think, after all," said Death to Winter, "reluctant as I always am to admit defeat." And without another word, he gathered his cloak around him and went away to bide his time.

Accordingly, Winter carried the witch to his palace. As they went up the staircase, the lamps grew brighter and the furniture took on a more polished appearance.

About midnight, a whole lot more of the ice-crystal, affected by Winter's angrily affectionate looks, fell off with a crash. Winter frowned at the unaesthetic noise. It would be, he foresaw, a slow and tedious exercise, defrosting his beloved – she *was* his beloved, he could no longer very well deny it, much as he would have liked to.

What a dreadful irony he thought, that he, coldest of all things, should have acquired a heart warm enough to thaw ice, which even the blazing heat of Summer could not melt. Every time he smiled at the witch, shattered rime would scatter the floor. He wondered grimly how long it would take before she was herself again.

One morning, mistily but unmistakably, she smiled back at him.

Unnoticed, Spring crept almost up to the very ramparts of Winter's palace. Winter went out secretly at dark of moon to pick a few primroses for his thawed witch, before he ragingly chased the Spring away into the south.

Elvenbrood

How beautiful they are,
The lordly ones,
Who dwell in the hills,
In the hollow hills.

"The Immortal Hour,"
Fiona Macleod (William Sharp)

When they moved to Bridestone, Susie had tried to be very positive. That was the key word, apparently. Positive. What you *had* to be. So Jack tried to back her up. She'd been through enough, they all had. Make the best of things.

He was seventeen and a half, and because of that, she said she preferred him to call her Susie, though outside the house, at college, he referred to her, when he needed to, by her true title, which was Mum. Luce still had the unchallenged rights to call Susie Mum, but she didn't either. Luce was fourteen, white-blonde, strange in the way girls suddenly got.

"Susie's a *person*," said Luce, seriously, bossily, "she has a right to have a *name*, not just be our Mum."

"She *is* our Mum," Jack pointed out.

Then Susie had come in, all Positive, and they had to start Positively cleaning the new house up, and unpacking.

It was a new house in every way, as several sections of the sprawling village were, part of a block of houses, all joined up, with big flat glass windows and doors. They were all presumably the same inside, too. One largish downstairs room, kitchen, cloakroom, three small bedrooms upstairs, and a bathroom. The house, though, looked out onto fields and hedgerows, woods. It was all right, better than the flat they'd all been crammed into in outer London, when Dad – Michael – was fired.

The firing had been because Dad drank too much alcohol. Or no, it had been because *Michael* drank too much. Jack could remember a few years before, when Luce had been nine and sweet, and Susie had been, not Positive, just happy, and Dad had been Dad, and brilliant. Michael worked too hard, Susie explained as things ran downhill; he was trying to keep them all going; they must support him. Then he got fired anyway, and they lost the house in Chester Road where Jack and Luce had grown up. They went to live in the flat. Once there, Dad – now truly Michael full time – went on drinking too much. He began to tell Susie, Luce, and Jack that he was sick to death of them and the burden they were, and also he started to hit Susie. One night, Jack smashed one of Michael's bottles over Michael's head to stop him. Jack had been crying, just as Luce and Susie were. Michael sat there on the floor looking stunned. Then he just got up, with a trickle of blood from his forehead running down his nose, and walked out. He never came back.

That had been a year and a half ago. Now they were here.

Which was the really stupid part, Jack thought. Mum had had a win on the National Lottery. Oh, not millions, but enough for a decent down payment on a small house, and some left over until, as Susie said, (positive enough she'd fooled the mortgage people), she found a job. Being Positive, they'd already found a local school for Luce, and Jack's college was only half an hour away on the train.

Jack couldn't help thinking it was a shame they hadn't won the lottery before all hell broke loose in their lives. Susie said that wasn't the way to look at it. It was wonderful luck. And of course, it was.

Bridestone, though.

Jack had stared at the place uneasily, even as the train pulled in. Susie's choice. It was one of those Kent-Sussex villages that had been picturesque, and still was in bits – ye olde smithy, ye olde pub, a church that was built just after the Norman Conquest of England in 1066, even the ruins of a Roman fort and a Norman castle nearby. But the village had also grown. It had put on weight since the 50s, got too fat with new houses and estates and silly shops that, Jack thought, sold stuff no one in their right minds could afford, or would want to.

There was a Big Divide here too. There were the Rich, who lived in old timbered houses along the hilly narrow streets or in flash mansions just outside, with gardens like parks. The Rich had huge dogs, rode horses, talked like things yapping to each other. They looked way, way down on 'That Common Lot' who'd bought the new houses.

Susie had been an actress once. She'd been on TV and everything, only no one remembered. But she wasn't *common* – she was *un*common.

"Look at the lovely view!" she sang as they saw it first, properly, from the upstairs landing window.

Well, it was a good view, Jack had to admit. He was going to be studying photography next year; he was just on his foundation course now. He could take excellent pictures of the green-golden fields, the clouds of dark woods, the sweeps of open land beyond…

Why didn't he like that view?

He tried, in a funny way, not even to look at it, not to look out of the windows. Nuts.

Luce *loved* it. She loved the tiny garden, too, with the blue, fake wrought-iron chairs and table Susie bought, the untidy rosebushes and lilac tree. She'd be out there for hours in the evenings, when he and Susie watched TV, alone, singing to herself like she had when she was little. Maybe it was good for her. Over the end fence, the fields buzzed smokily with summer.

At night, the moon sailed white across that countryside, owls eerily cried, and Jack found himself going downstairs about 1am, not for a drink of juice or a piece off the cold chicken, but to check the locks, front and back.

"Susie, do you think these locks are strong enough?"

"They're what we've got, Jackie."

"Yeah, but couldn't I fix for someone to put on better ones?"

"What are you expecting to break in…?" she chortled. "A *lion*?"

"Those bloody dogs are about lion size. One of those'd be through that glass in two seconds."

"I *like* dogs. Lucy and I might like to get one ourselves. But listen, Jack, thanks honestly, but we're out of London here. It's much safer, you know."

Luce said primly, "Jack never worried about locks in London. Once he left the front door unlocked all night when he came in."

This had been at Chester Road, so Susie changed the subject.

What was it that bugged Jack about this place?

A couple of Sundays they went for a walk around the lanes. Susie and Luce chatted about birds and wildflowers. Jack kept looking over his shoulder. Once he heard something following them behind the hedgerow – he got ready to thump it till two crows flew up.

But it wasn't just the wildlife, or the view, or the people here –

but – *something…*

Something…

Perhaps he was just a city boy, or neurotic, like Susie and Luce were now, a bit. Just that.

The fourth week they were there, Luce ran in one afternoon from school, breathlessly excited to tell them, "I met this *weird* man in the High Street."

Jack and Susie looked up, horrified.

"What do you mean, Lucy?" Susie asked, careful, gripping the edge of the kitchen table.

Jack, home early on what the awkward course tutor called 'An Assignment', waited.

Luce said, "I don't mean *that*. He's off his head, out of his skull…"

"On *drugs*, do you mean?" demanded Jack.

Luce burst out laughing. She still had this laugh, like silver bells… Michael had said that. No, *Dad* had said it. "I just mean crazy. Not dangerous. He just came up and said, 'You be careful, little girl' – as if I was a kid – 'careful how you go'."

"Did you speak to him? Lucy, I've told you…"

"No. Of course not. Why would I? I just walked on. Then he called after me, 'Just go careful with that hair.' And then something about the Romans leaving the stone, and knights leaving the castle – but I was by the bread shop then, and I went in like you asked and bought this loaf…"

"Forget the loaf. What did he look like?"

"Thin, old. His hair was long. He looked like a woolly sheepdog. His clothes were old, too. Sort of like Victorian for a fancy-dress party – only worn and mucky. But people like that stink. They smell like dustbins and garbage, and he didn't. He smelled…" Luce considered, "like grass."

"*Grass?*"

"Off a *lawn* – that sort. And he had green eyes, like me." Susie and Jack exchanged a worried, brown-eyed glance. "Tomorrow, Lucy," said Susie firmly, "I will take you in to school. I will collect you in the afternoon."

"Oh, *Mum*," Luce wailed.

Jack went out after tea, which was their early dinner at six o'clock. He walked down the hill from the grassy estate, past the quaint gate where sometimes cows grazed, and which led to a cornfield. He walked through a couple of narrow streets and into the High Street.

There was a village green with a war memorial on it. The church, with its square Norman tower, was across from the green and, on the other side, nestled among huge oak and beech trees, the pub. This pub had a strange name... Jack peered round the leaves and past the several posh drinkers gathered outside on rustic benches, with their wine and Real Ale.

The pub sign showed a green hill, and some people dancing together on it under a curved crescent moon. *The Lords and Ladies* said the lettering.

One of the drinkers had noticed Jack and pulled a face. *Ah*, Jack could see the man thinking, *that Common Lot have now produced a yob intent on underage boozing.*

Jack turned his back and strolled on, across the green to the church.

He was looking for the man who had spoken to Luce. In such a stuck-up place as Bridestone, anyone like that, surely, would have been run out of town long ago. Unless – did they still keep a village idiot here? Just for the twee charm of it...

What had he meant *'Go careful with that hair'*? A warning? A threat? Jack badly wanted to see the man, ask him which, and why. And if a threat, tell him that Jack didn't like old tramps threatening his sister, all right?

After a while, Jack left the church. He walked on, up and down roads and through the little between-house alleys. Someone was playing Mozart. Dogs barked, richly, in gardens with not one branch out of place.

Returning to the green, he saw the sun was going. It was getting on for 8:30. An hour at most, and it would be full dark, and Susie getting anxious because he'd only said he was going for a walk.

The church, too, bothered Jack. The graveyard was packed with ancient leaning gravestones with dates like 1701 and 1590. Age so thick you could cut it in slices.

And what had the nutter meant when he said that about the Romans leaving the stone, and the Norman knights? Jack had never heard that the Romans – or the Normans, for that matter – had left there at all. The air was cooling, and the smell of flowers blew over on a breeze. It was getting dark quicker than he'd expected.

When Jack got to the front door, Susie was already flinging it

Tanith Lee

wide. "Jack, Jack, thank God…"

"What is it? *What*, Mum?"

"Lucy's gone!"

Jack stood there, with all his blood turning to sand. It felt like the flat again, those times when Michael… the raised drunken voice rising in the other room, accusing Susie of caring nothing for her family, only for the career she'd given up, and then the sound of a blow.

"Are you sure, Susie?"

"Of course, I'm bloody sure, you stupid moron!"

Unlike Michael, she was seldom rude. She must be at her wit's end. He read the signal and said, "Yes, OK. You've checked. When did you realise?"

"She was up in her room playing her CDs, quite loud – one of those thump-thump people you both like so much…"

"U2."

"And it just kept on playing the same track, so I went up to say could she turn it down a little… Oh God, Jack, she wasn't there. The window was wide open, that was all – she couldn't have climbed out of the *window*, could she? I mean, why would she do that? I mean, she wasn't in the bathroom, and she didn't come downstairs – I was ironing and I had the radio on – but I'd have seen her go by the main room door…"

"Did you check the other rooms? Yes. The garden?"

"I looked *everywhere*. I even – I even looked in the blasted washing machine for God's sake!" Susie cackled weakly. "Am I being daft? It's all right, isn't it? She's probably somehow been up there all the time…" Susie turned abruptly, raced along the hall and up the stairs like a slim stampeding elephant. Jack followed. Upstairs, there was no sign of Luce.

They craned their necks out the open bedroom window, gazing down at the small patio below. It wasn't such a long drop.

The air smelled wonderful now, scented with flowers and hay and clean growing, living things – and *night*.

"Mum, *look*! I think…"

"Oh, oh there she is! Oh my God, what's she doing out there? Lucy! Luce!"

Across a couple of fields of ripening corn or wheat, or whatever it was, among the tall stalks, a short slender figure stood quite still, showing up with an almost luminous whiteness that must be because of lights shining out from the house backs. Luce, with her pale blonde hair…

Go careful with that hair.

Susie was already running downstairs again, throwing open the back door. Jack caught up in the garden. By then Susie was standing by the back fence, nearly crying, like a scared child.

"She vanished."

"The stalks would hide her from down here."

"No. When I got here, I could still see her out in the field. And then... she just wasn't."

The night felt chilly, or cold. It was moonless, too.

"I'll go and look for her." Jack sprang at the fence and over.

"Be *careful.*"

Jack grunted and pelted forward into the stinging coarse slap of the wheat or corn. He hated it, smashing it aside with his hands – he'd probably never eat bread or cereal again.

He heard Susie calling when he thought he'd travelled about a quarter mile. By then the dark shadow of the woods was looming through the stalks, sinister in some electric way.

Jack stood, bewildered.

Behind him floated the voice of his mother, vital again with relief: "Jack! It's all right, she's *here...*"

And then Luce's voice, "Jackieee!"

While in front of him, against the backdrop of woods, motionless as the unshaken grain, a white-skinned, white-blonde creature was looking back at him, smiling – quiet, and amused – with slanting cat-green eyes. Only a second, this. Then it melted away. Into shadow, into night – *into the ground?*

Jack shook himself. Nothing had been there – adrenalin and an optical illusion. He turned and ran back for the house.

"She says she was everywhere I'd just looked, doing something, not realising I was looking for her. We just kept *missing* each other."

Jack scowled. "That's dumb. We looked everywhere. You can't *miss* someone anyway in a house this tiny."

"It's what she says. She got bolshy and then tearful when I kept saying it couldn't have been like that. She said she's not a liar. But she is. I took the flashlight. There're scuff marks on the table on the patio. She must have got out on the windowsill, swung onto the shed roof – I can hardly bear to think of it. What if she'd jumped all wrong?"

"Yeah. Do you want me to speak to her?"

"In the morning. We've had enough for now."

He wondered how Luce had got back in. She must have sneaked in again when he was out in the fields and Susie at the fence. Crazy.

Crazy like the green-eyed man.

That night, Jack dreamed he was still running. Something was chasing him – a dog, he thought, a white dog. He woke up sweating, because he'd left his window shut.

He wondered if that other thing – that white figure Susie he thought they'd seen – was Luce's *decoy*, so she could get back unnoticed.

The woman behind the library desk was pretty tasty, but she was also pretty nasty. "The computer's crashed. I'm sorry." You could see she wasn't.

He told her he needed to research Bridestone. She raised an eyebrow. "You must have heard of it," he said, "one stop up the line."

"I'm from London," she proclaimed loftily.

The promised data hadn't been much anyhow. Just dates on the castle, and a plan of the Roman remains with some altar to a pagan goddess.

As Jack was stalking through the door, a man's voice sounded behind him.

"Were you asking about Bridestone?"

Jack looked around. A young middle-aged man stood there, frowning at him, as if it was forbidden for people like Jack to ask questions. Jack didn't like men of this age anyway. Michael had been one.

"Yes," said Jack shortly.

"Any special reason?"

"I live there. If that's OK."

Jack saw suddenly the man's frown was because he was squinting out into the sun.

"You might try an old guy called Soldyay," said the man. "That's spelled *Soldier*, by the way. He's dotty, but quite harmless. I've known him years, and he knows Bridestone village, the history and so on."

"Soldier? What do you mean, 'dotty'? You mean off his head?"

"Somewhat. But as I say, no danger. Gentle as a lamb. Really, I wouldn't recommend seeing him otherwise. I'm his dentist. He appears before me once a year to show off his truly wonderful teeth. They really *are* wonderful. Like a young tiger's. Not a single cavity."

"Has he got green eyes?"

"That's another thing. His eyes are as clear as a child's. Green? Yes, I think so. Also his clothes are horrible but somehow he's always fresh as a daisy. Anyway, if you want to know about the village, he's your man. Bridstane it used to be. It's in the Domesday Book and all that. Seen the ruins?"

"Not yet."

"Nothing much left. A few crumbling walls. The Roman fort is even less intact, plus it's up a mountain of a hill. I *don't* recommend *that*."

"Was it abandoned – the fort? Or the castle?"

"Sometimes Soldier seems to say so. But then he has times when he just talks in riddles. He's supposed to have a peculiar history himself. My mother used to remember him first turning up. Old then, she said. I don't know his age. He lies and says sixty to my receptionist, but he's well past that. Catch him on a good day, and you'll get some sense."

"When's a good day?"

"Waxing moon. That's today, in fact. You can call at his house, he won't let you in. You'll have to talk to him in the street. No. 7, Smiths Lane, behind the old…"

"Smithy," said Jack. "Thanks, Mr…?"

"Tooth," sighed the dentist. "Please *don't* say it."

On the train going back, Jack thought how he hadn't gone in to college to check. He had considered it – the computers there might work. But then a foundation student had practically to walk over blazing coals to get access to them. He hadn't spoken to Luce, either. She'd slipped off early to school that morning eluding Susie's escort, so Susie felt she had to phone the place to make sure Luce had safely arrived. She had. Then the phone had rung again, someone wanting Susie for an interview that day, some job she'd applied for – she hadn't said doing what. "Jack, I'll have to go out. Would you please pick Lucy up this afternoon from school? She'll like it better anyway, her handsome elder brother, not her Mum."

Before meeting Luce, he had plenty of time to run Mr. Soldier to ground. But first, lunch was on the agenda. Or it was meant to be. As he opened the fridge door, there was a multi-coloured explosion.

Jack yelled, staggered back against the kitchen table, soaked and gawping, as a double pack of colas, two cartons of orange juice and one of cranberry, and a bottle of fizzy white wine erupted their contents all over the room—and all over Jack.

He hadn't the heart to leave the mess for Susie when she got back. His note about the ruined food would be bad enough. Most of the stocks in the fridge were now spoiled – unless you really fancied soggy bread, wet butter, cold sausages in an orange and cola sauce. The fruit and salad might make it, if washed. Could you wash *bacon*, though?

Jack was glaring into the fridge again when the milk carton, somehow slower than the rest, also decided to blow its top, right in his face.

Eyes full of milk, Jack swore. Spilled milk stank, too. So, not only cleaning the kitchen now, but another shower and a change of clothes.

He got out of the house again about three o'clock and ran through the village to Smith's Lane.

The street was cobbled, the houses – drab, old, narrow oblongs – slotted together like a kind of jigsaw. Most looked uncared for, but No. 7 won the prize for worst. The door-paint peeled in strips, the windows were nearly black with dirt behind yellowed filthy net curtains. No bell. Jack went at the door knocker as if needing to hammer something in.

He thought no one would answer.

Then, silent as the fall of a leaf, the door opened, and Mr. Soldier stepped out to meet Jack in the street.

His eyes *were* green. They didn't slant, though. And, as Tooth the dentist had said, they were incredibly clear, the whites like enamel. The rest of him – he was old and crinkled up, like scrunched paper. His grey hair poured over his shoulders, over his face. His clothing looked more 1970s, Jack thought, than Victorian, but also as if he slept in it, slept too in a refuse sack.

"You spoke to my sister."

"Did I?" He had a good voice, not overeducated and yappy like the Bridestone Rich, more like an actor. So, was he acting now?

"Yeah, you did. Blonde girl, yesterday."

"Ah." Mr. Soldier smiled. His teeth were just as the dentist had said. "That was your sister, then."

"Why did you try to scare her?"

"Did I scare her?"

"No. But..."

"I did mean to, in a way. I meant she should be careful. Sometimes..." Mr. Soldier hesitated. He seemed apologetic. "Sometimes I'm not very coherent."

"You get *drunk*?"

Mr. Soldier looked surprised at the rage in Jack's tone. "No, not often. I can't afford to. I simply mean I'm not always myself."

"Do the police know about you? Do you have to attend at a hospital for treatment?"

"Not at all. I seldom cause any bother."

"You bothered my sister."

Mr. Soldier said, "I think it isn't I that bother her. Perhaps it's already too late. Maybe not."

Jack snarled. His fists rose.

Mr. Soldier did not react. He said quietly, "Something wants her. Something is *interested* in her."

"*Who*? How do you *know*?"

"I was the same. Once they were interested in me."

"*Who are they*?"

Mr. Soldier knelt down unexpectedly on the ground. He licked his finger and wrote in his own spit on a large cobble, one word.

Jack stared at it. ELVNBROD.

"Elven..."

"*Don't*." Mr. Soldier rose. He sounded oddly proud as he said, "Don't name them. They can be called the Lords and Ladies, or the Royalty. In Ireland, you know, they call them the Gentle Folk, or the Little People. Or the Lordly Ones."

Jack goggled. "*Faeries*?"

"Oh, *that* name. Well. Of a kind, maybe. In the faery tales and legends, it's true, faeries do steal human children. And that is what these ones do, the ones we have here."

Jack stood back. "You are out of your tree."

"They stole me. Yes. Though, believe me, I wanted to go with them. They make you want to go, more than you can bear. They're old as the hills, fair as the morning. They look young as children or adolescents, that's why they like the *mortal* young. In their country, you stay young too, and immortal. They live under the hills. It's like paradise there."

"So what's paradise like, then?" Jack demanded.

"Like the best and most wonderful place you can imagine, then better."

The sun beat on Jack's head. The word *Elvnbrod* had faded from the cobble. He felt dizzy. Did he want to shake the old man, or was he starting to believe him? Don't be a fool.

"So, then," Jack said, adult and cool, "these *things* want to take Luce away with them, like they wanted you when you were a kid. Only you didn't go."

"Oh, but I did."

"You – you what?"

"Listen. Something gives them the right to take a child. Myself, then. Your sister now. There is a stone in the old Roman fort. The Romans put it there, back in the time of Caesars. It was dedicated to the goddess of light, Brid. They left it here too, when the empire ended. This area has always been a center for *Them*. But the Stone keeps the village safe. Unless..."

Jack swallowed noisily.

The old man softly said, "There was a Norman warlord in the castle. He sold his youngest daughter and son to the Lordly Ones, in return for riches and luck for himself. He got what he asked, but later his knights learned of it and gave him to the church. He was burned as a witch. The castle was abandoned as cursed. Even the best luck can run out."

"Luck..." said Jack, dully. "Money..."

"After a long while, one of the warlord's children was returned. The Lordly Ones had to let him go, because the luck had failed. They didn't want to, nor did the boy want to come back. The moment he breathed the air of this world, he became old as the hills himself. Yet he lived on. The power of immortality preserved him, but not his youth. He lives still. Perhaps he always must."

The man's face was like a carved stone. Jack took a step away.

Just then, the church clock struck four. It didn't always strike, but now it did, and the chimes filled him with a terror without cause. Then he knew why. *Luce.* He reeled away up the lane and sprinted for the school.

She was gone. The teacher he found in the tree-planted yard told him she'd seen Luce running off. One of her friends had tried to interest Luce in seeing a new foal someone had, but Luce said today she had to be home.

Jack bolted back toward the house.

As he ran, the thoughts drummed in his skull. Normans, Romans, Brid's protective altar stone that gave its name to the village, Luce so mad to reach the fields she jumped out of a window, singing out there all those evenings in the dusk – to herself? Or *to what*? The figure among the grain, amused, patient – *greedy*. And Susie winning the lottery, such good luck.

When he burst into the house, Susie was sitting there with her shoes off, drinking water from a bottle.

"Jack! I didn't get the job, but there's much better news. I met Ken Angel in town – you know, that TV thing I did. He's down here looking for locations. He *said* – now *wait* for it – he'd like me aboard on this production. Oh, just two or three lines but... well don't look so astounded. I can still act, you know."

"Is Lucy here?" said Jack.

Susie's flushed face went white. She dropped the water bottle and he watched the water uncoil along the carpet. "*What do you mean*? Of course, she's not here – you just met her at school. *Didn't you?*"

Jack explained Luce had been gone, to a mother whose face was now blank with fear.

He thought, even if any of this were possible it couldn't be Susie's fault. She hadn't met *something*, made a bargain...

She was at the phone, rattling it about. "Damn, no line, now of all times. Where's my mobile...?" The contents of her bag tipped out on the water on the floor. She stabbed at buttons.

"You're calling the police."

"No, a pizza delivery. *What do you think?*"

Something slid into Jack's mind. He thought of foxes in London, on the streets in the early morning, sleeping in gardens – Man had taken over so much of the open country, now the foxes had come to live where the people were.

Were *They* like that? Did they in fact like to be close, maybe just in that wood up there – watching their chance, intrigued by cricket on the green, the pub with their name, the trains. Waiting. In case something might become available...

All this was madness.

Jack stood fighting with himself. Then he realised Susie wasn't talking into her mobile. She said, flatly, "I can't get a signal." Then she said, *"Where are you going?"*

What could he tell her? Nothing.

He ran into the kitchen, opened the back door, ran again. Behind him he could hear her shouting in panic and anger. He couldn't let that slow him down.

He was practiced now getting over the back fence. He heard her bare feet beating on the path. The fields were like a wall of dry white fire, into which, like a moth, he flew.

They were there.

Yes, he could feel them all around, unseen but *present.* Some primitive sixth sense had kicked into play inside him, though really, hadn't it done that from the very start?

Jack stopped running. He pushed forward through the grain. There seemed to be eyes behind every group of stalks. *Green* eyes, and hair that blended with the colour of the fields. Yet when they *let* you see them, they were luminous.

It was no good now thinking he was mental. He knew this was *real.*

Above the fields, the woods, dark green, with green-gold glitters of sun.

He strode through them, fast, looking everywhere. Birds shrilled warnings, squirrels darted overhead. They were like the heartless servants of what truly lurked here.

The hot, static air seemed full of mocking laughter. Sometimes he called out his sister's name. It had a hollow sound.

This was useless, but somehow it had to be done. A sick weight was gathering in his stomach. He refused to think about Susie. Even though this was no use, he must go on. He wondered vaguely how many times, since people first lived here, someone or other just like Jack had trudged across this hilly landscape, calling someone's name, knowing it was no use at all.

The sun moved west. He would have killed for one of those exploded colas – of course, *They* had done that, too – and messed up the phones? Some sort of electric psi stuff, like a poltergeist.

Jack came to a halt. Suddenly he'd stepped over dark tree roots, mosses, ferns, and come out on quite a wide road going sunlit through the woods.

The sense of being watched and laughed at lessened. Then he

saw there was an ordinary man standing under a tree.

"Thank God, there you are."

"Mr. Tooth the dentist," said Jack, confused.

"Thanks for the inevitable joke. Try Alan, if you wouldn't mind."

"A. Tooth," said Jack idiotically. He burst into childish giggling, appalling himself. Then he leaned over and threw up.

When he'd finished, Alan Tooth handed him an unopened bottle of water. Jack gulped; the water helped. He said, "How the hell did you happen to be waiting?"

"It seems everyone comes this route. They used to call it Lordly Way – there's an old track under the fields and trees. You can still find traces if you know where to look. I'm into amateur archaeology. That's how I first met Soldier. As for you – well after we spoke, I worked it out – abruptly, during my tea break. I cancelled a couple of non-emergencies and called on Soldier myself, this evening. Then I knew."

"Do you know... *does it happen*?"

"Yes, I think so. Not often. This is the first for about half a century. The police scoured the place that time. They said it was child abduction, the usual filthy human thing. It wasn't, though, I don't think. My mother told me about it. A boy that time, twelve years old. Very fair hair. *They* like the ones that look the most like they do, you see."

"He – Soldier – said it had to be a bargain."

"No. A certain kind of *wishing* seems to do it. The mother of the boy that time, she'd made a thing of telling everyone she wished she'd never had him, was sick to death of him, wanted a better life instead. And the funny thing is, after this child went missing, the police never had her under suspicion. Then she met a man with a load of dosh and married him."

Jack put his hand on the nearest tree to steady the rocking world.

Now he knew who had made the bargain that involved Luce – or formed the wish that wrecked the protective magic of Brid's Stone for her. It was *Michael*. Susie had never ever wished her family gone. She had been happy. But Michael invented a new personality for Susie – a woman who hated her kids and only wanted her old life back – and this was the Susie he slapped and punched. And all that time Michael told them all how sick of them *he* was. Sick enough to get up and leave forever. And with that thought he must have changed his loser's luck – and they received the edge of it.

They had also been dragged toward the nearest place where the payment for Michael's luck must be made. Jack remembered the three of them looking at the estate agent's stuff. Susie and Luce had fixed on Bridestone the moment they saw it.

"Come on," said Alan Tooth. "We'd better get you home. Your mother'll need you."

"Then it's hopeless – searching?"

Alan's face fell. He no longer looked particularly grownup himself. "Let's hope not. But better leave it to the police."

"You said..."

"I know. But going on the records, no one ever got them back. Not even a body."

"Unless they came back themselves centuries after – like Soldier."

Someone spoke out of the wood. Both Jack and Alan jumped violently. "It's waxing moon," said the voice of Soldier. "Go we up that highest hill. Go careful."

He came out of the wood, his face holy as that of a knight carved on a tomb. His speech was altered by time and memory, and *he* was altered – strong, perhaps irresistible.

The climb up the hill was hard work. Stony outcrops, beech and elder trees, interrupted the path. The hill was coated in tangled grass. Far behind, the golden sun was sinking into the land, taking away the light.

"See," said Soldier, "she is risen."

The crescent moon was up the hill, still faint in the sunset. The remains of the fort above seemed one with the jumble of the hill.

"This is where the entrance lies to their domain," said Soldier.

Alan added, "Yes, it's supposed to be under this hill. That's why the Romans had trouble here and brought in the druids – most unusual. They weren't normally friends. The druids suggested the Stone of Brid. Roman soldiers tended to prefer worshipping Mithras. Not here."

Alan was seeming more scholarly, and Soldier more insane. Defensive? Jack had no defence. He didn't even know why they had come up here – but again, the *compulsion* was intense.

Maybe *They* liked somebody to see what they could do, how beautiful they were, how clever...

The last sun was squashed out just as they made the final stretch. Both Jack and Alan were dripping sweat. Soldier wasn't, though he looked three times Alan's age. The darkening light now became actual darkness. Shadow sprawled from rocks, trees, down from the sky itself. The moon, though, brightened, a white rip in the dusk.

The jagged Roman walls were in front of them. Ruin and nightfall robbed them of any shape or logic. A portion of archway stood ahead, and beyond it a kind of grassy court that looked as if sheep had grazed it recently. Down a topple of slope, Jack saw a formless stone.

"There," panted Alan. "There it is. The altar."

"They will always come here," said Soldier softly, "when they have gotten, to show their triumph to the Stone. God wills. *They are already here.*"

Jack stared, hair rising on arms and neck.

Through liquid shadow, something pale, that shone...

He could see them. The Lordly Ones, the...

Elvenbrood.

He didn't try to count, but he thought there were fourteen – one for every year of his sister's life. Yes, they were beautiful all right. Their skin was pearl, hair moonlit clouds. Some were male, others female, but their clothes were the same, misty, clinging on slender bodies, but also flowing. There were jewels on them like nothing he'd ever seen or imagined, with great tears of light inside. They had daggers too, and swords of some silvery metal that couldn't be steel. And as he gazed at them, hypnotised, Jack saw Luce, there in the middle of them. Like them, she had flowers in her hair.

He wanted to shout to her. *They* were smiling and laughing, and so was she. Laughter like silver bells and silver daggers...

His mind yelled in the prison of his paralysed body – but he couldn't move, and neither it seemed could Alan.

The Lordly Ones danced their stately dance along the hill, with Luce dancing with them and coming to the altar they bowed, and their bowing was full of the most exquisite scorn.

Alan croaked something. "D'you see?"

Another thing had formed, beyond the altar, right there. It was a hole into emptiness, but down the tunnel of it was a pulsing, gorgeous glow.

"It's the *gate*, the way into the underhill..."

Trying to move, heart roaring, pinned to the spot...

Jack's struggle seemed to dislodge something outside himself. *Soldier.*

"Here I am. Here, your child that you loved, who loved you hundred on hundred years. The one you sent into exile, lost in this world that, to your heaven country, is hell..." Soldier moved among them, with extraordinary grace. He moved as *They* did. Not like an old man in clothes from the garbage in a dustbin. He spoke in some language Jack had never heard – almost a twisted sort of Germanic French – yet Jack somehow understood every word.

"Don't take that other child," said Soldier to the Lordly Ones, royally scornful as they were. "Do you really want *her*? Ignorant and unformed and knowing nothing of your glory. No, take me again, out of this bitter world. I love you so. And I have learned all there is to know here. I am like a book you will be able to read for a thousand years."

The beings on the hill had ceased to move about. They looked stilly at Soldier.

Luce, petulant suddenly, cried, "It's only that stupid mad old man..."

One of the beings struck her lightly across the face. He did not speak, but turning to Soldier, he reached up and breathed into the old man's mouth. Although there were no words, Jack knew what the being had said: *Let us then remind ourselves of how you were. Let us compare and judge.*

You could make no excuses. It happened in front of Jack's eyes. Age and decay fell from Soldier like a discarded shell. He stood there, straight as a spear, a boy of maybe thirteen, golden-skinned, unmarked, sun-gold hair to his waist.

Yes, said the voice that had no voice, *he is better.*

Laughing, Soldier looked green-eyed over his shoulder at Jack and Alan stuck there to the ground. "Farewell, men of mud. Farewell, world of dust. Know for always you could not have kept her, had *They* not loved me better than she."

A dazzle hit the hillside. Treetops and walls flared like neon, faded.

They were gone, the beings from the hill, the old man who had become a boy. Only one last pale shape remained, lying on the grass.

Paralysis left Jack. "Luce!"

When he touched her, she opened her eyes and looked at him,

annoyed. "Why did you wake me up, Jack? What time is it?" And then, surprised but not alarmed, "Why am I up here?"

Jack couldn't speak. It was Alan who had to spin her some yarn that she'd come up here on a dare. Oddly, as she listened, she seemed to believe him, to *remember* the dare – and nothing else unusual at all.

Alan and Jack talked later. It was a secret they had to keep always from Susie, and from Luce too. "It wasn't just they loved Soldier more than Lucy, Jack. It was because you and Susie love her so *much*. That other woman who hated her boy – Soldier could never have made a swap with him – I doubt if he even tried. I think he only warned Lucy to make her more likely to do it – you know how girls can be. Or maybe, when he was saner, he did try to stop those things. Would she have been happier *there*? Well, yes. But that's not it. We're supposed to live out *here*."

Jack and Alan often had talks now, since Susie had moved the family to the town, and Susie and Alan became an Item. Susie was rehearsing for her part in Ken Angel's TV drama – it had nothing to do with faeries.

It was a year later that police in Gloucester found the burnt-out Jeep Cherokee with Michael's body in it. It had gone off a country road into some trees. They said Michael would have been killed at once, the fire had happened afterward. It seemed, from bits of evidence, that Michael had become rich after leaving Susie. No one could find any trace of how, or where. It was a real mystery.

But Jack knew, he and Alan, though *this* they did not discuss: how Michael had come by his sudden money luck, the edge of which had rubbed off on Susie. Knew, too how Michael would not have been dead when his vehicle caught fire. Like Soldier's father, the Norman warlord ten centuries before, Michael had been burned alive.

Felidis

1

"Don't go in those woods – there's a terrifying girl – a *female* there – and she's a *cat*."

"What do you mean?" he asked, the young man standing on the road. "Do you mean she's bitchy – *catty*?"

"Nah," said the other man, the old red fat one on his cart, while the fed-up but poorly fed horse shook its ears. "I *mean*, boy, she's covered in *fur* – and her *hair's* fur. And she's gotten herself two ice-green *cat eyes*. She's bad – she's *evil*. Don't go in those woods. I've warned you."

And with a cluck to the horse, off he trundled in his cart, old red Fatty.

While Radlo still stood on the track in his thin coat, with – he later admitted – his mouth hanging open.

"He's mad," Radlo presently said aloud to reassure himself. In a nearby tree a magpie sounded its rattling scorn. "He didn't agree to give me a lift to anywhere either. So..." Radlo looked back at the cloud of late summer woodland rising over the hillsides about two miles off. "So, I might as well go on the way I was going in the first place. I like cats, anyhow," he added, if rather doubtfully. Cats, surely. But *girls covered in fur*? "To hell with it," Radlo finished.

And on he walked.

The second man Radlo met, three hours later, by then deep in the dusk woods, was the opposite of the other. The second man was thin and young, and pallid as egg white, and it seemed he came from the village just smokily visible over a rise.

"Here you," began thin young Eggy. "What you wanting?"

Lots of things, thought Radlo sadly. *A good meal would be nice for a start – or even a friendly word.* "Nothing," he replied.

"You're after *something*," Eggy insisted. "Be off! You're not wanted around here."

Radlo scowled. He hadn't meant to, but the scowl had been brewing for thirteen days. "You don't know me," he scowlingly growled. "So how d'you *know* I'm not wanted?"

Idiotic Eggy goggled at him.

"All right," Eggy idiotically said. "Better come with me, then." And led him down through the trees into the village.

There was dull yellowish lamplight starting in some of the cottage windows; the smoke going up from the chimneys had the tang of early cooking. Radlo's stomach gurgled. Near the well a few people lingered, women drawing up a last pail of water, and a woodcutter in conversation with a couple of huntsmen.

"You ought to go have a word with her," said the woodcutter to the hunters. "*She'll* put it right. And if it's a big beast like that you can't be too careful."

This sounded rather odd, but, anyway, having noticed Radlo and Eggy approaching, one of the huntsmen shook his head and made a gesture plainly meaning *Shut up*. All three men turned and glared at Radlo, while the women with pails stared.

"What's *he* want?" asked the woodcutter. "What you bringing him in for, you blitherer, eh?" This presumably to Eggy.

"Maybe he wants *her*," said the other huntsman. The first hunter shushed him.

"Says he's expected," said Eggy, inaccurately.

"*Who* expects him?"

Radlo, finding all this too tiresome to be funny – hungry and irritated and with nowhere at all to go, and no one at all anymore to want or expect him – lost his temper and roared: "*She* expects me. *Her*. The one you keep on about. Who *else*?"

It was impulsive and ridiculous. The moment he had done it he felt a complete fool. The Lord knew who this wretched female was they had mentioned. Probably the local jolly-woman, who charged coins for kisses, or worse – some well-off old nag in whose good books they were all trying to stay.

It wasn't he had forgotten red Fatty's natter of a girl in fur. It was only two and two hadn't yet become four.

"What do you think?" asked the woodcutter of the huntsmen. "Do we believe him?"

"Shall I thrash him?" helpfully inquired the bigger huntsman. "That'll get the truth out."

Radlo was not above fighting, but he and the hunter didn't seem a fair match. Radlo loosened up his muscles, ready to run for his life.

And just then one of the women by the well called out, "Look over there. Better see what *he* thinks."

At which everybody turned, Radlo too, and there sat a black cat with a white triangle, like a little breastplate, on its chest.

"Good eve, Jehankin," chorused the villagers.

The cat gave a flip of its tail – just one. It sprang away into the shadow beyond the houses.

Grumbling now, the men frowned at Radlo. To Eggy, the woodcutter said, "See the way the cat's gone? Better take this fellow up there, then. Go on, be quick. She may be waiting, for all we know."

Having not, until the cat appeared, put two and two together, at last Radlo did. And two and two seemed to make ten. The manner in which Fatty had spoken about the girl in fur, the way *this* lot spoke of *her* – they had seemed different females. But Fatty, the outsider, was scared of her. The villagers were in awe?

And there was no method to get out of it now, whatever anyone thought. Eggy was shambling off the way the cat had gone, along a side path that led from the village and up another thickly treed hill. While the big, thrash-threatening hunter gave Radlo a shove, and pushily fell in behind him. Just as a pair of guards might herd a prisoner to his doom.

Well done, Radlo, he congratulated himself sourly.

The woods now were jet black and thick with a night like a horsehair blanket. Somewhere an owl hooted, another bloody joker laughing.

The lamp in the window showed first, dark amber. Then, in the open doorway of the little house up the hill: a young woman, dressed in the ordinary village way.

She *had* gotten herself ice-green eyes. Her hair *was* fur – short and spiky and furry, in colour *tabby*. Her skin – flawless, of course – was covered by a furry velvet nap, like palest pearliest grey velvet.

Radlo's legs gave way.

He landed (prone) at her feet.

Fatty hadn't lied.

2

Did the cats pick him up, and courteously carry him indoors? There were certainly enough to have done it. So far he had counted at least thirty, and some were very alike, and therefore he could have *under*counted, and they could be twice that number.

He'd felt ashamed of fainting. He hadn't eaten anything, it was true, but grass and a withered apple for three days... but hunger had happened before. No excuse.

Hers was a rambly cottage, with one upstairs room. Up there she had her bed, behind a curtain most likely, and otherwise did all her work with herbs and potions. Unless invited, who would dare intrude?

The cats *did* go everywhere. Yet Radlo noted from the start none of them relieved themselves indoors or scent-marked walls or furniture. Nor did they spoil the herb and flower beds outside.

She was a witch, obviously. A witch covered in fur. And though he had seen later the green irises of her eyes had each a circle of white around them, as a human eye did, it was a *small* circle of white. And some cats had that too.

She was a cat.

A witch and a cat.

She'd told him her name was Felidis.

And she had been very kind, brought him some strengthening broth, and warm bread baked in her own oven by the hearth, and beer she had apparently brewed as well. Radlo was so hungry he hadn't, right then, had any problem with a cat-woman making and serving up his food.

That evening too, as he sat on the comfortable cushioned bench by the fire, he heard the huntsman, the big one who'd shepherded him there, telling her about a wild cat, a panther, he called it – no doubt a wood-lynx – that was bothering the village. (This was what they had been talking about when Radlo went into the village with Eggy.) And in her calm cool voice, witchy-catty Felidis had said, "Oh, that's fine. I'll go out tonight and have a word with the panther. I think I did catch sight of him a few evenings back, but I've been that busy...."

Later still, when the moon was well up, splitting the woods into ranks of black pillars and thin white-moonlight spears, out she went. And peering through one of the little windows, Radlo saw her at the edge of the clearing where her cottage stood, moving quietly up and down with a large shadowy cat-thing about the size of a hunting-hound. There wasn't anything dangerous-looking to this interview. If anything, it was like a couple of friendly acquaintances taking a short walk after church. (The black and white cat was out there too, the one Radlo had seen in the village. It sat on a tree stump, not seeming concerned about the *other* cat, which was three times its size. It must really trust *her*.)

Eventually she (Felidis) touched the moon-doused shadow-panther's head, and it rubbed once against her hand. Then the animal turned and sprinted from view. Surreal, all this. A dream? But Radlo knew he hadn't dreamed it. Nor the velvet silver of her hair and skin, the luminous green *flash* of her cat's eyes as she walked back to the cottage.

She had said he might sleep the night on the floor of the downstairs room, with a cushion and a blanket and the dying fire for comfort.

"I know how it must be," she had said to him mildly, "to be wandering about on your own in the dark."

When not looking at her, one would never know what she was. She sounded like a human girl. But even in the glow of the last embers – you could *see*.

That first night he'd barely said a word to her. He had gawped at her for hours. She made no remark on this rudeness. Nor had she told the villagers Radlo was quite unknown to her – *not* expected.

He did dream of her, between being disturbed by the bouncing and purring of cats. Of course, he dreamed. He was already part-afraid and part-fascinated, and entirely out of his depth.

"What do you want, Puss?" Radlo asked the black and white cat – Jehankin, had they called it – who was sitting about one-third of an arm's length from Radlo's face when he woke up. Radlo liked animals of all sorts, even snakes, even wolves at a safe distance. But his way of talking to this cat was falsely easy. And the cat gave him a *look*, as if to say, *You don't kid me, young fellow*. He was a young cat himself, strong and glossy and clear-eyed. Even assuming it (he) could take on such a grandfatherly attitude towards Radlo, this cat was a *boy*. (Daft way to think. Daft, all of it. But then, this creature wasn't afraid of a lynx.)

Felidis came in with some red flowers and a basket of apples and putting these down knelt by the cat and embraced him.

"Jehankin, my prince!" she said, with great happiness and love. And Prince Jehankin purred like a gigantically buzzing bee.

Radlo concentrated on the cat then, not to have to look at

Felidis, which with daylight, and feeling better, he decided was almost impossible. (He had a feeling too the witch had patted his forehead as he slept. He wasn't sure he liked the idea.)

However, she was engaged entirely with her cat. Radlo saw that, although she was loving and caring with *all* the cats, she made an incredible fuss of this particular feline.

They rubbed faces for minutes. And she too (oh the Lord!) made a weird purring noise far down in her throat. Then she brought for the cat a dish of meat, and another of curds, and left him to breakfast. When quite done, Jehankin groomed himself, polishing his fur end to end with his spic-and-span pink tongue.

Of course, Jehankin must be the witch's Familiar.

A while after Radlo, to his joy, was given breakfast too. Then he sat on the bench and Felidis inspected him. The cat sat by her and seemed to inspect Radlo as well, with a considering air.

"I must give you a drink of suitable herbs. That seems to be what you must have," Felidis announced finally. "Then you'll be well able to go on with your journey."

At that Radlo was covered by a cloud of depression. He had *nowhere* to go. Besides, a witch would want paying.

"I can't offer you a single coin," he said gracelessly, looking down at the floor now.

"No worry. People pay me or not, when or if they can," said Felidis, turning towards the narrow, crooked stair and the workroom above. The cat stalked before her and bounded up the steps.

"You've been generous," said Radlo. "Perhaps – are there any chores I could do to help you out?"

And to himself, *Be quiet, you total madman. Fly while you've gotten a chance!* But, not looking at her, her voice seemed only human, rather musical and pretty.

"That's honourable," said Felidis. "Well, if you will. There's some wood to be cut, if you're up to that. Or the berries in the raspberry vines are ripe to pick."

Outside, swinging the axe, Radlo was aware of endless cats, white patterned black, and black dabbed with white; ginger, and ale-brown, and a few pied like tree bark, and even some pale grey – like Felidis herself. Gold eyes and amber eyes and eyes of jade winked and glittered like jewellery in the bushes.

Radlo found he had begun, almost by accident, to sing. He sang rather well, he had been told. The sun was up and warm on his back. The clearing was attractive, the tall green canopy of woods all around, just lit in places by the first red and copper of fall.

When he had cut and stacked the wood in the shed, he picked two baskets of the lush raspberries. He only ate four – they were irresistible and very sweet.

About a mile off down the slope, and hidden by trees, the village sometimes gave off a homey sound, the tinkle of a sheep bell, the thump of a rug being beaten, or a hammer striking sharp from a forge.

They lunched. He alone, if with several cats. The witch up in her room of spells and medicines. Then she gave him, at his request, other tasks. He said he would move on tomorrow, if she would allow him the pillow and blanket one more night. She answered carelessly that he was welcome.

Radlo thought she wasn't afraid at having a strange man in her house, even now he was well again. After all, she was a witch who could talk to panthers.

3

Am I in love with her?

I can't even look at her half the time, not properly – but am I in love?

Radlo was upset even by thinking this. The one girl he had so far loved had dumped him for the local landowner's son, less than two months before. And after that (or because of that) he'd been in some trouble, and then been thrown out of his own village, and so taken to wandering.

He had no special trade, though he was strong enough to earn his bread – cutting wood, clearing paths, helping with sheep or horses, that sort of thing. Besides, he could read and write. He had been a scholar before the faithless girl ruined his life.

As the year had begun to edge towards fall, he grew nervous, wondering what he'd do all winter, holed up the Lord knew where, and that was if any village would make a place for him.

He had been aiming for the big old town that lay along the river, westward. But for a man on foot, and always having to stop to earn some food, the journey so far had taken a while. And in the last thirteen days too, someone had robbed Radlo, someone else had lightly but nastily beaten him up, and last but hardly least, a farmer had cheated him of promised pay.

Now here he was.

Her voice was sweet and tempting as the raspberries and apples he had picked for her. But in evening gloamings that green *flare* of her eyes...

No, he couldn't love a being like Felidis.

He had been sleeping on her cottage floor by now for five nights. By day he did work for her in the house or clearing, or went to the village on her errands. He had made friends with some of the cats – those that let him – and was always respectful to Jehankin, the beast that was her Familiar. Jehankin himself stayed with Felidis in her herbarium during a chunk of each day. At night the black and white cat went out on his own business, presumably to hunt or play, like the other cats, in the woods.

On the fifth afternoon (yesterday) a boy had come hurrying up from the village, and dashed past Radlo, who was mending the wall of the second shed. In the cottage, a call, and then the village boy's excited gabble. Somebody was riding directly up here, it seemed, to visit the witch. Somebody important.

Felidis stepped downstairs, swathed in her broad grey apron, wiping her slender furry hands – paws? – on a cloth.

Then they all – she, the boy, Radlo, and some sixteen cats – waited about. Until up the track from the village came an impressive group of callers. There were several mounted soldiers, heavily armed and in the uniform of a moneyed household. Also servants on mules. And in the middle was a rich man in a velvet coat, sitting on a big white horse he looked too sick to ride.

Felidis said nothing. She only looked up at the rich man, calm as cream.

One of the servants broke out haughtily, "Woman, show some politeness to my master..."

But the rich man himself cut the servant off. "She's polite enough. Hello, witch. I see you're as they say you are."

"So," said Felidis gently, "are very many of us."

"Maybe," he answered. "But do you have the skill they rumour too?"

"I have some ability."

"More than that, I hope. I'm not a well man. Can you help me out?"

"Dismount, sir," said Felidis, "and come into my house. We'll see if I can."

160

The important man was assisted from his horse, and went meekly into the cottage with Felidis, and the last any of the rest of them saw of events, for a while, was Jehankin trotting up and in at the door, before the door was firmly closed.

Then everybody idled about the clearing. The soldiers shared a beer-skin, and the servants muttered, while the other cats sat on stones, on the shed roofs, or up in the trees, and watched. And Radlo himself watched the plaster drying on the mended wall. The village boy who had brought the message idled about too. He began to talk to Radlo, showing off, knowing *everything*. "Oh, *she'll* get him right as rain."

"Will she? Good. This lot could turn ugly if she can't."

"Did you know, last year the great lady of Tall Trees came here, so sickly she lay on a *litter* – but within two hours she was up and out and pink as a girl. And since then, every month, our village gets a vat of wine and a barrel of grain, on account of the healing Felidis worked for her."

"You don't say," said Radlo. *Little liar*, he thought.

But the boy went chattering on, now about this wealthy patron and now that, or the old monk who was one hundred years old and wanted just one more year to finish painting in the book he was making, and the monk received several more, and Felidis was given a gold jewel from the monastery, which she in turn gave the village for their church, where it hung to this minute.

"She never keeps a thing for herself. Says she never needs it."

Radlo climbed up the ladder to check the shed roof, slightly aggravating the cats now roosting there. But anything to get away from the chatty boy.

It was almost sunset, the sun like a burning house low down in the trees, when the cottage door was undone.

Out walked the rich man. He looked, Radlo noticed, about twenty years younger, and happy as Christ Mass.

"By the stars, she's done it, lads." He had a flask of medicine too, which the servants took charge of.

When they had all ridden off, and even the boy had gone scrambling down the hill to tell the village – no doubt another pack of untruths (the rich man had singled him out, Felidis had confided the secret of her spell – Radlo left the roof.

He felt angry.

Either it was some trick she'd pulled. Or else she *was* just a jolly-woman after all, and an hour in her cosy arms was what had put Richy to rights.

Inside the cottage he could hear her singing, sweetly too, up in the herb-room. And Jehankin sat half down the stair, washing his paws. His white whiskers seemed to grin at Radlo.

"The hell with it!" Radlo snapped, and flung out for a stamp in the cooling, darkening wood. Here he disturbed a badger set, shocked a big clawed and militant owl, and ultimately stumbled over a tree root, ending in some mud.

I'm jealous. Don't be insane. Of what? A cat-girl with tabby hair. She probably even had whiskers too, if one went close enough and stared.

When finally he returned, something wonderful-smelling was cooking in a pot on the hearth. (The rich man had brought a present she *had* accepted, it seemed, a roast for dinner.)

And she had laid the table for the three of them: herself, Radlo, and the black and white cat.

His anger melted in the firelight. It was too chilly to storm off. Why not sit down and eat, facing her properly over the candles, and with Prince Jehankin seated couthly between them, sharing everything, having his own bowl exactly like theirs, and a little matching cup of beer?

Oh, in the candle- and firelight, after a little food, she looked – her skin was just... pale and velvet smooth. And her hair... so she had some grey in it before her time, as you might expect from a woman who worked very hard. And her green eyes? They were beautiful.

She told him a joke and it made him laugh. He told her one, and she laughed too. The cat sat smiling, and presently lay down on the table, like a nesting pigeon (or a lion), his paws tucked under him.

"Your cat smiles," said Radlo.

"Of course. All things smile. But – apart from humans – animals only when they mean it."

"Humankind. We're *false*, deceivers," said Radlo sadly.

"Maybe we feel we have to be. Poor things, we are."

"Not you," he said.

"I'm the lucky one."

"What did you do to that rich man today?"

"Helped heal him."

"*How?*"

"Herbs, things I'm lessoned how to use. And... a kind wish."

"I thought perhaps..." Radlo faltered. He said, "Were you a bit kinder than just in your wishes?"

She burst out now in a wild young laugh. It was so true and real it made him laugh again too.

"No," she remarked in a moment. "I don't make myself *kind* that way with men. With anyone. That isn't for me. I have no ambition, Radlo, of being any man's lady, let alone his wife. I don't want love or fun of that sort, or marriage, or children." (Radlo stared, astounded. Never in all his days had he ever heard any woman, young or old, say such things.) "My path is another one."

"But you've no family," he blurted, astounded now into astounding concern for her loss.

"Don't I? Look about."

Blankly he glanced around. All he saw were fire glimmers and warm shadows, and here and there a soft gleam of flame on fur, or a glint of a garnet or an emerald or a topaz eye.

"Yes. *They're* my family. All I have and all I want. You've seen what I am. Quarter cat at least."

Radlo sat dumbfounded. Strangely his eyes had filled with tears.

Then she told him quietly how it had been with her. Since she was her own living proof, he believed her.

"I don't remember any mother or father, or anything much until I was – I'd guess from my size then and abilities – about three years old. And how I'd gotten myself into the woods I've no notion. But I have a sort of set of memory *fragments* – things half seen or heard, felt, *hated*... these make me think perhaps I escaped from some sort of carnival or fair, where I was shown as a monster, jeered at and starved. But perhaps I'm wrong, and my parents simply abandoned me, having been scared of me from the start and unable to stand me another second.

"The woods are my first certain memory. They were so big and dark, full of night. I think, for me, it must have been how it would feel to be at the bottom of a lake, or under the sea. And it was cold. It was the end of fall, and the leaves raining down and frost shining white.

"But then there he is. Who? Why my rescuer, my prince there, Jehankin. He was younger then but still wise. He was warm and soft to touch, and *good*. He led me away to an old ruined barn, where he and his kind were living. There was a whole tribe of them, two hundred or more, a house full of fur. And they kept me warm and brought me a share of their kills – I won't tell you, Radlo, what I fed on sometimes. You'd go green. But everything that lives must eat, and they saved me.

"I stayed with them for years. Sometimes some of the cats went away to make new colonies, and sometimes new ones came in and proved themselves of use and stayed. And Jehankin taught me all I needed to know, for he's a clever cat, you can't think how cunning and brainy, and brilliant as a star. I even learnt the human language because Jehankin made sure I heard and saw the things I must in order to do so. But the cats were my people. They never despised me that I couldn't copy all their skills. They kept me safe and sane. And in the end, when I was about fourteen, Jehankin found this village, and this cottage, and he and I and some of his sons and daughters and wives came here.

"In the beginning the villagers were afraid of me. But with time they came to understand I could help with healing, and talking to wild panthers and such like – and they could ask for little magics like the lighting of a fire without striking a flint, or the unfreezing of water that seems to come from a single word. Five years have passed. Now the village is quite proud to have a witch, even a furry one. And sometimes, as you saw, persons come great distances for cures, or some spell of good luck. And none of them doubts for one moment..." Here Felidis broke off. She lowered her eyes as if shy. "...that I am a genuine witch. Although some more distant villages still fear me, the female who is part girl and part cat."

Radlo found himself speechless. But he also found next minute he said, "Jehankin must have been the tiniest kitten when you first met him. He's only a young cat now – and you've known him, by your own reckoning, nineteen years less three. Yet there isn't a grey whisker in his head."

To which she said nothing, but Jehankin himself sat up and stared straight at Radlo with his eyes of cool yellow clearness. If he was even six years old, never mind sixteen, seemed unlikely. But then, he was Felidis's Familiar, who had woken her true magic gifts.

Just then Felidis rose and Jehankin jumped down and followed her to the door. When she opened it, out he went into the moonless night. It seemed she had known what he wanted, it often did so, without any visible sign.

After that she went upstairs. Radlo put the cups and bowls into water and made up his bed on the floor.

Something in him, which had been soothed and glad, had grown edgy. And lying watching the fire reflection on the ceiling – above which lay her noiseless room – that question began in his heart and mind:

Am I in love with her? I can't even look at her half the time… Can't be in love… but am I?

4

How quick the last of summer and then fall fell away, like water through a sieve.

When the first snow came drifting down like flour over the grey-blue afternoon, Radlo was still living in the cottage. He still did the heavier chores, and also he had been teaching Felidis to read and write.

During these lessons Jehankin was nearly always present. He observed everything they did, both tutor and pupil, peering over the witch's shoulder. Though Radlo's writing the cat seemed to prefer to look at upside down.

Radlo grew accustomed to Jehankin, as he had to the other cats. He was used to Felidis saying they were her brothers and sisters, and the youngest ones her nephews and nieces. Once Radlo asked her, if that were the case, how were she and Jehankin related? "Oh, we're not," she said. "Though truly, he's been like the father I never had. But more than that, he's my Liege-lord, my prince. I owe him everything."

Radlo was not jealous of Jehankin.

Definitely not. Radlo was not going to be jealous of a cat. Even a cat like that one.

But Radlo had gotten used as well to being in love with Felidis, with finding her weirdly beautiful, and despite this, with never stepping out of line. He'd no more put an arm around her waist or bend to kiss her than – than what? Than try to bloody well fly.

Love. It was hopeless. But it wouldn't go away. And so, as she still made room for him, neither did he.

Winter wasn't a bad time there. They ate well, the villagers bringing her quite a regular supply of meat, the makings for bread, and other stuff. When the snow became serious, they were wedged into a loaf of white ice, but there was plenty for dinner, and at Christ

Mass a feast. Radlo fixed the cottage roof, cleared the chimney. He wrote poetry on the last of his store of paper – to her, of course, mentally kicking himself all the while.

Wait till spring. He could get out then. Go away. Make for the damn town on the damn river.

Each night in the firelight, if she wasn't there but working above, he spoke softly to her of her changing her ways, of courting her, of her trying him out.

When she *was* there, he talked about the grey foxes he'd seen, the dark pheasant stalking through the snow-glades, or the broken bucket he had patched up.

The thaw began about a month after Christ Mass.

Radlo could have killed it, that warmish, slick wet shiny scent in the outer air, the drip of icicles over the door. The first reddish buds filled him with rage.

"I think I'll be off in a few days, Felidis. Once the slush has cleared a bit. The weather's good. You told that woman who came to ask it would be a forward, lasting spring. Fine traveling weather."

If he had hoped to see her look upset, forlorn, she didn't. She smiled at him. When she smiled, the delicate pearly fur by her lips rippled like a rill along a brook. And her lips looked so smooth, nice...

"That's sensible, Radlo. And you've been such a help to me. Only think, with the spring I can send for books on herbal lore, to increase my knowledge. Now I can *read*. I must give you a thank-you gift," she added with – he felt – sudden tenderness. "I wonder, what would you like?"

You.

He stared at her bleakly, biting on the unspoken word. Then, "What I'd *like* I don't think you'd give." *Oh shut up, you dumbleskull.*

But she turned her cat's eyes on him, and he could no longer look at her. She said, very low, "No, I couldn't. Nor would you truly want it."

"You don't know me. Or that."

"Nor do you know it," she answered crisply. "Or yourself."

"But..." he shouted, getting up, flapping his arms like a crazed goose.

And exactly then, over the afternoon hill began to come a sound of voices and cartwheels, and Radlo knew someone else was about to arrive, needing her in the only way she'd recognise. A man or woman desperate for her sorcerous skills.

He turned and walked out of the cottage, and stood outside in the mud, watching the cart drawn by a big horse, and the escort of several villagers. The woodcutter lay on some straw. He was unconscious and had been bleeding. But anything like this, and to the witch they came. She had never failed them. And Radlo wanted to bellow with fury at all of them for the interruption; unfair and unforgivable, a spoiled brat. He took himself off into the trees.

Then about a step short of a mile from the cottage he stopped. He turned and went back. But this time moving carefully and stealthily, approaching the house and its out-buildings from the other side, where no one was. He knew every nook and cranny of the place by now, all but her upstairs room where he had never been. Yet, this winter, while roof-fixing, he had discovered there was a little window up there, completely hidden from below. He'd never spied through it. Even had he been so base as to be tempted, the old glass was thick back then with snow. But it was spring now.

"I'll tell you what I want, Felidis, since you asked me," Radlo muttered to the last trees beyond the house. "I want to see what the hell you do with your magic. If I can't have *you* – at least I'll have *that*."

It was about midnight that Radlo came back the *second* time. There was still a lamp burning in the lower room. When he pushed in through the door no sorcerous spell was spun to keep him out. Nothing seemed changed. The cats that stayed indoors were clustered here and there, sparring, washing, sleeping, as ever. Felidis sat by the fire on the bench, winding a skein of light green wool.

Of Jehankin there wasn't a sign.

But then, he was usually off all night, about his own business in the wood or the world.

His own business...

Radlo slammed the door.

Felidis showed no reaction; her hands never faltered on the wool.

"You're a liar," Radlo rasped in a rough lunatic voice.

It was a fact: anyone who spied on a witch was liable to be smitten mad, or blind, or simply dead. Serve him right, then.

Felidis did not reply.

"I say you're a liar, *cat-girl*, because you're no more a witch than I'm a – than I'm a *cat*."

At this she raised her face and smiled at him. And he saw, as he never had before, indescribably she smiled just the way Jehankin did.

"Yes," said Felidis. "I thought one day you'd come to find out."

Then Radlo hung his head. He slumped down on the floor and gazed into the fire. But all he could see in the flames was what already he'd seen earlier, through the little window in the roof.

The injured woodcutter, who had been deeply and nearly fatally slashed by a breaking axe-head, lay on a mattress, and he hadn't a flicker of awareness left to him, though he still breathed. Felidis stood mixing a beer-coloured fluid in a cup, but every so often she turned her head, and looked attentively at the black cat with the white fur breastplate, her prince, Jehankin. One couldn't miss that by this turning of hers, this pause and then going on with her herbs and the mixture, she seemed to be following a series of instructions. Yet nobody else, aside from the black and white cat and the senseless man, was in the room.

Meanwhile, Jehankin himself, fastidious and spruce from a recent thorough preen, sat about one-third of an arm's length from the woodcutter's face. At regular intervals Jehankin leaned forward and breathed out his healthy meaty cat-breath across the man's closed lids. And then, so subtly, the cat would put out a paw – usually the left one – and place it, claws sheathed, for a split second on the woodcutter's forehead. Radlo watched about five minutes of this until, at one of these touches, the villager opened his eyes. He saw Jehankin, and then he drew in a huge breath and let it go in a vast sigh, as if he'd just eaten a wonderful meal, or woken from a fabulous sleep. After which he blinked and turned and saw Felidis, by which time the cat's paw had been withdrawn. "Ah, lady Felidis," said the woodcutter, "I feel a whole lot better. You're a real wonder, you are." And Felidis had glided to him and held the herbal cup to his mouth.

"Drink deep," she had said. "You'll be right as summer rain by daybreak."

"It's the cat," said Radlo now, as midnight turned to the first hour of morning. "The *cat*. Isn't it? The *cat's* the sorcerer."

"Yes." Felidis's face was abruptly full of delight. She beamed, and threw down the wool, and raised her arms slowly up. The cat, himself, my teacher and my prince, Jehankin. He is the witch. He is the genius."

"Then what in the Lord's Name are *you*?" whispered Radlo, weeping now; he couldn't help it.

"I," said Felidis, with the pride and glory of a king, "have the honour to be his *Familiar*, who – while he found me ignorant and all alone – nevertheless woke in him the skill of his true magic.

5

"You didn't tell me what you'd like to say my thank you"

"I did."

"No, my dear. That *isn't* what you'd really like. Trust me – or trust himself there, for he *knows*."

"It's a cat," sulked Radlo.

She laughed. He loved her laugh. The cat took no notice.

Of course, naturally, obviously, when dealing with humans – (she had said, "Your *people* need to lose some of their family obsession with their own kind!") – it *had* to seem *she* was the magician. Who would accept the gentle paw of a cat could pass on such miraculous healing, such wonders? (Jehankin had healed Radlo too. Radlo had *not* thanked Jehankin. Jehankin, patently, didn't care.)

"*Listen*," said Felidis. "He told me of a mild spell he'd woven for you, dear Radlo. Please don't scowl. It was kindly done."

"Yeah, yeah," growled Radlo. "Well, I'm off now."

"The Lord bless you," she said. She was so happy and full of compassionate interest in everything – he could have slapped her. But he wasn't that sort of man. Nor such a dolt.

For any dolt who did try that might not like the result, not with Jehankin sitting by the cottage door. Jehankin the witch. The healer. The prince. Her Liege-lord. Oh, to hell with it all.

Radlo strode off through the sun-goldening woods and was as civil as he could be to the villagers, who also waved him off on his journey, the woodcutter patting his shoulder and giving him a flask of spiced wine. "You tell them out there, lad. Tell them we have a fine witch here."

"Surely," said Radlo.

Only ten days, nights after did he curse himself for his own foul behaviour. But they – she – wouldn't trouble. None of them would care. *He* was irrelevant. And so back came the anger. And full of anger's energy he travelled fast to the west and reached the town by the river in less than thirty days.

That summer in the town, set up by then as a scholar in the university and making a decent living, Radlo met a lovely girl. Her hair was long and the colour of sunset bronze. Her eyes were blue as coins minted from the sky.

When once they were friends, she told him she had dreamed, the previous spring, of a cat, black and white and wearing a little silver crown, who called her by name. First the cat, a male, read her a story out of a book – for he could read! Then he told her the love of her life would soon be in the town. And he had been right.

"They're magical, all cats," she said. "Extraordinary creatures descended from the old gods, the *good* gods, who ruled the world before the Lord, and who still sometimes move about here, with His approval."

Radlo kissed her. He loved her and she him, and in another year they would be married, a union that would last the rest of their lives. But Jehankin *hadn't* given Radlo this wedding of love, no more than Radlo had inadvertently taught Jehankin to read. Jehankin was a *cat*. And Felidis. Oh, Felidis... she was only a witch in a wood, a female covered in fur, and with hair that was fur, who'd gotten two ice-green cat's eyes. A girl who was a cat. Feline. Felidis.

Felidis.

Felidis...

Golden Hair

Twice he asked her, and twice she refused him. The third time he did not ask.

She had no right, in any event, to deny him. She lived on his land, drew her sustenance from his fields, her drink from his river and his well. Even her house was built of the wood of his trees. She was his property. And she had said no.

It was her hair that first made him notice her. She was working in the wheat fields with the others, scything beneath the late summer sun. Her hair was not the colour of the wheat. It was the colour of new-minted metal, coiled round and round her head and still falling from the coils to her waist. It was massy hair, but fine, gold in the shadow, silver under the sun.

It was four years since he had ridden so far on his estate to view the harvesting. He had not beheld much of interest; now he found this. He stopped his horse to look. She had a supple, well-made body under her serf's kirtle. He wondered if her face would spoil the rest. But when she turned, he perceived it did not.

He called the overseer.

"That girl, my lord? That's Clessy."

When the overseer had fetched her, she stood quietly by the horse, looking up at the lord of the estate, unblinking.

"I've travelled to many regions," he said, "but I never saw a piece like you before." And when she made no answer, and did not lower her eyes, thinking her bold, he said: "My bed's the place for you. What do you say?"

She paled then, and her eyes widened. And in a voice like winter ice, she told him: "I say no, my lord."

The blood burned his face. He thought the overseer had heard her.

"I might have you whipped for that," he said, but she only went on staring at him, and he spurred his horse and rode off in a rage. And on the way, he killed one of the serf children, riding it down in his anger, purposely, and breaking its neck.

That dusk he hunted the forest aisles by torchlight. A great stag loomed up from the glades. His stag – destined for his knife. And when it had been cut down at the end of the long chase, he sheared free the dripping antlers, like branches of the forest itself, and the blood and wine quickened him. Presently, he inquired after the house of Clessy. Everyone knew her, by that hair of hers; she was easy to discover. Easier than the stag had been.

He went alone to her door and smote on it. He called in a false voice, not his own, asking her help, for he had been informed that Clessy was a healer. When she opened the door, a cloak wrapped around her and her hair like a golden cloud on the dark air of night, he laughed. "It is I, witch," he said, "so let me in."

"I will not," she said, but now she spoke lazily. And then behind her he made out the dim shape of a powerful man – kin, lover or husband. "You had better go, my lord," she said. "I'm not for you."

And something unnerved him, not just the hulking youth at her back, but some essence in her pale smooth countenance.

Again he turned and came away. On this occasion, it was a girl he murdered, a dun-haired girl provided for his bed, who displeased him. He flung her from a window. She was his and the window was his, and the courtyard below on which she was broken, that was his too.

He lay in bed and brooded till the sun rose and touched the crown of the sky. When the sun began to descend, he sent twenty men to fetch Clessy Goldenhair from her house. "Slay any man you find with her, and burn the hovel, and her garden patch. And if she keeps any live-stock, slaughter that too."

When she arrived, he had them chain her to the wall.

"Now we shall see," he said.

And she spat in his face.

When he had finished with her, he ordered in his men. Some were strangely reluctant, but most were glad and ready. There were enough to kill her. She died in silence, her eyes wide open.

He remembered the scythed wheat and the stag, and just before they dragged her body away, he slashed from her head her golden hair, and binding it firmly at one end with a cord, he kept it by him. Stroking it and playing with it.

Next day, he rode homeward to the manor-fort, and the hair was tied on the pommel of the horse.

In the fields, his serfs watched him go by. They watched the gold cascade spilling over the withers of the horse. No one spoke of it.

That evening too, he toyed with the golden hair, but it irked him, even now. He wished it were all to do again, her death. It had not sufficed. At last he tossed the hair on the rushes of the floor and went to his bed.

In the dead of night, in the blackness of it, something like blown autumn leaves or like wheat sheaves in the wind, rustled outside his door. In the morning, there was only a faint track there in the light dust of the house. As if a broom had swept across the threshold of the chamber.

Today, he chose to go riding again. As he was waiting for the horse in the courtyard, he heard the sound of blown leaves along the ground behind him. He glanced about, but there was nothing there. The horse was brought, and he mounted it. He galloped through the gate, along the road above the orchards. Sometimes he heard the sound again, and when he looked, the grasses were moving at the roadside as if a fox ran through them.

He reached the priest's dwelling, and reined in. The priest emerged, bowing, agitated. The priest feared the lord of the estate more than any god, and showed his fear extravagantly, placatingly.

"Do you see the grasses move?" the lord asked the priest, and, gazing fearfully about, the priest nodded, not having seen at all.

"Perhaps one of your hounds is following you, my lord."

Somehow the priest could not keep his gaze steady. It wandered to a hastily dug grave that last night he had been persuaded into praying over.

The lord cantered back towards the manor-fort, and the movement in the grass returned with him. In the bright sunlight, he caught a gleam like metal.

He entered the hall of the manor-fort, and sitting at table, the joints and wine before him, felt a sinuous thing wind strand over strand around his ankle.

Wildly he pushed upwards from his chair, sending the trenchers flying. But, in that second, the wound presence slipped from him, and was gone. He apprehended only a dazzle of yellow wriggling into a crevice.

"Did you spy that great tawny rat?" he shouted. "Put out poison. I will not have vermin in my hall."

Later, he was playing chess with his trembling steward, who, terrified to win, gnawed his fingers. The amber and ivory counters clicked on the board, A pawn dropped from the lord's grasp. Heavily, a switch beat against his knee, as if a dog fawned on him. He brushed at his knee, and encountered silken rope, which sprang away, doubtless alive, but no dog to spring with it.

He was in time to glimpse a golden thing that shone and coiled and slid from sight into the shadows.

That night he kept from his bed until the candles were burned to stubs and the stubs themselves melted away. He went up sluggishly, and something moved after him, like a little dog that loved him, creeping always close.

True, he tried to shut the door on it, but he was not quick enough by half. It came in with him and curling about his ankle it twisted itself like a snake, lifting upward to his knee, his thigh, about his waist, his chest, to his throat. And at his throat, it tightened, and he could not hold it from him. It was so fine, so slippery, and yet, across his neck, like a band of iron. All was done slowly, a fragment of air squeezed from him instant by instant. And though he roared out at the beginning, no one ran to him. But soon he could not roar. And as he choked, by infinitesimal inches, to his death, his hands still plucked at Clessy's golden hair – the first of her he saw. The last he saw of anything. Until:

"That is the substance of my refusal," she said softly to him, yet looking unblinking in his face from where she stood among the wheat.

At that, he shook himself, and noted everything was as it had been. The late summer sun, the workers with their scythes, the overseer pausing nearby. And he himself, the lord, on his horse. And he had just said to her: "My bed's the place for you. What do you say?"

"Yes," she said now. "It is all a dream you have had. But it shall be real if you kill and hunt and come to me again, at my house tonight, and call me witch and demand to enter. Real as you dreamed it, and to spare."

The blood burned his face. He thought the overseer had heard her.

"I might have you whipped for that," he said.

But he spurred the horse away across the field.

And seeing the serf child in his path, he dragged the horse aside, in order to avoid it.

Herowhine

Whether she sits astride the white stallion, clad in bronze mail, sword on hip, eyes like angry stars; or whether she leans negligently on a pillar, clothed in velvet, her hair wound through with pearls and scented with roses, you can't miss the Heroine. At least, not often, for she's usually very easy to identify.

For a start, she has twice as much hair as anyone else. Even if it's cut short (generally it isn't) it's still twice as much. Then there's her willowy figure – strangely equipped with a luscious bosom – the slender supple waist, flat-stomached yet with curvaceous hips, beautiful feet and long legs. To head in the opposite direction, there's her neck, also the perfect length, and her chin which never doubles, and that face to launch thousands of ships. Between those succulent lips her teeth are flawless, and you can bet, if ever she lost one (in battle, maybe?) it'd be as far back in her mouth as poet's license could get it. Her eyes are large, lustrous, compelling. How about her nose? That's just fine, too. And of course her skin is immaculate. It's a happy thought that, even when you come on her, lost for months in the desert, and part dead of malnutrition and dehydration, she'll have romantic shadows under her eyes and she'll have grown thin in a fragile heart-breaking sort of way, but as for bursting out in sores or a rash – or anything else unpleasant – you can forget it. Her clothes get ragged, but she does not. If she swoons, she does it neatly, and is sufficiently light that any average Hero, even a Villain (the weaker species) can swing her aloft in his arms. If she gets ill, she might as well be drenched in dew as vile human sweat. You can dig her up after six years from somebody's dungeon, and her hair won't be greasy. That's a Heroine.

And now and again, when some Hero has lost her, why doesn't the dolt recognise she is the only captive in the evil lord's caravan whose complexion is still matt, who still smells of flowers, and faints elegantly on her back – when all the rest are perfumed with elephant and sprawled on their shiny noses?

And doesn't that idiot who dares lead out his troops against her *know* she's going to beat him? She's only a slip of a girl (bar the bust) but look at that sword-play – fabulous! And she's just drawn her bow and gone and split another acorn at five hundred paces. Besides, can't he spot that indicative hair from about ten miles off: white as snow, red as blood, gold as corn, black as ebony, or even, possibly, *lavender*? That hair ought to warn him, around fifty yards of the stuff, waving in the wind like a banner.

As for the Rapist, couldn't he have foreseen a girl like that would.... well, never mind, surely he could have foreseen it? As for the imploring Seducer in his stone castle, won't he ever get it through his stone skull that she loves another and will never yield?

Really, someone ought to supply them all a manual: '*How to Detect a Heroine. How to Cope When You Do*'. Ah, but wait. What's this?

A bald over-weight Heroine with acne, just cut herself on her sword, fallen off her horse, and spilled gravy on her velvet and armour, tottering along smelling of too-sweet scent and last week's roast swan. There now, the Rapist's got her – she didn't seem to mind – and she's yielded to the Seducer too, just fancy, and both R. and S. have threatened to run off to a monastery. As for the battle, her side won, but only because she wasn't there.

The Hero, a handsome youth, comes striding across the desert with a couple of dead enemies slung over his shoulders, and recognises the Heroine at a glance. You can't actually miss her, hammering on that monastery gate with a mad determined light in her short-sighted bleary eyes, and her triple chin wagging girlishly.

And the Hero faints. Elegantly on his back, naturally.

For heaven's sake, someone find a beautiful girl with roses in her hair to soothe his fevered brow.

In the Balance

Despite his training and his integrity, even in spite of his faith, on entering the small dark room, Cermarl became afraid.

Not that there was anything overtly dangerous in the room. Neither did he enter it alone, for as was customary, the candidates for Initiation came into the room in pairs. But this in itself was disquieting to Cermarl, for the man he had been paired with was Paitese, whom Cermarl hated, or, more precisely, loathed.

Apprenticed to the secretive Magicians' Guild at the age of eleven, there had followed for Cermarl nine years of rigorous study, unrelenting discipline, exacting labour. Yet never once had Cermarl regretted the profession the gods had elected for him. Even when his body ached and even his brain and the marrow of his bones ached, he was filled by a sense of wonder and striving. And with no pride or complacency, Cermarl knew he had kept the tenets and obeyed the laws of the Guild flawlessly. Not from virtue, no – he was no more virtuous than any average man. It I was out of joy that he obeyed, and out of a straightforward logic that told him there was no other way. For to be a magician, to have such powers at his disposal, a man would have to be insane to abuse them.

The Guild Creed was plain enough. And the Creed was taught to them as boys, before they learned the easiest of magics, such as how to charm birds or how to make the grass move without a wind. A magician must not use his ability in order to oppress others. He must take no more than the stated fee for any of his works; less if poverty decreed it. He must give help wherever he was asked, unless to help meant to commit some act which would do harm. He must not seek gain. He must not pursue vengeance. For the gods, who had gifted him with power, would behold his deeds. All men were in the golden Balance of Heaven, and for a magician, the scales were already dangerously tipped. Thus it was.

These things were taught to Cermarl and were accepted by him as a man accepts, for good or ill, his own flesh. Indeed, his brother apprentices appeared equally bound by them. The odd lapses, small matters generally, were repented of, confessed to, and penances set. Weakness passed, like summer heat

It seemed no evil could flourish. And yet it had, in one single place, in one solitary grey mind and one rotten wizened heart—in Paitese.

Cermarl could still recall vividly, and always would, that day when he was thirteen, and had been two years in the Guild School. Waking from an afternoon doze in the poppy-red meadows beyond the wall, he heard unexpected voices, the girl pleading and crying, Paitese insistent, softly yapping his threats, till the thing was done and he had had his way. Neither had seen Cermarl, hidden unwittingly among the tall stalks, too stricken and stupid to interfere – and too scared. Yes, somehow even then, scared of Paitese Not of his powers, which were no greater than Cermarl's own, but of something in the boy himself, the slinking dirty thing there was no name for, unless it was *devil*.

Later, other events... the innocuous lizard, blasted by sorcery, dead in the courtyard; the theft of a gold armlet and Paitese suddenly flush with coins; and more nebulous, nastier signs such as the manner in which the people of the villages round about shrank from Paitese, yet pushed their daughters toward him, offered him wine and fruit.

There were no complaints. No one dared, presumably. Obviously, Paitese used his talents as a budding magician to cow them, then do as he pleased. Apparently, he had broken every article of the Creed. Once his Initiation was completed and his full powers came to him, there would be no restraint on his corruption. But Cermarl, like the villagers, kept silent It was not in his nature to carry tales; he had no proof – he could not bring himself to sneak out. Besides his faith, both in the wise Sorcerer-Teachers of the Guild School and in the very gods themselves, checked him. Paitese too was in the Balance of Heaven. Surely, the genius of the Teachers should detect Paitese crimes without the sneaking aid of an intermediary. Surely, gods would curb Paitese.

But they did not. Through all the years, they had not. As if the Teachers, so farsighted in all else, were blind to this. As if the gods were blind.

And today, the day of Initiation, was the ultimate chance of proof Cermarl would have that the gods existed, that the Teachers were all-seeing and that the world was worth dwelling in. And this was why Cermarl, despite his faith and his integrity, was afraid. He could hardly avoid being afraid, so much hung on these moments – not to mention mere life and death.

The room of the Initiation was almost pitch black. At its centre rose a black chest as high as a man.

There were four openings in the chest, two on one side, two on the opposite side. It was a perfectly simple arrangement, with a terror only such perfect simplicity could engender. Each man of the pair of men faced two openings, both presently closed by shutters. Through the use of his training and his power, also by submitting himself to the judgment of Heaven, the man must select one of the openings on his side of the chest, pull aside the shutter, and thrust in his arm up to the elbow. And thereafter await the result of his choice, the verdict of the gods. The Initiates knew what the two alternatives were, having already been instructed.

"In one aperture," the Teachers had said, "there is a ring, in the other, a snake."

And now Cermarl stood at one side of the black chest, Paitese, the blighted but flourishing weed, stood at the opposite side, smiling through the gloom, for Cermarl could dimly make out the smile. And now the gods must show their hand, and Cermarl trembled, for himself, for Heaven itself, wondering if it would fail his trust.

"Frightened, are you?" Paitese whispered across the shade. "Perhaps you've not led the exemplary life that I have, Cermarl. Or perhaps you doubt your talents as a mage."

Cermarl did not answer. He willed himself to banish fear and the mocking voice which played his fear like the strings of a harp. He bent his head to stare at the dull golden shutters of the two openings before him. He drew he power up from within himself as if he called the sea to the beaches of his brain.

But the power was sluggish. Something – his nervousness, the awe he felt, the vile presence of an enemy – milked his spirit. Cermarl shuddered. He could not land his strength.

He prayed, hardly meaning to pray, to the gods, that they should guide him if they found the truth in his soul. He set himself naked before the gods. Then he reached out and pulled aside the shutter on the right-hand opening. Not pausing, he thrust in his arm.

For an instant, nothing. Only the thunderous gallop of his heart bursting against his eardrums and red lights bursting before his eyes. And then he felt the sinuous motion of a sentient thing over his wrist. Even as his heart stopped, deadened already by horror, the nearly painless razor-sharpness of the bite penetrated his forearm. He had chosen the snake; the snake had been chosen for him.

He withdrew his arm slowly. Now the pain was beginning, shooting up his arm into its pit, into the pectoral muscle itself, like thin, blue-hot wires. In a few seconds, poison would reach his already immobilised heart, and his death would be total. More than terror, he felt misery and wretchedness. Heaven had failed him. Or had it been that he was wanting in some fashion the Teachers had not warned him of?

As he stood there, the blood running from the two holes in his vein, Cermarl saw Paitese evolve triumphant from the dark on the far side of the chest, a shining ring gripped in his fingers. The cup of Cermarl's bitterness overflowed in a blackness deeper than that of any room.

He roused, Cermarl, in a lamplit chamber, but rejected the evidence of his own eyes as foolish. When a man whom he seemed to recognise as one of the Sorcerer-Teachers bent near, Cermarl asked him courteously: "Am I in Hell?"

"Indeed, you are not," said the Teacher. He indicated something gently. Looking down, Cermarl discovered his bitten arm, whole and still part of him, but the bite magically healed to a savage and enduring scar, the colour of old silver. "You are past the Initiation," said the Teacher, "you have become a member of the Magicians' Guild. You are welcome among us, brother Cermarl."

"I don't understand," said Cermarl. "It was he Paitese – who grasped the ring – and I – the snake…"

"Truly," said the Teacher, "you grasped the snake, as the Initiate must, if the gods mean him to survive. The snake has no poison, though it is trained to bite. The lasting scar you bear from its wicked teeth is the secret mark of our Guild. Take note." Here, the Teacher rolled back his sleeve, and on his forearm there really was a twin silver cicatricle. "We instruct you," continued the Teacher, "on what lies in the two openings of the chest. But not on their character. Behold…"

And Cermarl looked again, the third time, where the Teacher pointed. He saw a blue and twisted body being carried away through the court beyond the window: his evil rewarded, his evil deeds at an end.

"It is the ring," said the Teacher, "which is poisonous. The gods have chosen."

Iron City

IRON CITY

So says the green neon ten yards high, and under the legs of the tower, the lime-green girls plying their wares, *stop one and buy me...*

Raining, knives of water in the old gutters. The sky is made of cables, steel, the tops of buildings and the smog, city-breath, shut down like a lid.

Wet night to be out.

Better come in.

The girl with the long green tresses which, out of the neon, will be blonde, sees a client.

Rags of hair, pelt of rain, two glass eyes of a toy rat.

The girls of Iron City
Are cruel and seldom pretty

"Like me?" says the girl to the rain rat.

"You? Like?" The rat blinks his rainy eyes. He smiles, and takes her hand.

"Thirty," she says, "to you."

"Thirty blackbirds," he says, "baked in a pie."

Arm in arm, they. She doesn't understand the quotation, or that he has altered it.

Under the iron stalks of the bridge, up a stair of wooden bones, to an apartment. Below, the river runs. The walls are red.

When blood splashes up the walls, it doesn't show.

She has no time to deny him. Never argue. The customer is always right.

Right, right, left, right the rain knife goes.

Under the slope-roof of his garret, the poet writes. Fingers cramped from keying at the antique word processor.

Words of the city, the lost of its streets moving like rain along a window, empty hearts and open mouths longing to swallow everything. Shadow citizens singing songs of blood. He writes of night's dark perfume and tastes so strong they cut the tongue.

The poet sips his black gin.

Down on the street, a bottle breaks, shouts and the scraping of razors. Screeching. Feet which race, without haste, away, and one pair not.

The city kills. The metal jaws of its industry chew up carcass after carcass. Bodies fall from high sills like autumn leaves. That day saw twenty so accidents leaving a trail of maimed and dead. A train, mounting the rail of sky, fell from the elevated bridge through the glass roof of a pleasure dome. A thousand bits of overtime for the undertaker.

The poet taps out another line...

Something is out there. Bright eyed, lips parted, *waiting.*

Morticians, whores, engineers. Lovers. Others. The City's saliva creeps.

The teeth of night shut together, spitting out the body of the half-boy into the river's icy gloom.

3 a.m. sees his machine-mangled remains raked up onto the riverbed. An industrial accident, some might say. At the factory, the straws of his bones and overalls are picked from the steel jaws of a well-oiled mechanism. Metal racks hosed down, the gory rags of another nightshift sluiced away. Mark off one more time-card. No overtime invoiced.

What is left of the trainee is shovelled, dripping, into a labelled body bag. Removed. Off to a freezer to escape the chill.

A thousand crows perched upon the bridge, watch and wait.

Something is out there.

Something clicks and skips along the pavements, under the busted neons. Glimmer on wet teeth, wet eyes, knife. Not troubling to conceal anything, the face of the rat-catcher is only business-like. He has completed one transaction. There is time for another before the solstice of the winter dawn. Light comes late, goes quick from Iron City, snagged on girders and put out, loathe to make the morning struggle back up from the slimes and soots, the chemical sloughs; not liking its reflection in last night's sick, bloody street spillage.

Later.

A girl is on the waterfront. Against the low wall, where the walls of higher ships push out the sky. Light streaks the river. Orange rind and little bags of death, condoms by the million, armour against disease, filled, tied and floating with dead children strung out like mists into the water.

The girl is not touting for custom. She has lost her way from the upper levels. White face above water-proof garment. Low heels. Not a whore. Yet here she is, a twilight madonna. She qualifies.

"Got a light?" clichés the rat-catcher.

The girl looks blankly at him. Does anyone smoke anymore? Or does he only want a match to set the world on fire. In places, they have done that too.

"Sorry."

"What you doing here?" asks he.

"Walking."

"You never moved," he accuses her. Already condemned, but not for a lie. Contempt of caught.

"I..." she says.

"Want see?" says the rat. He shows her the knife.

She nods. She came here for this.

Did she come here for this?

He holds her and delicately slips the knife through the black layer of her waterproof, the white crystal layer of her skin. Red petals as from a broken rose shower on the dirty wharf. It's a pity to waste them. He sips. She hangs over the arm of her death as he portions her. Her eyes are still open wide. They look at the stars, as if there were any. There are no stars. It was all a con trick. One night someone pinned bits of cut-out glass to the black lid laughingly referred to as the sky. The moon was more difficult. When too many questions were asked, they invented pollution, and they made smog. That hid everything.

"No moon. No stars. You can close your eyes now."

The City kills.

The train, crumpled, still. Beached in pleasure dome ceiling glass. A man's body roasted on train's aerial. Audible static, next crackling snatches of voice... Jingle advertising something sweet. Terrible tunes playing on some new receiver.

The train:

Dead.

Silver, grey, blue-lined. Streaked with red now, nose down, this metal engine. The train.

Only a machine, not fitted for the thinking or the doing of things, except carrying the living, sometimes the dead, not able of such things as love, hate. Any emotion.

Only a train. A thing on wheels, never, no *never* capable of suicide.

So why is it glad? Why do the bloodied struts of steel turn upward, smiling, see?

Why is the train happy now it lies there? Iron of the iron city, smouldering, with only the faux sky for shroud.

Silver. Grey. A machine insane.

The girls of Iron City
Are cruel and seldom pretty.
They make you cum to the beat of a drum
And rob you without pity.

The sailor off the ship clutches madly at the girl in jade green corset and stockings the colour of canaries. Her red hair catches the dull light behind her as she rides him down. He sees the flash of her red nails too. Something sets him off, some twist of her practised loins. Or the slick of light on her bare breasts, the feeling of her heavy pumping thighs in his grip. He groans and gasps and arches into her, giving his seed, the generations of his body, not to her sterile inner core, but to the little bag provided.

No natural exits here. Leave in a body bag.

Farewell my sons, my daughters. Out on the river with you. Go float down the Styx with all the others. Massacre of the innocents. Farewell my lovelies.

Released, the girl dismounts, leaves him. She goes to her cubicle, sluices her internal parts. She towels, and rubs off his musk. She walks through into another place, a chapel of sisters of the night.

"Gotta light?" Yes, someone still does smoke. Lean little tabs, cancer-free, (but who can be sure?), all filter. Flavour: Wild Mint, choc ice cigarette.

"Jesus, he took a time."

"Didn't know you had Jesus in there tonight, Luly."

"That sailor. Reckon his cock was constipated."

Luly, foul-mouthed but fair, stretches her body to the raw crimson light. Oh, her hair is like unto a fabled garden of peonies, poppies. Red, so very red. Her eyes are cool green, paler than her strident corset. She wears laced boots, purple and black, striped over wasp-like yellow where the stockings peep through. Don't get stung.

"Did you hear, Luly? Two more tonight."

Luly shakes her blood-red hair.

"A girl by the river. That was the other. He unseamed her like a dress."

Luly doesn't care. Death is always out there. But she is here in the warmth, in the air made of aerosol scent and little trails of non-cancerous smoke. She drinks down a whisky laced with cream. She eats a piece of chicken. Nearly a whole half hour before her next client will be shown up. (Would have been three quarters if that clown hadn't been so lazy. What did he think he was doing, giving her a good time? Making her cum? Stupid. Only Death really cums. Death cums every time. Every time he takes. Multiple orgasm.)

She works to keep her little brother. Another cliché. Luly knows she is a cliché. Isn't everything? Her little brother has no arms. Such a pity. Beautiful, all the rest. Even his shoulders, like polished Adonis marble, ending in smooth round finalities. His breath is sweeter than any aerosol. His eyes greener than any choc-ice cigarette and bright as the real stars that maybe once there were. His long hair, dark as river, flows. Luly loves her brother. When she goes home she bathes and scrubs, wipes off all her make-up, ties back her wet flame of hair, embraces him.

Kisses. Makes him meals. Feeds him chocolate. He eats so couthly. She would like to eat *him*, too. Not in the sexual way, in the Bacchic way. Yet she would protect him against all the world. He never speaks. He can never touch her. Such a relief.

A thousand crows and more… The night.

The little boy wanders from shop front to gaudy shop front, not looking in at each and every delectable behind the glass but looking for his mother. His tiny feet carrying him here and there, there and over there, but he still cannot find her.

Watching, the crows shiver.

Rat, rain, man, eater of sweet fleshes, lurks in a doorway,

slurping down entrails, the noodle 'life'. Wipes whiskers clean on grey cuff, twitches, sniffs, ignores now the self-service body at his feet and sees them, two of them. Close. He and she, swaggering Nu-Forms with pretend lobotomy scars and stick-on misfortunes. Down from upper levels, must be slumming it here.

Closer. And then they see him and the bloody bundle in which he stands. No more swaggers, or bravado. Just terror.

Run, run, run!

To the beat of my drum...

The She's heel breaks. She topples, does not fall. The He has left her behind. Running past a blur of crows perched upon a blur of bridge, running for the rusted stairs leading up.

Scream and scream, the He and She.

Rat sniffs twice, two times, shuffles off.

Feathers, so many feathers, blue-black, fall, spiralling to the river. Oily shimmer ripples.

The little lost boy cannot see or smell the rancid gathering plumage, automatically takes for granted that the ends of his vision will finish in waters, dark and deep.

No waters. Only feathers.

The river swarms with countless crow feathers. The carrion birds have shed their winter coats.

Boy's eyes full of tears, cannot see straight, will fall down through cracks in the broken bridge, fall in to drown in the black heaven of a sea of crows. He loses footing, tumbles...

But no.

Rain in a raincoat with eyes and nose, catches the boy, holds him, holds him close.

"Want Mam, my Mam."

"Course ya's do."

Tight incisor smile now. Rat paw reaches into manky pocket. Pulls out small, white. Thing.

Watching

Pain in a raincoat takes the boy's hand.

"Shut eyes, and them to be kept shut, hear?"

Nodding, obedient the lost one, shut, bolted.

"There."

Only feathers.

Just the boy now, no rat, no raincoat, no footsteps scampering off, just the lost boy by the broken bridge.

One eye opens, nothing, nobody. Two eyes. Looks down. In his hand, a present. A bone.

A perfect finger bone.

Still lost, motherless, uncaring of such things now. The boy plays happy with a new toy.

Lifting limply from the bridge, one by one, myriad featherless crows fly off, following the rain rat, following their shepherd. One by one, flying off, making morning.

Factory sirens scream. Clocking off time for all the night-shifts.

Home they go, some pausing to piss in gutters, to augment the filth there, the rinds and blades, the blood and grief, the weeping of the city's wounds.

The poet too is venturing home. Back to his unmade shabby bed with the horrid patch where once the black gin spilled – or he wet himself at a vile dream of a rat in a raincoat, wiping his knife upon a woman's hair. "Stop dreaming me, stop *writing* me, you cunt," had said the rat.

The young man had recently been brought in. Another accident. Just half of him now. The mortician takes her time, stroking her fingers through his dead blonde hair. Tracing a slow, painted nail along the lips of his blue-crow feather-black open mouth.

Smeared with dirty tears the dawn is in the east. Luly walks home in the part-light of day, and sees the clot of vehicles round the upstairs room near the bridge, where a blonde blushed red last night from her pelvis to her eyes. Luly stares, looks off. Notes the shards of glass and squinnied metal from the train that fell into the Palace Hotel. (A stately pleasure dome decreed.)

Luly reaches her street.

Steps inches thick in unmentionable stuffs. The hallway grows rare algae. The lift is stuck between floors. A drunk, or corpse, hangs out of it.

Luly extinguishes her cigarette and climbs up slow to her one true love.

He is lying in his bed asleep, like an angel. The sheet reaches to his perfect shoulders.

He looks normal. Only too clean, too pure to be any of that. Luly creeps to the shower and scours herself of all the night, before she will come back. She plants, with naked washed lips, a kiss on either temple, on the eyelids, the long lashes, either cheek, the space between upper lip and nostril, the chin, one shoulder, the other shoulder. Then as he sleepily awakes and smiles at her, Luly whips off the sheet and climbs in. She lies along him, as if neither of them has any sex, and she is able to forget it. Luly sleeps her one-hour sleep of morning, her lips pressed to her brother's side where the arm should be and isn't, and if it were, would he not be out there in the muck and shit of Iron City, besmirching his soul with all the rest of the rotten world?

The rat-catcher rat sleeps in darkness. Curled up. Where he is quite invisible.

Does it even exist, this city of rust? Some forgotten undreamt dream, some concocted hole; The anus of the world which may also be another imaginary poet's unwritten shameful fiction.

The cats are running from the intersections up the rails and posts and broken-glass-topped cliffs of the city. Black masks, dominoes; White masks as if the eyes had been drawn round with chalk. Morsels of dead rats between their teeth. Good hunting.

A big black wagon stops outside a brick tenement.

It is full grey-brown day, eleven o'clock if anyone knew or cared.

A nasty great box is being uncrated from the van and borne slowly down into the road.

Someone has knocked on a door. A young girl stands there. She looks frightened, as if being scared would do any good.

"He was your brother?" says the man in black overalls.

"I ain't got no money," says the girl.

"No charge," says the man. His face a wedge of stone.

Already the girl is crying, as if it could help.

"Got in the way of the big one. Can't turn that one off. Against orders. Dangerous machine. Very quick, you see."

Nailed down in the past. The water of life dripped away.

Drip, the tears and running nose of the girl who won't dare say a word.

"Can't have felt it. Never do. Always happening. Not even time to cry out. He's in that box. Where do you want it?"

"Just put it in the hall."

"Sign here. Nice and tidy. The Collector will be by later, unless you want to make funeral arrangements."

"Thank you," says the girl. White as the dawn, tear-stained. The wagon goes.
She looks at the box in the hall, which is her brother.

Luly makes breakfast at three in the afternoon, or fifteen by the old clocks. Eggs in an omelette with a pinch of flour, spices and black pepper, cream and cheese for filling. Black market bacon. Real food, not synth or fake, not dubious. Nothing if not the best. Wheat toast. Oranges and maple syrup. A green apple – green as his eyes. He eats with economy and neatness as she gently fork feeds him.

When he was three, Mumma tried to poison him. With petrol. Luly remembers this like an evil story told at bedtime. Mumma's dead anyhow. Mumma went under the wheels of the one shiny car Luly never saw.

Luly reads to her little brother, a foot taller than she is. She reads during the afternoon old tattered books (rat-gnawn) got off bookseller patrons, when they finished kicking against her body, biting her basque. Often the books miss pages, have neither start nor end. Just like life really. But life did have an end, if you could believe *that*. Or she reads him newspapers. She expurgates these. No news of crashes, accidents, rippings.

She doesn't know if he understands any of it. He likes the sound of her voice she thinks, the only one who does. "You're the only one what loves me, you are, an' you do, don't you?" His dreamy smile. So beautiful. If their old whore-mother knew – Christ, what a thought.

Sometimes she just sits. Looks at him. It's enough. Ain't it?

D Section. North West. Level 88. Bars and brothels heaving with factory overspills. Sweaty blue-collars, shoulder to shoulder loud with excitement and bad ale. They've come to watch the hanging.

Vast screens taped to exterior bar walls. Public execution as entertainment. Keep the workers happy. Top brass have even sent a camera crew down, nosing in at drunken oafish faces, missing teeth and industrial facial scars worn with pride.

Rat slides through the scene, liquid.

The crowd stamps its feet, punches fists to air, chants, calling for the Drop. Epic screen music distorts through dodgy overhead speaker drones. A '4D Family Extravaganza.' Apparently.

Eyes in a raincoat, blades of vision peer through the bodies, lunches? No. No women. Just laborious male flesh. No tenderness, no succulence.

A hooded figure fills the huge screens. The hood is pointed, a dull red fluffy clown's nose stitched beneath the two torn slits of eyes. The mob roar. It's the WireMan. The jovial executer with his arm draped casual-like round the shoulder of the tied, gagged, squirming accused; a thin metal noose collars his neck.

"Drop! Drop! Drop!" they bellow, not knowing why.

Drones spit out the accused name, Brian E. A disgraced employee of the month. A fatherless son and guilty of failed youth theft.

"'Ang 'im! Fuckin' 'ang 'im!"

Brian E has pissed himself. His crime – to have wound back watches, to be a pre-dater of calendars, to polish his hair and whiten his crumbs of teeth. Condemned for wanting to recapture his prime years, the long-gone heyday of his life. So selfish. No one memory is sacred. We are all in this together. We must all work, grow old and die. That is the way it has always been. (Or so they were told) No slackers needed. All he's fit for is the Drop.

"Drop!"

WireMan pulls the lever. The crowd holds its breath. Brian E slips in slow-motion,

his feet fall down through the trapdoor, his body follows. The metal rope around his neck tightens,

sinks into his flesh, severs bone as his head with eyes stretched wide, sliced clean off, topples to

the studio floor in a fountain of blood. There is a close up to show the eyelids flashing their last.

Cheesey music plays as the WireMan cavorts about the televised stage as if on an imaginary horse.

Crowd is wild. Throwing its arms around itself, hugging, jumping up and down, singing violent nonsense words. Vindicated. Just, in its belief of born, toil, die. Not chancing to think of younger days however rotten they were, or of a clock's second hand pushed sly back. Not knowing that time is a forgery.

There is a fear in knowing.

An extendable fish-eye camera lens is pushed into rat's pinched face. He backhands it out of the way and exits through gaps in the jubilant heat of strong, scared bodies.

The rain-rat-man with a blade in each pocket and one upon his tongue, would have made a commendable WireMan, but for his deformities.

Ah, such a pity to be perfect.

Four and twenty blackbirds,
Ripped in a pie...

There are dead men under the bridges. As the light begins to go – get out quick – they settle in the mud like a warm bed. On the tall buildings the lights start to come back on. An electric confession. All is forgiven. Not.

That was day. Short. But the night is so big, outside. Limitless. It was always this way, from the first cave-mouth with its lick of flame, with endless sabre-toothed darkness beyond, to the cave-pocked buildings 160 storeys high, putting on their diamanté lights as if it mattered, as if it could do any good.

Old sun, crust crimson, sinking down behind the docks, where sooty birds dine out on dead men.

The poet is wrapped in the amber glow of the word processor screen. Hasn't written a word all day. Still thinking of a title for an unfinished poem. He looks at his notes, cuttings from pale papers, smudged newsprint. Witness testimonies. Is it true? Could it be? Did he really kill a nun?

Slice her up, breakfast upon her? Some say he did. Others that this is impossible. Eating her body would be like consuming the Holy Ghost in reverse. They say he cooks some of them on a little stove. Crisped white flesh tanned in the oven. Choicest cuts. But it's the street-walkers he takes, or girls he thinks are prostitutes, out alone in the night-place, the woods of the world. Fair game.

All the city must be a market for him. Just imagine how the street looks to him, shelves and cupboards. There a pastry on legs, there a girl in gingerbread with angelica feet. That one a delicate chicken, in a rich cream sauce. Offal isn't awful.

But up there, off sidewalks, levels so high, they're out of the danger zone. Prey which has climbed trees.

In the glass towers, on the concrete balconies, level 1, they are safe... as houses.

Straw houses.

I shall huff and puff and....
Sweet dreams, little candy Juliets.

And it is only from that safe height that the unspoken past can
sometimes still be viewed.

Over there, far-away off, beyond the Tannhauser perimeter,
shifting, searching, the tall, lumbering silhouettes in the marshlands
and swamps. Steam and clockwork relics left over from the Cola
Wars.

Luly puts on her purple corset and green stockings and sits painting
her nails (scoured for her brother). She feels pleasantly dirty now,
garnished with powder, lipstick, gloss, mascara. Quite a dish. Only
waiting. She tries not to think of kissing him goodbye. It had been
so poignant, it always almost makes her cry. Even now. Daren't let
him see. He cries easily if she does. Can't bear to see those silk-
strand tears slip down the smooth planes of his face. But here,
where she is not allowed to think of her brother, Luly scratches
herself under the arm, drinks urine-coloured gin. By midnight her
piss too will reek of alcohol.

Too easy. The third girl of that early night, (still a wisp of rose-red
in the west) slips down among the garbage. Her exquisite entrails
taper out, coils of jewellery. The heart still gives a tiny tremble, an
aftershock.

The rat carries his knife sadly through a sluggish rain, which
washes it, wiping off the badge of his red courage. Sighing, he
nibbles only one thin rice-paper of young skin.

It was untrue about the nun. There are no such things any more,
more myths like the stars.

Moon, stars and nuns extinct.

"One extra she says. An' you're to do it. Tipper, she says."

"Long as he's quick."

"Can barely hold himself. Probably do it in his pants."

Luly opens the door and lets in her unexpected guest. He is
small and thin, slick black rainy hair, rain eyes like those of a toy
animal. Had brought the night in with him, stinks of it.

"You take a wash," says Luly. "The things are in the dispenser.
I'll put it on for you. Full protection guaranteed."

He goes into the bathroom. Does not wash. Comes out without the condom and stands and looks at her. Jesus. A fool. But he may be easy, then. Not even need one.

"Nothing to worry at," says Luly.

As she walks over to him, she had a feeling she is on a midnight pier. Strings of light are all out, hanging in dead clusters, like amputated eyes. The river feathers by. She is suddenly afraid.

"No," she says. "You got it wrong. I ain't wanting it. I've *got* someone – I have things I wanta *do*..."

She feels the knife go in softer than a petal brushing her skin. When she looks down, through a mist, her breast is in his hand. She stares. No longer *her* breast, as no longer attached to her. She feels the pain only as terror, and screams. There are frequent screams here. How often she has screamed in simulation for clients. No one cares. (As if they would.) The rat-catcher, catcher of rats, son of rat-catchers, father to none, observes the whore with her white and purple and red, and red and red. He shakes his head and slits her in half.

Sing a song of sixpences
Covering your eyes.

Easy then, this time, only a success. Slip down the stairs, head bowed. Fate accomplished. Before they send her the next punter, he is away. How many brothels he can visit like this. Why did he never try before? So simple. So perfect. He carries beauty in a carrier bag. The nicest take-away.

He trots along, clicking, skipping beneath the poet's window. The processor suddenly clacking noisily out. The ratty-rat pays no heed. Who cares who immortalises him? He can do the job himself, will never be caught. Not even stopped, though the rain streaks him with white along his mask of blood. She splashed him. (Sip) He, too, flushed with pride. The gutters swill with blood and
horrors. What's one more? There are no nuns, or stars. No Moon. No gods and no policemen.

The poet reads aloud what he typed moments earlier.

"The beast the beast
The feast the feast

At least at least
There's plenty to eat
On the iron plates of the city."

"Doggerel," says the poet, disgusted.

He deletes all of the files. Wiped clean. He wrenches the plug from its socket, heaves the word processor up, kicks open his room door and exits, carrying the weighty machine down to the riverside where he hefts it into the watery muck. Bubbling, gobbled down. Swallowed.

Iron City eats everybody alive. Merely to live is to be devoured, years, inches and yards at a time. The jaws of steel will have everything. A cream tea, sudden and sodden, sucked in without a murmur.

Gone.

At Luly's funeral (the brothel staff had insisted there be one) everyone cries.

They throw roses on her grave, a compacted two feet (anyone buried must be put in folded up, the graveyards yawn not only, but overflow. Easier with Luly, partly depleted). After the ceremony, at which the Madam reads the lesson, drunk, there is a booze-up, knees-up, throw-up ultimately.

Luly will not be forgotten.

They never knew, she did not want to stain him with their knowledge, about her little brother.

The poet escapes. Gone over high walls, picked his way through the dried-up barbed wire canals, negotiated the forest of ashes and wild boar to find himself in the everglade. There he will find the inspiration to write (with a found crow feather cut to quill) of a dynasty of blind herons and their eternal battle against the Messiah-Toads.

She is standing on the corner in her old ragged coat, skirt and cardigan. Some cheap beads at her throat, perhaps an ancient rosary re-painted. Her eyes are black with shadow, and her lips crayoned red. She tried to dye her hair. It has turned three colours, all of them wrong.

Scarecrow. But here on the corner of night, available, and not so far from the neon of green welcome – the other whores moved her off a ways – the stalks of the bridge where tonight the smog is thick as rancid butter.

She shakes. Chicken. She didn't want to.

She stands there, thinking of her brother in the metal mouth of the big machine they wouldn't turn off, let it chew him, and gave her back the pieces in the box. Three days it was in the hall, waiting for collection. The second night she opened it, and ran to spew her heart into the dark. Her brother. Who kept her. Who worked and saved her and was eaten my a steel machine and left her here alone with nothing to do but this.

"It ain't me," she says to him and the night. "And when I have to – *then*, it won't be me neither."

But it will, she knows it, and he will see, her brother gone to Jesus meek and mild, who will love him, and both Jesus and her brother will watch when she – when she lies back on the wall and lifts one leg and lets…

Someone stands there, even though she pulled the smog closer around herself, trying to hide from what be done.

"Like me?" she asks, coy, the way she has heard them say, under the stalks of the bridge.

But she senses he has only paused out of a kind of courtesy, on his way to somewhere more urgent and important, seeing her standing here alone in the murk.

"You? Like?"

A rat-like man with rainy eyes. Romeo in a raincoat.

She leans forward, unbuttons herself. She is full of dreadful aching agony. Don't let God see. Hate him, the man, the bastard, it's the only answer.

"Ten," she says, knowing what she's not worth.

"Room?" he says.

"Oh – no. Here."

Juliet down on the ground. Oh, bid me leap…

He too leans forward.

Suddenly she sees he is offering her a knife. She takes it from his hand and pushes it home into his gullet. He makes a gurgling noise. The right one. She has heard it before, outside.

She is glad. Glad when he slides down into the mush of foulness underfoot. Jesus saw. Jim saw, too. She runs away crying, but not sorry.

Only later does she wonder if he truly was offering her the blade, or if he was offering to kill her. Did she make the right decision? Incision?

The feast
The feast.
At least
At least.

Where he sits, the light gets in, through the broken window. At first he waited here for Luly to come back. Then he only waited. At first he cried, too. Then crying gave way to other things, some sublime introspection of nothing.

He is thick in filth now. Without her to help him, he is all the dirt and foulness, the ordure and puke of the streets. He *is* the Iron City, once fine, now architectured over in decay and dung, in bad and bitter things.

But his eyes have stayed the way they were. Calm and beautiful. No iota of filth has reached them, or inside them. Windows of the soul, their lights go on burning against the coming night of death.

And when he topples over, any day now, gives up the ghost as they say, pegs out, *leaves*, his eyes will stay open until the flies and mice and microbes have eaten them. His eyes will remain focussed on stars. Perhaps upon the moon.

And when all the flesh of him has been picked clean, his skeleton will lie couthly on the floor, its white and peerless bones in a pearly alignment.

You can't ruin everything. No, you *can't*. See?

Last Drink Bird Head

Having been doomed to death, the condemned man must choose his last meal and his last drink. By law also he must declare his preference publicly. And he could ask for anything.

He was jet-black of hair and handsome, and besides that, though he had killed many it had been in war for the good of the people, who loved him.

They urged him therefore to choose something wonderful.

But the meal he selected was simple – bread and cheese. Then they wept. It was what the people ate most often.

"And your last drink?" demanded the officer of the law.

"I will have," said the man, "Bird Head, in a wide glass."

Uproar. No one had heard of such a drink. Yet by law whatever he asked for he must have.

The City Authority offered a reward of gold to anyone who would search for thirty days for Bird Head. The problem was this: if after thirty days the drink was not discovered, the condemned man must die without it, and so must the one who had volunteered to search for it. The Law's arm was long.

None did volunteer. Though thousands wanted the gold, none wanted to risk death.

Then a woman stepped forward.

She had loved the condemned man for years, without his knowing this. He had perhaps seen her here and there, perhaps even smiled at her, but there had been other matters on his mind. She thought, *I can at least give him the drink he wants most. Or, if I fail, I can die at his side.*

For twenty days and twenty nights the woman searched.

She heard false ideas of what Bird Head was – an ecstatic liquid drug, a wine with bits of twig and beak in it. She learned nothing of any use.

On the twenty-first night she came upon the house of a sorcerer.

"Ah, is it you at last?" he foreknowingly cried.

By the light of a green fire he opened a jar and showed her the head of an enormous owl with great amber eyes.

"Bird Head," said the sorcerer.

"But," said the woman, "how is this a drink?"

"Place in a glass and just add water."

She reached the city barely in time. In the square where the gallows stood, the condemned man sat eating his dry last meal.

The woman placed the head of the owl before him in a wide glass. Then over it she poured a jug of water.

No sooner did the water touch the head of the bird than the owl grew whole, breaking the glass and swelling to the size of a stallion, with wings the width of six houses. The condemned man leapt on its back. To the woman he said, "Will you have the gold – or me?"

"You," she replied.

He drew her up beside him.

The soldiers of the state fired at them in vain as, laughing, they flew away into the sky.

The Origin of Snow

A Story of the Flat Earth

Over the midnight desert they rode. One from the norther, and one from the south, and one from the west. He from the north was white-skinned and clothed in gold, and thirty men rode behind him, musicians and priests. He from the south was smoky-skinned and clothed in scarlet, and fifty men rode behind him, armed to their teeth – which were also capped by steel. He from the west was black, and clothed in silver, and what rode behind him were not men, more like great cats, thought they too carried musical instruments and weapons.

At the edges of the scene, the mountains crowded, and above the sky was full of stars.

The three riders met.

"Are were here for the same reason?"

Which of them spoke? All three, and each in a different language. But all three too were scholars, and all three understood all three.

Then they stared upward at the sky.

"From there?" asked White-and-Gold.

"It must be from there. From the country of the gods," avowed Smoke-and-Scarlet.

Meanwhile, Black-and-Silver, who had the keenest sight, added, "But who is this, now, coming from the east?"

The one from the east did not ride, he walked. However, with every stride, it seemed he covered half a mile or more. No man, no *thing* accompanied him – and yet, the whole night seemed to do so. He was pale of skin, black of hair. His garments were black, and a great cloak blew all about him like a storm, though there was no wind. His beauty was – unreasonable.

They did not know him. Though, being wise, they knew of his kind.

"He is a demon."

"He is, without doubt, from their high caste, the Vazdru."

"*We* must be wary."

"Greetings," they said.

The Vazdru stood looking up at them. Never before had any of the three been looked *up* at, by one standing *below* on the ground, who seemed in fact to look *down*.

At last, he spoke.

"Your threefold journeys made some noise across the ceilings beneath."

"Your pardon, sir," said Black-and-Silver. "We did not mean to disturb you, or your people in the fair city of Druhim Vanashta underground."

"But here we are," said White-and-Gold, "to attend the arrival of a new god – or at least a might magus..."

"Or most holy messenger," said Smoke-and-Scarlet.

"The advent has been predicted," they said. "He is to fall from heaven like a star."

Azhrarn, the Vazdru, who – at that time – was not yet *Prince* of demons, laughed softly. Never had music more wonderful been heard, or with such a knife-like edge.

"Neither god nor mage, nor, for that, messenger, will fall. The gods keep to themselves."

"Handsome sir, the constellations, who movements we study, tell us otherwise. Tonight, a great wonder will occur."

"The stars do not move," said Azhrarn. "They hang like diamonds, from roots of air."

Perturbed, the three riders glanced at each other.

Eventually Black-and-Silver said, "Then we are ahead of our time. Perhaps this gift from heaven is due in some other age."

"If so," said Azhrarn, "the earth will then no longer be flat, as now it is. And the gods will be otherwise, for now they have no interest in mankind. Save sometimes they are disgusted by you."

As the three riders frowned in disappointed and uneasy silence, the demon vanished. Instead a coil of shadowy sand sun away – but whether north, south, west or east – none of those three wise men could tell.

Azhrarn, mere prince among princes, waited alone on a rock in the desert, and gazed towards the mountains, pondering.

At length, he leapt forward, and in another moment was instead on the highest peak of the furthest crag. Here a cave opened, within whose darkness burned a flicker of emerald fire.

"Who are you?" demanded the dragon, when Azhrarn appeared in its lair. "No matter," it graciously conceded, "you are a most fascinating creature and I shall enjoy dining on your flesh."

Jaws full of points like swords, clashed.

Azhrarn stood smiling a little, as the dragon regained its balance affronted.

"Give up. I am no prey of yours."

The dragon took no notice. It flapped its wings about him some minutes, hawking up fire, snapping and rending – and achieving nothing.

Then finally Azhrarn struck it across the head.

The dragon collapsed, stunned. Rather than hurt, the blow had been exquisite...

"Now," said Azhrarn, "you will carry me to the Upperearth."

The dragon snorted and regained its confidence. "Though you are glamorous and a magician, I will do no such thing."

"You have seen some of my powers. Do this, and I will give you a reward."

"What? What can you give me?"

"Your recompense shall be in proportion to your work."

Up through the night sky, past a rising crescent moon, who seemed to avert her gaze in a veil of cloud. Up through the starry gardens, whose stars now did swing on their roots at the gust of dragon wings – perhaps causing more astrological predictions below.

In through the gates, invisible, un*actual*, the doorway of Upperearth, the country of the gods, they flew.

Though night lay beneath, and all across the plate of the Flat Earth, it was always morning in Upperearth. Cold and shining blue, the polished and almost empty landscape, where also mountains distantly gleamed, rimmed with adamantine. In those days – a memory even long ago – groves of strange trees existed there, thin and long and silver-golden, and in their branches sat weird elementals, that the gods then kept as (neglected) pets.

These showed some interest in Azhrarn, but mostly in the dragon. The dragon sank down.

"The weight of the magnetic gravity of this place exhausts me. You must go on alone."

Azhrarn, indifferent to most gravities, left it in the groves, among the whizz of tiny chirping steams and atoms.

He walked over the plain of heaven.

In one area stood a well of glass, filled with some sort of sludge. Three guardians lay muffled and asleep on a bench. He ignored such trivia.[1]

Whatever else, Azhrarn, from the moment he had heart the hoofs galloping above Druhim Vanashta, had known this night was pregnant with some bizarre event.

Curious, prescient, untender, he reached a godly palace, like a shaft of sunlight changed to crystal.

A god was inside. (Flawless, fly in amber.)

There he poised, the god, in the even-then moronically self-absorbed over-intellectualism of these particular deities. They had made Man, then lost interest in him. But demons they had *not* made. The demons had made themselves – and very marvellously too. *Their* design was much better.

Azhrarn touched the glassy sunbeam. It shivered but did not give way. The god however shot him a look.

Through the god's transparent skin and mirror eyes, violet ichors dimly showed. He (or she) was perfectly lovely, and in a way that was, frankly, repulsive.

"What do you want?"

Gods did not speak. They did something, however, which we must believe amounted to speech, since the stories are sometimes full of their chatter.

Azhrarn heard the question. He said, "Mankind has smelled something cooking up here. What is it?"

"Nothing. It is nothing," said the god.

By his, or her – or *its* (only the gods themselves might know what gender they were) *denial*, proof was given to Azhrarn. Such beings would never deny what was not a fact.

Azhrarn ran. He raced across the plain. All types of indescribably and ridiculous god-stuff flashed by – pavilions, gardens, *devices* – fruitless to attempt to see, let alone consider them.

He came to a square of open land (if it *was* land). The square was of a colour the earth did not, and never would, have. Nor does it now. A group of gods were here, and they unwound together a long, long parchment. And as they did this, they fed it into the mouth of a hideous but also – be glad – quite indescribable object. Perhaps it was animal, perhaps machine, or vegetable, even. In any event, it ate the parchment up and swallowed it down.

Azhrarn asked no further questions. Truly there *was* an aroma, a smell like burning. He knew instantly what they were at.

The endless scroll was the writing of fate. That was, a fate not yet made accessible[2]. Inchoate and free-flowing, still it contained, obviously, many predictions, a whole rota of events that must and would occur.

Azhrarn leaned forward, trying to see what was written there. He noted only one awful sentence, in letter no human could decipher: *One day the earth's flatness will be roundness.*

The gods were still young enough at this hour that they were by then trying to block his view.

"Humanity snuffling after this like a dog – three troublemakers in the desert – Man the cockroach must not learn too much – such matters must be hidden…" voicelessly they screamed.

And he, Azhrarn, still only a prince among princes, did not know *not* to reach out and snatch…

In that glimpse, he saw that every letter written there was unlike any other…

Then the parchment – which smelled of burning – burnt him, savagely. It was like clutching the whitest, hottest fire. But he bore it, and he tore that fragment away. And in that instant the furious gods, still capable, in their elderly youth, of real annoyance, evicted him from heaven.

The glacial blue cracked. Through the sudden gap Azhrarn was cast – and fell.

He fell like a dark star. Like a premonition of many other things to come. Yet in his hands he retained the smouldering fire of parchment.

This, meeting the atmosphere of the Flat Earth, became abruptly a white and splintering whirlwind.

Only then did Azhrarn let go. He took charge of himself in contrast, and stopped his fall. On an island of cloud close by the moon, he found the dragon, which had, it seemed, left heaven of its own accord, irritated beyond endurance by the attentions of the eager pet atomies.

Together, they watched the shreds of fate's scroll scatter down towards earth.

"The gods will punish you," opined the dragon.

"I tremble," said Azhrarn, idly.

"You have burnt your hand."

"That is your reward, then, for taking me there," said Azhrarn.

"You may lick the roasted meat of demonkind."

The dragon pleated its scaly forehead in a scowl. Then duly licked the alluring scorch.

Down on the desert, the three wise men saw the flakes of white begin to ascend.

"What is that?"

"It burns…"

"No… it is cold…"

On the tops of far-off earthly mountains, white fire-flakes of unreadable fate gathered in sparkling hoods of ice. Elsewhere, upon forests and rivers, upon the shores and hills of the world, glittering like tears of sorrow or laughter, in they came.

While in his high tower, a fourth wise man, who had analysed the stars more carefully, and had not left his city, caught on one finger a single fleck of the falling white.

Through a magnifying lens he examined it. Then another, and another. Each was of wondrous pattern. Each was unique and unlike all the rest.

Across the face of the Flat Earth, mankind at its windows and doors, staring.

"What is *this*? Are all the stars falling? They *burn* – no, they are cold – what shall we call this thing?"

Azhrarn, young on his cloud, looked silently and named the fluttering white *Broken Letters*.

In his tower the fourth wise man named the phenomenon *Flowers*.

A king's favourite wife called it *White Bread* – but the king's favourite slave called it by a different, saucier name.

Everywhere, it *was* named. And by naming, made perpetual, since words are magic, then, now.

Letters, stars, flowers, breed, *seed…* One day, perhaps, we of this foretold and altered earth will decode them. And so learn the rules of Fate in the secret alphabet of snowflakes.

Notes:

1. Actually, the Well of Immortality, as he would later know.
2. Or manlike – later in the stories Fate will be Kheshmet, one of the Lords of Darkness.

The Pain of Glass

A Story of the Flat Earth

1. *The Third Fragment*

That very afternoon a caravan had entered the city. It had journeyed from the Great Purple Sea, which lay far to the west and was so named for the preponderance of purplish weed that massed its waters, and at certain seasons dyed them. After the coast, the caravan negotiated many lands. It had crossed serpentine rivers, dagger-like mountains, and finally the Vast Harsh Desert, renowned for waterless and unobliging terrain. Small wonder then that the caravan might be supposed to bring with it much valuable stuff, not to mention travellers' tales, whose vividity was matched only by their tallness.

Prince Razved stood on a balcony of his palace, staring out over high walls and lengthening shadows, to the marketplace.

"Oh, to be merely a merchant," sighed the Prince. "Oh, to have no destiny but the discovery of new things, adventure and commerce."

He did not mean this. What he actually meant, and partly he knew it, was that he yearned to be freed from the direly irksome situation into which Lord Fate had thrust him. For though he ruled the city, he might enjoy neither it nor his full power in it. A single awful obstacle kept him always from his rights.

Just then a voice arose at his back. It was wild, quavering, and disrespectful.

"Are they *here*? Are they *near*?"

The Prince clenched his jaw and his fists. He paled white as fresh ivory. Young though he was, the weight of extra decades slumped upon his shoulders.

There in the chamber behind the balcony stood a filthy and dishevelled old man. Two hundred years of age he looked, and the colourless thin wires of his hair rained round his face, which was like that of a demented hawk. He was mad as the word, and none

207

could help him. Now too he began to weep and scream. Razved locked his fists together behind his back and bellowed for assistance.

It came instantly in the person of three men, frenzied with dismay, who rushed into the room, where they flung themselves on their faces before the Prince.

But Razved only said to them, in tones of steel, "He has got out again. How has he done this? Are you not meant to care for and contain him?"

"Mighty Master – only a moment was the door undone…"

"Only ever is it undone for a moment," replied Razved, his tone now composed of stifled rage and black despair. "Or it is the window-lattice. Or some other pretext. Take him away. *Hide* him from me. If you transgress again, you will meet the doom those of his last retinue suffered."

Whispering shrieks of terror, the jailor-retinue leapt to their feet and gathered in the mad old man, bearing him instantly off, crying and calling, along the corridor to renewed detention.

But Razved could not rid himself of the memory of the encounter, which had been so often repeated through countless years. He strode to another chamber. There he donned a disguise he sometimes employed when wandering about the city. Razved believed none of the citizens had ever penetrated this. And although, of course, many of them had, and did, none were recently foolish enough to confess to him.

As the sun burned down behind the palace, the Prince also descended. Before the first star blinked, he was in the marketplace.

Soon the whole market, infused by the caravan and lighted with torches, was like a lamp against the blue night.

Razved strolled from place to place, forgetting for a while his plight. He beheld an indigo snake of extreme size and patterned with gold, that danced to the intricate beat of drums. It twisted itself into hoops and spirals, coils and knots, that each time seemed impossible for it ever to unravel – yet always it did so, rising and bowing to the crowd. They threw coins, which the snake caught in its mouth. And there was a silk from the edge of the Purple Sea, coloured with the purple weed-dye, and this material seemed to burn with sapphires in the shadows and rubies in the torchlight. Also Razved tasted bizarre fruits with thick cream skins, that had no juice but gave up the flavour of honey. Elsewhere stood books the height of a man and twice his width, with covers of hammered bronze, and pages of blond wood incised with silver – but often what they said was nonsense. Or there were birds which could recite poetry in the voices of beautiful boys or women, tiny exquisite models of temples and shrines cut from green pearls, wines which were black and scented with roses, swords both straight and curved, in the blades of which were supernaturally-written spells of invincible power...

After a while Razved grew weary. He sat down by the booth of a seller of glass and drank some black wine.

Behind him the Prince could hear how the glass-seller was complaining, some tale of half his wares, including the most expensive mirrors, being broken, the fault apparently of a vulture-like desert witch. Razved paid little heed, only thinking, *the man does not know his luck. He has only loss of trade, and poverty to fear. While I...* And once more he clenched his fists, pondering how the full rule of the city might never come to him, nor the title of King. Dwelling too upon the awful haunt of the insane old man in the palace. *I shall never get what I am owed. I shall never he free of him. Would not death be preferable?*

But despite his bitter thoughts, Razved was not yet ready to make the close acquaintance of Lord Death. And presently he turned his head to glare at the complaining glass-seller.

At once the man broke into smiles. "Best sir, what might I show you that may tempt? It is true, many of my finest articles were destroyed as I travelled here, but even so certain elegancies remain which, though quite unworthy of your discerning gaze, may yet briefly amuse you."

Razved yawned. He passed a jaundiced look over a surviving mirror so liquid it suggested a tear from the full moon, and a curious magnifying glass that stared back at him like an elemental eye.

"Well," said Razved, with unencouragement, "what is your finest *remaining* piece?"

The glass-seller, whose name was Jandur, bowed his head as if in thought. He had heard rumours concerning the city, and of a strange delaying fate which hung over its King-in-waiting. Jandur had also been told that sometimes this Prince went about the streets in disguise, but was easily recognisable, the disguise being a sloppy one and the Prince himself equally brooding, ill-tempered, and unmissably regal in his manner. Yet those who gave away their recognition, the rumour added, were normally found deceased not long after. Jandur now guessed that here sat the very man. To be cautious was therefore prudent. To make a *sale*, however, must be a prize. Besides, there was too another matter.

"Wise sir," said Jandur, after a moment, "one item there is that I feel inclined to show you – though I am uneasy at doing so."

"Come," snapped Razved, "your task is to sell, is it not?"

"Quite so, intelligent sir. My unease rests on two counts. Firstly, I hope you will pardon me – but I perceive from your garb you are neither rich nor high-born…"

Razved seemed coquettishly pleased. "You speak honestly."

"…yet," continued cunning Jandur, "what strikes me forcefully is a great refinement of spirit and judgement immediately apparent about your person. Because of these qualities I would wish to reveal a treasure. Yet again…"

"Yet again!" Razved had now risen and was impatient to be shown.

"…I am loath to part with the thing. It is charming, and unusual beyond all my other wares, yes, even those exquisites smashed to bits amid the desert sands of the Vast Harsh."

"Come," said Razved, with a dangerous glint in his eye. Life had baulked his wishes, this pedlar should not.

Jandur gauged all perfectly and now exclaimed, "You shall see the wonder! Pray follow me, illumined sir, into the back premises of the booth."

In the dark beyond the light beyond the dark, then – that was, the shadowed space inside the lighted market and city, which themselves rested in the dish of night – the ultimate inner brilliance shone. It was very small.

As Jandur lit the candle to display it, Razved peered. What did he see?

"Only that?" he said, in ominous disappointment.

The object was a little drinking vessel, about as tall as the length of a woman's hand. The stem was slender, and the cup wide, like the bowl of an open flower, but it would hold, Razved believed, less than three gulps of wine. "And this is your most astonishing vendible, is it? Your brain must be as cracked as your broken mirrors."

"Pray examine the item."

Razved sullenly reached out and wondered somewhat why he bothered to do so. But then his fingers met the texture of the glass. As they did this, the candlelight caught all the vessel's surfaces, and for a second it seemed to the Prince he held in his hand a mote of softest living flame – it was like phosphorescence on water, or like fireflies glimmering on a marble trellis. The colours of the goblet woke, shifted and merged, now dawn-pink, now flamingo-red, next a limpid golden green. Not meaning to, not knowing quite what he did, Razved touched his other fingers to the lip of the cup. Instantly there came the sweetest and most poignant note of music, slender as sheer silk passed through a silver ring. And in that moment, standing in the cramped booth, Razved felt within his hands not the glass of a vessel – but two perfect breasts – crystalline, silken – that sang back against his palms, while on his lips he tasted the glass-girt wine of a longed-for lover's kiss.

Jandur, who had predicted with some cause an intriguing result at contact, stepped swiftly forward, and steadied both Razved and the precious goblet, though Jandur wrapped the latter in his sleeve.

Razved seemed nearly in a swoon. Jandur sat him on a bench and replaced the foremost treasure of his stock safely out of reach.

"What occurred?" eventually Razved asked. He no longer had the voice of a Prince, he sounded like a child. "Is the cup ensorcelled?"

"I cannot definitely tell you," Jandur answered. It was a fact, he could not.

"It is – *what* is it?"

"Alas. I cannot say. Mystical and magical certainly."

"Does it affect all – who – touch it?"

"In various ways, it does. Some weep. Some blush. Some begin to sing."

"And *you*," said Razved, with another warning note suddenly entering his voice: that of jealousy, "what do *you* feel when you take hold of it?"

"Fear," Jandur replied simply.

"Ah," said Razved. "It is not meant for *you*, then."

For a while after this exchange, neither man spoke or moved. Jandur stood in the dark beyond the candle, thinking his own thoughts. The Prince, still physically overwhelmed, his manhood urgently upright and his blood tingling and thundering, slumped on the bench. At length however, he bethought himself of his status, and drew himself together.

"Well, an astonishing trifle," said he, with the most ludicrous dismissal. "But what price do you set on it?"

Jandur now realised his peak of cunning bravado.

"I will confess, sir, I am so taken with admiration for your natural gifts that, while acknowledging your obvious penury, I believe you may after all be able to summon the amount. For surely such a man as yourself will have *another* admirer from whom you will command the present of the vessel – an admirer even more smitten than I. The value I require is seventy sevens of white gold."

Razved snorted piggishly. He now cared, it seemed, less for his deception. "You are astute, glass-vendor. Just such a sum was handed me by a lover, in order I might buy myself a trinket." And reaching into his poor man's apparel, he drew forth a bag and spilled the contents at Jandur's feet. "Wrap the thing in a cloth," he commanded in a feverish undertone.

Jandur, ostensibly ignoring, even stepping on the spilled money, did as he was bid, he himself taking great care not to touch the goblet once. In a few more minutes the King-in-waiting had hurried from the booth, and any who noted his rushing figure, saw it fly off around the high outer wall of the palace.

But Jandur sat down on the bench and murmured a prayer of thanks to a god of his own country – both for the riches Razved had given him, and for his release from proximity to the glass goblet.

Deep in the dark thereafter, Prince Razved repaired alone to his most isolate chamber. Not even the moon might look in, save through the sombre vitreous of thick windows clad in gauze.

Dark was in the flagon, too, the black wine aromatic of roses, which he had had his servants bring him.

The haunting madman had been locked away, shackled tonight for good measure. Not only were merchants prudent, after all.

Razved, bathed in hot water and spices, clad in loose and sensuous garments, unwrapped at last the goblet. Holding it only through a piece of fine embroidered cloth, he set it on the table by his couch.

Despite the lack of light, even so the faintest and most mellifluous tinctures of colour began at once to flutter to and fro in the glass.

They were like birds in a cloud, or fish in a ghostly pool. Dilute crimson melded to opalescent rose – to amber – to emerald. All this – just from his touch through cloth, his hungry gaze upon it.

In a while he leant forward and filled the vessel full of inky wine. Rather than dim the spectrum in the glass, the blackness seemed to bring it out. Gold shot through the other tints like benign lightning.

Razved sighed. He had put away his woes.

He placed his fingers upon the rim of the goblet. At once, it sang for him. He could hear again a woman's voice in the notes, clear as a silver bell, and as he kept just one finger on the vessel, the melody – and melody it was – went on and on. Razved was not afraid. Unlike the shoddy glass-seller, he was royal, a warrior of a warlike and powerful line – although he had never ridden to battle, nor seen what battle may produce aside from valour. The glass was neither evil nor any threat. It was enchanted, and enchanting. It was a delicious toy the gods had sent him, in recompense for all the other frustrations of his days.

Unable any longer to detain himself, the Prince now put both his hands on the goblet. Intoxicating heat raced through his arms and filled his body, as he drew the brim towards his lips. He drained the wine, and the act of drinking became instead the act of kissing, while the singing notes entered his brain, and floated there like iridium feathers.

He found he had lain back, the cup held firm against his heart. And then it seemed the cup too had taken hold of *him*. Female arms, slender and strong, encircled his body. For an instant he glimpsed, lifted above him, a maiden made of flames and waters, flowing down on him in waves and foam and sparks, more sinuous than any serpent. Then a mouth famished as his own fastened on his lips, a tongue like smoothest myrrh and ice-hot quicksilver, drank deeply. Against him in his delirium he felt the movement of a frame that was softness and succulence, pliable and limber as a young cat's – but all this, the plains of skin, the pressure of slim muscle, the downfall of shining hair – even the narrow hands whose tips were like bees, the flawless breasts whose tips were like buds – all this was cool and composite, and made all, *all* of it, of *glass*.

Yet still Razved feared nothing. As his hands swept over the crystal curves of a phantasmal yet actual shape, as he drowned in the silver notes of a song that had, as yet, no words, as he began to ride in the primal race of desire, not one qualm interrupted Razved's intense and scalding pleasure. For it did not trouble him *she* was all of glass, and that *she* flamed with shades of flowers and gems, and her tongue was of glass, her lips and hair, her little feet that gripped him, glass that kissed, caressed, and sang in ecstasy. Even her centre, the core of her glory, that too, where now he lay, fixed and explosive as a sun, *that* was formed of glass. And it rippled and embraced and grew molten, better than any human vessel; wine and darkness; jasper, asphodel: fire, ash, sand.

2. *The Second Fragment*

That very morning, they had entered the expanse of the terrible desert known as the Vast Harsh, Jandur the glass-seller received an omen. He did not, at the hour, much consider it, but later it came to him he had been awarded one of those useless portents the gods tended to throw before mankind. What the omen presumably was, had been a solitary black vulture crouched on a sycamore, which weirdly held upright in its beak a shard of glass. This caught the light and flashed, amusing many who saw it. But they, and Jandur, soon forgot, since a mile or so later the desert began.

There lay before the caravan now countless miles of that inimical landscape, which separated the more abundant lands from the towns and cities of the north and east. And though provided with all necessities, none of the travellers viewed the desert prospect with much joy. The Harsh was famed not only for its personal cruelties, but for those of various men driven out there, and making their desperate livelihoods by the robbery and murder of passing human traffic. Well-armed guards had joined the caravan at Marah, the last town on the desert's edge.

The Harsh opened to receive them, grinning.

Jandur journeyed glumly among the rest.

By day the caravan wended, though sheltering sometimes at noon, when the predatory eye of the sun centred the sky. Once there it turned both heaven and earth into a furnace any glass-maker might have valued. *Perhaps*, thought Jandur then, *the gods also are glass-makers. The earth is their kiln and we, mortals of siliceous sand, suffer, turn and burn in this sun fire, and likewise the flames of pain and sorrow, in order to become creatures as pure and beautiful as glass.*

But really he was well aware that people rarely grew beautiful or pure through suffering and burning. Normally ill-treatment made them worse, and wicked. Those who did achieve virtue no doubt might have become just as wonderful, even if they had *not* had to suffer, or to burn.

At night the caravan spread itself out like an exhausted yet demanding beast. It lit torches and fires, cooked its meals, sometimes told stories or danced, frequently bickered, argued, or even came to blows. Above, the myriad stars blazed bright. *If each were a glass*, thought Jandur, *what a fortune they would make for those that formed them. But alas, when they fall*, he added to himself, seeing one which did, *they shatter.*

Jandur had himself never made a single piece of glass. He only *sold* glass, but that in quantities. In the very next town they would come to, which was called Burab, and which still lay ninety days and nights across the Harsh, Jandur's brother-in-law had charge of the family's second glass-makery. He was a quarrelsome brute, dark red from heat; and scarred all over with the white bites of burns. But Jandur had already enough stock and thought he would not need to trouble his brother-in-law. Which thought cheered Jandur in the desert, even when jackals howled, or the dust-winds blew.

Despite the reputation of the Harsh, they met no robbers. Probably any robbers spied them first and found their numbers, and their armed escort, off-putting. Meanwhile, on a certain evening, they reached one of the few oases that served the waste.

This was a poor enough specimen. A handful of spindly trees led to a well no bigger than a washtub, the margin spiked with black rushes that discontentedly chittered.

Leaving his servant to go for fresh water, Jandur dismounted from his mule and took a walk among the stunted trees. The sun was already low and veiled in sandy gold, and a reluctant breeze smoked along the dunes. The impromptu caravanserai was being settled for the night, cookfires breaking into red blossom. Jandur went up to a little rise, idly following the prints of some now-absent, small desert animal. From here he looked about at the world, as mortals did and yet do, both pleased and displeased with it, suspended in the quiet melancholy of dusk.

"Where is the glass-maker?" shouted a baleful voice behind him.

"I do not know," muttered Jandur. But he turned nonetheless.

And there on the rise with him perched a most ungainly and

uncouth female figure. She was clad in a mantle of vulture feathers. More, her long and ragged hair, lucklessly dark as was the hair, they said, of demons, was stuck with other such feathers. On her wrists and at her long, thin neck were ornaments of what Jandur, not illogically, concluded to be vulture bones. She smelled of vultures too, a smell that was of chickens, and of carrion.

If he had been going to admit to an acquaintance with glassware, perhaps now he thought better of it. But this was all in vain. For she announced immediately, "You are *he*. You are the one named Janpur or Jinkor, a glass-maker and vendor of such."

"What, assuming I am he, would you have with him?" inquired Jandur.

The female ruffled her feathers. It was difficult to be sure, when she did this, if rather than a mantle, they were not actually growing from her skin. "I am Morjhas. I perambulate the desert. I have no trepidation in the Harsh, for my powers bring me all I need."

She was a witch. Jandur nodded politely.

But she reached forward and thrust her skinny talon of a finger at his breast. "Come you with me. I will show you a strangeness. I am bound to do this, for my talent carries with it a certain onus. A strangeness, I say. And what you do thereupon I shall advise you."

"I may not leave the caravan," protested Jandur. "If you are often here, you will know the place abounds in villains."

"What care I for villains? They are all afraid of Morjhas — and rightly. Those who annoy me," she added, fixing Jandur with a tar-black eye, "regret it. If you behave, you will be safe enough in *my* company."

They flew.

He had not, and maybe he might have done, expected this. But the bird-hag lifted him straight off his feet and bore him away. He suspected he screamed, but none heard him over the din of the caravan; twilight doubtless screened the view. And she — she spread her wings and rushed both of them on.

However, they did not travel a very great way. The 'strangeness' Morjhas meant to reveal lay only some half mile from the camp.

At first, having been landed, Jandur gaped about him. No trace of sun remained, only the huge translucent violet dome of nightfall, where they were lighting the million cobalt, ferrous, and pewter cookfires and torches of the stars.

The vulture witch pointed with her eldritch claw.

"*See there.*"

Some sixty or seventy paces off rose a mesa, scorched black by weather, and below, as elsewhere around, lay sand, slightly patched paler or darker, denoting seemingly depth, variance of consistency, or only shadows.

"At what do I look? That rock?"

"*Hush*, fool. Look and listen and learn."

So there they stood, and the night gathered all about, glowing as always in such open places, yet also black behind the stars. And coldness came too, for the desert, even the Vast Harsh, presented two faces, furnace by day and iceberg by night.

Jandur was frightened, but not out of his wits. He stared at the patch of sand below the mesa that his unwanted guide had indicated, and in a while he started to note a disturbance in it. A dust devil appeared to be at work there, but one which did not move from its origins. And after a time, the motes which circled upward and round and round commenced also to shine.

"Is it a ghost?" asked Jandur in a whisper.

"*Hush*," said the witch.

And exactly then the spinning busyness began to chime. An eerie carillon it was, bereft and lorn, like the cries of the wolves and jackals which prevailed in the desert. Yet too it had profound beauty, an insistent music. Like a song it seemed, lacking words, though once perhaps words had belonged to it, a song of longing and loss that only a poet might create, and a human throat emit.

This uncanny and emotive recital continued for several minutes. Then came the night wind, and breathed on the spot, as a mother might with a weeping child. And the song ended, and the dust of the sand drifted down. It slept, whatever it had been, whatever it was. And silence returned, composed of the shift of the dimes, the sigh of the flimsy wind.

Morjhas spoke. "There, then."

"But *what* then?" asked Jandur.

"I cannot tell you. I, even I, do not know. But it cries out, does it not? I cannot ignore that cry, nor shall you."

"But what am I to do with it?"

"*Fool* of a *fool*, *son* of fools to seventeen generations, *father* of fools and *grandsire* of *imbeciles*!" ranted the vulture-witch. "Are you a glass-maker? Gather up the sand there, take and make it into glass, for glass is made with sand and fire. Take it and shape it and see what *then*, it does – for long enough it has lain and lamented here, unheard by any but myself and now you, O *fool*."

"Take and make…" cried Jandur in horror, for he did not want any part of this scheme.

"Take and make. For my powers are generous and I must be kind in turn to the tragedies of the Harsh. But you I will punish if you fail in this. Heed me, Jumduk, if so you are named. Either scoop up the sand there and have it worked, or I will send my minions to smash every item of your saleable glass, even within the cosy caravan. I will begin, O *fool*, with a certain mirror…" Here the vulture held up her wing and gave a screech, and from far away – about half a mile in fact – the appalled merchant seemed to detect a glacial splintering. "I will smash all and everything, until you have dug up that place of sand which sings and sobs. Go now. Hasten back to the camp and get your slaves and your spades, for with every second you delay, another delicacy *breaks*. Be assured also, that if the sand is not then rendered to glassware before three more months elapse, I will break anything you may have left, or thereafter acquire! You had best believe this."

Jandur was uncertain if he had only gone mad, but he credited every word. He bolted for the camp, and endlessly along the route as he ran, he heard the shattering of glass – the whole while becoming louder and louder.

Indeed, Jandur's bivouac lay in some confusion, when he reached it. People stood about amazed, and bits of glass lay around sparkling prettily in the firelight, but there was a deal of shrieking and praying too. "Vile winged shadows fell upon your wagon, Jandur!" some explained, hurrying gladly to convey bad news. "We heard the vandalism upon your wares but dare not enter! No other among us is attacked – only you, poor Jandur. Whatever can you have done to incur this supernatural wrath?" While as a background to their verbiage, yet other breakages sounded.

But Jandur paid no heed. Seizing his servant, two spades and some sacks, Jandur pelted back again, now on foot, across the desert. Regaining the spot where the dust had lifted and sung, the two men dug and transposed sand for all they were worth, until they had filled the sacks.

No sign of the vulture-witch remained, and truly the general site was so unremarkable that, saving the mesa, it was probable Jandur would not have found it again. A large dug hole now marked the dunes. Yet soon enough the sands would refill it.

"Hark," said Jandur. "Does it seem the wrecking has ceased?"

Presently he and the servant were agreed, any noises of destruction had stopped.

They trudged back to the caravan then and loaded the sacks into the wagon, where there was now some space for them, Jandur having lost a fair portion of his most valuable goods.

No other event of any moment befell the caravan, or Jandur, until they had entirely crossed the Harsh, and reached the town of Burab.

Jandur went, albeit with no delight, to the house of his brother-in-law, Tesh the glass-maker, which lay behind the smoking chimney of the makery. Here Jandur's sister, Tesh's wife, greeted Jandur with affection tempered only by her husband's censure. Tesh himself banged in and out of the place, upbraiding Jandur for the loss of his goods… "A witch broke them? Ha! A likely tale. Your donkey of a servant packed them improperly, either that or *you* lost them at gambling. What a simpleton you are, Jandur. Your father must whirl in his grave at your incompetence."

"Nevertheless," said Jandur, gravely, "I have collected in the desert a most fascinating sand, and this I would request you put to use instantly. Fashion some fresh articles that I may sell them in the great city markets."

Tesh was not the man to be given orders by such as Jandur. He made a colossal fuss, shouted at his wife, tried to kick the dog – which eluded him without effort, being well-practiced in the skill – and rained curses on the earth in general. However, since Tesh had had no items in the original wagon-load, and might now get profit from future sales, he eventually complied, making out that he did Jandur the sort of favour that was known, in those parts, as a 'Full day's holiday, with a feast at its end'.

Jandur then retired exhausted to his bed. The caravan would not quit Burab for some while, and there was time enough. The sand had filled three sacks to the top, and he expected several pieces to result. Unease he put from him. If the sand were possessed by some supramundane force, Jandur himself had had no choice but to take it on. What the resultant glass might be, or do or cause, Jandur did not permit himself to consider.

The next morning the chimney of the makery gouted, as always, thunders of smoke and sparkling cinders.

Jandur busied himself about the town, buying presents for his sister and the dog.

Evening fell and the smouldering chimney cooled. A little after the regular hour, in came Tesh – both Jandur and Tesh's wife jumped up in startlement.

The red-hot man was pale as one of his burn-scars, and glassy tears trembled from his eyes.

"My darling wife," said he, and she so addressed almost fainted with the shock, "can you forgive me for my temper and my foulness?"

"Are you ill?" she cried in panic. "What ails you?"

"Alas," wept Tesh, and gentle as a lamb he went and knelt before her, burying his face in her skirts. And when the dog came worriedly to sniff him, Tesh, without looking, stroked its head and murmured, "Poor boy, you shall have a bone, you shall have a dish of meat. I will buy you a collar that reads: *Faithful Under Duress.*" After which his words were drowned in his tears.

As she embraced this strange, new-made husband, Jandur's sister said urgently to Jandur, "Go to the makery and see what has gone on!"

And Jandur did as she asked, his mind buzzing between curiosity, amusement, pity – and sheer fright.

The makery was a significant and hellish area. It rose up on many levels, that were dominated by the dark yet fiery hulks of kilns and braziers, and silvered stoops and founts of water, and all the while the crackle and bubble, the trickle and shiver, the rush and gush and whoosh and push – things altering, melting, expanding, blooming or dying. And always, even now, the ebb and flow of fire flickering on walls and roof, the glycerine rivering and drip of molten glass, the stench of hot metal and clay and combustion, and gaseousness, the nasal glitters and sumps of stone-dust, silica, calcium, and black natron.

Below on benches sat Tesh's work-gang. One was nursing a blowing pipe, three or four some smallish empty moulds. These fellows seemed bemused beyond speech. At a table sat one, though, who was polishing little beakers with the rubbing stone. He glanced up and said to Jandur, "I will tell it. There has been a peculiarity here. Either you have brought us bad luck – or good luck. We are not sure as yet."

Jandur put a substantial coin before the man. "I hope you will all take some wine to comfort you. But for now, go on."

"The sand," said the stone-rubber, "when emptied, was only enough for a single slight item."

"But it had filled three sacks!"

"So we thought, too. But opening and emptying them, all that was there was this miniature amount. Be sure, Master Tesh ranted he would waste none of his *other* sand to pad it out, and next he made oaths worthy of the demonkind. But by then he must make something else of it than vulgar language, so we set to work. Then, when all goes in the crucible, a wild scent comes from the mix."

"A scent of what?"

"Of women's sweet skin and garments and young clean hair... so *then* we are all afeared, but Tesh rants on, so on we make. Then when he comes to blow the piece, soft light shines up above the brazier. Like green iron, or the rose-red that comes from glue-of-gold. But Tesh blows on, and then the vessel comes from the fire and is finished and firmed with a speed not very usual."

"What had been made?" demanded Jandur.

"One slender goblet with a flower-like drinking-bowl."

"And then?"

"Master touches it," put in one of the other men. "And his face goes rapt, as if he saw the gods. And then white. And then he staggers out to his house."

Jandur collected his wits. "Where is the goblet?"

"He took it with him."

When Jandur pelted back in at the house door, he halted as if he struck a buffer of some sort.

For there sat his sister, with Tesh adoringly leaning on her, and the dog with its head on Tesh's knee. And Jandur's sister sang in a light and lovely voice, an evening song. And in her hand Jandur beheld a glass drinking cup, no *longer* than a woman's hand, and full of mutable colours, as the stone-rubber had said. But just then the servant girl came in, and singing, Jandur's sister handed her the cup.

In consternation and excitement, Jandur watched the girl, to see what her reaction to the goblet might be.

For a moment she only stood quite still and gazed at it. She was not more than thirteen years, and next she turned away, rather as a child would who has found out a secret. Jandur though saw she smiled, and her face blushed like one of the tints in the glass.

Jandur went to her and softly said, "What is it you feel?"

"Oh," said the girl, without either shyness or boldness, "only that one day I shall be in love."

"You must give me the cup," said Jandur. "It is mine."

Without any hesitation the girl did so, but the smile did not leave her, just as Tesh was yet affectionate, and his wife yet sang to him.

When Jandur took the cup he braced himself, thinking all manner of insanities or ecstasies might overwhelm him, and that despite them he must not let it fall and break. But all he felt was a speechless fear, the very same which had already visited him on the goblet's account.

He walked out into the little garden of the house. The moon was rising over the wall, where a mulberry tree grew, its leaves tarnished by exhalations of the makery. Jandur raised the glass, and the moon shone through it, grey and silent, telling nothing.

What shall I do with you? Jandur thought. *You may work miracles or do much harm. I will take you with me because it seems I must, and in the first city I will sell you, if such is possible. If I am wrong in that, forgive me, spirit of sand and glass. I have no other notion what is to be done.*

Then the wind blew through the mulberry leaves, and the wind said *Yes*, as sometimes, they reported, it did. *Yes*, said the wind among the leaves. So Jandur wrapped the goblet carefully and placed it in a box. A handful of time later he bore it to the city, where Prince Razved was King-in-waiting, and the Prince bought the goblet at the price of all the other broken glass. And after that Jandur took his own way through the world again, in prosperity or misfortune, as each man must.

3. The First Fragment

That very night, years before, the King of another country was to enter the town of Marah.

In the south, on the coast of the Great Purple Sea, there had been a war and much skirmishing, and this King, whose own city lay north of the desert, had brought his troops to assist a southern ally. The battles done, and victory secured, now the young King was returning home. The bulk of his army had marched ahead of him, but he himself stopped here and there on his route. That he should honour Marah was a source to the town of pride and pandemonium.

Most of the townspeople too were knife-keen to view the King. He was said to have that rare combination, pronounced beauty of person, intelligence of mind, and goodness of heart.

Marah, however, was not then as it would come to be in the time of Jandur's maturity – which time was yet some two decades in its future. Preparations were frantic and extreme.

Came the night, the young northern King rode through the main avenue of the town. In the glare of many hundred torches, it was seen that while his black horse was caparisoned in silk from the Purple Coast, which burned sapphire in shade but like ruby in the light, the King was dressed well but plainly, and his only jewel was the ring that signified his kingship. In himself though, he was jewel enough. His hair was like darkly gilded bronze, his face and figure were so handsome he might have been some wonderful statue come to life.

All about exclamations rose, and sighs, and after these – dumbness. How lucky was that northern city, to be ruled by such a paragon? How lucky his young wife, who had already borne him a son? How lucky his son, in such a father? How lucky the very sky there, and the air itself, to be seen by *him*, and breathed into *his* lungs?

Her name was Qirisn. She was by trade a musician, adopted and trained by an ancient school of the town, for her parents had died when she was only an infant. Marah, and the desert beyond, were all Qirisn knew, or supposedly. Since also she knew music, and knew it flawlessly, for she possessed great natural talent both as a player of stringed instruments, and as a singer. Music had, it seemed, taught her that incredible elements lay beyond the mere facts of existence, and far outside the scope of human law and rational thought. A fine and feral inner landscape existed within the brain and spirit of Qirisn, and something of it showed in the night-blue of her eyes, though few noticed her until she sang. Her voice was of an almost supernal quality, very flexible and silken, and superlative from its lowest to its highest notes. "So stars must sing," her last tutor had remarked of her, although not in her hearing. But she did not need to be made either modest or vain. She knew her worth and where it lay; it made her happy, and others happy also: there are few greater gifts than such genius.

It had been arranged that the best musicians of Marah should entertain the northern King, but they would do so, as was the custom then in the town, behind a screen. That being so, they went out on a little terrace above the street to watch, with various others, the monarch's arrival at the hall of banqueting.

Among these witnesses there was no change of opinion from that of all the rest who had glimpsed him.

"How fair he is!" they said. "Better than sunrise."

Only Qirisn did not say a word.

She was not, certainly, the only one to look upon the King and love him instantly, but with her the blow sank much deeper. Not simply had she never experienced the lightning strike of physical love before, she had, conversely, when involved in making or listening to music, experienced the phenomenon over and over, never then having a point of reference. It had seemed to her always until this moment, that the passion of her inner sight was impossible to realise in the outer world. Now she found otherwise. Panes like ice shattered before her. Her heart itself seemed to break like a mirror. To her, love was the most familiar and least known of any emotion. She went in to play and sing, moving in a trance, aware solely that he would hear her music. As of course he must, since now he would be the cause of it, and even in the past, before ever she looked at him, he had been so. It was plain to her, if in the most dreamlike way, she had known him elsewhere, in some other life perhaps, or on the outer fringes of this one. Or else, she had known him forever. And yet, in her current sphere, they would never meet.

The banquet began, the lamps burned bright, flowers and incenses released their perfumes. The diners were regaled by performances of magic and mystery. Doves burst from bottles and flew away, lions spoke riddles and could not be answered, diamond rain fell dry and cool as the moon's kisses.

The musicians played and sang too. If they were noticed above the general hubbub, who could be sure? Yet, when Qirisn sang, and tonight it seemed she sang more exquisitely than ever before, some did fall quiet to listen. And the King? It was noted he turned his head a fraction and, for a second, he frowned. But he was not unkind, not capricious, not heartless. Perhaps only he did not much care for music?

On the following day, the King resumed his journey, which, having once left Marah, must take him out over the boiled shield of the Vast Harsh.

He had, naturally, no concern for robbers, his retinue of servants and soldiers were more than enough to make cautious the most vulpine robber band. Nevertheless, he himself led forays among those bandit strongholds which were sighted, wiping many felons from the desert's face with efficient economy.

Otherwise, the King seemed somewhat preoccupied. He had trouble sleeping, and restlessly walked about the nightly encampments, chatting with the guards. Or he might write a letter to his wife – a foolish exercise since he would see her in a pair more months.

A sunset happened which was the colour of a damson. The King stood watching it, and then he turned to one of his officers, a man who had been close to him during the recent campaign.

"Did you hear ever, Nassib, was there much witchcraft in that last town?"

"In Marah, my lord? No, rather the opposite. Some of them talked of a witch who will shape-change to a vulture, but she is a desert hag and who knows, may only be a vulture and nothing more, save in a story."

"Quite so."

"Why do you ask, sir?"

"Oh, a little matter." The King watched the last of the sun's disc as it hid itself in some slot of the horizon. He added rather slowly, "I heard a girl sing at Marah, one of the musicians at the dinner. She had a lovely voice. But it is more than that."

"You fancied her, my lord? Surely you might have had her brought to you?"

"Well, but I never saw her even. And I do not wish to force any woman."

The officer laughed, between approval and envy, for very few women would not desire the King.

Returning to his tent, the King however wrote on the paper he had left ready for another letter, only these words: *In Marah, at the desert's brink, I heard a girl sweetly sing. And ever since that night, her voice has stayed with me. I do not know why. It seems I have been much disturbed by her song.*

The crossing of the desert, what with the forays upon bandits, and the King's mood, lasted longer than it might have otherwise.

But they lay over at a small oasis when the King called Nassib to him.

"Listen, my friend, I have a task for you if you will accept it."

Nassib declared he would willingly do so.

225

"Wait first to hear the commission. If you wish to refuse, I will find another to undertake it. You know I have been wed these past three years, and my wife has given me a healthy son."

Nassib agreed he did know this.

"Custom allows me to take other women, and also to wed them, but I have never thought either act necessary since my marriage. Now I am in love. I am in love with a *voice* and – oh, Nassib, you will think me insane – with a vision I see of her in sleep, or awake, when sunlight fails a certain way, or a cloud scarfs the stars. Am I bewitched? I do not know, nor any longer care. Go back if you will to Marah and seek out there the woman with the voice of silk and crystal. Though never having seen her, I can tell you how she is. Little and slender, with light hair, and eyes like blue midnight. If you doubt, ask her to sing a single note. Then you may be sure. Give her this ring with a crimson stone. Tell her, you will bring her to me, if she will go with you. I think she will. Her soul calls out to mine, Nassib, as mine to hers. Long ago, on some other earth, we have been lovers. More, we have been two halves of a solitary whole, and so remain. Tell her she shall be my second queen. Tell her," and here the King's face assumed such a look of bliss, his words rang strangely with it, "tell her I am dead without her, and wish to come alive."

Nassib stood bereft of speech. He was shocked beyond calculation at his own response. For it was as if all this while he had known the King uttered only the truth, and there could be no other choice.

But "My regrets, Nassib," said the King, taking his hand. "No, I do not think I am mad. I am at the sanest moment of my life. If you will trust me, do what I ask. If not, remain my friend, and I will send another. For she must be brought with some subterfuge to the city. There will be many obstacles to overcome, both of courtesy and faction. There may be dangers."

"My lord," said Nassib humbly, "I believe the gods have taken you and she into their hand. I cannot gainsay the gods. I will do everything you ask, as best I am able."

Before moonrise Nassib, accompanied by eight hand-picked men, was racing back across the Harsh to Marah.

She had dreamed of him every night, as he had of her.

Awake, in changes of light she had seen him, in the faces of others or the faces of statues, or in the pouring of water, or the dazzle of sun on the strings of an instrument.

Qirisn grieved yet, seeing him so often, still she did not lose her quite unfounded hope. She could be nothing to him – yet surely she was. They could never meet – yet surely they would.

Some months after the night of the banquet, a young man, garbed like a desert wanderer, sought her in the court of the musicians' school.

He asked her if her name was Qirisn, and if she had sung in the hall when the King of the northern city dined there. He looked intently at her soft hair and small frame, and long into her eyes.

He asked she sing him one single note. She sang it. "I am Qirisn," she replied.

"Yes, so you are," said he. Then he gave a savage laugh. Then he begged her pardon for it. "When he was here in Marah, did you see the King?"

Qirisn assented. She was very calm, long-trained in means of control, as the musician must be, but pale, so her eyes seemed black rather than blue.

Nassib took a breath, and asked her, "Would you see the King again?"

To which Qirisn quietly answered, "I would give my life to do so."

Then the rest of the message was detailed, and the ring of rose-red topaz pressed into her hand. And she carried it to her lips and kissed it. Nassib next told her how they would leave the town before sunset, and start out over the desert, he and his eight men her escort. She nodded but asked nothing at all, only the colour of her eyes came back and filled Nassib's mind with a kind of blank serenity, and after this all was easy to do.

How easy indeed it was, as it had been easy to say to him, as she had, she would give her life to see the King once more.

And thus, while Qirisn and Nassib were crossing the waste, at long last the King reached his city.

Near to evening he entered the palace, and his wife the Queen came to meet him, her look radiant, her glorious hair twined with hyacinthine zircons. He greeted her publically with great affection, and then they went away into their private apartments, and here, after a slight interval, during which the radiance faded from her, the young King spoke of his love and respect for her, but then told his wife what had befallen him, and what presently must come to be.

She paid close attention. When he had finished, she raised her face, now like a paper never written on.

"What of your son, the Prince?"

"He shall continue as my heir. I will love him always – love does not cast out love, only increases it. He shall reign as King long after me."

"And I," she said.

"You will ever be my first wife, First Queen, and I will hold you dear. You need be afraid of nothing."

"Need I not," she said. And then, "Well, my lord. I wish you every felicity in your life with this second queen, who is your highest love, your spiritual mate through time. After the aeons you have waited to regain her, how marvellous will be your reunion." And rising she bowed to him and went away.

The Queen paced slowly to her own rooms, and there she drew off her body every rich thing which she had gained through her marriage. She called in the nurse, and gazed at her son, less than one year of age. "Be blessed, my darling," she said to her child, and gave the nurse seven zircons from her hair. Alone again, the Queen went into her compartment of bathing, and there she lay down on the marble floor and cut the vein of her left arm. Some while she watched the white stone alter to topaz red. She said to it, "He has not broken my heart, he has broken my soul." But then she fell asleep, and soon thereafter she died.

Such was the rejoicing at the King's return, no one discovered what had gone on until that night had passed. The King himself did not receive the news until noon of the next day. When he did, he wept. It was proper that he should, and his court and subjects revered him for his tender sorrow. The Queen meanwhile they reviled for a madwoman. Even those who knew the truth avowed he had not meant to hurt her, she was unreasonable. And of course he had *not* meant to, for no man wants, unless an utter monster or fool, to saddle himself with such a dreadful scourge of guilt. Yet through the anguish of his tears and remorse, his love for Qirisn stayed like a pearl within contaminated water. The days of mourning would be long and scrupulously he would attend and mark each one. Beyond them, heaven-upon-earth awaited him. He could endure till then.

A storm was coming to the desert, it blew from the north. Lightning flared through the clouds, littering them with thin fissures of grey-gold. The thunder drummed on the sky's skin, as if to break through and plummet to the ground below in heavy chunks like granite, and each larger than a city. No rain fell. The dunes lit white, then brass, flickered to black, seemed to vanish underfoot.

To begin with they rode on, the escort of nine men on their horses, the girl in the little open carriage, she and its driver protected only by a canopy. But in another hour a strong wind gusted from the mouth of the storm, smelling of metal and salt. Soon enough it had the horses staggering and snapped the posts so the canopy flew up to join the roiling cumulous above.

Nassib came to the carriage.

"There are tall rocks there. We must shelter, Qirisn-to-be-queen. No other way can we keep you safe."

They sought the rocks then, a narrow mesa like one segment of the backbone of a dead dragon.

Lightning carved about them still, and the thunder rolled. Men and animals waited, stark or trembling, and only Qirisn was composed, afraid of nothing since her fate had found her, and she had trusted it.

Eventually another sound grew audible. It was that of men, unlike all others. Around the rocky hill came a cavalcade of sorts. They had lighted lamps too, and they were jolly, smiling and calling out invitingly to those who took shelter at the mesa's foot.

One of Nassib's men spoke in a voice of death.

"In number there are at least thirty of them. They are bandits. This is their stronghold. The gods have abandoned us."

Nassib drew his sword. It made a rasping, jeering noise, as if it mocked them. "While we may, we fight. Do not let them take you living." He had seemingly forgotten the girl. If he had remembered, he would have turned and offered to slay her at once. He could see his men had no chance, and nor would she have any, since these felons were everywhere noted for their profligate viciousness.

After this the bandits sprang from their donkeys and rushing up they killed every other man that was there, Nassib too, the bandits grabbing and their leader beheading him at one blow. They recalled Nassib from the King's forays on their kind, but tonight they lost none of their own.

When even the carriage-driver had been slaughtered, they drew the valuable northern horses aside. That done, the leader went swaggering and laughing to Qirisn. "And what are you? Not much, for sure. Yet a woman, I will grant you that."

Perhaps she had gone mad in those minutes. Perhaps she had only been mad from the instant she fell in love.

She addressed the bandit reasonably, without fear or anger. "You cannot touch me. I am meant for a king."

"Are you? His loss, then. You shall have me and my lads instead."

The storm watched, missing no detail of what was next enacted at the foot of the dragon's backbone. In the lightning, flesh blazed white, or golden, or grew invisible; blood ran like blackest adders, or inks of scarlet or green. Cries became only another melodic cadence for the thunder and the gale. Storms frequently carried, and carry yet, such crying. Who can say if it is only imagined, or if it is the faithful report of the elements which, since time's start, have overheard such things?

At length, no one was there beneath the rock, but for the dead and Qirisn. In her, one ultimate wisp of life remained, although swiftly it was ebbing. *Come away*, life whispered to her urgently, *come away, for you and I are done with all this now.*

But Qirisn's eyes fixed on the sky of storm. The gods had forsaken her, love had, truth had. Worse than all these, *she* must now forsake *him*.

Something in her screamed in mute violence, a wordless, unthought prayer to the sky. Which, pausing, seemed to hear.

The cacophony of the cloud settled to a kind of stasis. The flutter of the lightning fashioned for itself another shape, that of an electrum knot. From this, long strands extended themselves, like searching arms. Long-fingered hands, resembling tentacles, reached as if most delicately to clasp the world. Then, from the core of heaven, a Levin bolt shot downward. A flaming sword, the white of another spectrum, struck deep into the ground, at the spot where Qirisn lay dying. And after this it stood, the bolt, joining heaven to earth, pulsing with a regular muscular golden spasm. It fused all matter, sand and soil and dust, body and bone and blood, together in a disbanded union of change. Then the sword diluted and was gone. Everything was gone. And darkness sank into the space which was all the heaven-fire had left.

It is said, and possibly only Jandur, those twenty years later, propagated such a tale – for he was secretly a romantic – that hours on, when the storm had melted, demons came up onto the Harsh to enjoy its refreshment under a waning moon.

Passing the spot, those beautiful dreamers, the Eshva, paused only to sigh, before wandering away. If Vazdru princes passed, they paid no attention. But two Drin, the dwarvish, ugly and talented artisans of Underearth, did halt beside the silicate residues of Qirisn's death.

"Something is here worth looking at!"

But a desert hare, a female, gleaming platinum under the watery moon, and with ears like lilies, galloped over the dunes. And lust stirred up the Drin at such loveliness, and they vacated the area to pursue her. Such a master was love, then, for demons, and for men.

4. The Fourth Fragment

That very moment, as he entered the highest vortex of pleasure, Razved heard his phantasmal partner call out his name in her joy. It was not a moment otherwise for anything, let alone for thought. Nevertheless, it seemed not inappropriate she should know his name. Then the colossal wave bore him through the gate and dashed him among stars, and after that flat on his back again amid the pillows, with a maiden of glass gripped in his arms.

Only now did he unwillingly feel the chill and ungiving texture of her unflesh, and sense the folly, and maybe the *error* of what had just been done.

Only *now* also did he understand it was, after all, not exactly *his* name that she had called aloud in her voice of glass.

No, not *Razved*, that was not the name she had uttered. It had been Raz Vedey. *Raz Vedey, my beloved lord.*

Drained by ecstasy, stupefied by confusion, Razved lay there. There rushed through his befuddled mind a memory of his mother, who had slain herself before ever he had known her, and of an old man locked up and enchained in a dirty room below. Down there, amid the irons and the skittering of rats, that was where *Raz Vedey* might be located.

In his mind, Razved asked of himself, *whatever she is, what would she have with my father?*

Because, of course, the mad old man, who constantly escaped his imprisonment, but who haunted Razved even when safely stashed away, was that father, that very Raz Vedey.

Razved himself knew well that, along with a disgraced mother who had cut her wrist and died, he had a male parent who, while yet young and strong, the victor in a southern war, had one night, during a galvanic storm, started up shouting that his soul had perished in the Vast Harsh. And who, despite the subsequent care and attention of the best physicians and maguses, quickly became and stayed entirely lunatic. Razved, growing to maturity, was reared sternly by tutors, and when only thirteen made the regent of his father. Since then Razved had ruled the city, but without full authority and without the essential title of *King*. For did the King not still live? The city's moral code forbade his removal save through natural decease, and crazed though he was, the King ungraciously refused to die. Razved, to be sure, had engineered a clutch of clandestine attempts upon the wretch's life. All of these had failed. Yes, even the strong poison, or the block of stone cast from an upper roof. It was as if, Razved had long decided, his devilish sire awaited some news, or even arrival, and would not himself depart the world until assured of it. His constant wail: "Are they *here*? Are they *near*?" seemed infuriatingly – or piteably – to confirm this last suspicion.

The Prince's eyes now remained tightly closed. He was partly afraid to open them, for the fragile weight of *her* still lay over him. What would he see? What must he do?

"Remove yourself from me," he muttered, but there was no reaction.

Instead his brain brimmed suddenly with uncanny images – a glassy girl, shimmering green and rose, who drifted through the chamber on feet of glass, and her eyes, curiously, were dark, and gazed at him and did not see him. Perhaps they saw nothing, for they were made – not of eyes, nor of glass – but of *pain*, of *agony*, and of despair. A bride, brought forth from the carcass of Harsh Desert, the true meaning of whose title was *The Illegitimate Vessel*, a bride who had died in horror and waited in blind lament for two decades, next entering the city of her lover, her beloved, and mistaking for him one who *was* flesh of his flesh, if *never* spirit of his spirit. Where now then for her? Where else was there to seek or to fly?

On Razved's skin the glacial glass turned to ice, and with a howl he burst from his trance.

He bounded off the couch, slinging the succubus-creature from him, and opened wide his eyes. And in that instant, he saw and heard a shattering of glass – as if a million crystal windows had blown in and whirled about him.

"Help me!" yowled Razved, King-in-waiting, descendant of warrior-lords, spraying his robe with the waters of his bladder. "Assassins! Demons!"

But when his terrified servants entered, they found him quite alone, not a mark upon him, and on the floor by his couch only one little plain drinking goblet, smashed into bits like sugar.

Qirisn was now finally and fully dead. Free therefore, she glided through the wall of the prison-chamber and stole quietly to King Raz Vedey. She touched his ravelled face, and looking up he saw her, her light hair and blue-midnight eyes; he saw her soul. And shedding his ruined mind and form, he came out to her, strong and young and beautiful as he had been in Marah, and kissed her hands and her lips. After which they went away together, wherever it was and is that lovers go, after physical death, when they are two halves of a faultless solitary whole.

But in the red dawn, when someone came to tell the Prince that his father had abruptly departed the world, Razved buried his head in the pillows and wept, over and over: "At last, at last, *I am the King*!"

Persian Eyes

I

The Roman stood looking at his slave. She was one of many, in the fine house on Palace Hill. They came and went barely noticed, across his vision, like shifting columns of sunlight, or the diurnal shadows that changed shape over the floors. But something, now, had made him see this one.

"Come here," he called. Not harshly, he was not a cruel man to his slaves, did not believe in it unless it were needed – and then a sound beating usually settled the offender. The female slaves especially he did not like to chastise unduly. Like flowers, or animals, they looked better, and were a nicer ornament to his house, if well kept.

The slave came across the garden toward him. It was the fifth hour[1], late in the morning, and the sun gilded the little fountain, and the marble statue of Apollo with his lion. The slave, too, was polished a moment with light gold. And then she was in front of Livius, her head lowered.

She had black hair, plaited back and held with a thong. She wore the coarse linen tunic of her status, but of a pleasant soft cream in colour. It made her honey skin look darker. She was about sixteen years old, or probably younger, for like most slaves, she would tend to appear older than her years.

Livius regarded the slave carefully. Had his wife said something about this girl? He thought so – what had it been? That she, his wife, had bought her privately, a favour to some rich friend – Claudia Metella perhaps, or Terentia... *Why* as a favour?

There was nothing wrong with the girl that he could see. And, if there had been, his fastidious Fulvia would hardly have wanted her, nor would he.

"Look up," he said.

The slave looked up. For a second, a flash of her face, small and Eastern, triangular in form, the nose long and lips full. The eyes...

She had glanced down again.

"No, I told you to look up."

A slightly longer flash of face then, but not much. Obviously, she was frightened of him, the Master, thought she had done something wrong and would be punished. Maybe she had been badly treated elsewhere.

"I'm not angry. Where were you going?" This was the voice he used for a young nervous horse.

She whispered some words, his slave, which did not sound like the Imperial Tongue. Not even like the argot of the lower orders. Some Eastern muttering. But she had known enough Latin, of course, to understand his orders, if not to reply to them.

"All right. Go along, then."

She dipped her body before him, graceful, mindless, then turned and walked away across the garden.

A strange creature. Like having a tamed but shackled leopard in the house.

Livius smiled at his idea and returned into the cool of his library.

"She has strange eyes, that slave," said Livilla to her mother.

Fulvia took no notice.

They had been having their hair dressed in the summer courtyard that opened from Fulvia's summer bedroom. Fulvia's hair, bleached by quince juice, was ornately curled and crimpled; Livilla's dark hair had been dressed more simply, as became a maiden. The slaves who had seen to this were now gone, and none of them had been the slave to whom Livilla referred.

She tried again, "Mother, that new slave – where did she come from?"

"Which slave? What? What are you talking about? Why should slaves interest you?"

"They don't. Or only this one. The one with green eyes."

"Yes," said Fulvia. She sipped her wine, mixed with the liquefied pulp of roses. She looked thoughtful, considering. But said nothing else.

Livilla would not be put off.

"Mother, the other slaves dislike her. You know it can cause trouble when they get upset. They get careless. Look at how Lodia nearly burned you with the tongs…"

"Yes, yes. But I hit her with the mirror. She won't do it again."

"She was nervous, Mother. Unsettled."

"Livilla, that shade of yellow doesn't suit you. I've thought so for a long while."

Diverted, disconcerted, Livilla looked down in outrage at her yellow stola, figured with anemones. And forgot to say any more about slaves.

Fulvia, bored with the Livillan torrent of insecurities now released, in the matter of dress, hair, and skin, sat with apparent patience, offering calming words. Fulvia was used to being bored. It was her life.

Of course, she wanted for nothing, and she did not wish to change this. She did not really *wish* for anything.

Birds sang. She thought about the slave.

It had only been ten days ago that Terentia Austus had sought Fulvia out, arriving in person that morning, sitting frowning and hard among Fulvia's pretty things.

"I want," Terentia had finally announced, "you to take a creature off my hands."

Fulvia had raised her brows. Terentia was several years older, and looked it, her makeup much too heavy and her grey hair covered by an auburn wig, of a colour known as *Flame*. Terentia was also powerful, the wife of an electoral candidate sure to do well, a rich woman securely fastened in a prestigious marriage. What did she want? One could doubtless not say *No*, whatever it was.

"A creature, dear Terentia? What kind of creature?"

The Austus family kept a menagerie, as Fulvia knew. She suspected a snappish wolf or porcupine was about to be unloaded on her.

"A slave," had said Terentia.

Fulvia was almost relieved. "A slave. I see."

"There's nothing unsuitable about her. She's biddable and not work-shy. I'll be frank with you, Fulvia. My husband pays her too much attention."

Fulvia waited behind her polite mask. She thought that if every married woman worried about her husband's activities with *slaves*, the gods knew what would become of them all.

However, "Yes, it sounds absurd," said Terentia, seeming even more aggravated. "Why should I care? I have my sons, and besides Austus is still most attentive to me. I've no complaints. Also he keeps a woman near the Circus Gorbus. I've never had any concerns about *her*."

"Then...?" prompted Fulvia, sensing a prompt was expected.

"This slave came to me from my sister Junia's household. She begged me to take her, wouldn't say why, or only some rubbish about the slave's being disruptive. And of course, her husband's a drunk, so one never knows."

"No."

"Then I take the wretch into our house. She does her work perfectly adequately. And then Austus – becomes obsessed with her."

"Obsessed…"

"Yes. I choose the word with care. Perhaps it's his disappointment last year in the election…"

"Oh, but, *this* year…"

"Exactly. And he must concentrate on that. So she goes. Will you accept her? A gift. I won't ask a sesterce for her. It would be unlucky."

"Well, but, Terentia – couldn't you merely…"

"No. I can't explain. Are you willing? That's all I'm waiting to hear." Terentia had risen abruptly from her seat in a flare of costly garments and a clash of pearls. The severing of valuable connections twanged in the air. Fulvia did what she must. Terentia nodded. "I'll send her to you before the dinner hour."

And so the slave arrived. Looking her over, Fulvia thought her nothing much, simply an inferior from an Eastern country, which Terentia had actually said was most likely Persis. She had wondered, too, what Terentia would say to the obsessive husband, and if he would presently storm across Palace Hill after his property. This did not happen.

The girl seemed to sink into the household with very few ripples. The slaves were not notably antipathetic to her. In Fulvia's experience, they often took a dislike to newcomers, particularly females.

Her eyes were a little odd. That glassy grey-green, unusually clear in the dark skin, between the black lashes.

But there.

(Livilla had stopped lamenting and was instead admiring herself in the silver mirror.)

Fulvia had mentioned the new slave to Livius, naturally. He had been quite uninterested, as one would predict.

They ate the evening meal in the garden, then lingered there. From beyond the house came the low rumble of heavy-wheeled traffic on cobbles, the occasional shouts of some party or other revel. Above, the sky deepened until, undimmed by the uncountable lamps of Rome, the stars were put on.

"The snails were good," said Jovus.

"No, too sticky. Cibo still doesn't know how to cook them," added Parvus, the connoisseur.

Livius listened to his two sons, neither yet a full-grown man. He had been reading and had fallen asleep in the thick heat of afternoon, like some old grandfather. Now, leaning here, he felt curiously alert, as if expecting something. But nothing, nothing at all was expected.

A girl had brought more wine and was pouring it into his cup. Her.

He wanted to say again, *Look up*. But the eyes were downcast, she might not have had any eyes…

Outside a wild raw shout blew up. Palace Hill was a select area, but it got noisier by the night. Perhaps he should buy a farm, move out into the country among the olives and vineyards, vegetate... But there was Jovus, the eldest, to secure first in a worthy career. And Livilla to marry suitably, to someone or other.

None of this, his duties, caught his attention greatly tonight. But there, the lamp was being lit by Apollo, and she was standing straight again, and the flame splintered in her eyes. How green they were. Fig-leaf green, yet cooling, like marble.

He glanced at Fulvia. She had been watching him.

"Did you like the pork liver?" she asked, solicitous, as a good wife should be. And he sensed her boredom, both with ordering the liver and its cooking, and now asking. His answer, his approval, also bored with those, as *he* was with all of it, including his children, his house, the noises of the city, the city, the night…

"Delicious, Fulvia. How clever you were to think of it. Aren't the stars fine?"

Fulvia lay sleepless on her bed. It had been made in Egypt, and sloped a little, keeping her head higher than her feet, and tonight this gave her a peculiar feeling of weightless drifting, as if she might float up and out of the door, and over the high walls into the city.

What would she see? The lit porches of festive houses not her own, hung with garlands. The seven arched spines of Rome, crowded with their temples, gardens, mansions, and the dark valleys between, where the markets, dens, brothels, and slums lay twitching and surging, also sleeplessly.

Fulvia turned on to her side. At this ninth hour of the night[2], it was very quiet on Palace Hill. There was only the faint stir of the plane tree in her private courtyard beyond the curtain. It sounded like the moving coils of a snake.

She had thought her husband might sleep with her here tonight. Generally, she knew the signs – little attentions, a kind of heat which came from his body. She had been anticipating the visit, had taken down her hair and freshened her perfume. She no longer thrilled to his sexual attentions – all that had left her with the birth of Jovus, the first son. As if sexual pleasure (as she had) had done its duty, and so now she need no longer experience any. She had been sorry at first, then philosophical. These things happened. And she still enjoyed his arousal. The manifestation of his continuing desire, however infrequent, was a compliment.

Why had he not come in, then?

Perhaps he was tired. He had eaten a large meal and taken a little too much wine. And it was, though the summer was so young, a hot night.

I must sleep, Fulvia commanded herself. She listened to the tree rustling and glimpsed inside her mind a silvery snake winding through leaves, in the instant before she fell from consciousness.

Livius woke with a start.

What had disturbed him? (He listened, hearing nothing, even the noisy neighbours were silent now.) And – where was he?

Ruffled, he got to his feet. He had come back to the library and stretched out on the couch here to read for an hour before going to Fulvia. She would have realised, and he always gave her time to prepare. But again – he had slept. Now he could tell from the feel of the house, it was only an hour or so from sunrise.

Far too late to disrupt Fulvia's slumbers. He was a considerate man. It had been different, of course, when they were young. They had shared a bed every night and kept busy.

The lamp was guttering on the desk. He trimmed the wick and took the lamp with him along the corridor. When he reached his garden, he paused between the pillars. The stars were dull now. The garden was moonless, ghostly, and the fountain shivered like a piece of silk.

As he turned into his own room, the light of the small lamp

flared fierce as a torch against furniture and hangings. Livius winced at the heavy gold, the bright inlay of ivory, the blast of scarlet curtain. How much had he drunk? Too much, it seemed. He blew out the lamp and undressed in blackness.

I'm not old, he thought, lying there. His vision seemed a little disturbed, and in the blackness, weird faces leered and smoked at him from near the ceiling. The wine, or even the pork – *I wish the gods would make me young again, he resentfully mused. Even five years younger.*

He thought of fig trees – he did not know why – their shade, the glow of their leaves filtering the summer sun.

We should be like that. Sleep for a while in winter, and then grow strong and new again, like leaves.

Livius smiled now at his own foolishness. He slept.

The slaves of Livius curled in their tiny cubicles tucked deep and windowless within the house. Most had a bed; that was their Master's kindness. Now and then one would creep to the privy, a dirty, stinking place, without the fitments of the rich man's easements, let alone of the lavish thermal bathroom with its sheltered terrace facing south.

Cibo met Lodia in the dark, between the privy and her cubicle. As the house cook, he had somewhat better quarters behind the kitchen, and also some power in the slave-world.

"Well, Lodia. Like a moment with me tonight?"

Lodia grinned. It was her way of saying she knew she had no choice.

Cibo guided her, and when they reached the corridor with the lamp burning, he saw the bruise on her arm. The Mistress had struck her today with the polished silver hand mirror, for carelessness. Now he joked about it, telling Lodia she was an idiot and had better watch out, or Master would sell her off to the mines.

Lodia was used to his foreplay. She said nothing. Cibo led her into the kitchen, past the man-tall pots and burned-charcoal-smelling oven. He gave her a piece of bread, a leftover, smeared with pork fat. In a corner, his two assistants lay on the stone floor, snoring.

Cibo took Lodia against the wall, in a hot rush and snuffling almost-silence. He finished quickly, scowling. "All right, you can be off now. You're not so juicy as you were. Next time I'll take that new girl. The Persian."

Lodia said, "If you do, don't look in her eyes."

"Eh? What does that mean?"

Lodia was once more – dumb.

Cibo said, "It's not her eyes that would fascinate me, Lodia. Go on back to your pit."

Jovus dreamed he was a man and wore the Man's Toga. An augur had been taken and it foretold great things for him – though what, he was unsure. Even so, he was making a speech in the Forum, and older men nodded, and the crowd was all applause.

Then a girl walked through the crowd. She moved like a breeze through a cornfield, and the human figures swayed away from her, and back again when she had passed, but took no notice of her otherwise.

Jovus, however, lost the thread of his oration. He stopped speaking entirely, and an enormous quiet filled the Forum, and in the blue-scorched sky, another colour came, as if an awning had been erected, as they did it at the circuses.

Beyond the wall, Parvus, nine years old, dreamed he was swimming in a deep green pool. He was rather anxious, for he knew that he was tiring, and the sides looked sheer.

Livilla, on her own bed across the corridor, was sobbing in her dream because she could not bear the saffron colour of her stolas, and they were all like that, every one, even those she was brought that began as pink woven-air muslin, or delicate white silk – and none of them therefore suited her. She looked blotchy and too fat, unmarriageable, so she wept.

II

As he gazed about him, the Artifex Iudo was puzzled. But then, his clients often puzzled him with their requests – a perfectly serviceable pillar to be removed and replaced by a carved prop that made the room into a stage set; a wall with charming nymphs changed to a bacchanal of the wine god, lewd female companions, and goats.

This, though. This did intrigue him slightly.

"Yes, sir. Certainly, it can be done. I have a new colour that has come from the Libanus region. They call it *Sea-Wave*. Or, then, from Egypt..."

Livius said, "The colour of this perfume pot, like this."

Iudo accepted the pot with its hint of nard. One of the lady wife Fulvia's, probably. It was a deep, nacreous green. He thought perhaps he would not be able to match it at all. Green was a colour which so often turned, like milk. One painted it on, and as it dried, something in the plaster made it too shallow, or too strong. Which normally might not matter. But now, with this insistent instruction...

"And the subject? As I have it here?"

"Trees," said Livius absently. "Leaves. Pools. Green things."

Of course, more unusual than all the rest, (than the commission for the Artifex and his assistants to paint the two dining rooms, the library, and the rich man's bedroom, all in greens and variations of green) was the straw hat, such as a farmer might put on, clamped down on Livius' noble head, even here in the shade. And beneath the hat, a band of thin cotton, itself dullish green in colour, perhaps to catch sweat from the forehead?

Livius' eyes were watering in the sun. They looked inflamed.

Iudo had noticed the elder of the two young sons also had this problem with his eyes, although not so badly, nor had he put on a hat against the sun.

The boy was there, now, out in the garden court, sitting on a bench, brooding the way they did at that age, whether patrician or citizenry. (Supposedly the plebeian poor, in their sties, did not have time to brood in youth. They were already out pimping, whoring, stealing, cutting throats, or training in the gladiator schools. Or at the very least, standing in line for the free food the city offered.)

"Well, then. You may do it."

"Thank you, sir. We shall try our best."

"Begin today."

"Ah – very well. That may be somewhat..."

"Take this." The bag clanked heavy as a legionary's full campaign armour.

Livius sighed. He hooded his lids.

Iudo, hurrying off to organise his men and paint, did not see the rich man pull the green cloth right down over his eyes.

In the garden, Jovus *did* see this.

He stood up, nervous, his inner, nonphysical body attenuated, like the eyes of a slug standing on stalks.

Jovus picked a way across the sunny court, as if avoiding

invisible obstacles, between the beds of roses and late iris, whose reds and purples seemed to be on fire.

"Father?"

Livius did not answer.

Was he asleep again? He had fallen asleep at dinner yesterday.

"*Father,*" said Jovus, more loudly, and then his father's face turned toward him, and Jovus saw his father's open black eyes staring at him through the band of thin Egyptian cotton.

For some reason – every reason – this frightened Jovus. He was fifteen, almost a man, but he was afraid.

"Sir..."

"What is it?" The voice was weary, dismissive. Jovus knew that really all his father ever was to him now, at best, was courteous. The happy man who had played with him as a child, the grieved man who beat him when he skimped his lessons, who took pride in every achievement – that man was gone. But where?

"Which rooms are to be painted?"

Weary, short, Livius told him.

Jovus went away and slouched through the house into his own rich boy's bedroom, with its carved garment chest and bed of ebony and pine. The crimson panels painted on the walls offended him, but he stared at them until his eyes ached.

Past the doorway, then, she went.

It was just like that. As if there were no other in the house, it was all vacant but for himself, and then for her. Jovus watched her.

She *slid* along the corridor, vanishing suddenly at the turn, as if merely to turn a corner were supernatural.

He had seen his sister Livilla earlier throw a cut piece of her own hair into the flame before the household guardians in the larger dining room. But then, too, he had heard her whining about wanting to make an offering to Juno Viriplaca, to ensure her marriage.

Jovus thought the gods would not be concerned with this. They never offered help, even his family ancestors did not. Rather like Livius, they had lost – in their case with immortality or death – all involvement in the human world, save where they could be harsh in it.

The house of Junia Lallia, Terentia Austus' sister, stood behind the Gardens of Fortuna, screened by the massive poplars and ilexes. Fulvia approached uneasily and in full panoply, in the closed litter with curtains of Indian silk, with her bodyguard and two attendants.

At first, sitting in the vestibule, on a hard, gold-adorned seat, Fulvia thought that perhaps Junia might not see her, despite the delivered gifts of goose offal in honey, early-ripened peaches from the coast, and spikenard.

But then one of the house slaves conducted Fulvia into Junia's private sitting room, which opened on a courtyard garden depressing in its glory of trees, a terraced water course, tame doves, monkeys, and a peacock marred only by its rusty shrieks.

Junia was a youngish woman who scorned to bleach her hair. Her clothes and jewellery said all there was to say on such matters.

"It's most kind of you to see me," murmured Fulvia.

"Such lovely presents," replied Junia coldly. "Is this about the elections?"

"No – no, dear Junia Lallia – I wouldn't think of bothering you, but…"

"Then it is," said Junia, staring now into space, "the slave."

"Oh," said Fulvia.

"Yes," said Junia. "The Persian woman," she added. "Her name – did anyone tell you? Roxara. Or so they called her in the market at Ostia – or again, so I understand." She paused. Then she clapped her hands. A girl came in with wine and cinnamon-water and little cakes. After the girl had served these and gone, Junia said, "It had to be faced. Of course you would come here. Terentia told me what she did. But I think she didn't tell you what I had done, or why."

Fulvia gave over caution. "Tell me."

Junia lifted her brows, that was all. Then she told.

"My eldest son, who as you know lived here in my husband's house when not away in Gaul, bought this slave, as men do, on a whim. He presented her to his wife, a poor virtuous little ninny with the wits of a pigeon. I suppose he liked the looks of the slave, and meant to sample her, and the poor little ninny wouldn't even have noticed, very likely. However. My son didn't sample the slave called Roxara. Instead, Fulvia, he went mad."

Fulvia felt herself whiten. She felt the blanched and rosy makeup standing out on her skin like a *separate* skin, and herself, all horror, glaring through.

Junia Lallia said frigidly, her eyes on nothing at all, "Firstly he wouldn't return to Gaul. My husband covered this up by saying our son was ill. All sorts of devices then had to be resorted to, in order to avoid disgrace. I won't tax you with those. Meanwhile physicians came and went. And my son – my beautiful son…" shocking Fulvia once more, this abrupt break into emotion, as swiftly mastered, "…lay raving in a darkened room, unable to bear the light, or any bright colour, wanting the girl – not for any proper reason, but simply to *look at her.*"

"To – look at her?"

"He couldn't keep his eyes from her. She had to sit in the room with him. I witnessed it day after day. She sat and looked at the ground, and then he would go to her – grovelling along the floor like a dog – staring up into her face…" All at once, Junia sneezed. Having done this, she made a sign against the bad omen. She said, "We tried to keep her from him. He would cry for her. I mean he would scream for her as if he were in agony. Oh, then, I called priests to the house, from various temples, and other persons. Because it was sorcery, what else?"

"What else," gasped Fulvia, shuddering.

"They had some effect – mostly through drugging him to insensibility. But then they told us we must send the woman away."

"But surely – if she's a sorceress – you should have killed her – your husband, excuse me, but really, he should have killed her at once."

"He didn't dare to," said Junia. "Another strong man brought to his knees. We were afraid… And so – I sent Roxara to my sister, a very reasonable and sensible woman, who assured me it was all nonsense, and she would put all to rights. But, as you know, in the end my sensible sister, who fears nothing, and will walk through a cemetery on nights when the ghosts hover in the moonlight, she, too, became fearful, and she sent this evil being away to you. Forgive us, Fulvia. We are in your debt forever."

Fulvia thought, *so you are, but how will that help now?*

She, too, controlled herself. She said, "And your son?"

Junia turned her head, but not before Fulvia saw why she had sneezed – her eyes were bursting with tears she did not permit to fall. Junia said, "He's gone."

"To… Gaul?"

"No, not to Gaul."

"Then – can he be *dead?*"

"I don't know if he is dead."

Fulvia blurted "But you must know…"

"He vanished. My son vanished. When Terentia's slaves came to fetch Roxara, he was already gone, and we knew nothing. Each of us thought he had wandered to some other part of the house. Then that he was in the city. Searches were made. It was discreet. Then less so. He hasn't been found. If you have heard no rumours, that is due to my husband's connection to the Flavians."

Among the forgotten cakes, Fulvia was panting, but Junia now sat icy, stone still.

"Perhaps he will come back," Fulvia faltered at last.

"Do you think so? Now you sound like his dolt of a little wifelet. Of course, he can never come back. She cast a spell on him, and it took him somewhere he can never escape and never be found, out of this world."

Junia rose.

Fulvia staggered to her feet.

"I'm in your debt," said Junia. "If I can assist in any way at all, I will do so. What will you do?"

Fulvia drew in her lips. She said, "There's only one way."

"Yes, perhaps. If you're brave enough."

The litter raced over the hills, the bearers running, the bodyguard thrusting lower citizens from its path.

At the portico of Livius' house, they came to a halt. The door was knocked upon. The doorkeeper opened it.

Fulvia got out of the litter. She was trembling, it was true, but she had crossed this threshold many hundreds of times, only once carried over it as a bride. Now, as she moved forward into the familiar house, her foot caught in the tile of a second step, *which was not there*. She felt herself falling and watched surprised as she flew out on to the mosaic floor. She heard the crack of her head against its ungiving surface, from some way off. And then nothing.

It was the Greeks and Egyptians who had thought everyone but themselves to be barbarians, as alike in their limitation as sheep. Romans, though, were also inclined to this idea – the barbarity of other races... the Egyptians and Greeks by now not always unincluded.

So, she was a barbarian then, from Persis, that land Great Alexander had subdued, a country of crags and brown dust and lions, of green gardens mysterious under an alien moon...

Livius looked about him slowly. The walls of the library were pale and painted over by green, green fruits, green leaves, green figures that danced or swam in a distance of green waves and green dolphins. The Artifex and his men had worked swiftly, perhaps with not as much agility as speed. A curtain, (green), hung at the yard door. The summer sun was always too bright. He found lamps were better. And sometimes he shut one eye and looked, through the spyglass of flawed emerald, at their green flames.

This amused him. But he was waiting. He knew that he was.

Once, a child, a boy, had come to the inner doorway.

"Father – the physician says..."

Something unimportant.

Who was this child, addressing him as *Father*? One of the slaves? Perhaps. In certain patrician homes, the Master was called Father.

This child-slave had been distressed, wet-eyed, and snotty. Parvus, he was called. A nickname.

Someone had told Livius his wife Fulvia (he thought they called her Fulvia) had hurt herself. He had gone to see, starting at the loud colours – raucous red, orange – in her room. He did not recognise the woman stretched out on the bed, over whom the physician bent. The smell of medicinal resins turned Livius' stomach. He did not stay there long, thinking maybe he had made a mistake, and come to look at the wrong woman.

The door curtain moved. Who would it be now?

It was her, of course, the barbarian Persian. She came in with a wine jug. She was pouring the wine. Seen through the emerald, the wine was black-green.

Livius waited for the Persian girl to raise her eyes so that he could look into them. But she would not do it.

"Sit," he said, "sit over there." She moved so adeptly, as if alive. But really he did not think she was. None of them were, nor he himself. This girl, however, although unliving, was *moved* by something live *within* her.

She sat down on the couch.

"Look up."

She raised her eyes, lowered them.

How could he ever have thought her afraid or nervous? She had no feelings or emotions, and probably no brain inside her skull, under its covering of amber skin and coarse rich hair.

"No, let me see your eyes."

A look. Gone.

He wondered if he should have her whipped for insolence. If that happened, or if he cut her with the little knife he kept here, for breaking the edges of wax seals, would she bleed green, like the sap of a plant?

Livius got up and went over and sat on the stool, gazing up into her face, and so into the lowered, half-obscured depths of her eyes.

The flames of the lamps were there in the green irises. It was like looking into a hall under the sea, lit by torches.

"Where do you come from? From Ocean? Or out of a tree – a tree nymph or a water nymph?" Her lids drooped lower. "Don't close your eyes. Obey me."

Her face – expressionless, mindless. All slaves were of this kind, unless singled out and made pets of. Would she change now, since he favoured her? Livius thought she would not.

He did not want to touch her, let alone take her to him in the sexual act. He found it restful – and yet curiously exciting – simply to sit here like a boy, and stare up at her, trying to see in at the tiny glinting cracks between her eyelids.

When Fulvia opened her eyes, the room was a rippling dimness smeared by lights.

She said, alarmed yet imperious, "I can't see…"

"It will pass, madam. An effect of the drug I've had to give you. You banged your head when you fell. Your cranium is bruised but whole. And I've bled you. All's well."

"Did I fall? Where? I don't remember…"

"At the house door. You entered in a hurry."

"Did I? I don't remember…"

"You'd been visiting the lady Junia Lallia." (The physician – a know-all.)

"I don't remember…"

Livilla had appeared, white and terrified. She ran to the bed and made a grab for Fulvia's hand. "Mother – Mother…"

"Gently, child," barked the physician, annoyed at seeing his handiwork disarranged.

But Fulvia said quietly, "Where is Livius?"

The physician turned and busied himself at a table loaded with his salves and infusions. The air smelled of burned beetles, mint, and Greek incense.

"This doctor is Idas," said Livilla, trying to be adult, "he is the doctor Claudia Metella recommends for all things to do with the head…"

"Yes. Where is your father?"

"In his library," said Livilla. "He came in once. Then he went away."

"He mustn't be troubled," said Fulvia. She felt bitter at his lack of care for her, and resigned, because this was only what she would anticipate. Virtuously and grimly, she put him first, and did not know how thin her lips had become. But she was also sleepy from the bleeding, and the potions. "Make sure," she said to Livilla, "your father eats a good dinner."

As she slipped back into sleep, Fulvia thought, *this isn't right. I should get up and go and see to something. I know it was to be done – that was why I was in such a hurry coming in, and so I fell.* But her head ached. She thought of the thing she could not remember. *Never mind it.*

Parvus was standing behind Jovus just outside.

"Don't go in," instructed Livilla. "She's asleep."

"She's slept for days," said Jovus.

"I know," said Livilla. "But Idas says she's in no danger and must rest."

"He's a Greek," said Parvus, a red-eyed racist, "and he may be useless, too."

Jovus put his hand on his brother's shoulder. "Hush. The Metellas sent him. He's all right."

Livilla said, "I have to go and see to the kitchen, since Mother can't."

When she had stalked off, dismayed at her (temporary) position, Parvus said, "What's Father doing?"

"What he was doing before."

They had seen him. Both had peered around the edge of the green curtain. Seen Livius, their father, a man, sitting at the feet of the Persian woman in the green darkness.

"Is she a witch?" whispered Parvus, "like the sorceress Medea?"

"It's nothing to worry about," said Jovus. He lied, wanting to be alone. "A man – does these things with his house-women. It's just some fancy of his."

Livilla entered the kitchen, and saw that it was empty, and although the day was advancing, nothing much had been done toward the main meal. Oil, onions, and herbs lay about, and some fish – one of which the cat had got hold of, dragged under a bench, and was now eating.

The girl clapped her hands, and no one came, and Livilla had a strange horrible sudden fear that all the house was as empty as the kitchen seemed to be, but for herself and the cat. Everyone was gone, the slaves, her brothers, her father, and Fulvia, too, borne off into the air.

The urge to cry ripped through Livilla, but she tried not to, for she would soon be a woman and married, and she must not let go of her dignity.

Then Lodia crept in.

Her slave's face was pale and deranged, an almost exact match for Livilla's own.

"Cibo choked," said Lodia.

"What – do you mean?"

"The cook – he choked on something. Look – he's there, by the ovens."

Livilla turned and saw Cibo's fat, impossible-to-miss body sprawled in a shadow that had somehow hidden him, and now did not. His face was turned away, and Livilla was glad.

Lodia stood swaying, holding herself in her arms. In a sort of chant, she announced, "He must have tried to have her. He must have tried to." Then she sank to her knees and cowered, wondering if one of her masters would come to kill her.

But when Lodia looked up again, the Mistress-daughter had run away.

"I was glad to leave that house," said Idas the Greek. (Rather as Iudo the Artifex had felt, if Idas had only known.) "Something goes on there. A great house, and full of people and slaves, and workmen, and so *silent*. And you know how now and then I see things other men are unaware of?"

His acquaintances in the tavern, attracted by the wine he had bought them, nodded.

"Well, then, in the walls of that place – oh, at first it was aswarm with artisans painting everything green, yes, even panels in the tables and chests – I never saw the like, such a dingy, leaden colour. But then, as I came from the sick lady's chamber and was passing one of these rooms, now all green-painted – and so badly..." the

acquaintances waited, to see what the old romancer would bring
out now, "...I saw faces in the walls, among the painted leaves.
They watched me. Oh, not *painted* faces – they moved – not human
faces either. The gods know what they were. Not animals – not
quite that – perhaps like the faces one sees in the trunks of trees, or
leaves clustered together, or in weeds under a pond..."

The greened house lay silent about its green courtyards. Green
shadows dappled Apollo with the panther-skin of Bacchus.

No one went out. And yet it was as if they had *all* gone out.
Even if you glimpsed them move there, in the rooms, along the
corridors, shifting the sunlight and the hangings, even then, it was
as if they were not really there. But if they were not, what was?

For a kind of energy filled all the cells. Time had passed. Some
tens of days, thirty, forty. And no one called, not a single trader, and
no visitors. Behind the door, in his alcove, the door-slave slept. Yet
it was as if he were not there. It was as if the *house* were no longer
there, merged into a green shade or green wave. Become one more
grove or fountain of the decorated city.

People on Palace Hill, going by the blind outer walls, failed to
glance at them, as if – the house of the patrician Livius had
vanished.

III

At noon, Jovus went to the kitchen and took some of the olives and
figs that lay on the table, and some of the stale bread. A slave – he
had forgotten the man's name – had slunk out when Jovus came in,
rather as the cat had been used to do, before it ran away. The slave
had also scrounged some of the leftover food. Although it was
spoiled, there still seemed to be enough. And somehow Jovus did
not think about when it would all be gone. (He had noted the body
of Cibo was no longer there. Someone must have dragged it away.
He did not *like* to think of *this*.)

But the house had no Master, so what could you expect of it?
Or, it had one, but a Master who stayed in his library and did not
move, no, not even to seek the privy or the bath. And the house
had a fragile Mistress, who had been sick from a fall, and walked
only a short way from her room, and back again.

The hotter colours faded from Jovus' bedroom walls, he

thought, as they had faded from the flowers in the garden. Livilla's saffron stolas were now the colour of soured cream.

Jovus ate the figs and bread standing in the garden, and he looked up at the sky, which he did not think was blue, not truly, or else something came between him and the sky.

The city was deeply quiet. Occasionally he thought he heard traffic on the roads, or vague cries, but it was perhaps only the rustle of blood behind his own ears.

Moss grew in the mane of Apollo's lion. Jovus was examining this, when he heard his mother's voice from the colonnade.

"Where is your father?"

Fulvia had asked this a great deal, but then she had stopped asking, as the answer was always identical.

"In his library," said Jovus, as always. "Mother, would you like this fig – look, there are raisins, too."

"Never mind," said Fulvia.

She turned, and then she turned back. She said, her voice like pearls which had been crushed, "He isn't there. I looked. He isn't anywhere in this house."

Jovus felt panic spring in him like a tiger.

Fulvia wore no makeup. This made her seem both younger and quite old. Either way she would be no help.

Nevertheless, together they went again through the house, through room after room, into each of the courtyards. They pulled aside drapes and let sunlight into the spaces – was sunlight green? They walked through the three rooms of the bath, steamless and unheated. They searched the cubicles of the slaves. Sometimes they met these slaves, who shied, but seemed deaf and dumb, or who bolted, and this made Fulvia irritated, and so more like her previous self, a remote and pragmatic woman, offering calm words that snapped with repressed rage.

At some point, too, Livilla joined them, crying a little, but stupidly, like a small child who had mislaid what it was upset about. Parvus also appeared. He was quite naked, and very dirty, but none of them reproached him, though Fulvia clicked her tongue.

They did not find Livius.

At last, they were back in the library, where, in the curtain-dusk, the scrolls and wax tablets shone dull in their cubbyholes, like ranks of peculiar skulls.

Fulvia stood there at the room's centre. She glanced now and then demandingly at the couch, the chair, then at the stool, which had fallen over. She seemed to think she might still find her husband. She tapped her fingers on her gold bracelet. (The gold was discoloured.)

"It's what she told me," said Fulvia, frowning, concentrating. "I remember now. Her son. They disappear. And now Livius has done it."

Livilla snivelled. Parvus picked at a scab on his knee, embarrassed.

Jovus thought, *I don't know them, these people. Who are they?*

Fulvia thought she heard her elder son thinking this, but she did not care. She hated him really, her son Jovus, who had, with his birth, robbed her of sexual pleasure. Even the wretched, time-consuming Livilla had not done that. As for Parvus, what was he, some spawned thing, like a frog...?

But there had been something Fulvia meant to do. That was it. This thing had been the reason why she had rushed home from the woman's house – which woman? It did not matter the one who told her about a son who disappeared, as now Livius had.

What was it Fulvia had meant to do, been so concerned with that she had tripped over an unreal tile loose in a stair that was not there under her feet?

Fulvia turned to Jovus.

"Where is *she?*"

Fulvia wondered if she should go back to her husband's bedroom. She had not looked beneath the bed. Livius would not be there, but *she* might.

"Who?" quavered Jovus, but Fulvia saw the tiger of panic smouldering under his skin.

"The Persian – what was her name – *Roxara*."

The name sounded in the room incredibly, as though it was actual, and the only thing that could be so.

And after it there followed the most subtle, silky feather of sound, the noise something might make, uncoiling over a bough heavy with leaves.

"Ah," said Fulvia. She moved quite quickly and pulled the curtain right down from the courtyard door, and then she put her hand on Livius' desk. She took up the little knife he had always kept there. It was only a small knife, but a young woman's neck was usually slender, and the vital vein unmissable.

Yet now Jovus was in her way. Fulvia did not care enough about her son to wish to kill him, and so she only said, "Stand aside from her." Not using his name either since she had forgotten it.

But Jovus went on lumpenly standing there, between Fulvia and the slave called Roxara, who all that while had been, presumably, sitting motionless and invisible in the room's other chair.

Then Fulvia lost patience. She struck the boy across his shoulders and thrust him aside.

Fulvia herself stood then only inches from the Persian Creature. Fulvia could smell her. She did not smell human, but spicy, like mummia. Her head was not bowed. She was looking back at Fulvia with her opaque serpent-scale eyes, and Fulvia lifted the knife in a steady hand, because this Roxara's snake-neck was very slim, and the vein was plainly to be seen there.

And Jovus screamed, "*No* – no – Mother!" And punched her hand away. And he was strong after all, it felt as if he had broken Fulvia's wrist, there under her green-gold bangle.

"Leave me alone, you fool!" she cried. She was exasperated.

"No – *no*!" shrieked Jovus. "No – Mother – you can't kill her – you *mustn't* kill her. Mother – no – *look in her eyes!*"

Fulvia snarled like a wild beast. But even so, with the Creature's face so near to her, almost inadvertently, she did what he said.

Then she saw the eyes' real greenness, and then she saw through, to *within* their green. She stared. She stared into a limitless hall built of glaucous nothingness, like the depths of a sea. Here and there currents moved in it, like liquid winds, and faint glimmerings, like drowned stars. And there, too, deep down and far away inside it, and in miniature, Livius was wandering – she made him out exactly, his every detail, even to his dishevelled hair and filthy toga – her Livius, her husband. Beyond him, were some other smaller figures, farther off. She could not yet quite make them out, although they seemed, as he did, familiar to her.

---

[1]. about 11 am

[2] about 3 am

Question a Stone

About twelve miles from the city of Sincash Mahr, the inn called *The Chameleon's Arms* rose from the salty plain. Unlike the plain, or the massive mountains – so cruel and skeletal and tall – that themselves loomed about a hundred miles beyond the city, this inn was a paradise.

Once a palace, now a lodging-house of endless rooms and suites and courts, kitchens and libraries, gardens and cultivated forests, fountains, statues and secretive glades, it cost a fortune to stay there, even for one night.

But sometimes a single night is quite enough to turn a quartet of lives on their collective ear.

Amongst the weaponic admixtures of metals, those which use black iron, or red iron, are considered superior, whilst those which also employ the subtle and serpentine ore known as mercurix are both typical and unique. The natures of such blades possess quite distinctive characters. Arguably genders. Allegedly souls.

From *The Book of Swords XIV*

Talzen was tired, but hopeful. He had ridden for three days and much of the two nights between, before he came in sight of *The Chameleon's Arms*.

"There, Cinnabar," he said to his mare as they walked between the high gates. "Did you ever see a finer sight?"

The horse, with unconscious wit, shook her head, her bronzy mane catching the many lights of the inn. Talzen laughed softly and stroked her neck. She was a princess among horses, strong as a lion and far more polite.

The gates, which were heavily gilded, were covered in myriad wrought-iron depictions of chameleons. The broad avenue that ran towards the front of the inn was columned on either side by fifty-foot flame-cypresses, each like a black plume, in the well-trimmed branches of which twinkled little chameleon amulets. Beneath the trees, spaced at intervals of twenty paces, stone chameleons held up lamps. There were plenty of live examples in the grounds as well, so Talzen had heard. This was an eccentric place, worth the hardship of finding. His last employment had been both dangerous and dull, an odd combination. But it had provided enough coins that Talzen could now wallow in chameleon comforts for a whole Sincashian tlok, approximately nine days. He was in fact only planning on a qath – four. His next bout of toil lay in the city.

After dark, as now, you could just make out Sincash's own lights in the distance, a muffled glow like a fallen rosy cloud.

The mountains on the far side were a different matter. He had been looking at them for quite a while as he rode. Others had named them The Bones of Fate. They looked it carved now from the night and only sketched in white at their upper ridges with early snow. But the plain was still hot as a cauldron, and even once the sun was gone, the rough pushy breeze, strident from blowing for thousands of acres without any upright opposition, came in warm and tindery gusts, smelling of burnt grasses and scorched rock, russet dust, and the ghost of a sea long drained away into the south.

It would be good to lie in a bath for an hour, thought Talzen, with a Sincash flagon of plum qvass to hand. Then dress up and go down to a good dinner. And all the while knowing the horse was being groomed and burnished and stuffed with royal roots and oats and sweet water.

Then, just as they came into the first courtyard, with a courteous servant gliding bowing towards him, Talzen experienced a premonition. He had had them before. This one was of the usual type. A heaviness in his gut, a sense of vague physical unease, as if at the onset of a fever; a sort of momentary flicker across his vision – as though the scene had trembled, like a backdrop in some theatre far to the west.

Talzen stood still and waited. The mare, accustomed to his ways, did as he did. Perhaps half a minute passed, or a handful of seconds. Certainly, the bowing servant had only just reached him when Talzen felt the hunch lift away and fade into thin air.

He did not often have to suffer such things. Which was as well, since invariably the prediction was a true one, yet the character of the presage was never immediately revealed. Unhelpfully, it was always a simple warning, as if some spirit whispered aggravatingly in his ear, "No, I can't say *what* it is – but be *on guard*. Be wary. *Something* is about to occur."

To all appearances, Talzen was quite at ease as he spoke pleasantly to the servant – handed over Cinnabar with a list of instructions to a ready groom, tipped each man generously, and walked on into the entrance hall of the inn.

But Talzen barely saw the blue-washed walls and garnet-coloured pillars, nor the hundreds of chameleons painted or made from semi-precious materials, that covered almost every inch, including the mosaic on the floor.

Talzen's trained gaze went everywhere, unhurriedly and thoroughly, for the moment dismissing anything purely decorative.

However, ironically, when finally he spotted the Trouble of which he had just been warned, it did take a very decorative form.

The man was one of a company of five men, himself obviously their leader. Tall, straight and lean, with wide shoulders and the longest legs in the finest incised leather boots, he had hair blacker than any night and a pair of eyes the exact shade and quality of a tiger's. That he was the pivot of the foreboding was also undeniably clear. If not why.

All five strode across the foyer and off on the long walk that led a quarter of a mile to the main dining-room.

Even after they had vanished from sight, Talzen lingered by a pillar, pretending to study a small chameleon perched on a pedestal and seemingly made from a ruby, until it winked at him and turned grey as his cloak.

By the stars, thought Talzen, between amusement and alarm, *is that black-haired man the one I'm to be careful of? As if I wouldn't anyway. My God.*

With which his heart rapidly agreed, not to mention his loins, which were also determined to inform him that they, too, were now very hungry.

What a beautiful man. Handsome as a panther. Twice as dangerous, from the look of him. That sword – that's black iron and haematite – and mercurix, unless I've forgotten everything I ever knew. You don't put anything else into a scabbard of that sort, unless you're a total idiot. And he doesn't seem to be.

Inadvertently, Talzen found he had put his hand on the pommel of his own sword, which was itself of red iron and mercurix.

At this instinctive and lascivious pun, Talzen almost smiled. But he was taking no chances. Instead he followed the servant to his allotted room, and in fifteen minutes was lying naked up to his chin in water at first scalding, then as heady and relaxing as the flagon of

Tanith Lee

plum qvass he drank.

Presently, irresistibly, Talzen's thoughts turned themselves again towards the black-haired stranger. They imagined him in other circumstances and rather less formally dressed. Almost sleepily, Talzen found his hand now strayed along the lean length of his own body to the *other* sword, which like a firm-fleshed, greedy water lily was raising an inquisitive head above the lake of the bath.

Talzen reminded his thoughts of the warning. He told the ardent flower to lie down again and removed his hand from its temptation. Nor was he an idiot. He would not have survived this long at his trade of swordsman, if he had always indulged himself. And tonight he had better be sharp.

Andreis, black-haired and tiger-eyed, was not especially tired. He had, by that evening, already been lodging at *The Chameleon's Arms* for nearly two days. The work he and his men had carried out in the city of Sincash Mahr was accomplished. Remuneration had been prompt and extravagant.

The four men of Andreis's band had also decided to treat themselves at the inn, which he had gone along with, of course. They were never, except in a fight, his chosen companions.

At the inn, he had been able to spend some well-earned time by himself, nevertheless, leaving them to their normal hobbies of boozing, sex and gluttony. He spent hours in the libraries, poring over scrolls, books and manuscripts, or listening to recitals by the two-stringed cinorit and the sgy, the throat-flute. His men were due to leave after dinner tonight on another errand, travelling to the east. Andreis had therefore, with cheerful social deception, come to dine with them. He had also made private arrangements to couch, later on, with one of the inn's very appealing Honey Maidens.

Meanwhile, out in the spacious stables, his patrician stallion, Ruffian, who was the colour of black slate and with the most rare blue-grey eyes, would already, doubtless, be mating with *The Chameleon's* own chosen mare.

Andreis valued these oases in the desert of his labours. Valued them so much perhaps because aware he would, too, grow bored with an alternate overall oasis of rest and relaxation.

The entry' hall, as ever, was full of people – arrivals, departures, servants, and several live chameleons, changing their colours with sorcerous abandon and occasionally sprinting across the hall to accompanying screams of fright or wonder.

Andreis additionally noted a young man in the foyer. Though travel-worn, he was a beauty of his kind, or so Andreis judged. A thick mane of hair, the shade of some light brown, polished wood, fell to his shoulders. Something about him, a sort of swagger apparent even as he stood quite still, studying a small chameleon on a plinth, suggested he too was in the sworded trade. There was a feral female quality attendant on his youthful masculinity, though nothing at all feminine.

Andreis turned into the corridor that led to the dining-room. His men were joking and jolly. He had trained them long ago to behave themselves in decent places. Only Bracer was sometimes a problem. Andreis decided he had better keep an eye on Bracer. And so Andreis forgot the young man in the foyer, and never even considered that the sword at the young man's side was, most likely, of the best, admixed, as was Andreis's own, from two or three blended smelts of Boar Iron Steel, climaxed by mercurix.

When Talzen had bathed and put on his best clothes, which were quite impressive, he too set off on the walk that led to the dining-room. He was entranced to find the corridors wandered circuitously between inner gardened courtyards roofed by crystal, and lit with painted lanterns, galleries of statues, armour and mechanical toys, and alluringly curving staircases guarded by marble chameleons, and each ascending – but to where?

His famishment had been stayed by the qvass, and in the end curiosity got the better of him. Already able to hear the faint welcoming rumble of the dining-room, he detoured and went up the very next stair. Its curve took him swiftly from the corridor, and next out on to a flat roof of the inn. Here was another garden, with exquisitely cut shrubs and small trees in urns of sandstone and alabaster, and a fountain playing from the translucent jaws of a chalcedony dragon. It was now quite a breath-taking night. The enormous stars of the plain were wheeling with unseen motion, like giant jaspers and diamonds, from the east to the west, and even the Smoky Way was quite visible, like a colourless rainbow of ice.

As he stared appreciatively upwards, Talzen became aware of a different sound than that of splashing water and the wind-rushes of the leaves.

He had heard such noises enough times to know he disliked them.

"Honourable sir, let me go," entreated the girl. But the honourable sir failed to comply.

God above. Was there never to be peace anywhere?

Talzen did not, for a second, stir. He watched shadows and dim lights struggle in among the foliage and heard now the clank of a metal jug falling to the tiles of the roof.

At this, Talzen went forward. He parted the branches and regarded a tall, well-built man, who was holding the servant girl by her arm and her hair. It was blue-black hair and a petal-soft arm, but that was not why Talzen spoke, and extremely loudly in fact.

"Excuse me, I regret the impairment to your hearing, old man. Let me help, as you're so deaf. She asked you to LET HER GO."

The man was glaring at him. He seemed oddly familiar – had Talzen already seen him tonight?

"Flounce off," said the man.

"No," said Talzen.

He moved forward between the trees and instantly the other drew his sword from its scabbard. It was a good blade but made only of cobalt steel.

A buzzing and murmuring was audible. Some other people, until now up on the roof to watch stars or bill and coo, were clustering round to view what now went on. They had, of course, paid no heed at all to the girl's entreaty; it was a commonplace.

Talzen did not draw his sword. You did not draw a sword like Talzen's for such an impoverished little event, and thus were equipped in other ways. Talzen simply did this: slapped his right hand on the pommel to attract attention there, while shooting out his left foot to stamp down hard on the bastard's right foot; Talzen then clubbed him foursquare on the under-jaw as he leapt in the air. Down fell the unknown-known man and lay still as a bundle of bones.

Some of the watchers laughed, and a couple applauded. The poor little girl ran away. Talzen wished he might have calmed her, but she was gone.

He gave the amused audience one glance. Then he took himself back off down the stair and on towards his dinner. It was only as he entered the huge, ornate room, with its transparent ceiling and picture-painted walls, that he recollected his premonition. Trouble had been before him... it had even revealed its source. How could he have associated that oaf upstairs with such a source? Yet he should have done. For now, Talzen recalled where he had seen the oaf before, and with whom. It was not hard to do, for there across the crowded room the other was the panther with the tiger's eyes.

Ah, excrement on excrement.

"Forgive me that I must interrupt your meal," said Andreis, as he stopped beside the table. "But unfortunately, you and I have something to discuss."

Talzen looked up at him in dreary self-annoyance. Which, with a flick of expression sometimes bewildering to others, he changed to the lightest arrogance. "Pray sit. Have some wine. It's from Khavalisc. The 18th Year."

Andreis raised an eyebrow. "That won't be necessary. But I will sit." He sat.

Was ever such male grace surpassed?

Damnation, thought Talzen.

"Perhaps an apple, then? They're at perfect ripeness."

"Forgive me again," said Andreis, who had too quite a wonderful voice, "but I dislike to share food or drink with anyone I shall presently kill."

Talzen's face settled. He looked at Andreis under his long lids and with grey immovable eyes. "Go on."

"I run a company. Our business depends on public perception of our shining skills. Where this fails, compensation is needed. Upstairs on the roof, it seems, and in front of quite a throng, you set on a man of mine. You knocked him out, which made a fool of him."

"No," said Talzen. "God did that."

Andreis did not smile. Nor lose his temper. He was cool as twilight on the frozen mountains. "You'll meet me tomorrow morning at an hour convenient to us both. The gardens here are licensed for duelling. What sword do you have?"

Talzen, whose face was now like pale bronze, stood up and let the other man see the sword, where it hung concealed in its revealing advertisement of sheath.

"That's good," said Andreis. "Red iron, yes?"

"And yours is black."

"Exactly. Well suited, then."

"Suppose I refuse," said Talzen.

"I shall have someone or other drag you down, and then kill you anyway. If you discredit members of my company, you lose me my livelihood. Commercially, I'm bound to eradicate the fault. No hard feelings. It's nothing personal."

Talzen sat down again. "I have things to do tomorrow morning. It had better be the seventh hour. Then I can get on afterwards."

"You shouldn't anticipate that," said Andreis.

"You are so sure of your talent."

"None more so."

"I, unfortunately, know nothing about you."

"My name is Andreis. From Ateni, and Khinai."

"And I am..."

"I know who you are. Some of your audience upstairs were thrilled to inform me. Talzen of Bucaresa Ruman. I regret I'd never heard of you 'til then."

"'Til seven, then. If it suits you."

"It will do," said Andreis. He stood up once more. "Don't be sulky," he added, with a freezing laugh that might not be feigned. "I won't keep you long tomorrow. It will scarcely hurt."

Talzen managed to give Andreis his most gorgeous and charming smile. "It won't hurt *me* at all," he said. "I can't promise the same for you, I'm afraid."

The dining-room all about had fallen deeply silent, as some hundreds of ears were stretching, and eyes peering sidelong or over wine glasses, or into handy mirrors to get the view second-hand. Once Andreis had quit the hall, another swarm of conjectural conversations flurried up.

Looking now as sulky as he wished, Talzen drained his glass and, leaving another generous tip, left the table.

Although he swore by them continuously, he did not think he believed in any gods. Had he done so, he decided, he might have visited one of the tiny shrines and temples scattered about the grounds of *The Chameleon's Arms*. And there thrown a raw egg at the god of good luck.

Andreis climbed the longer stair to his private apartment. He had taken a suite, comprising a bedroom, two parlours and a large bathing chamber. Just as well, since now he wanted space to pace around, unseen.

He was very angry, but the anger of Andreis was generally cold. Bracer was a numbskull, and he, Andreis, should have kept a tighter rein on him, for sure. But then the dolt had only gone off to visit the latrines; for God's sake, did he need a nursemaid for that? Besides, his rank conduct – also reported by the crowd from the roof – had caused Andreis to dismiss him temporally from his duties. The other three knew better than to grumble and had ridden off on their own mission. Bracer by now, sore head and all, was on a waggon trailing back to Sincash.

Andreis ended his prowling and went to a window to gaze out on the night. It was a fine one, the sky an orchard of stars. He clearly observed the icy Smoky Way, to which twice women, and once a man, had compared Andreis himself – a cold and impossibly distant display, the heart of which might never be reached.

But Andreis was not inevitably cold. It was only a part of his armour, as, he suspected, that vivid charm and over-confidence of Talzen's might be.

How old was Talzen? Andreis believed some four or five years his junior. *And I am not old.* It was a tragedy and a bitter crime to kill a man so young and... promising.

I would rather have taken him to bed than packed him off to paradise in the morning.

Which reminded him he must now cancel the Honey Maiden also.

Soon after, Andreis stripped, laved himself with water, and darkened the lamps before he kneeled to his own gods. He *did* credit other beings, supernatural and more complex, though they would have emerged as he had, and all men, from the vast potential of a faceless, formless, all-encompassing God.

"Forgive me tomorrow's sin. It is unavoidable."

A chameleon the colour of the night perched, glittering faintly, on the window's sill. Then, as if only to demonstrate that it could, it altered in one swift tidal blush, from silver-dark to scarlet, burned there an instant like a fresh ember, then slipped away along the wall.

A female sword is often likely to be outgoing and adventurous. She is most frequently found in the keeping of a strong and masculine man and will very probably represent a number of his more secretive or aesthetic qualities, while additionally revealing some of those traits he himself has restrained. A male sword, conversely, may be flirtatious and inconsistent when not engaged in actual combat. He will often be found in company with a man whose female elements, while perhaps not overt, run parallel with his masculine side. This sword is

canny and has something to him of the magician. However, under extreme stress
he may be prone to break, if seldom physically then in some deeper and more
insidious way. It is never wise to underestimate the personality of either the male
or the female sword, nor the inner world where, partly, they always remain after
mining, smelting, casting, smithing and seething.

From *The Book of Swords* XXI

This place is not like the inn. Not like the plain either, or the mountains. There are no cities, even distant ones.

Constantly the surface of the ground moves in slow, rippling waves. Decidedly it *is* ground. It is covered by a velvety lawn of moss or unusual grass, of a scintillant blackness. This resembles, maybe, the dense short fur of a cat. Yet it is constantly in a dancerish motion, not as grass – or fur – moves in a wind, but rather as the plangent and regular, muscular movements cross a tidal lake.

Strange tall plants rise from the lake-like earth. They are inky, or of a soft pewter shade. Transparent blue crystals hang from some, and quietly chime as they stir and swim forward, backward, with the rhythm of the ground-lake.

The surface is also fairly flat. Ghostly low hills seem to contain the area in a rim of deeper blue. Above, the sky – is it sky? – is hazy, milky. It holds light, mild, and very cool.

Now and then, only noticeable if a viewer can be very quick, veins of another substance, a sort of liquid copper, seem to glisten along the smooth curved edges of the rippling ground, or to spangle a moment in the crystal buds of the plants.

Sirrib is standing on one slope of a rounded hump, perhaps a rock, staring away over the landscape. She is visible only from the waist up. She has long white, streaming, gleaming hair, the white skin of a very young woman, and large coal-black eyes. Her lips are red. She is wrapped in a kind of stole or shawl of black and silvery fibres, which describe artistically her slender but definitely female shape.

Gradually you become aware that she keeps raising to her eyes a sort of spy-glass. She scans in all directions, and this way any other watcher is able to take in the full beauty of her form, as far as it is visible, and her face. She has a passionate face, frankly. Despite the priestess-like immaculacy of her features and bearing, her perfect mouth is nearly – dare one say – greedy. Greedy in a *lovely* way; who, that has themselves any appetite, would not *desire* to be eaten by such a lovely, beautiful, ravenous rose? Imagine the perfume, and the holy pressure. But then, she is looking, not for *anyone*, but for someone. So much is evident.

Inadvertently or not, the watcher may then move about the contour of the rock. That way at last they must see plainly enough how Sirrib is herself growing up from the rock, since below her hipbones she seems embedded there. This does not impede her circling movement, but surely it must otherwise hold her in place. And she seems not to mind this imprisonment, if such even it is. In any case, the round rock also moves in constant ripples, and over them fleck tiny sequins of gilding, a serpentine highlight.

She lowers the viewing glass in both beautiful pale hands. A flock of slim, black and white birds flies over.

Sirrib shuts her eyes. She appears to sleep. And when she does this, all of her sinks slowly down into the slot in the rock. Only the platinum-blonde crown of her head is then to be noted.

Ripples of luminous tiger's-eye follow in the wake of the birds across the sky. And a mellow darkness, debatably nightfall, closes the vista.

His country is not like hers. It is all blood-ruby, brass and mahogany.

It is too, from horizon to horizon, a type of sea, certainly an enormous body of water, in which peculiar sub-aqueous creatures are in some form moving about, but in the slowest motion, like snakes indigenously active in treacle. Above, the sky may be a sunset, or a dawn. It is orange and crimson.

Flamuro himself is held in the hot, baked-to-a-cake solidness of the water, from just below his narrow hips. His torso is clad in a fabulous breastplate of brazen metal, incised with gold. His skin, where bare on face, neck, and muscular arms, is tawny as an eagle's wing. His hair is like a fire. His eyes are violet, almost purple in tone.

Flamuro too scans his world, from side to side, in all directions – if directions even exist here. He does not use a spy-glass. What he holds in his strong musician's hands is a set of pipes, each of which plays a weird and animal cry, sometimes like the fluting of a bird, or like the howl of a wolf, or the purring of a cat. He tries these sounds out, one by one, or sometimes in a chord, then waits a minute, as if listening to hear if any resonance is struck, away over the edges of the limitless and generally unmarkered sea. It seems also sometimes he thinks he can make out a reply. Then he tries that special sound again; aiming it in the exact direction as before. But in every instance, after each second attempt, he frowns slightly and gives up.

Once, once only – at least at this time – a pearly whiteness evolves and quivers through the nearly solid amber of the sea about him.

Flamuro is visible below the sea's surface only as a dark, possibly tapering pillar. A sort of merman? The pearly whiteness however, circles the dark extension of his physical presence below the lid of the sea. When this happens, he seems briefly pleased, looks down, lowers one hand into the surely-impassable syrup which, nevertheless, allows the hand to enter and – very slowly – to move. He tries to catch, or to caress, the glimmer of white, which, at his attention, flares abruptly to a lightning flash of sapphire. Then it goes out.

When this occurs, Flamuro curses. He has a voice, even if it is composed of similar sounds to those of his pipes. He seems angry, then sorry. A single starry tear that might be made of lava leaves one amaranthine eye. It drops in the sea and immediately vanishes, through being a perfect match.

The sky, if it is, is draining to mournful greyness, and suddenly Flamuro sinks straight down into the fixity of the water. Only the crown of his fiery head still shows.

Something with claws, and a lethal-looking tail, wends idly along through the sea.

A moon like yellow jade appears out of a hole in the perhaps-sky, and its light blanches everything to a blank, as darkness might have done but never does, here.

When mercurix is added into the composition of a pure sword, it will further inform the sword's nature. An occult empathy and random telepathy may then be experienced between a sword and its human keeper. But also, it has come to be thought, exclusively between certain swords. Some swords will accordingly seem to take against other weapons, though never those of inferior structure. Other blades may form between them bonds of friendship, or of the greater emotions. Several stories are recorded of such events, and of bizarre outcomes dependent on the effect. The curious sage, Solis of Zyre, when commenting on this alchemistry, claims that it is reckoned a phenomenon as unreadable as it is unpredictable. 'It has been said it would be far easier,' he tells us, 'to question a stone, for all the lesson we might gain from trying to fathom the metallurgic hearts of blades. '

From *The Book of Swords* XXE

An hour before the duel was due, Talzen woke, bathed, and otherwise prepared himself. After a light breakfast of rice and santh, he cleaned his teeth scrupulously and pared his nails. He felt miserable and had not slept well.

In the past, he had fought a number of duels. Of the ones which demanded a death. Talzen, self-evidently, had been the victor. But he disliked killing, which was either a curiosity or an obligation in a professional swordsman. On the other hand, he would, he had long ago decided, dislike *being* killed even more.

The notion of dispatching Andreis of Ateni and Khinai was dreadful. Perhaps it would be undoable, anyway.

But Talzen had also the occasional handy attribute of a swordfighter: he found it next to impossible to believe he himself could die in that manner.

Across *The Chameleon's Arms*, Andreis as well had risen and made himself ready, with the addition of certain short private religious rites and physical and mental exercises. Andreis had, by this era of his life, killed sufficiently that he accepted it as a task. He attempted only to make the act as clean as each situation allowed.

He too, however, despite all his habituation and preparedness, felt depressed.

The notion of dispatching Talzen of Bucaresa Ruman seemed wasteful and unfair. Andreis did not, though, for a split second, imagine Talzen could kill *him*. This was less a swordsman's egoistic faith than the result of a prediction given him in his youth. He had been informed he would live into old age. And from various other things also then hinted at, and which had since taken place, he credited the prophecy...when he thought of it.

As both men descended to the inn grounds, the sun contrarily was just rising. Most of their fellow guests meanwhile were already up, drinking and eating hearty snacks before filing excitedly out to witness the fracas.

Upwards of five hundred people, estimated both Talzen and Andreis, were intent on providing an audience for the show. As the swordsmen walked out, by separate doors, onto the sandy paths among the glades, they were aware also of another crowd, this bundled up on the inn roofs, and looking down eagerly through telescopes.

The sky had been lavishly polished and broomed by the night wind, now fallen quiet. Birds trilled throughout the gardens. Many miles away, the mountains were barely to be seen, moltenly absorbed into the apricot east. Chameleons sat or clung on tree limbs, or the white arms of statues, but the chameleons, like the mountains, had copied carefully the colours of everything proximitous, and unlike the energised crowd, they went for the most part unseen.

The duelling ground was a wide-open area, kept always mown and clear. It was surrounded by low flowering shrubs, which would obscure nothing of what went on. At the south end of the patch was a soapstone image of the Sincashian god of justice, who was represented as discouragingly eyeless, and besides lying down as if asleep. To the north stood an altar to all-gods, available to any worshipper, a kind gesture for anyone who might want to offer a quick one to some personal deity. Neither Talzen nor Andreis even glanced at these icons.

The sun of course was still low and would get in both their eyes from time to time. Then again, it would not be directly overhead, scalding down and splashing on the blades at every twist and turn. Each man had fought in enough inconvenient spots and awkward lights, he scarcely bothered with the sun's angle.

One of the inn clerks ran up with a paper tablet for both to sign. This would safeguard the corpse's property for any heir. Andreis signed a signature of bold simplicity; Talzen a signature of flamboyant unreadableness.

At that, one of the inn's intercessory priests appeared and spoke a brief prayer to grant one or other protagonist reasonable judgement beyond death and/or alive following his successful kill.

Virtually everyone murmured the closing response, as politely did Andreis. Talzen only unnecessarily inspected his faultless nails.

The crowd withdrew to the margins of the open space. It had become the Field of the Duel. A deafening silence fell.

Even the birds, suddenly alarmed by something or perhaps having seen such matches before, disapproved and took off *en masse* like a shower of upward-tending, feathery hail.

With an obsidian rasp, both men drew from their scabbards their wonderful metallurgical weapons.

The sun, the day, time – the world – stood still.

Could anyone then look at anything save the naked blades? They were each like a searing flame or coal shot from the sun's core. One was black as death, one red as hell, and both visibly singing with mysterious inner rays, ambered on the black, lapis lazulied on the red. Who would doubt such swords could ever now be sheathed, until one at least had tasted the blood of a living heart?

Before that second, neither man had fully looked, today, at the other. Now, turning face-on, they must.

Talzen felt every bone in his body change to a liquid like red-hot qvass. It was not fear. *I am in love with him*, he thought, incredulous and horrified. *What can I do? I can't kill him – must I then let him kill me instead?*

Andreis felt his heart flinch inside him. This was not fear either. He thought, *can it be I want this man more than I want my reputation? Do I have to call off this bloody farce of a duel, and make myself a laughing-stock worse than that dunderer Bracer?*

"Yes," he said, half aloud, cold as the southern continents.

"Yes," said Talzen, bleak as northern winters.

Any who heard the joint avowal took it for an oath of properly murderous intention. The audience itself went severally pale or dark or flushed with vicarious fear. It was a sacred if dire moment. Unmissable.

And what the audience had obviously relied on to happen next, next happened.

Both combatants were seen to raise their sword-arms, and leap together across the open turf.

Talzen thought: *No – what am I doing...?*

Andreis thought: *I never meant to run at him...*

Each thought: *The blade has come alive in my grasp...*

Never ever before, through all their battles elsewhere, light or treacherous, threatening only or entirely merciless, had either man felt such vitality, such literal *life* in the sword he used. Now indeed, the blade used *him*. He had, for the first time – Andreis and Talzen equally – no control over any movement. It was the *sword* in each case which moved. Which *chose* to move. Nor could he let go of the fiery serpent, tusked iron and volcanic steel and quicksilver, that flared and lurched and *struck...*

They *struck* together, both blades, like clashing planets, they *struck* and veered away and roared with a soundless noise that was like an avalanche, or a great chunk of the sky that fell – and swung at each other and struck *again* and struck *again...*

Later the bystanders, some of them, declared they had been

quite startled at this barbaric and ultra-powerful mode of combat. They had expected the more playful finesse, the sallies and retorts and ripostes and tricks and nicks, which fine swordsmen generally utilized. But this, in its way, they must admit, was deeply engaging.

The air was sizzling and ringing, as if it were a glass bell being struck over and over from within, spinning and echoing, though never giving way.

Certain of the ladies and gentlemen fainted. Others felt drunk out of all proportion to any inebriant taken at breakfast.

On every tree or statue, had anyone noticed, the chameleons too were blazing like bits of the sun, ruby and jet, sapphire and topaz.

And the swords *struck*.

Now they *struck* like stars.

And then, in one cawing and coruscating wheel, blindingly they became a single *erupting thing* – which flew off on its own, sloughing the duelists so they staggered, and only a practiced athlete's balance saved them both from plummeting headlong.

There on the field of death, the sword of Talzen, *Flamuro*, and the sword of Andreis, *Sirrib*, plunged together into the ground. Which shook.

The irradiation and the swarms of sparks showering off, made complete accuracy of view difficult. Yet most or all present saw, and ever after swore they had, each sword, though still a metal blade, take on also the distinct likeness of a beautiful, partly-human but mostly spirituous creature. *She* was white and *he* was gold. That much seen, the rest was not in *any* doubt. Mouth to mouth, breast to breast, clawing and clinging, writhing and arching and calling like entities from some other far-off melodic yet blood-wringingly uncanny sphere, they were *coupling*. They were making the most willingly violent and gloriously will-less love. They were in congress. The sexual act. They were in paradise-on-earth.

How long coitus continued, very few persons were able to estimate. It seemed to last an hour at least...only the gods knew. But subsequent orgasm lasted, or so one scholar stated – if some years afterwards – for at least seven minutes by the shadow-track on a nearby sundial.

It was naturally, that climax, like a lightning strike. People believed they had been incinerated, and understandably shrieked. But no one was harmed. In fact, quantities later claimed assorted ailments had been cured, or a lost tooth grown back, such items.

As for the swords, they had seemed dissolved in the colossal light, and in the bellow of sound that *made* no sound. Then when the brilliance faded, there they lay side by side on the turf, not even dented, straight and still, lovely and unliving. Wonderfully fashioned inanimate objects of an ordinary and everyday world.

"Will I ever draw that – that *creature* again? How can I?"

"Neither of us knows. Maybe not. Or, maybe we can do nothing else. We'll nostalgically recall, won't we, Talzen, how their infamous lust brought us together here."

"In your luxurious bed. My God, Andreis, you must be rich as the King of Pazt, to rent a suite."

"And you only want me for my money."

"Oh, I *want* you. No, my turn for that."

"Be my guest. Like this?"

"Gods of fire... yes. Exactly – like..."

The day, begun in flame, but not blood, had gone on in flame.

They had picked themselves up, these two handsome men, from the place where they had, metaphorically at least, fallen on the field. They walked back, a couple of feet apart, courteously fending off the hysteric crowd, and each with his particular miscreant sword now firmly once more ensconced in its – her – his – sheath. No sooner up here in Andreis's opulent rooms than both unbuckled the swords and dropped them in a corner. Admittedly side by side. And then anyway other clothing unbuckled and undone, and scrambling on to the bed, or wherever first they came together – where *had* it been? Ah, yes, over there. Odds on, they were not the only couple to have been galvanised by the sorcerous dueted orgy seen in the gardens. Who cared? It had been of the best.

And no stigma now, no need to fight to a death. A miracle had occurred. Not the most stringently commercially-minded swordsman in the Six Hemispheres could argue with that. No one lost face. Only the impediments of garments and procrastination.

"I suppose you'll be off tomorrow," said Talzen, after a further suitable interval of ecstatic exercise. "Off you will go. I'll never see you again. Just as well," he added, "I have no time – for this."

Andreis held him close enough for comfort. "I should have killed you, shouldn't I?"

"You have, my prince. You've stabbed and run me through more times than I can reckon. *And* killed me. Ah. The bliss of death."

"And likewise, you returned the compliment," said Andreis, adding with a mocking paternity, "my boy."

Days come and go. As do nights. Sleep makes demands and cannot be gainsaid. Even swords who, over vast distances both temporal and ethereal, telepathically meet and desire each other; even swords who manoeuvre their so-called 'keepers' into random action and related duels, in order blades can meet, mingle, meld and mate – even swords sleep sometimes, albeit, where feasible, side by side.

But when Talzen woke next midday, his lover, and his lover's sword, were gone. Talzen and his were alone.

They made their peace, as old friends usually must. By evening, sore but stoical, Talzen made on to Sincash Mahr. He noted as they went that his mare, Cinnabar, was relaxed and mysteriously smug, and was glad for her. He would try to be glad for Andreis, too, for Andreis's freedom – since Andreis would forget soon, of course.

And Andreis himself all this while, thoughtful and slightly melancholy, his own weapon secure at his side, rode the sleek stallion Ruffian towards the east.

Nothing is forever. But then, forever, possibly, is also nothing.

The sage, Solis of Zyre, near the end of his treatise, however, adds that the questioning of a stone is, in actuality, not entirely foolish. He points out that any piece of stone, when closely studied by magnification, will render up certain truths. These may involve, through revealed strata, the ages of the earth, or even minerals, some valuable, or tiny fossils enfolded there.

Once, he claims to have found in a stone, the pristine mummified footprint of an ancient beast, now extinct. 'Stones,' he adds teasingly, 'are sometimes worth an inquisition.'

From: *The Book of Swords* XZ

From a letter by Andreis of Khinai
To Talzen of Bucaresa:

And so I shall be journeying back across the plain in about a month. It would be a pleasure, and much more than this, to see you again, Talzen, at *The Chameleon's Arms* – I trust you'll permit me the honour of taking care of all finances during the visit?

I admit I have some hopes you'll still be in the region.

Having only recently learned my devil of a stallion, Ruffian, ignoring a pre-arranged tryst, instead possessed your charming and acquiescent mare, when last we all stayed at the inn. She'll be in foal. They always are. A nuisance for you, but I can promise the result will be a stunning horse. We might sell it, or rear it ourselves, what do you think?

On the other hand, I *can't* promise you faithfulness, my boy. Nor you me, I believe. Maybe we can promise each other something. For the sake of the horses, not to mention the swords, which will be pining to renew their acquaintance. Not for ourselves, obviously, never that.

While you wait for me, count all the chameleons. They say there are over three thousand. Tell me the total when we're together. It will help us pass all those long, tedious nights.

Andreis, yours.

The Three Brides of Hamid Dar

Now there was a beggar, the son of a beggar, who would each day take up his post under the date tree by the Well of the Wall. His name was Hamid-Dar, and he would tell a tale of himself in his youth to which, it was said, even the Caliph had once listened, although of course in disguise.

As a young man Hamid-Dar, who was lame, had yet been very comely, and for this reason now and then certain adventures had befallen him. One morning, as he was at his usual trade, leaning upon his staff by the Wall Well, a covered litter approached, borne by four slaves of a black that was almost blue. And out of the litter as it passed had slipped a fair female hand coiled with bracelets and rings, and this let drop at Hamid-Dar's two feet, the strong and the lame, a bag of that which clinked.

Can it be, thought Hamid-Dar, bending to pick up the bag, *that I am summoned again to visit the wife of the silk merchant? Surely that litter was not hers? Perhaps it is the spice merchant's widow's sister, of whom I have heard stories, but whom I have never yet met.* And with mixed feelings he took the bag and, assuring his fellow beggars that it contained only some nuts and figs, (their unripe hardness causing the rattle it had made), he went away to examine it.

On opening, the bag divulged several coins, and these of gold, so Hamid-Dar was amazed. Next he found a little parchment, which read as follows: "The astrologers inform us, to all men, high and low, Fate awards great chances. But they must be risked. Come then, if you will, to the House of the Black Doors, as soon as the evening star has risen."

Now then, thought Hamid-Dar, *this is one of whom I have never heard.*

And he went straight away to the bathhouse and the barber's and had himself prepared there like a dish for a queen's supper.

At the proper time Hamid-Dar found for himself the appropriate building, for he had been earnestly inquiring for it all afternoon. *The House of the Black Doors* lay in an elder quarter of the city, an area reckoned by some to be of ill-repute. But Hamid-Dar had no fear, for all his life he had prospered by courage and foolhardiness.

There was an ancient archway, partly ruined, and beyond stood the house, with its three black doors instantly visible, but not a window to be seen. And there on the roof like a polished diamond perched the evening star.

Hamid-Dar made so bold as to go immediately to the middle of the three doors and knock there. At once the door flew open. Inside was a dimness and a darkness. Hamid-Dar paused at it, and as he did, he made out the porter who had let him in. This was a monkey in a coat and a turban of scarlet. Bowing low, the creature beckoned the beggar youth to follow, and scampered away through the house.

Hamid-Dar made no further delay, but went after it, and quickly too, seeing it travelled so fast. Until, led only by the glimmer of the red coat and turban, he came out into an open court that had no other door, but all about on a gallery many blind windows.

The monkey had vanished, and the sky above was laden with night. A second time Hamid-Dar paused, and now he wondered. But before he could decide, a voice called down from the windows above: "If you are Hamid-Dar the beggar, then be welcome."

"I am Hamid-Dar," said Hamid-Dar, "and I am of the profession of beggary."

"That is well," rejoined the voice, "but answer also this. Are you ready to take your chance with Fate?"

Hamid-Dar looked up and about but could see no one.

Nevertheless, the voice was that of a young woman, very musical and very sweet.

"I should not have come here otherwise," he declared.

"That too is well," said the musical sweet voice. And then there came a strange rustling and scraping. And suddenly there fell down something from the sky and covered Hamid-Dar and cast him on his knees. And when he tried to do battle with this something, it rolled him up and pulled him over headlong, and presently he was trussed crown to toes in a net of metal mesh. He gave vent then to some complaints, but on this occasion no one replied. Only the monkey frolicked over him and batted him with its tail, gibbering.

Then the net was hauled up and swung off into terrible space, and Hamid-Dar tumbling and crying with it. Up into the stars it seemed to go, and as it did so, whether by desire or oversight, his brow was dashed against a corner of the house and for a while he knew no more.

In his childhood, some three or four times, Hamid-Dar had journeyed with his father along the roads that led out from the city gates upon the desert. Therefore, the scent of the desert and the pressure of its enormous silence, which contains all sounds like seeds within a jar, were known to him. And waking from his daze in a moving darkness, yet Hamid-Dar knew instantly where he must be.

Now this is some trick and I do not care for it, thought the young man, *and though I am lame, let me remember I have one leg and two arms and my wits.* And he braced himself for what might come next, while giving no clue to his captors that he had roused.

The net was gone, and instead he lay inside a litter such as a rich woman might employ – and indeed perhaps it was that very litter from which the fair hand had let drop the fatal message, for it had a pleasing perfume. The rocking of the litter gave him to believe that the bearers advanced at a steady trot and were those same four Nubians he had seen previously.

After perhaps an hour, the progressive motion slowed. Hamid-Dar heard, in the vast silence of the desert, the bearers begin to converse as they paced onward.

"Our mistress Zulima," said one, "has put a burden on us, setting us to carry out this troublous deed alone. Suppose we are discovered? For what we do is unlawful, to abduct this fellow and bear him to her secret home in the desert. And she has only to say, 'I know nothing of it,' and we shall be burned and hacked, and may be hanged, for we are only her slaves."

And another said, "Besides, the desert is large, and we might mistake the way. Lions may find us, or some evil spirit that lurks here."

"And say then," said a third, "the litter is found. Who will find our poor bones, picked clean by demons and jackals?"

Then the fourth Nubian spoke, and he said this: "But if we were to cast down the litter and flee, there is no one here to gainsay or prevent us, or to pursue and catch and punish us. And possibly we may come to the river and a boat, or to a camp of brigands who will succour us for our strength, and we may live then as free men do, and *spit* upon the city."

At that, all motion stopped.

There followed a long wait, during which no word was said. And then abruptly Hamid-Dar discovered himself in a falling litter that crashed him bruisingly to the earth. And as he lay among these bruises, he heard the eight blue-black feet of the Nubians loping off as fast as they might go…

When all noise of them had faded, Hamid-Dar came from the litter and looked about.

The moon had risen and bloomed high like a white lily on the lake of night. All around, beneath the moon and the sky, lay the wilderness, her changeable hills and valley of sand, and not a single other thing in sight, not a road or a rock, but only the footprints of the slaves who had run away, and even these sinking and powdering over as the little breeze of night erased them.

"Now am I lost," said Hamid-Dar.

But presently, he saw how the moon moved into the west, and that the footprints of the Nubians, when they had carried the litter, had tended to the opposite direction, the east. Hamid-Dar resolved he would continue their course, having no other, and turning his back to the moon, set off. "For do they not say, he that seeks in the desert will always find something, even be it only his own death." And since he was young, Hamid-Dar did not yet properly believe in death.

Hamid-Dar walked a long while, leaning on his staff, which had been left to him, and the moon at his back sinking. Now and then he heard a jackal singing out among the dunes, but he had no other company.

At last there began to be a lightness in the dark before him, and Hamid-Dar knew a touch of fear, for once the sun rose, his chance and risk would be great indeed. But a moment after, coming over a rounded slope in the sand, he beheld before him a rocky defile, and there, on its far side, not a mile off, an edifice that looked to be a house carved out of the cliff, with a stairway and a large black door above.

Another black door, is it? thought Hamid-Dar. *Well, they were to bring me to her secret house, they said, those wretches, the desert home of Zulima.*

And just then the sky took orange fire and the edge of the sun began to slit the horizon like a sword. Plying his stick, Hamid-Dar hastened down into the defile, and into the shade of the rock, and made toward the architecture and the doorway like a man on urgent business.

The stair he climbed with difficulty and some curses, and reached the door, which was immense, in anger. For he wished very much now to confront Zulima and demand some recompense. Thus he smote the bastion with more yet than his usual bravado. It responded by giving off a terrific clanging, such as made him stagger, while from the caves about a storm of bats shot forth and whirled around in fright before they sank down again into the dark. Thereafter Hamid-Dar waited several minutes, but even he did not knock again.

At length, a voice spoke to him, from somewhere I above. It was not the voice of the city court, being masculine and greatly amplified, yet also *whispering*, so he did not like it.

"Who knocks?"

"It is I," said Hamid-Dar fiercely, although he must nerve himself to it.

"Who is I?"

"In that case, it is yourself," said Hamid-Dar.

"Cease stupid games," sizzled the voice. "Tell me your name, and your purpose here, for clearly you have one."

"I am arrived at the invitation of the Lady Zulima, who has treated me poorly as does not befit her, nor myself."

"Zulima, you say? For what does she want you?"

"That is not my place to guess."

Then the unnice voice gave an awful laugh. "You shall come in and meet with your Zulima. Only be patient."

Hamid-Dar prudently sat down, and endured the sun, which now came over the top of the cliff to gaze at him with burning curiosity.

When the better part of an hour had elapsed, and Hamid-Dar was debating deeply on cups and pots and entire caldrons of water, the voice broke out again.

"Are you yet here?"

"As you see."

"Then you shall enter."

No sooner were the words uttered than the massive door shuddered and ground slowly open. Hamid-Dar stared this time into a cavern of blackness, but it was cool, and the sun had not claimed it, and he stumbled in.

He was not twenty paces inside before the door once again closed itself up, and at that a lamp began to come towards Hamid-Dar, borne by a tall and burly man dressed oddly for a steward, and carrying in his other hand a pitcher.

"I beg you," said Hamid-Dar, "for the love and common passion of God, if that is water allow me to drink."

"It is not water, but drink you may," said the steward. And he gave Hamid-Dar the pitcher with a glare for relish.

Hamid-Dar drank. The liquid was wine. But though had seldom tasted it, now he could not refrain, so raged his thirst.

"I am required to ask of you," said the steward, fingering at his belt an enormous knife, "If you are acquainted with the Lady Zulima, and know her appearance."

Hamid-Dar perceived in this a test. He said, "As she is aware, I do not know her."

"The greater your joy, then," said the steward with a loathsome snarl, "when that you look on her. Come follow." And he went off again the way he had approached and Hamid-Dar after him, lamenting now on the night's wreck of his anointing and barbering more than on his righteous wrath.

Up many granite stairs in the dark they went, detailed only by the steward's lamp, and came at last into a smoky stone cubicle lit by half a dozen torches. This did not resemble a lady's chamber, but Hamid-Dar took heart, seeing that the space was divided off at one end by a fretted screen.

"I have brought the rogue. Here he stands," announced the steward to the screen.

Then over its top was seen a fan, beckoning Hamid-Dar nearer.

He advanced with a sudden misgiving.

When he was three steps away the screen split and parted, and there before him on a stone chair sat…

"The Lady Zulima!"

At the steward's roar, Hamid-Dar deemed it wise to abase himself. Glancing up again, his first dismay was thoroughly confirmed.

The Lady Zulima was a giantess. Though seated, she gave evidence of being more than six feet tall. Besides she was both fat and brawny. However, from her bulk, which was swathed in brindled silk, protruded two hairy and bulbous arms, wreathed with quantities of bracelets of gold and precious stones. Sapphires and carnelians blazed on uncouth fingers having nails of uneven length, but hennaed red. Her feet, mercifully, were hidden by her swathed skirts, and her face by a thick veil. Yet upon her head was a headdress sewn all over with sequins of silver and gold, on which flawless large pearls dripped like rain from a flower. All these things Hamid-Dar saw and noted. And with his dismay became mingled a doubting avarice which nevertheless quailed. Plainly, the summoner by the Well of the Wall had been only a servant of this monstrous apparition – yet even she had been adorned like a princess. Such wealth in the mistress was not to be taken lightly. Yet neither was the lady's girth and hirsute complexion, when coupled to her presumably amorous intentions.

And now she spoke.

"Pray draw nearer, gentle visitor," cheeped the Lady Zulima, in a high and extraordinary tone, somewhat between the falsetto of a donkey and the twittering of a goat. "And tell me, charming youth, why it is that you have sought me."

"Madam," said Hamid-Dar, thinking the horror was perhaps bashful – as she had some cause to be… "it is your own message, and your own gift, which invited me. And your own slaves who captured me in a net, and your own Nubian bearers who brought me here, or partly so, for I was abandoned in the desert by them and might well have perished. Yet Fate conducted me after all to your door."

"But tell me, pray, what can have been my wish, that I invited you?" scrape-tweeted the lady.

"That, madam, I dare not conjecture."

"Conceivably my weak and sinful sex," girlishly brayed Zulima, "have drawn you before in secret to their houses, and there tempted you to dalliance."

"This has happened," admitted Hamid-Dar, with genuine reluctance.

"For shame!" screech-chirped the fearsome lady. "But still, come closer yet. For if that is what you suspect of me, how can I escape blame? Thus perchance we may dally a little, pretending you are my lover, and I your blushing and timorous bride."

Hamid-Dar would at that instant gladly have found himself elsewhere, it is probable even upon the desert's burning-glass. But it seemed to him, without turning to be certain, that other men had come into the chamber at his back, and stood there as the steward had done, hand to knife. And meanwhile, the Lady Zulima was stretching out her hairy hands, tickling his cheek playfully with her fan, and seizing him by the shoulder in a grip of Damascus steel.

"A little dalliance, so-lovely one, let us have," she coaxed, hauling Hamid-Dar upon her bulky lap. And as he sprawled there, to his ultimate alarm, he found she had taken him by the neck. In a much-different voice now she bellowed: "What? Do you chance, you puny squit, to breach the cavern of *Hashan, the Thief of Thieves?* Who sent you? How have you dared? I will have answers to these questions of mine. Go down and view my treasure, and there you will meet those who will move your tongue to chat!"

And Hamid-Dar had scarcely the time to realise that the Lady Zulima was in fact a huge man, with a huge man's voice and a huge man's fist, than up were raised the skirts of brindle silk and there were too a huge man's two huge feet in two huge boots that stamped twice on the stone under the chair. And at once the stone opened, and below gaped a glittering pit, and into this the man's brawny, hairy arms hurtled Hamid-Dar with a final hugely-booted kick for good luck.

No sooner had the unfortunate beggar landed, and that hard among spiked and jagged items, than a gang of frothing bandits leapt upon him and dragged him up.

"See, son of a she-gnat, what jewels have been amassed by Hashan, the Thief of Thieves. See, for these may be the last sights your eyes shall look on."

Hamid-Dar struggled and begged for pity, sternly reminding the robbers that God had better eyesight than he and missed not a single deed.

"You have only to reveal your true purpose in arriving here," staunchly maintained the robbers. "Speak the truth, and our lord will be kind."

"But I have told the truth already!"

"Thus! To the wheel with him! Heat up the oil and irons."

And in this way Hamid-Dar was propelled between towering hills of rubies and emeralds, by inland seas of pearls, through forests of golden things and wastes of silver, to a deep chamber hung with hooks and pincers and lit by the flare of fire.

For several hours did Hamid-Dar suffer in the torture-vault of Hashan, the Thief of Thieves. In pure verity, none of the greater inflictions were used on him; here the robber band contented itself with promise and description. Nevertheless, they did him some harm not only to the mind and spirit, and when at last they took him from his chains he was barely conscious and mostly beyond reason.

In his dinning ears then were breathed these words: "Get you hence, for we too are pious, and would not have your death charged to us by God. It seems from your mewing you are a fool that happened here by mischance and not design. Therefore, we free you. Take with you those scars and hurts we have given as tokens of what worse thing will befall you should you ever return to the treasure-house of our Lord Hashan."

And after that Hamid-Dar was flung some miles away upon the cruel sands and lay there in his pain until the lidless eye of the sun went down, and the cool of the night walked over the desert, and brushed his battered body with her dusky hand.

"What now?" inquired Hamid-Dar of the evening. "For what have I deserved this injustice?" cried Hamid-Dar to the dunes. "Here am I, who have lived only by my bravery, taken in a trap, scourged and blistered, and lost in the wilderness as before. To this the Lady Zulima, whoever she may be, has brought me, may God hear my plaint."

Soon enough though, Hamid-Dar rose to his feet and set off in an easterly direction, limping and sometimes falling down, but having no other direction.

There is in the desert, by day or night, a sweet odour that surpasses all others, even the oil of roses or the vapour of. olibanum. And this odour is that of the oasis.

To Hamid-Dar the fragrance ascended, like a water-smoke, and he turned toward it in delirium. Before the dawn, yet after the moon had sailed beneath the world, he stepped upon a carpet of sand that was sown with grass, and up to a shore bladed with wild reeds. And here lay the sky in a mirror, and he plunged in his face, and when he lifted his head, he saw below the tall palms that grew with their fronds in the earth and their trunks upholding heaven and the stars like fishes under his fingers.

There was no other present but for a slender snake that sipped from the water as daintily as a cat. But looking beyond the trees, Hamid-Dar thought he saw a dismal low building.

"Now what is that?" said Hamid-Dar, not cheered, for it looked to him mostly like a tomb. "Whatever else," he added, "it is not the sought-for secret house of Zulima, the unknown seductress. I cannot be deceived a second time."

Then he drank again, and on lifting his head started violently. For before him stood a man in clothes of fine quality and having three gems in his turban.

"Peace," said this man, although he spoke with a strange accent, as of a foreigner. "You are wrong in what you say."

"What have I said?" asked Hamid-Dar cautiously.

"If you seek the house of Zulima," said the man, "be sure, there it lies before you."

Hamid-Dar got to his feet, the sound and the lame, and leaned on his staff which the robbers had left him, and inwardly bemoaned the wounds they had also left, "This lady gifted me in the city and invited me to come," said Hamid-Dar, "but her slaves abandoned me and her service, and since then I have been set on and sorely hurt."

"Come then to the house of Zulima," said the man. "You shall be cared for. But you must enter at your own will. My mistress cannot command."

"How far is the house of which you speak?"

"Why, it is there."

Hamid-Dar looked where the servant pointed, and he saw in the mysterious aqueous half-light before dawn, that there was a magnificent palace beyond the palms. That he taken it for some derelict tomb a minute earlier surprised him, but he supposed his faintness and the twilight bemused.

If that is the house of Zulima, thought Hamid-Dar, *then after all Fate has not been malign.*

The palace rested in a garden of flowering trees, where fountains played. At the door two damsels like slim pale moons came to assist the traveller. He was welcomed in and conducted to a splendid chamber where, in a bath of brass, abrasions were soothed. He was cleansed and consoled, and presently they brought him a suit of clothing fit, so he imagined, for a caliph. And then he was served a delicious repast, to the strains of most eloquent music.

Finally, the servant of the jewelled turban entered and bowed low. He inquired if everything had been to Hamid-Dar's satisfaction, and Hamid-Dar assured him that it had.

"Then, if you will, the Lady Zulima patiently awaits your presence."

Hamid-Dar, feeling not merely restored but remade into twice the man he had ever been, hurried to follow the servant to his lady's private apartment. On every side were riches beyond hope, and all set out with such charm and taste that they nearly caused the young man to weep. Soon they reached a doorway of marble into which was set a door of palm-wood ornamented with gold.

"You have only to knock upon the door," said the servant. "At her entreaty, you have only to go in." And this mentioned, he bowed himself away with a stately gliding tread.

Hamid-Dar knocked upon the door, employing customary force. At once a dulcet voice replied: "If you will, enter!"

Hamid-Dar thrust at the door, which slid wide, and he stepped over the threshold into a chamber that reduced all the other teeming glories of the palace to a shadow-show.

At the marvel's core, on a couch of crimson satin, there reclined a maiden of such beauty that Hamid-Dar, on some deep abacus of the brain, commenced to count his blessings. She was dressed in garments whose colour and texture could not be divined, they were so thickly covered by work of gold and silver, and at her waist was a girdle that blossomed with tawny topaz and green jade. At her throat and wrists were rings of gold torched by rubies and cinnabar. Her lustrous hair, which was blacker than ebony, was also barely to be seen, being woven with hyacinths and beryls and hung with silver pomegranates. Between her eyes, which were large and wonderful themselves as two agates, hung a yellow pearl bigger than a pigeon's egg. Her countenance was not veiled and might have put out the moon. She had a train of golden stuff that quite hid her lower limbs and her feet, although there was a footstool under it that was a tortoise made all of one solid emerald. Hamid-Dar threw himself upon his face.

"Rise up, bold traveller," said the Lady Zulima, in her harp-song voice, that had too its trace of foreignness – in her, most fascinating. "For you have journeyed far and endured much, to visit me."

"That I cannot deny," said Hamid-Dar, arising. "And although I take all now in equal part, I am sorry you saw fit to capture me in a net, to dash my skull against a corner of your city house, and to entrust me to four slaves who basely, at a whim, threw me down in the desert, where I next fell among thieves who tricked and almost slew me."

"And is this so?" asked the Lady Zulima, and she smiled a clandestine smile behind her jewelled fingers, and at this Hamid-Dar could truly find no fault with her. "But now you are here with me, at your own will, and have partaken of my hospitality."

"Which hospitality outshines the sun at noon," decreed Hamid-Dar. And he noticed then that her feet under the train of gold gave a little twitch upon the tortoise footstool of a whole emerald.

"Come nearer, dear traveller," said the Lady Zulima. "I am parched for your companionship. Come nearer, as the bridegroom approaches, tenderly, his bride."

And Hamid-Dar, as he went forward, saw that again the feet and limbs of his hostess twitched rather vigorously under her golden train. And he thought, *how eager she is to caress me*! and went to take another swift step. But unexpectedly something checked him, and he could not have said what it was, but he found he stared at the footstool, and at the train.

Then Zulima said, in a most enticing way that sounded like silk rippling across pieces of money, "Why do you hesitate, bold man? Will you not risk me? I am only a woman and can command you to nothing. You must steal upon me and bend me to your wish."

These words stirred Hamid-Dar, and he took the swift step he had meant to take, which brought him almost to her couch. But in the middle of the step, Zulima smiled at him, and her exquisite teeth glittered, and something about them made him check once more, although immediately she hid her lips with her ringed hand, and he was confused, for it almost appeared to him that every stone upon her hand was *pointed*... And in this puzzling moment, being lame, Hamid-Dar stumbled and lost his footing, and his staff slewed in his grasp and with a fearful thwack it struck the footstool and sent it spinning.

As the great emerald went, so did the train of gold. It sloughed away and unveiled the lady's feet. And when it did this, Hamid-Dar perceived that she did not have, under the edge of her skirt, any feet at all, but the enormous rounded scaled yellow tail of a serpent.

"May God and his angels defend a hapless sinner!" screamed Hamid-Dar and turned rapidly to leave.

The Lady Zulima sprang upright on her couch, and her skirts now tore right off, and there she was, a woman with the lower body of a snake, who reached after him with hungry claws, and snapped with her pointed fangs, and flickered her thin black tongue. "Foul morsel, return to me. It is my due. Have I not nurtured you? Have you not come to me of your own accord? Return, you joint, and let me feed upon your flesh, for it is many months since such a nourishing dinner entered my house."

Hamid-Dar, as he rushed toward the door, looked back once and saw that the serpent woman was clad in grave-clothes thick with dung-beetles, and at her throat and on her arms and in her hair were tangled asps with glowing eyes, and scorpions, and spiders, and human bones. While it was the grave-stone that had lain where her feet should have rested. Just in this way were also the riches of the house, which, as he sped and clamoured through it, proved to be nothing other than that it had first seemed, a ruinous tomb. And as for the bath and the supper and the music, they did not bear thinking of. Nor was there space to do it, for as he plunged by, the servants of the snake woman, themselves now in their proper shape of snakes, and one of these with three eyes in its head, lunged and hissed at him and tried to throttle, trip, and bite him. But though lame, Hamid-Dar recalled he had one good leg and two arms and his staff and his wits, none of which commodities had they. And he won into the outer air alive and burst into the oasis shrieking and reviling all the earth and all the things that God had set upon it.

Nor did he slow his limping and hopping flight, nor cease his blasphemies, until he was far off and the sun – for time had been impeded in the serpent's house – rose from the desert's rim.

Perhaps prevented by the onset of sunrise, the snake demons had not hunted Hamid-Dar, and as the day scorched on, he saw nothing of them, nor much of anything. He found, after an onerous walk, a rock, and there he stowed himself in the shade.

"What an unfortunate am I," said Hamid-Dar. "And what has brought me to this state? Why, a woman, may God heap miseries upon her."

Nevertheless, the bath and the ointments and the food given him in the serpent's house, (though they did not bear thinking of), had done him an amount of good. He resolved that he would sleep until the sunset, resuming his trek at night. For although he had lost all his luck, yet he was not dead, and did not believe that death awaited him. Therefore, some other thing would come his way. But he had no aim to be duped a third time.

At sunset he rose and rejected the eastern path, to walk along beside the sun, into the south. For surely, the city might lie in that direction.

His shadow went beside him, and the sand turned blood red, and then the sun became a gilded dome, and next a band of scarlet, and eventually was gone. Then the wind, the breath of night, blew over the desert. The stars came from their doors, and on his other hand appeared the moon.

"What woman is there on the earth," said Hamid-Dar, "that can compare with the beauty of the world?" And later, as the moon stole up the sky, he said, "What cash can I buy anything so fair as God's night?" And later still, he murmured, "It is to know these truths that holy men wander into the waste." But it began to be chill, and Hamid-Dar began to be weary, and then he said, "I am not happy with my lot, nor have I been dealt with justly."

Less than a minute after, Hamid-Dar came over a high dune, and below beheld a strand of river, blue-white as lapis in the moonlight.

"God be praised," said Hamid-Dar. For now he could find his way to the city, nor would he thirst.

It was as Hamid-Dar climbed down toward the river that he noticed a house built among gardens near the water's brink. Such was the appearance of this edifice, being dilapidated and decayed, and haunted by noisy owls, that Hamid-Dar was quickly alert.

Sure enough, no sooner had he got within a hundred paces of the spot, than out of the broken gate there raced a pair of muscular men who, bounding up, suddenly accosted him.

"So be it," said Hamid-Dar to himself. But aloud he said in a whining tone, "Can it be at last I have reached the secret home of the beauteous Zulima?"

At this the two men exchanged curious glances, then the larger of the two seemed to recollect himself, and grinning, he bowed low. "Just as you say, *Zulima's* house."

"And I," said Hamid-Dar modestly, "am Hamid-Dar, a poor beggar, upon whom the unprecedented favour of your mistress has fallen. But I have been lost in the desert and undergone there many irksome trials."

"Oh, if you are *Hamid-Dar*, proceed at once with us, to the house, where our lady has been pining for you."

"Be it so," avowed Hamid-Dar to himself, and put a firm grip upon his staff. But at the men he fawningly smiled and declared they might lead him.

Thus he was escorted down into the garden, where the owls peered and muttered ill of him in their own tongue, and next through an unhinged door, and across some sunken passages and empty rooms into a small chamber.

Here, upon a wooden stool, sat the form of a woman, though

she was heavily veiled, both face and hair, and clad with no richness, her long plain skirts covering her lower person and her feet in a manner that caused Hamid-Dar to tighten further his grim grip on the staff.

"Madam," exclaimed the escort, "here is he that you have sought. Hamid-Dar! And he has called you by name already as the Lady Zulima."

The veiled head was inclined, and in a soft voice the lady thanked her servants and permitted them to depart.

When they were gone, she seemed to peruse the beggar carefully through her veil. At length she said, "Since you are here and name me, I am encouraged, and will allow you to step closer."

"My thanks," said Hamid-Dar. "First let me acquaint you with my adventures." And then he recited them, the netting and stunning, the throwing by Nubians, the assaulting by Hashan, the events of the serpent's house and the flight from the serpent woman here. "Therefore," finished Hamid-Dar, "I have learnt a thing or two. And now, O vile demon or felon, whichever or both you are, do not suppose I am to be made a mock of three times. No indeed, it is in this hour that I shall take revenge for all the wrongs awarded me." And that said, he pounced upon her. He ripped her veil and her skirts and would have taken his staff to her, but she, screaming, gave him such a push that being lame and weary, he toppled down. Next the two servant men rushed in and got hold of him in a savage way. Hamid-Dar looked up from the earth in fury, and he saw standing before him, with one foot behind the other, a handsome young woman wearing a necklace of diamonds at her throat which the veiling had concealed, and some fabulous gold work in her shining hair likewise.

"Beast of a man," cried she, "my monkey has more courtesy and sense. How am I humiliated, nor do I deserve better for my rashness." Then she added to her servants, "Take him from my view and beat the wretch. But render him too the story I have entrusted to you. For it is my correct reward that he should gossip of me, that my shame should never end."

This uttered, she turned her face from Hamid-Dar, and the servants pulled him away into a court, where they surely beat him, and very grievously, with rods. And that done, when he was barely sensible, they rendered him the story of their mistress.

Zulima had been from her birth, though fair, lame in one foot, and for this reason, having no male kindred living to protect her, she despaired of marriage with one of her own station or fortune. Having heard of the comely and clever beggar, Hamid-Dar, she bethought herself that all men are made by God, and this one might consent to matrimony, seeing he would understand her disability, and would also gain considerably thereby. She accordingly decided to test both his bravery and his integrity. She had him abducted from a deserted house, intending that he should be delivered to her, knowing nothing of her, neither her name nor her status. For the meeting she chose a dilapidated mansion in the wilderness. Here she would plead that the money she had sent him as her gift, and her few garments and jewels, were her only dowry, along with the decaying manse and two or three servants. She would then ask if he would take her for herself, unveiling her feet, her face, and her diamonds, in mathematical order only as she had judged his responses.

When Hamid-Dar did not arrive, Zulima was at a loss, and in distress, wondering what fate had overtaken her possible bridegroom. At her order her servants quartered the sands for him, but when Hamid-Dar strayed to her very walls it seemed God had attended to her prayers. Naturally her servants recognised the young man, since they had been searching for one of his description, although they had been disturbed he already had learnt their lady's name, such was her hope of secrecy.

Alas, it is a fact she would have wed him if he had behaved one part graciously before her and given over her delightful person and her considerable wealth to his care. But this chance Hamid-Dar had now precipitately cancelled. And as he crawled lamenting toward the city, from the house by the river, Hamid-Dar, striped by blows and broken of heart, could only exalt the peerless omnipotence of Fate.

This then is the tale of Hamid-Dar the beggar, which he told of his youth, by the Well of the Wall. Its meanings are many and each must sift them as he may, and act upon them or discount them as he wishes. For there are only two constant truths in all the universe: That man is a dunce of great wit, a wise and wily fool. And there is no God but God.

A Tower of Arkrondurl

Alas, poor ghost!
From 'Hamlet' – *Shakespeare*

1

He had been dead so long, the Sorcerer, here. Yet the tower, tall and iron-grim, was still deeply feared and scrupulously avoided.

To come into that region therefore was to discover no human conurbation, not a single human dwelling, for miles. The woods flocked over the rise and fall of the land. But these even seemed empty of animal life or birds. Once he saw a white owl cleave the twilight with its wide-winged passage. Before suddenly it veered aside again. But the sun shone by day, and by night the stars; the moon rose, though she was thin as a nail's edge with waning. The moon... one second he allowed himself to dream of *her* – candlelight on amber hair – then closed the dream away.

Cyveth's horse was tired by now, the seventy-seventh evening of this particular trek. Tiredness was not unreasonable. Not only must the horse support Cyveth, but his personal baggage, which included a sealed casket heavily containing one of the reasons for the journey. When the horse spontaneously stopped, Cyveth allowed this. He looked out across the dusken countryside. Below lay a valley, already mostly smoored in shadows. Bridging the gap, a broad stone causeway stretched with, at its farthest end, a tower.

Cyveth recognised the tower at once. Aside from all else, he had been told of it throughout his current ride north. They had spoken, those that did, in forthright bursts, or in whispers, of Arkrondurl the Sorcerer. It was as if they *must* speak of him. As if to speak about him, one way or another, was like uttering a prayer, or – now and then – vomiting. Since these procedures relieved them, if only for a little while.

For minutes, or hours, they recounted his supernatural cruelties and murders, his evil games and horrendous raping scourges. Nothing they said of him was good. Nor ever dull. A new if freelance vocabulary had required to be coined in order to illustrate what he had done. The occasionally extraordinary descriptions had always made an implacable sense. By the time anyone, and certainly one such as Cyveth, reached this causeway and looked across at this tower, he must have become a *scholar* of Arkrondurl.

And Arkrondurl was *dead*. While, according to every muttered or shouted sentence, rumour, tale or inadvertent proof – the one-eyed man three days before, the *three*-legged man a month ago – death had only briefly interrupted, and then transfigured, the malevolent concentration of the Sorcerer. Flesh and blood he might no longer be, but intransigently vile and inexorably powerful he had remained.

Bats flickered now over the hills, like the paling-darkening blink of sudden eyes.

Cyveth dismounted, heaved off as much of his luggage as was needed, and left his well-versed horse to stand at ease. He crossed the causeway alone and on foot.

Beneath the tower he did pause to stare up at it, and saw with no surprise it was still, despite the intervention of decades, in full repair.

As he pushed open the metallic door, its hinges hardly creaking, he noted that after all, there were no living bats in the upper air. It was merely some disturbance of the dying light.

2

For things were not always what they seemed.

Cyveth had learned that years before. His father had been a magician of some ability, who used his talents mostly to entertain the crowds for money, or to process cures for illness or injury – generally also to make a living, but sometimes unpaid, from compassion. If ever Cyveth's father had committed any wrong act through his gift, Cyveth never either saw or subsequently heard of it.

Even so, there had been others in that trade. The tall thin man, for example, known as the Waspion. Or the shorter, plumper man known only as *Myself*. What *they* had done, or were said to have done here and there, was in itself a lesson, both in wickedness – and the human knack for uncovering it and awarding it great publicity.

Yet there had been warm and multi-starry nights in those southern regions of the past, times seated in the open, or in various secluded dens. And then the magical miracles were wrought – the horse which flew on the wings of a swan, the girl who walked – and danced – though the rock fall had broken her back twenty days before.

Sorcery was not only for villainy, or for gain and show.

Nor was the reality of the world formed from granite, merely *seemed* to be. The world's reality was *malleable*. And death, of course, was not the *end*.

3

Inside the tower was a hollow gut of stone, out of which a stone stair hauled itself upward into an overhanging stony enclosure that hid it. The coming of night was hiding it too, draping long thick curtains of shadow, veil by veil...

Lugging his essential gear, Cyveth took the stair and climbed into utter black.

But he was counting now. Formerly it had been on the thirty-third (twice), the seventy-seventh (five times), the ninety-ninth (once) step that a response took place. Not, however, here.

Moving on to the hundredth stair Cyveth nevertheless hesitated. Remarkably strong and well-conditioned, he was not yet either weary or winded. But a sensation – less caution than expectancy – caused him to halt. Despite this no reaction came. The tower felt empty – not of sentient occupancy, but of the presiding *unlife*, the un*dead*.

Presently, Cyveth resumed the climb. A hundred and one, a hundred and two, a hundred and *three*...?

And something *rolled* across his feet.

It failed to stagger him, physically or mentally. The ever-awareness of a number three, seven or nine in the equation could never be lost on the son of a magician.

The stair itself moved, then. It swung smoothly along and to the side, bearing him, primed and balanced, with it, and so into another wide gulp of open stony space. Which, as Cyveth was borne in on the magic stone carpet, bloomed up into ghoulish, greenish visibility.

Corpse-lights, the kind to haunt marshes, blossomed on all sides. They illumined like verdigris a high vault and the mathematics carved into it, the meanings of which were partly translatable by the visitor. Strange pillars, like misshapen limbs fossilised to basalt, strained up to support, or only clutch at, the ceiling. On the vacant floor was scattered a vague yet ominous type of dust, marked with indecipherable tracks, very narrow and broken, and always dimming out before they reached anywhere – or indeed before they had *come* from anywhere.

Cyveth jumped off the stair. He dropped his luggage on the dusty floor. It did not matter. If he succeeded, he would bear it out with him again. If he failed, he and it would simply remain to blend with the rest of the filth.

Along with all the other disparate training he had received, Cyveth had learned, from childhood, an actor's resonant and controlled voice.

"Greetings, if you are present, peerless and mighty Mage-Lord, Arkrondurl of the Towers."

Nothing stirred. Cyveth had not anticipated it would. As an actor, this was not the first and only time he had given such a performance. And though the setting of the stage might vary, the other leading actor must normally arrive on cue, despite the fact his *timing* was his own to choose. It was a law of sorcery as much as the theatre.

The curtains of gloom and gris green parted.

The master performer entered, from nowhere, and the silence rang with its deaf applause.

"Who speaks?" he inquired.

"I."

"I do not know you," said Arkrondurl the Sorcerer.

And Cyveth sighed. It was the only indication, infinitely misinterpretable, that an iota of his tension had left him.

"How," he said, "*should* you know me, Lord? I am nothing. While your golden name is fame itself."

Vanity. Playing to it might – did – often work. Fairly infallibly. And did so now.

"True," affirmed the hellish ghost. And flexing his long-fingered, pallid hands, Arkrondurl spun a brief episode of showy lightning round the space. "Yet, I am a revenant only. What need you fear?"

Cat and mouse then, it seemed. Not quite unknown...

"I have heard the stories, Lord."

"Have you. *All?*"

"I have heard enough to freeze my heart and turn my bones to powder."

"And even so," said the Sorcerer, "you are *here*. Do you wish to become, yourself, a *story?*"

Cyveth laughed softly. "Perhaps."

Arkrondurl's long, pale face, intellectual and severe, ugly in its aesthetic elegance, terrifying in the sour and sadistic cant of lips and fleer of toneless eyes, now gelling in a kind of – pleasure?

Cyveth said, "For a nonentity such as myself, Lord, glory can only come through service to a far more dynamic being."

"Which being could that be?" (This was like verbal fencing with a flighty girl.)

"None other than yourself, inestimable Sorcerer."

"Let me show you," said the ghost, "a few small pictures; past events that have gone on here in my tower, as at other times in others of my towers. There are nine in all. Did you know this?"

"Oh yes, my Lord."

"It seems you have studied me like a book. It shall be your reward to learn a little more. See, then."

The lightning roiled again, and in the ropes of it, vivid and sudden, awful scenes splashed up in fragments, like splintered panes of coloured glass, each spiteful and foul enough to tear any eyes that looked on them, men and women – children – were caught inside the broken pieces; human creatures that suffered torture and obscenity beyond (beneath) description, and struggled, shrieked and died, in adverse tints, to a music of sounds that, in their turn, rent the hollows of a listening ear. Another man would have crumpled, puked, swooned; maybe died too. But Cyveth, if sufficiently white now to rival the ghost's bleached visage, stayed upright, motionless and quiet. He watched all, attentively. Although, of course, as with so much else, he had seen such stuff more than once before.

4

Nine – the number of the unholy lives of Arkrondurl. And the number of his towers, built, unalike yet siblings, and dotted all about the north and eastern map of the earth. In woods or a forest you would find them, on hillsides, as here, on mountaintops, on a tiny isle that stood up from a lake, on a rock that had set its foot deep into an open sea. One, so it was said, (and so at last it had been found to be), rose underground, far down in a cavern, where neither night nor day ever came – and glad perhaps they were to be excluded.

How he made the nine towers was easily comprehended: through sorcery. And in them, one by one, his nine separate mortal lives had followed each other, after certain accidents – when he had overreached his own perfidious cunning, or Fate, as once or twice it had, sent a hero wise and swift enough to tackle and destroy him. Through his nine lives, Arkrondurl, returning, had persisted on every occasion (until once more slain) in unspeakable power and ungrace. The whole span had amounted to three centuries. But then there followed his *alternative* existence, as exemplified tonight. A *ghost*. It was, always, a phantom in which the perverse and soulless expertise and sagacity remained, if anything enhanced by non-corporeality. His ghostly practices, they said, (they did not lie), exceeded those encompassed by him when simply living.

How had Arkrondurl managed, post mortem, to linger in the world?

They said, again, and some believed them, that no god at all would let *that* spirit through the gate of Otherlife. And even the demons of the icy pits of hell refused him. Only the long-suffering world, it seemed, had no say. And so he lodged on with her, abusing, as ever, his domicile, nor needing any more to pay the rent. A squatter unworthy of the name, as also of the name of man.

The stories and their trappings had been absorbed by Cyveth years prior to the evening of this call upon the ninth tower. He had heard tell of all of it and been at a loss. Until he learned, elsewhere, a mystery – which was itself the second half to another, the first portion being already known to him. Both were benign, though doubtless prodigious – and according to the majority of sources blasphemous and unforgiveable.

Till that second knowledge, the question had gone unanswered, the demand as to how to destroy a ghost, when exorcism, (it had been tried with Arkrondurl so many ghastly times), had fearsomely failed.

For could there be any alternate way to render back to death that non-sentient being that would not, *did* not die? You could not rob the dead – of *life*.

5

The show of moving pictures was done.

Arkrondurl poised, another pillar – this one of poisonous salt amid obliging shadows.

"Well. And did you like what you saw?" The relentless voice probing, turgid with pride and satisfaction.

"Lord, whatever you see fit to do, in *my* eyes, has the gleam of gold and the brilliance of diamond. In my eyes, Lord – the only sin is to *deny* you."

Not all the self-in-love were blind. Arkrondurl, it would seem, had been, and was. Impassive and flaunting as a peacock he waited there, evidently grasping the idea that a gift was to be offered.

"My Lord," said Cyveth, "will you permit me to assist you?"

"*You.*" Arkrondurl laughed. "You... to assist – myself."

"In the most fundamental and servile manner, Lord. Solely that. May I detail my plan?"

"Amuse me. Do so."

Cyveth bowed low. And obeyed.

How many performances had he given in this role? Was he confident? – as much so as any fine and tempered actor. Was he *word perfect*? Oh yes.

6

It was the Waspion who had disclosed the first secret to him. Cyveth, then just sixteen, and always curious, and – sometimes to a foolhardy degree – eager to learn, had risked half a day in the Waspion's uncomfortable company in order to be educated. Cyveth had also worked out a strategy with the Waspion, as with others one was ill-advised to trust. Cyveth pretended that he had only a slight talent in the magical arts. He could perform the odd crowd-pleasing trick but had no aptitude for much else. In this way he had been shown, and so picked up, quite a number of skills. Then again, Cyveth was abstemious in their use. Magic both fascinated and perturbed him. As with fire, it could keep you warm and improve your diet, but you stopped short generally of burning down the house.

The Waspion was prone to drunkenness. He revealed the terrifying formula of the spell under the influence of black wine and red brandy. If afterwards he recalled what he had done, he did not allude to it, nor did Cyveth give any indication, let alone demonstration, of having found out anything unusual he could copy.

Of course, also it had been obvious the gambit involved two processes. One could not be fulfilled without the other. The second and perhaps most needful of these Cyveth set himself to master some years further on. And that had been when first Cyveth heard of the Sorcerer Arkrondurl, his nine towers and nine lives and the enduringly indestructible problem of his ghost.

7

"Behold, Lord. Here in this box…"

The casket, about half the length of a donkey's back and the width only of a man's arm, lay out now on the dust. It was very plain, and its clasps of inferior steel had not yet been released.

(The ghost stood watching adamantly enough.)

Cyveth clicked his tongue – once, twice, three times.

The clasps scraped rustily from their sockets, the lid reared up, and fell back on the floor with a clatter.

"What is that?"

Did the great Sorcerer not know? Surely – no, no. He did not.

"It is, inimitable sir, a man. Or, the body of a man in miniature. May I invite you, Lord, to examine it?"

"Why should I trouble?"

"Because, Lord, it might be worth your while. I could not dare suggest it otherwise."

For a moment, nothing. And then Arkrondurl gliding forward, gazing down.

Though less than the size of a year-old infant, the male figure in the casket was in every and all ways adultly in proportion, and perfect. Had it been full-grown in stature and girth, plainly it must have been a figure of more than seven feet in height, wide-shouldered and lean of pelvis, muscular and formed – not well but *flawlessly* – with a complexion like fine bronze, hair black as death's river, and – for the eyelids stayed open – silver-eyed. So Arkrondurl had been, in youth, they said, at least in his colouring. The heroic and beautiful stature here possible was never his, except in illusion, through sorcery. The face too, no mistake – even at doll size – was that of an Arkrondurl not only young, and physically without fault, but of exceptional handsomeness. No mote of the sadistic, the debased or rotten had infected any aspect. Few women, or come to that few men, would look unmoved on such a sunrise of mortal gorgeousness.

"Very pretty," said the Sorcerer. His offhand tone would deceive only the most obtuse or silly. "But what does it *do*?"

Cyveth, showman, actor, trickster, mage, quietly and reverently told him.

"First, Lord, through my lesser and far subordinate art, I can make it grow to its full height and dimensions, strength and virility. Then, also through the one other huge secret I have learned, I will open it to receive your lifeforce, and your colossal intelligence. Beside which, my own meagre craft, or that of most, is like a sigh to a sound of thunder."

Arkrondurl turned on Cyveth then the blaze of his awful eyes. No more were they silver, but – a *nothingness*. Some colours were spectres never even born.

"And then – I shall live... in the flesh once more?"

Inside the voice was there the vaguest childish tremor? Or not? Who could tell? *Cyveth* could. He had, before, unforgettably, heard these giveaways.

"You will live, my Lord," said Cyveth passionately and fiercely, "not merely as in the flesh you did, but to the extreme capacity your power, your genius and your knowledge deserve and have merited. So, lesser men must die to please you? Let them make room – make room for *choicer* men. You have *earned* this renewal, exalted master. *Let me serve you.*"

Only then did Arkrondurl toss towards him one slightly, playfully questioning look. "And your own reward?"

Cyveth laughed. "To live in legend. The wolf in shadow – blotted out – yet *there*. A mere human – who gave Arkrondurl back his life."

"You will be cursed. Perhaps sought and destroyed."

Cyveth shrugged. "But *not* forgotten."

It was now Arkrondurl who truly laughed. Inevitably, a repulsive noise. "Or *I* may kill you. You will know too much."

Cyveth lowered his eyes, (another falsely modest and flirtatious maiden). "Let us see," he said. And lifted the creature free of the casket.

8

Making the spell was, once the technique had been gained, comparatively straightforward, even rapid. And by now Cyveth was well-versed; he had performed it several times before. (The construction of the mortal receptacle – the miniaturised male figure – took far longer and was an act of many scenes, every version involving thirty-three days and nights. As with the ordinary miracle of conception, the creature must be securely planted and next grown, but this inside an alchemic crystalline womb, the nature of which was so bizarre it had, on each venture, startled Cyveth afresh.) But *now* – the spell was activated…

The quickness with which the figure expanded was epic. Within three minutes it had grown to the size of a twelve-year-old child. In three more it had achieved the fully-proportioned height and girth of a statuesque male deity. From its head the thick river of hair poured out. Within its open eyes moisture glittered; its lips parted to reveal the white and polished teeth of a healthy man some twenty years of age. By the ninth minute all was complete. If perfection had been merely obvious before, now it was overwhelming.

A god would *not* be shamed to put on such a physical garment.

Cyveth did not glance towards the Sorcerer. Cyveth, by now, had slight doubt as to Arkrondurl's reaction.

But when Arkrondurl spoke, the greedy lust anyway dripped from his voice. "Yes," he said. "I will inhabit that. Never fear, I shall reward you. Now get on – make haste. *Rehouse* me."

Cyveth gave a cry of acquiescence.

He rushed to obey.

And as he drew, in palest light, the necessary arcane symbols on the ground, the walls, the air, and sprinkled there from pouches needful tinctures, smokes, sands, Cyveth held his own racing brain in check. The only danger in these final moments was that he might after all, though never before had he done so during the past teem of years, make some mistake. Less from carelessness than over-familiarity…

Far off in his mind as he worked, he glimpsed the sections of Arkrondurl's prologue. The heroes with swords who had come to slay the Sorcerer while he *lived*, some successful, most not. And the exorcists who had, all of them, failed. And the countless innocents and undeservers who had perished. And time itself. And eventually a hero who was not any such thing and his deed that, for the major part, could not earn him fame or lasting glory, being too unglamorous, and too subject to repetition. Or, seen another way, potentially too doomed, too *un*conclusive. For *this* 'hero' (Cyveth), was as yet young, and strong. But later… later… What then?

In the seventieth minute of his being with Arkrondurl, Cyveth grew still.

"Great Lord, all is prepared. There are three seconds of passage. In the first you will vanish. In the next you will enter he that waits to assist your avatar. In the third you will be within his envelope of flesh, anchored as any living man in his mortal frame. You will be *him*, and he – will be yourself. Your vehicle and your kingdom. Live long, and to the most entire scope you may, unsurpassable Lord, in this well-earned and apposite mortal life."

Arkrondurl, like a grinning scar on the grizzled sheen of the tower. An image made only the more disgusting by duplication.

And then the two words spoken.

The showman and trickster missing nothing, getting all right, as he must, and always had. Again word perfect. All perfect. Perfection.

A flash of flame, like that of an exploding star. Searing brightness, tumbling dark. Soundless cacophony. The deafening quiet.

Cyveth turned, slow and stiff as an ancient a hundred years of age. The ghost of the Sorcerer was gone. On the floor, the beautiful and full-grown man was stirring.

Wrapped in his own half-paralysis of horror, Cyveth watched, breath stopped, heart shuddering, all eyes.

A god, re-bodied, rising up in returning vitality, flexing and smiling, laughing as a lion roars – *No*. Not that. Instead – the creature on the ground – was writhing, rolling, foaming at the lips, its eyes wide and wild, noises spewing from its throat and nostrils, hands clawing – and now all of it, a composite chaos, leaping to its feet and at once falling down again, crawling, sprawling, mewling and screeching – slamming its handsome flawless skull against the stony wall over and over.

Cyveth swept up his magician's luggage, the emptied casket with it. A hero with a sword? The baggage Cyveth carried, *that* was Cyveth's sword.

Springing past the howling slathering mad thing, which did not somehow seem to see him, Cyveth reached the steps, jumped a perceived gap, and pelted down them. As he descended the length of the tower of Arkrondurl and sprang out through the doors on to the causeway, the mindless outcry echoed on and on behind him, inside the stone. And while Cyveth ran back across the causeway under the star-prickled night, the notes of torment and despair continued, if anything more loud. The godlike body was strong. It could support an incredible amount, as it would be required to. Like the tower, the creature had been built to last.

Safely returned to the woodland on the causeway's far side, Cyveth found his horse. It was staring at the tower sidelong, less in fear than in a disapproving recognition. Which again was not unreasonable. Like Cyveth, this horse had witnessed eight times already an identical tumult.

Cyveth spoke the finishing word, the third of the spell – there must always be three (or seven, or nine).

Despite the lack of light – the starved moon was hiding in the trees – anyone might notice a peculiar change occur then to the tower. It appeared to have grown – solid. That was, solid all through, as if the mass of stone had knitted suddenly internally together. Not a window now or door, facing out. Inside, no staircase or space or vault or ceiling, no smallest hole or crack. A block of granite only. With, somewhere inside, locked, packed, trapped, the tortured and wailing new-gained body of the Sorcerer Arkrondurl, and the lifeforce of Arkrondurl. Which was in turn, doubly held, in body and in tower, *both*. It went without saying, had Arkrondurl been as he *had* been, flesh or ghost, he could have smashed instantly any prison, stone or flesh, to pieces. But Arkrondurl was not, *now*, as he had been. Why not?

As a living man, able once to be born and thereafter to return himself to life – if only eight further times – his ability had been virtually infinite. And as a ghost, his powers stayed incorrigible and supreme. Since the lifeforce, disembodied, and keeping still its personality, retained unimpaired the will and acumen of its physical former brain. If next this non-corporeal but vital force were reinvested in an unoccupied but viable fleshly form, it would at once control the new physical brain it had inherited. However.

9

As he rode the horse, at a regular yet peaceful pace, back towards the distant south, Cyveth allowed himself (at last, at last) thoughts of home.

Certain family members still lived there, in the mild warm lands, among the orchards and the vines, under a yellower sun and those nocturnal stars, burning thick as meadow flowers, and held up only by the low brown mountains and the faith of men. But he thought of *her*, too, free to do so (at last) – or for a while. She was the young woman he would marry. A year his senior, tall and slender, with hair like an amber waterfall. *Myself*, the other untrustworthy magician Cyveth had known in youth, had foretold such a lover and been proved, that once, honest and correct. Three future sons had been promised too, born without trouble, lucky and bold. Whether they might inherit showman's gifts, and the knack of learning sufficient magic, *Myself* had never said. Cyveth must trust that one at least would do. Or, failing this, that Cyveth might *find* another boy able and prepared to serve an apprenticeship, and, when Cyveth had grown old and lost the flair, who would agree to take on Cyveth's unavoidable, repetitive task. For of course, one could not lie to oneself, someone would have to do it.

While he lived and had his strength, Cyveth might well be called on to do it all again. And again. It might only be one single time, but he doubted that. It would be at least three times. Or seven. Or, once more, the full set of nine. Just as for the past many years he had done it, and ended only here, with the ninth tower visited, and the ninth undead version of Arkrondurl confined to his total internment. Again.

How to destroy the deathless undead? Make them *alive*. Yet an aliveness with a proviso.

Despite its faultless beauty, the alchemically-fashioned male human body that had so lured – and captured – the ghost inside it, was in fact imperfect: it contained one invisible but pertinent omission. *A brain*. Certainly, some of the vestiges of the organ were present, enough to allow consciousness, a type of sight, and of vocality, gesture and movement – but these nevertheless active only in their most crass and fundamentally useless capacity. Presumably the Sorcerer would have essayed some check of the creature, as it lay tantalisingly on offer before him, but any supernatural scan he had tried had been satisfied. For sure, he would have noted workable heart and lungs, stomach and other intimate inner areas, a skeleton and muscles of flexibility and endurance. For the brain, however, there was only a facsimilous shell equipped with feeble rudiments, a wheelless cart that no mind, small or great, could cause to move one inch. But it had fooled him, that self-enamoured monster, his evil genius *blinded* by self to all reality. So sure he was of the flawless case into which he was about to be poured – for he credited only his own ultimate triumph. And in he went, and behind him the door of flesh was slammed. And there Arkrondurl found himself, trapped in a body where he could enjoy no single second of sorcerous power, let alone individual governance. He would be now like any human thing whose brain and mind no longer functioned. While remaining always *mindlessly* aware, *mindlessly* awake, helpless, hopeless. Howling.

And the body was otherwise so healthy and virile. It could live for ten decades or more – unless, as had three times happened, in his transports of agonised physical uncontrol, the Sorcerer should accidentally kill it. Then, out the ghost would seethe again. Nor only one ghost, for like his lives there were nine of them, one for each tower.

These nine ghosts never remembered, it seemed, anything of Cyveth – nothing of the trickster who had promised ideal rebodyment and glory, and instead condemned to hell-on-earth. Brainless, they had not kept the memory. And therefore Cyveth had been enabled to return and spring the cage again. (Cyveth, travelling these paths over, months and miles, listening to the gossipings of nightmare all heard before... Cyveth the jailor, himself perhaps also condemned – to his quest, forever.)

Or not forever. When old, weakened and exhausted – then his son, or some adopted heir, would take on the leading role. Three times, seven times, nine. Over and over, over and ever, for Hell's pit would not accept Arkrondurl and any sweeter Otherworlds were shut. Earth must imprison him, and men of earth, the men of Cyveth's line, see to the business.

Cyveth, riding south through the sun-petalled days, the high-roofed full-mooned nights, wondered how eventually he could come to tell his son about the quest and that he too would, ever after, be shackled to it. And Cyveth grasped it would be far harder, this telling, than going to see a tower of Arkrondurl and risking there everything in order to save the world. But he would do that, too. For though they mostly do not wish to, with no choice all mortal men one day must die. And perhaps, although this also they do not always wish, must return to life again.

Two Lions, a Witch and the War-Robe

To come on the apparently unguarded forest city of Cashloria was often a surprise, since it lay, as its name implied, deep in one of the vast ancient forests of Trosp. Enormous pines, cedars, beeches, oaks, poplars, and other trees towered up, for hundreds of miles. A single wide road, in places rather overgrown, eccentrically bisected the area. Once night began, the city was quite arresting. Then its thousands of lamp-lit windows, many with stained glass, blazed in slices between the trunks. Huge old stone mansions, public halls, and various fortresses appeared, but all smothered in among the forest, with trees growing everywhere about them, in some cases out of the stonework itself. In the narrow central valley to which the road eventually descended, where lay the city's hub, ran the thrashing River Ca, along which only the most courageous water-traffic ventured, and that in the calm of summer.

It was now fall. The forest had clothed itself in scarlet, copper, magenta, black, and gold. Audible from a day's ride away, the Ca roared angrily with pre-freeze melt-snow from distant mountains. Sunset dropped screaming red on the horizon and went out, and utter darkness closed its wings.

Zire the Scholar had been traveling a long while. He was weary and aggrieved. Yesterday, forest brigands had set on him and stolen his horse. Though naturally he had tracked and tricked them and stolen it back, the horse next cast a shoe, so now both of them must plod.

As night gathered and he spotted the lights of Cashloria, Zire gave a grunt of relief. He had read of the city over a year before, and set out to see it along with others, but during the last hour doubted he would find it at all. Benign unhuman guardians were supposed to take care of the conurbation, for example by protecting it with sorcery rather than city walls. This evening Zire had begun to think they had also rendered the place invisible. But lights shone. Here he was.

Zire was young and tall, and well-made. His hair was, where light revealed it, the rich sombre red of the dying beech leaves. His eyes were the cold grey of approaching winter skies. His spirit was not dissimilar: fires vied with melancholy, exuberance with introversion.

Presently, the young man reached a promontory, thick with trees and pillared buildings. Below, the landscape tumbled down, still clad in darkling foliage, roofs, and windows of ruby and jade, to a coil of the angry river. A few lights also marked the river's course, but mainly it was made obvious by its uproar. They said, in Cashloria – or so Zire had read – "The Ca is foul-mouthed and always shouting."

Nevertheless, here was an inn, by name *The Plucked Dragon*.

Lanterns burned, and Zire, having tethered his horse, and maneuvered through a hedge of willows, thrust in at the door.

At once a loud outcry resounded, after which total silence enveloped the smoky yellow-lit room beyond. It was not that the several customers had reacted in astonishment on seeing a newcomer; they were reasonably used to visitors in Cashloria. It was simply that, during the exact moment Zire stepped into the inn, a man standing at the long counter had swung about and plunged his knife between the ribs of another. Everyone, Zire included, watched in inevitable awe as the knife's unlucky recipient dropped dead on the ground.

The murderer, however, only wiped his blade on a sleeve, sheathed the weapon, and turned to regard the landlord. "Fetch me another jug, you pig. Then clear that up," jerking his thumb over-shoulder to indicate the corpse.

He was, the murderer, a burly fellow, with dark locks hanging over a flat low brow. He wore a guardsman's uniform of leather and studs, with a gaudy insignia of two crossed swords surmounted by a diadem. Certainly, no one argued with him. Here rushed an inn-boy with a brimming jug, and there went the landlord himself with another inn-boy, hauling the dead body off along the floor and out the back. Even the third man, on whose sleeve the murderer had wiped his knife – not, presumably, wishing to soil his own – made no complaint.

"Cheers and a hale life!" cried the killer and downed a large cupful in one gulp.

All present, with the exception of Zire, echoed the toast in fast fellowship. And some of them added, for good measure, "And hale life to you, *too*, Razibond!"

"Yes, long life. That dolt had it coming to him."

Razibond, satisfied, belched. Then his small eyes slid straight to Zire, still poised in the doorway. Those little eyes might just as well have been two more greasy blades. If looks could kill, they might.

"And *you*," said Razibond. "What do *you* say, Copper-Nod?"

"I?" Zire smiled and shrugged. "About what?"

"Oh, you're blind, then, as well as carrot-mopped. Come, let's have your opinion. You saw I slew him."

"That? True, I did see."

"You seem offended," said Razibond, ugly voice now sinking to an uglier growl. "Want to make something of it, eh?"

If Zire had been in any doubt as to what Razibond meant, further evidence was instantly supplied, as all the other drinkers withdrew in haste, plastering themselves to the walls, some even crawling beneath the long tables. Even the fire crouched down abruptly on the wide hearth, while the girl who had been tending a roast there sprinted up the inn stair with a flash of bare white feet.

"*Well?*" bellowed ugly Razibond, seemingly further incensed by Zire's speechlessness.

"Really," said Zire, "what you do is your own affair. After all, perhaps the man you stabbed had done you some terrible wrong."

"He had," Razibond declared. "He refused me use of his wife and daughter."

"Or, on the other hand," continued Zire smoothly, "you are, as I suspected, merely a drunken thug who throws his weight about, that being considerable since he is now running to podge, and slaughters at random. One day, you will answer in the afterlife, to an uproar of furious ghosts. Don't think I joke there, friend Razi. Another life exists than this one, and we pay our dues once we are in it. I imagine your reckoning will be both long and tedious, not to mention painful."

Razibond's face was now a marvellous study for any student of the human mood. It had passed through the blank pink of shock to the crimson of wrath, sunk a second in superstitious, uneasy yellow, before escalating into an extraordinary puce – a hue that would have assured any dye-maker a fortune, had he been able to reproduce it. More than this, Razibond had swollen up like a toad. He cast his wine cup to the ground, where it shattered, being unwisely made of clay, and, disdaining his knife, heaved out a cleaverish blade some four feet long.

Zire raised his eyes to heaven, or the ceiling. Next instant, he, too, had drawn a sword, this one fine almost as a wand, and going by the name of Scribe. As Razibond lumbered at him, Zire moved, easy as smoke, from his path, extending as he did so a booted foot. This brief gesture sent the homicidal guardsman crashing, at which Zire leapt onto his back, landing with deliberate heaviness and knocking the breath right out of him. Then, with a casualness truly awful to behold, Zire drove his own bright sword straight in, through Razibond's leathers, skin, flesh, muscle, and heart. Blood spurted like a fountain and decorated the blackened beam above.

At the inn once more, only silence held sway. Zire did not wipe the sword; he kept it ready in one hand. He looked contritely about at the stricken faces.

"My apologies," said Zire. "But I object to dying at this late hour. I would prefer supper. Oh, and my horse needs shoeing. Otherwise, if you want, we can continue the violence."

No one answered. None moved. The landlord himself, who had ducked below his counter then re-emerged to witness the short fight's climax, stared with mouth agape.

Then there came the sound of bare feet, and down the stair hurried the inn-girl. She alone seemed able to move, and now, too, proved capable of speech, although it came out in a sort of a quavering shriek.

"Rash sir, you know not what you've done!"

"But I do know," said Zire. "Let me see, killed a killer. Maybe all you here loved him, and now wish to attack me. If so, let's get on. As I said, I'm hungry."

"*Love* him?" wailed the girl. "*Razibond?* He was a fiend."

At this, the strange inertia that had held the room broke in pieces. Voices from all sides honked and whispered: "He was a monster…"

"A bully – no woman left alone, no man of honour safe…"

"May he rot in the swampmost belly of the worst-devisable hell…"

"But," yelled the girl on the stair, "he was one of the False Prince's guardsmen. None must harm *them*, no matter what their crimes. Or the False Prince will seek obscene vengeances. He is in league with dark magic, too, and will already know you have

310

trespassed against his soldiers."

"This inn," intoned the landlord, gripping the counter white-knuckled, "may be burned to the earth, and all of us whipped. As for you, sir, he will hang you by your feet above a pit of snakes, whose poison dispatches in the slowest, most heinous stages..."

"Or else..." vocalised another, "he will sentence you to the death of two hundred hornets, each the size of a rat..."

"Or the live burial amid fractious scorpions..."

"Or..."

"Yes, very well," interrupted Zire, apparently tired. "I have inferred the correct sting-laden picture of my proposed fate."

"Run..." shrilled the pale girl from the stair. "It's your only chance! We dare not shield you."

Zire grimaced. He sat down on a bench. "First, serve me some dinner," he said. "Also my poor starved horse must eat. Both he and I refuse to run on an empty stomach."

Silence once more submerged the room. The noise of the river, always angrier after moonrise, filled it instead.

Some half-mile below, at a second inn, whose name was *The Quiet Night*, and which directly adjoined the thunderous River Ca, Bretilf the Artisan sat over the remainder of his dinner, thoughtfully slicing the last roast meat from a bone. Beside him rested a jug of Cashloria's black ale. His tankard stayed full. He was concentrating equally on the bone and on a shape he could detect in the bone's surface. Once all the meat was gone, he intended to carve the figure free, but an interruption came.

Two drunken bravos, belonging – judging by their cross-swords-and-diadem insignia and studded-leather garments – to some guard militia of the city, had begun to quarrel.

Bretilf watched them sidelong through narrowed, tawny-amber eyes. His hair was of a similar shade, a type of ginger-amber, marking him out through the gilding of a stray lamp. He was otherwise young, tall, and well-made, and, had he but known it, bore a definite resemblance to another man, who only some minutes earlier, and half a mile above on the promontory, had stuck a sword straight through the heart of space-wasty Razibond.

"Damn it all, Kange," ranted the bigger of the quarrellers, "I say we *shall*."

"I don't deny we have a perfect *right*. But the house walls are high, and she is protected by loyal servants and hounds, the latter of which will snap off a man's leg soon as make water on it." This was the retort of the smaller though no less repulsive Kange.

Bretilf could hear all clearly, even through the general din. He suspected others in the room heard the dialogue, too, but pretended deafness.

"Pahf!" went on the first guard. "No need for that. We'll knock at the gate and remind the girl the False Prince has given us permission to delve any wench we fancy. Besides, when she sees our beauty, how can she not succumb? Failing that we'll poison both servants and dogs and burn the house to show we called."

"True, you're wise, Ovrisd," relented Kange. "But before we set forth on our mission, let's see what money we can squeeze out of that foreigner over there, with the pumpkin-coloured mane."

Bretilf put down the meat bone.

The guardsmen were advancing, smiling winningly upon him, carefully ignored on every side by the rest of the inn.

"Greetings, stranger," said the unpresentable Kange.

"Welcome, stranger," added the revolting Ovrisd.

"To you also," replied Bretilf, rising. "I believe you wish me to render you something," he presumed.

"Oh, indeed! How perceptive. We would like all of it!"

"And pretty fast."

"Perhaps not all, but certainly a great deal. All that you deserve," said Bretilf. He finished mildly, "Nevertheless, once is enough. To seek me later for more will not be to your liking." And, leaning forward, he grasped both their unlovely necks and, in one sleek, quick movement, smashed their heads together. Like two halves of a severed pear, each guardsman fell, thumpingly senseless, to the floor.

Instantly, every person in the inn, including the landlord, his slim wife, and large cat, fled the premises.

Bretilf placed coins in generous amount on the counter, and toting the jug and the sculptable bone, walked off into the riverine night.

A golden moon howled radiance like wild music in the sky. The insane river answered. Bretilf sat awhile on the bank and started the carving of the bone. But his own bones guessed the night's difficulties were not done.

Sure enough, about an hour later, two sore-headed and bleary-eyed guardsmen came staggering to the bank with drawn blades and antisocial motives.

"I said," gently reminded Bretilf, as once again he rose to his feet, "it was not advisable that you ask for more."

Seething and blathering, Kange and Ovrisd leapt ungainly at him. Bretilf flipped back his cloak. The moon splashed like hot lava on a sudden broadsword, that had the name Second Thoughts. *Swish, swish* went the two severed heads of Kange and Ovrisd, plunging off the land's edge into the hungry river. Their now leaderless bodies slumped, this time conclusively, to the earth.

Bretilf strode away into the slinks of Cashloria. It was his creed never to kill, if at all possible, at an initial encounter. But so many people were determined to try his patience. Reticence and extremity coexisted always with him. Presently, he found a much less clean, and more secluded, inn where he might spend the night in peace asleep or carving the figure of a militant stag.

Bretilf awoke to find, with some bemusement, he was staring at himself in a mirror. Zire awoke to find exactly the same thing.

Neither man recalled a mirror placed before him, in either of the inns they had last night occupied. In fact, Zire had fallen asleep at the table in *The Plucked Dragon*, after his first cup of wine. Bretilf had done much the same in his own inn, *The Affectionate Flea*. Besides, the mirrors were unreliable. Bretilf immediately noted that his own reflection rubbed its eyes, which Bretilf had not done and was not doing. Zire noted that, though he had rubbed his eyes, his reflection refused to copy him. In any case, said reflection's eyes, in both instances, were the wrong colour.

"Oh," said Zire then, boredly, "are you some sorcerous fetch summoned up to haunt me?"

"No," returned Bretilf. "I think rather your – or possibly my own – father played his flute away from home. And I, and you, therefore, are half-brothers."

"Hmn," said Zire. "You may be correct. We're certainly nearly doubles."

Then each got up, conscious as they did so of three further things. First, that in height and build they were also neatly matched. Second, that the faint beeish buzzing in their skulls, and taste of dry wool in their mouths, was very likely the result of their having been drugged. The third revelation was that, rather than remaining at an inn, whether wholesome or squalid, they were now in a cramped stone room with iron bars across the window.

Glancing at each other, they observed as one: "Dead guards. Royal disapproval. The False Prince."

A moment later, the door was opened, and several more guards, these ones with whom Zire and Bretilf were unacquainted, bundled into the space. They seized, then dragged Bretilf and Zire, the foray ornamented by a selection of punches and kicks, up many stairs and into another cell, plain but less prisonlike.

"Lie there, you scum," the guards instructed. "And prepare for horrors. The prince will arrive soon to judge you." They departed, slamming the door.

"Do you have a knife or sword?" inquired Bretilf.

"Yes, my knife. And Scribe is still with me."

"My Second Thoughts, also," said Bretilf. "And with my knife, the carving even that I was fashioning with it."

"Not disarmed, then."

"Nor bound."

It would seem," said Zire, "this prince has enough magical power to deal with us, whatever we try. A great shame," he added. "I had hoped to visit Traze next, over the river. And then the Red Desert."

"And I to finish my carving."

A spinning began in one of the cell walls. The two men watched attentively as it grew black, then electric, and roiled away, leaving an opening into a vast white marble chamber, its ceiling high as a full-grown oak. This was easily gauged, too, since live oak trees formed a colonnade along it. But they had trunks and boughs like twisted ebony, and blue leaves that quivered on their own, filling the air with a serpentine rustling.

At the room's far end rose a tall black chair upholstered in violet velvet. On either side of this squatted a fearsome beast, something like a wolf crossed with a raccoon. In the chair sat a stooped, thin man. He was a young man, but with an old man's face, and weaves of grey and white ran through his own light-coloured hair. His eyes were like shards chipped from something blue and long-dead. But he wore fine clothes, and on his head a silver circlet. He pointed with a long, thin finger.

"You are here for punishment. You have slain my men, my chosen guards. For this, only the worst deaths are given. What do you say?"

"Oh, dear," said Zire.

Bretilf added, "Since Your Highness has already decided, what point for us to say anything?"

"I will have you speak."

Zire said, "It would be redundant to attempt to placate, please, or obey you. We're dead. We can be as rude as we like."

"Yet," said Bretilf, however, "why are you called the *False* Prince? Or is that only because all Cashlorians hate you? Just as they hate your guards, who seem, all told, a pack of cowards, rapists, thieves, and cutthroats."

The elderly young man cursed. He reached up and pulled at the silver circlet, next sending it bowling along the floor, until it fell over into a rug. The two monsters by the chair snarled.

"Hush," said the prince to them. "I am called False because, although I rule here, by right of direct descent, I have never inherited the one artefact that would ensure my rule, and my power. It was stolen, during the last years of my father, the Old Prince's, reign – due to some foolishness of his. At once the Benign Guardians, said to protect the city, left us. Efforts to recover the sacred item failed. They fail always – for several have gone to reclaim it for me. All here know where it is interred. But that counts for naught. None can master the resident magics that hold it in. And all who try perish on the quest. Perish *horribly*, I have been led to believe, and have indeed witnessed.

"For example," said the prince, settling himself in a doleful mimicry of some storyteller, "there was the famous hero Drod Laphel. It was well known that he alone had, twice or thrice, bested five or six men together in a sword fight..."

"Only five or six?" grunted Bretilf *sotto voce*.

"My revered granny," hissed Zire, "could beat off eight at least at a go. Albeit with a special cloak-pin she possessed and not..."

"You would do well to attend," coldly broke in the prince. "It is an option I have, to torture you a little, before sentence. This can be waived or not, as you like."

Zire and Bretilf composed themselves meekly.

"Drod Laphel," went on the prince, "was also handy with spear and throwing axe, and besides learnt certain charms that enabled him to bewitch serpents. When pausing in this city, he soon fell afoul of my guardsmen. Ten set on him, and accordingly he slew them single-handedly, if admittedly in two batches of five. Following the episode, I had him dispatched to thieve back the vital article I miss. I even had, numbskull that I was, some faith that he, of all men, might succeed where no other ever had. But no. Drod Laphel, the snake-charmer, athlete, and magician of swords, returned empty-handed. Quite literally, since he lacked both of them. And he was deader than a coffin nail, besides being the awful shade of rotted plums."

Zire cleared his throat. Bretilf regarded his boots, as if counting the cracks in their leather.

"Are we then to conclude," said Zire, "our punishment for culling your degenerate guards is, personally, to be forced to undertake the self-same quest?"

"You are brave men," said the False Prince with dreary jealousy. "Bold and reckless as lions. Yes, you will be made to go. That much sorcery I can command. Understand this, too. If I were able to reclaim the needed object, and my rightful power given to me, I would not require a single human guard. I would throw the degenerates out, nor would they dare return here. Additionally, though it hardly merits saying, as you will never succeed at this challenge, whoever is successful will find his reward proportionate. Rather than death, riches beyond comprehension would be rendered you." Sourly, he recapped: "But best not to dwell on futile daydreams. Nor have I any pity for you. Why should I pity others when my own lot is so cruel? The supernatural agencies that should guard Cashloria are gone, or in hiding. The heart of the city itself refuses to acknowledge me, and conversely does me ill-turns. Only those guards, and these two creatures here, stand between me and the vengeance of a rioting populace. Were all my weakness known, I should not last a minute. But my days are scarce enough. Cashloria's thwarted energies are already killing me. Can you see? How old would you say I am?"

Neither Bretilf nor Zire replied.

"Fifteen," said the False Prince, lowering his blue, dead eyes. "I am fifteen. And if I leave Cashloria, its stony atoms will tear me in pieces. While if I remain, they will drain me of all life in another year. Yes, you shall go and try to snatch back for me the sacred artefact, the Garment of Winning, as it is called. Why should I spare you? Who, in the name of any god, has ever spared *me*?"

"So, tell me of your father," said Zire, as they rode over the long stone bridge above the Ca.

"A minor lordlet, killed by assassins before my birth. My mother and grandsire raised me in the irksome shadow of his death. At eleven I broke free."

"Then I believe your father died too young to have coined *me*."

"Who was your own?"

"A chalk merchant. I grew up white as a sheep, till at seventeen some foe threw me down a well. Crawling out, no one recognised the red-headed youth who then stole the local grandee's horse and pelted for freedom. I doubt my father, either, sired you. He was less white than uncouth and uncomely. No elegant lady, wed to – or widowed of – a lordlet would have let him touch her maid, let alone herself."

After this they rode awhile unspeaking. The river gushed green below, and on the farther bank the daytime forest was massed like a russet storm cloud.

They had no choice but to undertake the lethal task, so much had been made clear to them, not least by the False Prince's wizards, whose spokesman was a man in unfriendly middle age. "You are already under Cashloria's *geas*," he had told them. "It will avail you nothing to essay escape. You must travel to the place of dread, there enter in, and do whatever you're able to retrieve the Garment of Princedom – which is otherwise known as *The Robe Which Wins All Wars*."

At this news, Zire had yawned convulsively and Bretilf's hungry stomach grumbled. They had been from the start well aware some coercive spell was on them. They were its captives until either they had gained the trophy – or died, 'horribly', in the attempt.

During the breakfast that was eventually served them, and that might have been enjoyable, including platters of fresh-baked shrimp, clam, and prawn, good ham, and eggs curdled with white wine, the indefatigable wizard informed them of all the conditions of their unwanted and unavoidable quest.

The original thief of the Winning Robe was allegedly a mischievously malignant elemental of the forest. It had next created a bizarre castle in which to hide the Robe, ringing it prudently with a labyrinth, unknown yet frightful safeguards, and energising all with a sorcery so strident none had ever survived it. More than fifty men, all intelligent, cunning, and courageous, and well-versed in the use of stealth and weaponry, had been sent to the castle. And all had returned – but in disturbingly dead states: headless, footless, heartless; lurid with alien venom, rigid with stings of weird sort, skinned, scalped, or dissected. This multitude of squeam-making ends were duly attributed to the prince himself, in order the citizens might fear him and be kept down. "Hence the tales of scorpions and snakes," Zire had muttered.

"It seems a perfect genius is needed," said Bretilf, "if mere cleverness, cunning, and all other skills are no use."

"Well, whatever we have to our credit, there being two of us, it's doubled," hazarded Zire.

They were awarded two horses, a bay gelding for Bretilf, Zire's horse being his own grey, nicely reshod. Both animals were well fed, saddled, and burnished.

Now on the bridge over the Ca, the farther bank having become the nearer one, Zire abruptly drew rein.

Bretilf copied him. "What?"

"Let us," said Zire, "see if we're able, after all, to turn back and make off."

Bretilf looked once over his shoulder. "Each of us is aware he can't. The *geas* prevents it. Or else we would still be escorted. We can only go forward to the goal of the castle. We were told we did not even need a map, the compulsion on us being so strong we can only follow the compulsory direction."

"Perhaps, however," suggested Zire, "the *horses* can carry us in the opposite one, despite whatever spell binds us!"

They turned the horses' heads. Grimly, Zire and Bretilf faced back down the bridge to the city, gripped the reins, and kicked both mounts lightly in the side.

The horses instantly reared as if confronted by flailing flames or slavering demons. Jumping about in a shriek of metal hooves on stone paving, they reversed themselves with such enthusiasm their riders were nearly unseated. Both mounts then tore the last quarter of a mile along the bridge in the unwanted direction and plunged off into the forest beyond.

Only with great awkwardness and noise were they persuaded to calm down and stop. They were deep into the trees – bridge, river, and city out of sight. Bretilf and Zire scowled about at the red-leafed gloom, to which they were so well matched.

"So much for that, then."

The morning waxed through the coppery forest canopy toward noon. Glumly, Zire and Bretilf rode along the track the *geas* had selected. Birds sang, and once a deer broke across the path. A pair of squirrels mocked them from a tall black pine.

Not long after, something appeared ahead at the roadside. At first, both men took it for a marker of some sort. It stayed completely still. But, presently, Zire exclaimed, "Look there. It's a young woman. Why, it's the inn-girl from *The Plucked Dragon*, who was so full of warnings."

Bretilf added, "I seem to know her, too. Either she served me at the first inn, or the second."

The girl, drably clad, and with a tattered white shawl over hair greasy from constant nearness to roast meat, just then raised her hand – not in greeting, but to beckon.

"Perhaps she was thrown out of work because of us," said Zire.

"I can spare her a coin," said Bretilf.

The riders reached the girl and halted. She gazed into their faces with dull eyes. She spoke:

"Alas! The False Prince has ensorcelled and sent you to your dooms. Oh, you'll be done for like all the others. The Robe That Wins is untakable. Poor souls, poor lost souls!"

"Exactly," said Zire.

Bretilf remarked, "But it's kind of you to wish us luck so encouragingly."

The girl took no notice either of pragmatics or sarcasm. Solemnly, she cried, in a high, self-important voice, "My name is Loë, and I am of no account. But seek the house of Ysmarel Star that lies along this very track. There only may you find assistance."

"What is Ysmarel Star?"

"Seek the house and learn," melodramatically declaimed the rather aggravating Loë. "You can hardly miss the mansion. White roses crowd the walls and white owls flit around it, while a huge diamond star hangs low above."

"Not modestly self-effacing then, as are you," said Zire.

"I am nothing. I am only Loë."

And the girl ran suddenly off the track and in among the copper-gold patchwork of the trees. Bretilf and Zire stared after her thoughtfully.

"It seemed to me..." Bretilf murmured after a second or so.

"...also to me..." agreed Zire.

"...that where the shadow of that cedar falls..."

"...girl ceased to be girl..."

"...and became instead...?"

"…a weasel," concluded Zire. "Perhaps," he added, "we hallucinate from hunger. Let's enjoy a brief rest and dine on the provisions in the saddlebags."

During the afternoon, the autumnal forest changed from metals to wines, and so to lilacs. That evening the track, now very overgrown, and interrupted by the strong claws of neighbouring trees, meandered out into a series of clearings. Here dusk filtered, littered by tiny bats.

A sweep of land was rising upward on their left, the trees thinly scattered about on it. Then a hill was to be seen, clear on the mauve-glowing sky. One star had risen there of unusual size and brilliance, and beneath lay a dark, rambling house, here and there pierced by the needles of lamps.

"Ysmarel's mansion?"

"So it seems," affirmed Zire.

"Do we visit?"

"Why not? The track winds close, and the *geas* allows intervals."

"And anyway, to the doomed," Bretilf appended, "all delays are *good*."

The grey and bay climbed the hill.

High stone barricades appeared, smothered with moon-pale flowers, whose scent seemed enhanced by darkness. Above, six or seven gigantic bats flew about. But the low-strung star illuminated their wings, which were white. They were owls.

Purple glass and glass like saffron was in the lighted windows. A bell hung over the gate.

The two men observed the bell, but before they could decide to ring it, it pealingly rang of itself. At this, the owls descended together, and perched along the tops of the walls, looking at Zire and Bretilf through the stained glass of their eyes.

Some moments later, the gate swung wide, and inside was framed a dark garden, full of white roses that caught the star shine and ghostly shone. About twenty paces on, a broad door stood open and, even as they watched, soft lamps bloomed there. It was all most enticing. So much so that neither man advanced. They sat their horses, and the owls sat on the walls, and not a sound was to be heard, as if time had grown cautious, too, and stood still.

After a while, Bretilf stirred. "Do we go in? Or retreat?"

"All's lost, it seems, whatever we do."

They dismounted, tethered the horses among the roses, and walked straight in at the soft-lighted door.

They were at once in a charmingly informal hall, lit by depending lamps of fretted bronze and lavender glass. Luxurious rugs clothed a floor of delicate rainbow tiling.

A long table had been loaded with tall gilded flagons individually filled with black ale, red wine, blue spirit, or honeyed beer. A selection of pies, smoking roasts, cheeses, dewy salads, fruits, and sweets of many kinds waited on plates of gold or in dishes of silver decorated with pearls and zircons.

"Do you trust this feast?" asked Zire.

"Less than I'd trust a starving thief who jumped in the window."

"My own thought. Shall we dine?"

"Let's do so."

But even as they pulled out the gilded chairs to sit, a curtain across the length of the room blew back, and out stepped a vision that stopped them, once more, in their tracks.

A young woman, again, but this time of surpassing attractions. The undeniable beauty of her face was made yet more marvellous by two large eyes of velvet darkness. From her lovely head cascaded darkly shining hair in loose curls, that each took a chestnut highlight from the lamps. Her slim but voluptuous figure had been clad in a filmy gown of amethyst silk, caught at the waist by serpentine twists of white gold.

"How rewarding that you should call on me," said this apparition, in a musical voice that suggested the colour of smoky peach mixed with platinum. "Pray sit."

Bretilf the Artisan and Zire the Scholar – sat.

Instantly, some bowls of scented water were brought to them, by a pair of white rabbits. Without comment, each man rinsed his hands, at which two black rabbits appeared to offer linen towels. All four rabbits had come from under the table draperies, to which area they next withdrew. But, unceremoniously yanking up the drapery, Zire and Bretilf peered beneath – to find no sign of rabbits, bowls, towels, nor any hatch that might afford entry and exit.

Re-emerging from under the cloth, the two found instead their beautiful hostess had herself sat down at the table's central position. Her serenity was exquisite.

"Brave sirs, do choose whatever you wish to eat. Munch and

Janthon there will serve you."

Anticipating further rabbits, Bretilf and Zire were startled when a handsome, long-haired white cat appeared, walking upright out of a bouquet of pale flowers at the table's southern end. In another breath, a larger, but also handsome, short-haired black dog manifested at the table's northern end. This being stood on the floor by Zire's chair. The dog, too, walked upright, which meant its head was level with Zire's own – it was a large canine indeed.

Zire pulled himself around with a little effort. "Good evening, Janthon," said Zire. "If you'll be so kind, I will have..."

"No trouble, sir," replied the dog with faultless articulation. "Your mind is read." And, taking the proper implements from the board, dexterously began to slice for Zire the very cooked fowl he had been intent on. That done, Janthon stalked to Bretilf's place and, unasked, extended agile front paws and carved up for him a paté and a pie. Munch the cat meanwhile filled Bretilf's crystal glass of spirit, and now came to Zire to pour his silver tankard of beer.

Un-noted during these operations, three white owls had entered through a high window. Perching upon golden stands, they now began to sing a quiet but melodious trio, to the accompaniment of three black, crow-like birds, which seemed to have arrived via the mansion's open door. One beat a drum with its claws, another performed on a small harp, which it struck tunefully with one wing. The third whistled through its beak.

Zire and Bretilf ate and drank some while without a word exchanged.

At last, Bretilf spoke levelly to Zire. "Have we gone mad?"

"I think so," answered Zire in an offhand way. "Probably some effect of the *geas*, or else too strong a drug used to subdue us in the city."

"Or, alternatively, perhaps it's a dream." Bretilf turned to their delicious female companion, who sat quietly sipping a goblet of sherbet laced with wine. "Would you say so, madam?"

"All life is a dream," she replied, smiling. "Or so it is said."

"You are then a philosopher, lady," said Zire.

"No. I am a witch. Whose name is Ysmarel Star."

Zire and Bretilf put down their silver knives and drinking vessels. Each man rose.

"A witch. What else? I fear," said Zire, "we must be on our way."

"Urgent business at a castle," elaborated Bretilf, "involving doom and horrible death."

Ysmarel Star nodded. "So many have passed by, en route to such a fate. Few ever listened to my messenger, Loë."

"Perhaps, unlike ourselves, they knew your true vocation – witchcraft – and were too... respectful to call. There is sorcery enough in the city and the forest, surely. It tends to make even desperate men – among whom we must be counted – reluctant." This, from Zire.

"We trust not to offend by such frankness," finished Bretilf.

But Ysmarel paid no attention. She went on as if neither of her guests had spoken a word. "Of the few who did heed Loë, none before, suspecting a trap, dared enter my house. There were others who, having seen Loë, failed to see my gate, or anything else. It takes, gentlemen, a particular type of acuteness and sparkle, to note such things. Even that a rabbit, cat, or dog waits on them at table. That owls make music. Let alone the presence of my humble self."

"Any man who missed seeing *you*, fair lady," said Zire, "would need to be blind, and other things besides, perhaps more personally unhappy in his lower regions."

Bretilf said, "Any man who failed at seeing you, Ysmarel, would need to be *dead*."

"However," continued Zire, "we must get on."

"To be late for a doom is the worst bad manners," augmented Bretilf.

Ysmarel still gave no heed. "I have known for long months the imposed task which the False Prince of Cashloria sets any transgressor: to steal back the Robe of War-Winning. It is a hopeless venture. Men of great courage and genius have gone to the doom you refer to. Even thirteen women of unusual battle-skills and wisdom. But all perished, male and female alike. And each, it's true, ended horribly.

"For example," continued Ysmarel Star, modifying her stance rather in the manner of certain feminine storytellers, "the glamorous and gifted sword-mistress, Shaiy of the Red Desert, having killed two guards who attempted unwanted affection, was sentenced to seek the Robe.

"Shaiy was well known for her varied warrior talents, not to mention her learning and quick wit. It's said she could compose an ode worthy of the greatest poets in twice ten minutes. Or a bawdy song inside three slow heartbeats. Riddles she could answer while asleep. She was a notoriously sage robber, said to have stolen the Great Emerald of Gullo. Though she then kindly gave it away to a destitute lover. But even Shaiy only returned from the evil castle dead, and *minced small*, everything of her in a tiny box, all but her dainty white ears – which were pinned on the lid in the exact form of a butterfly."

Zire studied his boots; Bretilf cleared his throat.

Ysmarel simply clapped her slender hands. At the signal, every light in the mansion died, every waft of perfume, tasty dinner, or music – fled. A dog barked once, a rabbit squeaked, and a cat spat. A rattle of wings and clatter of discarded perches and instruments revealed where crows and owls beat it at top speed through a window and a door. The room had become black as tar. Only the star gleamed on the garden outside.

Male voices uttered.

"Are you able, Bretilf, to move at all?"

"Not I. And you, Zire?"

"Neither."

"Rest, my friends," murmured the seductive tones of the witch. "I have concocted, for your intelligence and reckless natures, another destiny than you predict."

"A witch, what else? That food," said Bretilf next, now in a slurred and impersonal way.

"Or that witchy bloody beer," grumbled Zire. "To the lowest hell with it, we have yet again…"

"…been drugged and enspelled," explained Bretilf.

In the darkness, there now sounded a discordant slumping couple of thuds, as of two muscular young men dropping on a tiled floor, amid their boots, garments, a part-sculpted stag, swords, and other accessories.

There followed a woman's provocative laugh. And night extinguished the scene both inside and out, as the low diamond of the abnormal star capsized in clouds.

In sleep, there was no respite either. Each man dreamed a selection of episodes concerning those luckless heroes – and heroines – who had entered the infamous castle.

Bretilf beheld Drod Laphel, tall and powerful, with golden locks, striding through an enormous sable building, sword ready, while a huge serpent oozed toward him. It was scaled like an alligator, yet black-blue as midnight. It opened its scarlet jaws and made a noise as of steam rising from a hot spring. At that, Drod chanted some spell so hypnotic even the actually ensorcelled and drugged and anyway non-serpentine Bretilf grew helpless. Surprisingly, the serpent did not. It surged forward, a scaly wave from a midnight ocean, and the golden swordsman vanished in its coils.

Zire, too, dreamed, but his surreality concerned the beautiful Shaiy. She was a lightly sturdy young woman, with skin of cream and eyes like green embers. Now, standing inside a huge vaulted hall, she confronted a sort of puma, with the head of a falcon and falcon wings. The falcon-puma had challenged her, it seemed, to solve some conundrum, and to sing her reply. This Shaiy proceeded to do. But no sooner did her excellent mezzo-soprano fill the space than the echo of her voice itself became a living entity, which boomed and howled like thunder. Blocks of masonry started to fall. And both Shaiy and the cat-bird-sphinx were lost to view.

Thereafter there were endless such dreams. Maybe even fifty or more of those condemned to seek the Robe appeared before Bretilf and Zire. All foundered. In each case, definite clues were given as to the vile methods of their ending.

Then at last Bretilf dreamed, and Zire, too, that they themselves – each solo – entered the same lapideous building. Their names had altered, for some reason. Zire was called Izer, Bretilf – Ibfrelt. Knowing this was less than useful to them.

Upon Zire, from the shadowy architecture rushed flapping creatures, most like colossal books, and he, spinning and leaping, wielding Scribe to parry and slash and pierce, the knife to stab and slice, still battled them in vain. They closed on him and slammed him shut inside their covers.

Bretilf found that he had tried to draw, or carve out on the walls, talismans of beneficent gods. But they erupted like boiling black milk, grew solid, ripped away his weapons from his grip. After which a giant stag rose out of the floor and tore at him, and stove in his ribs, with antlers and feet.

Slaughtered personally over and over in their dreams, Izer-Zire and Ibfrelt-Bretilf longed for day and awakening, whether in a hell or heaven, or – the favourite choice – the world.

Dawn though, as was its habit, took its own time.

A century later, perhaps, it seemed, the metal-leafed forest flooded pink as a blush. The sun rose. The things of darkness... fled?

The mansion of the witch was sombre and deserted-looking in the morning. No owls, or any birds, were evident. The white roses had folded tight as buds, as if only after sunset could they open.

Even so, the door to the mansion remained wide. As did the outer gate.

In a while, something might be seen to be moving through the garden.

If the sun watched for Zire and Bretilf, the sun was due for a disappointment, since what presently padded through the gates on to the hillside, though two in number, were a pair of young lions. Once outside, both paused to sniff the gate-posts, the air. One growled, the other lashed its tail. Roughly of an age, and having the same lean girth and obvious male stamina, tawny and limber, white-fanged, and tail tufted and maned – one dark red, the other more a tangerine shade – they might have been brothers of a single pride.

A look of slight unease was swiftly concealed by them, in the way of animals. They turned and cuffed each other and rolled about play-fighting – until suddenly rolling right across on to the track. Here they got up, shook themselves, touched noses, and glanced around, one with topaz eyes, the other with eyes of shined silver.

To anyone who knew no better than to credit all sorcery, they would be taken for Bretilf the Artisan and Zire the Scholar magicked into feline beasts.

Both lions, anyway, now raced off along the track, perhaps coincidentally in the very direction the *geas* prescribed.

A lion knows it is a lion, even if it has no occasion to tell itself so. Had it found occasion, it would, and using whatever words make up the lionesque language. All animals, naturally, employ language. Human ignorance of this results from the fact most humans have never understood most of the animal tongues. The reason being perhaps because, beyond the very obvious, animal language is formulated to convey states, ideas, and principles of conduct quite out of the range of human grasp. Certain schools of thought even maintain that what man sees in himself as 'acting like an animal', rather than a sign of degeneracy, is a sadly inadequate effort on mankind's part to copy the philosophical intellectual animal technique in the mastery of life, love, and death.

Zire, then, knew himself a lion. And Bretilf likewise knew himself a lion. That they were brothers was undeniable, fundamental, and largely irrelevant. As for a strange jumble each vaguely noticed as being a name, and a *distorted* name, neither bothered with it.

Nevertheless, both lions were slightly conscious of bizarre concepts, which sometimes swirled about in their maned and noble heads. To these also they paid little attention. What they knew was this: the day was warm, the earth and trees smelled good, and everywhere blew the scents of interesting things both to experience and to eat. Something excited and pushed them on in a particular direction. It went without saying therefore this direction was desirable and promised much. To resist the tug of it was not even considered.

For hours the lions bounded through the forest. By now verdure was thick, and the track less than a thread between the roots of trees and laceries of fern. Now and then they paused to investigate some interesting odour, sight, or noise, rested in shade under the sun-flamed canopy, drank from a streamlet dark as malachite. All was as it should be.

Noon filled the sky and so the forest. From safe tree-tents, squirrels, chipmunks, possums, and wood pigeons watched the lions, most respectfully.

To a man, the scene that now appeared between the trees was that of a huge clearing. For almost a mile all vegetation had been mown down or dredged up, and then a floor laid there, made of odd triangular flagstones, which seemed of polished basalt. In this surface the unhidden sky reflected, so it glimmered like a black lake. At its centre rose a building. To a man, again, or a woman, it was instantly apparent this structure had been formed from the trunks and heavy summer crowns of many living trees. Yet they had also been deformed. Some leaned askew, some were warped in unnerving hoops, and some forced together at their tops to provide a roof with branches, boughs, and foliage. After that, sorcery had struck them. They had turned to stone – not the smooth basalt of the paving, but petrified coal of dense, ashen black.

As no men were in the clearing, but rather lions, that analysis did not occur. The lions saw a cave-like mass, cool in the day's heat, and having to it an olfactory tang of human flesh and blood. In other words, recent fresh corpses.

Pausing only to dip cautious paws into the lake which surrounded the caves, and so learn it was solid, they sprang forward, and vanished through the entrance.

Izer, the lion who had been Zire, darted through a succession of lowering, gaping, all-black vistas. Space led into space, some more narrow, others wider or more winding. Izer galloped blithely through them all. Their enormity, and cranky arboreal sculpting, did not faze him. He did not feel made small and vulnerable, as a man might. Instead, curious as a young cat, he climbed where able up the malformed sides of the stone trees, and stuck his long, big nose into holes and fissures. He raised his paw and scraped the petrified material with a single claw. At which blue sparks flew and he veered away.

From the guts of this inert yet nastily intestine-suggestive labyrinth, came the most insidious wavering drone of sound. It was the sound of utter *soundlessness*, disturbed only in the ear of the listener by the tempo of pulse and heart. Izer paid it little attention. *His* hearing was honed for more informative noises. Of these there seemed to be none.

Then with no warning, something rushed sharply through the air, about three lion-lengths above him. Izer raised his head.

It was a bird. But a bird Izer had never seen, nor been self-trained to expect. It had no beak, nor even a head. Its outflung, fluttering wings were dark above, with complex paler featherings below, but they supported nothing. The bird had no body either.

Izer did not identify the flying object as a book, which, to a human, it would appear to be. For him it was only logical to classify it as a bird. And as lions are generally a match for most birds, save those of supernatural size, such as a roc, he leapt straight at it, bore it to the earth and smashed it there. The book's spine broke. Izer tore at its feather pages, champed and spat them out. The bird was not good eating, good for nothing, aside from a bit of swift exercise. When the next one came flapping at him, Izer took this in sporting spirit, sprang at it and batted it about a while, before destroying it on the ground. Other books followed in streamers, though not very many. Izer danced about with them, enjoying himself. When the last was felled, he noted tiny scurrying things that were spilling from the carcasses. He put his paws on them, bit and squashed them. They were written words, yet Izer did not know this. They meant nothing at all to him beyond a playful moment or two. They tasted only of ink anyway. He also spat their shredded bodies forth, rolled on his back, shook his henna mane, and trotted off deeper into the petrified maze.

Elsewhere, Ibfrelt, the lion who had been Bretilf, was nosing around some knots in the floor that might, once, have been edible fungi. He, too, was uninterested in the persistent yodel of the silence. However, presently he heard a curious scraping noise, and looking around saw some sharp implements worming out of a wall. No sooner were they ejected than they began to crawl over the floor, scratching irritatingly as they did so. Ibfrelt went to examine them, batting at them rather as Izer had at the books. Their steel edges made no impression on his well-toughened lion pads. In the end, he became bored with the things and loped off. He did not actually realise that they then pursued him in a highly sinister manner. To Ibfrelt, there could be nothing sinister about them. Nor did he see when, by then some way behind him, they lost momentum, rusted, flaked, and fell apart.

Wandering on into another chamber of the building, Ibfrelt paused only when a sudden form reared up from the floor. A man would have known this figure at once for a fellow man – a sword fighter for a fellow swordsman, and a dangerous one. He was tall, and laden with muscle, clad in mail, and armed both with a broadsword of considerable size and a dagger of extraordinary length. At Ibfrelt, he glared with flashing, maniacal eyes, and from a sneering gob let out a challenge: "Match me then, you damnable nonentity!"

But Ibfrelt evidently only knew men – when he *had* known them – as menu-worthy pieces of prey. Shows of weapons, of aggression, protective armourings – they meant nothing at all, to a lion. Ibfrelt smelled live meat, and he gave a snarl of appetite, then launched himself, like a vast ginger firework, at the threatening hulk.

Over went the hulk, amid a resounding bash and clamour, sword flying one way, and dagger doing no more damage than to shave four of Ibfrelt's impressive whiskers, before a couple of jaws, equally impressively toothed, met in his oesophageal tract.

Ibfrelt was already feeding greedily when, to his disgust, his kill dissolved like a mist and faded into thin air.

Some snaggle of labyrinthine turns away, Izer was just undergoing a similar disillusion. *His* adversary had been a rapier-brandishing swordsman, with a back-up ax. But Izer had simply jumped on him in the midst of the fellow's posturing, fangs seeing to the rest. When this nice hot meal vanished, Izer let out a complaint so loud even Ibfrelt paid attention and rumbled back.

Rising from the teasing absent carcass, Izer padded through the maze and, with leonine instincts of scent, vision, hearing, and *sub*thought, located Ibfrelt inside two minutes.

The lions commiserated with each other. This was a poor place, after all. It would be better to depart instantly.

It was then that a blazing light flared up in the next cave or chamber. They were lions; they took it for the undoing of an exit into the afternoon forest. Shoulder to shoulder, they flung themselves toward it...

They found themselves contrastingly inside a gargantuan inner region of the complex. The compartment would have evoked, to most human eyes, a colossal temple hall. To the lions, it was just an especially oversized cavern. Yet light from some invisible source filled it full.

In the very middle of the space stood a solitary *living* tree, or so it appeared. The tree was a sort of maple, but of absurd dimensions, and with autumnal leaves coloured raspberry, orange, and ripe prune. From the boughs hung a dowdy banner – or a garment? It seemed stranded there, whatever it was, by mistake, shoddy and threadbare, stained, and itself the hue of over-cooked porridge.

Neither lion glanced at it. A spectacle of greater fascination pended. The living trunk was slowly splitting along a hinge of softer, more elusive light. When the gap was wide enough, a form burst from within. It cantered into the cavern, a sight to render any warrior numb with astonished horror.

Directly before the lions epically bulged a stag of unusual size. It was almost spotless white, its antlers like boughs, its eyes glittering like fires. It snorted, and from its nostrils black smoulders gushed out.

Lions do not shake hands or smite paws together to announce brotherhood. If they did, these two would have done.

Without preamble, both vaulted headfirst at the stag. They hit it square, one to each side of the breast. Fearful splinterings, jangles, cracks, and clangs engulfed the air. In a thousand shards, the stag, which seemed fashioned from one house-huge bone, collapsed. The giant maple shook at the detonation. Leaves rained like – *rain*.

One other item was dislodged and drifted foolishly down, like dirty washing. Izer and Ibfrelt, Ibfrelt and Izer, ignored this. They were busy. The bone of which the monster stag had been constructed had once belonged to some improbably prodigious roast. They were engaged in extracting the marrow, any shreds of meat, savouring the cooked tastes, finding every splinter on the ground. In this way, they missed the dim phantasmal wailing of something, which, seeing all its ploys, even those untried, would never work, lamented in the stony masonry. They missed the dislodgement of the building, too, and how its walls and halls, openings and enclosures, came apart and smeared into nothing. They even missed the last descent of the unappealing porridge-coloured garment, until it fell over both their heads.

"So, what do you make of it?"

Trudging back through the forest, stark naked, and with the fall weather turning a touch more chilly, Bretilf put this question to the matchingly unclothed and chilled Zire.

Zire said, "It seems, now, perfectly obvious."

"To me also. Yet maybe we've drawn two different conclusions."

Bretilf carried the item from the cave-labyrinth, bundled up and tied tight with grasses.

From the trees, which overnight seemed themselves partly to have disrobed, leaving great swathes of cold and unclad sky and blowing wind, birds and squirrels threw nutshells at them. Foxes and wild pig distantly passed, snorting as if with scornful laughter. Snakes seemed embarrassed by the stupidity of men and slipped down holes.

Bretilf and Zire had not decided what they *made* of anything, despite their exchange. And some hours on, when they reached the mansion of the witch Ysmarel Star and found only the hill – they made not much of that, either. The grey and the bay horses were tethered nearby, however, and adjacent were neatly folded clothes, swords, and so on. Bretilf examined the part-finished carving he had begun of a stag.

"Just as I thought," said Bretilf.

"Oh, indeed," concurred Zire.

There followed a short conversation then, on whether it was worse to eat men or words, not mentioning meat bones. The consensus on this was that probably none of those items had been strictly real, more elemental, if potentially fatal, and so no moral issue was involved.

They rode the rest of the way to the city of Cashloria. Zire had taken his turn at carrying the rolled-up wretched rag from the maple. Neither man had wished to try it on, not even when naked in the woods. Just the first swipe of it across their heads had changed them back into men. That was enough.

Even so, sitting once more above the crazy River Ca, they held their horses in check and stared at nothing.

"It seems to me," said Bretilf, "the witch Ysmarel..."

"Yes?"

"Ensorcelled us into animal shape less to cause us trouble in the manner of ancient legends..."

"...than in order we might survive the maze and regain the Robe. Any intelligent or gifted man or woman who intruded on that spot," Zire went on, "was seemingly destroyed by demons conjured from their own abilities."

"The singer found her song turned against her in so dreadful a way, it tore the ears from her lovely head."

"The charmer of snakes found a snake he could not charm, which poisoned him."

The horses cropped the grass. Both men digested the effect of the beautiful witch's spell. By making them beasts, she had released them from any true engagement with their everyday beliefs. Though ghosts of their human preoccupations were yet accessible to the sorcery in the labyrinth, when presented with nightmare elements of them, as lions, they had either had no interest, or made short work and dined.

The humanly superior had perished in that place. But they, as lions, had had another agenda, *another* superiority. Which was why, too, they had gained the Winning-of-War-Robe. It had meant nothing to them; they had only run out growling with it tangled in their manes – then hair.

Modestly, Zire and Bretilf re-entered the city. Yet on the streets people swarmed to gape and cheer. At the False Prince's villa, they were admitted after a wait of only an hour.

The prince lay on a couch like one almost dead. He gazed up with weary dislike. "Who are these ruffians?"

"Highness," said the affronted servant, "can't you hear the

joyful uproar outside? These – *ruffians* – have won back the Robe – the Robe of the Winning of War With Oneself."

"Garbage," said the prince and turned over on his face. Another hour on, when he had been, rather roughly, convinced by his attendants, Zire and Bretilf had the dubious pleasure of beholding the transformation. With some revulsion, they saw how the War-Robe, when the prince had put it on, altered from a sartorial non-event to a glowing sumptuousness of colours and gems. The prince was also changed. In a matter of seconds, he grew young and strong, handsome and profound, pristine, pure, and kingly. And then, with pleasing open-handedness, from the coffers of the city, stunning riches were obtained and loaded onto mules, all for Bretilf and Zire.

They were by then incorrigibly drunk. They had sampled much of the royal cellars, and also rambled about the city, where everyone was eager to stand them a drink. Sometimes they drew into corners and spoke in low tones of the anomaly of such a man as the prince, so sticky with cruelty and crime, now entirely changed into a genuine paragon, worthy only of loyalty and praise. But they heard, too, a rumour of a kitchen girl, named Loë, who had that very day ridden off in a carriage that sparkled like a diamond, and with her many animals, owls, and crows from neglected temples, rabbits kept for the pot, cats and dogs who had earned their keep in various inns. Loë, or Weasel as she was sometimes called, or Ermine, was now said to be one of the Benign Guardians of Cashloria, who had lingered on the premises in disguise during the city's troubles. The Robe's return had freed her, it seemed, to go back to her own mysterious life on a distant star.

"I could sleep a million years," said Zire. "Alas, it's farewell now between us."

"Perhaps neither, yet," said Bretilf. "I've heard another rumour – that those villainous guards the prince is about to expel have vengefully scored our names on their swords. Will we fare better alone or in tandem?"

"Where are the horses and mules?" asked Zire, with respectable common sense.

"Below," said Bretilf, ditto.

As they jumped from the window to the backs of bay and grey, they picked up the nearby threatening roar composed of rejoicing, rage, and river. But soon the happy pounce of hooves, blissful jingle of coins and jewels, rumble of determined mules and carts, muffled all else. Heed this, then. The more noisily and threateningly the torrent bellows below and around, the louder make your song.

The Woman

1. *The Suitor*

Down the terraces of the Crimson City they carried her, in her chair of bone and gold.

The citizens stood in ranks, ten or twenty men deep.

They watched.

Some wept.

Some, suddenly oblivious of the guard, thrust forward shouting, calling, a few even reciting lines of ancient poetry. They were swept back again. As if a steel broom could push away the sea of love.

But Leopard did none of these things.

He simply stood there, looking at her. At *Her*. He thought, and even as he thought it, he chided himself, telling himself he was quite mad to think it, that her eyes for one tiniest splinter of a fractured second – met his. *Knew* his – knew *him*. Knew Leopard.

But then the chair, borne by its six strong porters, had gone by.

All he could see were the scarlet, ivory and gold of its hood, and the wide shoulders of the last two bearers.

Many of the citizens had fallen on the ground, lamenting and crying, cursing, begging for death. Like a tree which had withstood a lightning strike, Leopard remained on his feet. He was upright in all senses, bodily, mentally, in character and in his moral station. Also sexually.

For he had seen her. At last. His predestined love.

The Woman.

In the village where he had grown up, the birth of Leopard had been a great disappointment. He had been aware of a coldness among his family from an early age. By the time he was six, his mother was dead of bearing another son, and Leopard began to see neither he, nor his newcomer brother, were liked.

One day, when he was a little older, and had been playing 'catch' with the boys on the flat earthen street, under the tall rows of scent trees, Leopard heard one of the village's pair of ancient hags muttering to her sister: "Accursed, that boy. And, too, the infant boy that came after him."

"Why's that?" quacked the second hag.

"Ah. The mother was frightened by a leopard when she carried that *older* one. So he was turned into something useless."

"And the infant?"

"Think of *his* name," said the first hag.

Then both old women nodded and creaked away into their hut.

Leopard felt ashamed. He had vaguely thought he was called Leopard for the beast's silken handsomeness and dangerous hunter's skills. It would seem not. While his poor little brother, Copper Coin – had Mother been scared by a piece of *money*?

Copper Coin, however, rather than cursed, actually proved very useful later on, when he became popular for his beauty, and their family grew both respected and well-off.

Today, several years after, Leopard removed himself from the crowd and strode away along the wide white streets of the Crimson City, to the wine-house Copper Coin now owned. Leopard had a thing of wonder to tell Copper. Leopard's heart buzzed and sang within him.

A single enormous scent tree reared outside the wine-house; it was somewhere in the region of three hundred feet tall. At this season it rained down orange blossoms that smelled of incense and honey.

Patrons sat in the courtyard to catch the perfume on their hair, skin and clothes. And while they did this, of course, ate and drank. Trade was bustling.

Inside, Leopard had to wait. His beautiful brother was occupied for another quarter of an hour with a favoured client.

Leopard drank hot green alcohol and ate two or three river shrimps roasted with pepper. Seeing who he was, the food and drink were on the house.

Then the client, dreamy-eyed and flushed, rattled down from the upper apartment. He passed Leopard without seeing him though Leopard had met the man before. He was a prince of the High Family of the Nine, immensely rich, always courteous and good-natured. But also he was crazily in love with Copper, and usually came out of the bedroom in a trance, between shining joy and dark despair. This morning Leopard sympathised. For now he, Leopard, was also insane with love.

The servant took Leopard upstairs.

Copper, just fresh from the bath and belted in a dressing- gown of embroidered white silk, lay on a couch. His hair, worn some inches longer than any merely male man would wear it, coiled over his shoulders, gleaming black as sharkskin.

"Gorgeous as ever," remarked Leopard, between praise and banter. "Prince Nine tottered down, almost dead of love."

"So I should think. We were together three hours. It wouldn't look good for me, would it, if he pranced out bored and burping? But you," added Copper, "you're pale as a marble death-stone."

Leopard stared at Copper. Then Leopard went and kneeled at his brother's feet and laid his head in Copper's lap. Murmuring gently, Copper stroked Leopard's own hair, shortly thick as a cat's fur. There was nothing sexual between them. Copper had become like a mother-sister for Leopard at about the same time Copper also found his own inner femaleness.

"Ssh, what is it, darling?"

"Oh, gods of the seventy hells…"

"Don't invoke that uncouth nasty mob."

"The eleven heavens then. Oh Copper, Copper… Did you know?"

"Know what, my baby?"

"*She* was shown in the city today."

"The *Woman*? Gods, yes, I'd forgotten. No wonder half my best lads' clientele was absent. Damn it, there was I cursing them. And they too stupid to remind me."

Leopard shook, but with laughter.

He sat up and gazed into his brother's exquisite and surprised face.

"Listen, Copper. I applied."

"You – my own spirit! *When*?"

"Last Rose Moon."

"Three *months* ago? And all this while you never told me…"

"I was afraid I'd be thrown out from the first examination. But I passed them all."

Copper sank back on the cushions, fanning himself. "Wait, sweetheart. You go too fast. I'm staggered as an old hag on her last legs."

Leopard gripped his hand. Glowing with pride, he detailed every contest he had entered, and passed, always well, and often with the brilliant coloured inks of his competency and genius marked on the scroll. There had been reading and writing, in which, though village taught, he had had the luck of erudite masters, and the added learning Copper had later bought for him. There had been philosophy and debating too, humour and drama. There had been the art of painting, and the arts of war – crossbow, staff, moon-sword and bare fist. Finally he had had to compose a love poem of four lines only, each line containing only four words. Leopard modestly said he did not believe his own work one twelfth as good as others' he had seen inscribed on the judges' parchment, but by then he had also been physically examined by physicians and dentists, some of his skin and hair, his urine, blood and saliva scientifically evaluated. Lastly his semen was checked, having been gathered after the use of a certain drug and a dream, as he had thought, of The Woman herself. Only the finalists of the examinations were ever given this hallucinogen, but after it he could not recall what she had been like, the goddess of his orgasm. Now, naturally, he need not wonder for today he had seen her in person. Her eyes had – surely? unbelievably? – rested on him in turn.

In a restrained tone Copper observed, "And they allowed you to stand close to the road where she travels by in her chair. Only finalists may stand so near. Or the most wealthy, they say, who can afford to buy places. But, Leopard, my sweet one – these contests concerning The Woman occur only once every year…"

"I know. And now *you* know why I've lived in this city for a year, the parasite beneficiary of your bounty, and never a hard word from you though I earned myself not even a single bit of lead."

"I've plenty." said Copper, "why should I mind – yet Leopard – Leopard…"

Leopard raised his proud young head. "Say nothing to bring down my mood. *Nothing*. Don't tell me how many others have almost won her yet failed the Ultimate Test. Say *nothing* of that."

Copper lowered his eyes. The kohl on his long lashes glistened. They might have been wet with tears. "I say only this. One hundred men have died, in only the brief years *I* was here in the Crimson City, because of The Woman, and the Ultimate Test."

"I love her," said Leopard.

When he spoke of love, which was a common enough word and a concept often enough employed, love's very soul seemed to brush across Copper's elegant reception chamber.

Copper Coin had been named, at birth, for the copper coin their mother had bribed an itinerant hag to fix in the neck of her womb and stopper her, following the previous birth of Leopard. It was rumoured their mother had told the hag, "I can endure no more. I can *bear* no more." But the hag, though a villainess, had nevertheless been also either inept or cunning, and the coin had not saved Mother from conceiving, carrying and ejecting her last son, even if his advent killed her.

Copper had always, though glad to have been given life, felt very sorry for their mother.

Not himself desiring women, which he found a blessing, Copper had space to respect and pity them. Even the old ones – especially they perhaps. And even The Woman, maybe, the demon-goddess, cold and distant as some far-off planet, whose surface, if ever one *did* reach her, smashed men like brittle dragonflies on her rocks of razor and adamant.

The sky was green as young-grape wine.

Alone, Leopard stood on the roof of his lodging. Below, his city room, a cell equipped with a pillow, a writing-stand, and the fixtures for elimination and ablution in one corner, had also a ladder, which had often led him up here.

He watched evening stars like molten silver burst from the greenness. So love was. So it seared forth from the dusk of life.

Leopard had dimly heard of The Woman in the Crimson City since the age of six. But, at sixteen he *heard* with more than his ears. Thereafter he had had only one goal, which he kept secret from all who knew him closely, until this day.

Now Copper had been informed. And now Leopard had beheld, in flesh, not two arm's length away in front of him, The Woman.

Oh, to win her, to retain her – which must be impossible.

Yet to see, to have, and *then* to lose her – also impossible.

In the balance of the gods of balances, his weighted hopes and dreads must lie level tonight.

He had visited various temples about the city, sometimes passing other finalists he recognised, or they him, each man nodding politely, heart hidden yet well understood. He had travelled the white streets for miles, and made his offerings lavish, financed by Copper's generosity. And Copper had said nothing more. And yet, at their parting, Copper's perfect eyes truly had been full of tears, like diamond pearls. Such beauty.

If only Leopard had loved men, as Copper did.

But no. Leopard loved women – loved The Woman.

Nothing else would do.

Even if so many other hundred thousand men had perished, Leopard believed he alone would prevail. He would pass the Ultimate Test, have her and keep her. *Him* she would love. But too, of course, he knew such a thing could never be. He could only become one more shell smashed upon her steely beach. One more dead, useless man.

2. *The Lover*

Unlike the dusk, the dawn was a peach. The moisture of it put out the blazing stars yet lit the lioness of the sun, who leapt up high above the city.

"Oh, Sun Lady, give me my dream. ..."

Leopard climbed the three hundred marble steps to the Palace. He did this alone. For no finalist of the examinations ever made his final journey in company with any others.

Leopard noticed, despite the haze which seemed to envelope him, and the burning turmoil inside him, how the huge vistas of the city fell away and away. Long avenues and dwellings with roofs of carmine, purple or jade-green tiles; squares where fountains restfully played and gold and amber fish swam in pools among the lotuses; gardens of scent trees or sculpted pines and cedars... the world of the city, flawless and mathematical, grew less significant, nearly of no importance. *So death must be*, decided Leopard, strong enough he did not need to pause on the great stair for breath, only now and then to glance back and downward. For death too would be to leave the colourful world of life, ascending to some heavenly plain – or otherwise falling, of course, into some abysmal hell.

His reflections then were quite appropriate.

Who climbed this stair to the Palace of The Woman would indeed afterwards enter a heaven, or a hell.

At the vast doors, guards were absent. Servants drew him in like a welcome guest.

For many hours he was prepared, bathed and massaged, dressed in costly robes, given to eat and drink light and ethereal foods of great nourishment and strange pale wines.

Leopard grew calm through these ministrations, but in the way of one deeply shocked by some colossal calamity or happiness. Even though such an event still lay before him.

Of the other finalists there was never any sign, and no mention. This day, this night, were unique to Leopard, as to each finalist there was given always one such passage of hours in light and darkness.

During which he would undergo the Ultimate Test, and win or lose The Woman, and his life.

In the last recent years, a hundred dead, Copper had told him. Leopard had been amazed there were so few. None had ever won her. None.

In the afternoon, flocks of pink birds flew round and round the upper arches of the Palace where Leopard was now standing. He did not see them.

Before him lay a door of bronze inlaid with gold.

It opened after only half an hour.

No one remained on the gallery save Leopard, and in the room beyond the door, there would be only one. She.

He seemed to move through air, weightless as a ghost. He crossed the threshold. The door drew slowly shut at his back.

The Woman sat on a golden chair, with her feet on a footstool shaped like a crouching elephant.

Her hands rested on her knees. Every finger had a ring of silver or gold and assorted jewels. She wore also a wig of indigo hair, plaited with blue gems.

She seemed neither pleased nor dismayed at the sight of Leopard. He found he could not fathom her expression. But then he was stunned by her wonderfulness, by her female aura and her sexual glory.

He greeted her ritually, and musically spoke aloud for her his four-line poem, then knelt on the patterned floor to await her commands.

Silence snowed heavy as old blossoms.

He smelled incense and perfume from his clothing.

Partly afraid to go on gazing at her, he stared at the floor and the painted animals there began to waver before his eyes.

"Oh, get up," she barked suddenly in a hoarse high little voice. "Rise from your knees before you faint. So many of you do. How I dislike this fainting. Get *up*!"

Unsteadily yet quite gracefully Leopard obeyed her.

"Your poem's thought clever," she said. "That use of the one word *see* three times, then a fourth time but altered. How admirable. I suppose. Well," she said. She reached her small plump hand towards a silver side-dish and selected a sugared plum. She ate it slowly, looking at him.

And her cold-sheened eyes slid over him. *They* were entirely expressionless, like pieces of opaque black slate. Over and over him the slate eyes slid.

How wondrous she was.

Oh gods, he could hardly bear it – and already in a kind of desolation, fearful she did not like him, even so his sex was upright and ready, the most potent weapon of love.

"Come here, then," she said. "Since you must."

He went to her, stood there, standing once again in every sense.

"Well," she said, her shrill voice rather more dull, "take off your garments. Let me see what you are, you – what do they call you? – *Leopard?*" And at this, his name, she laughed, more shrilly, like a flute warped by rain.

And yet *he* laughed as well, vibrantly, loving her mockery even, loving *her*, and burning.

Naked, Leopard was a man like a perfect statue, made of satiny tawny wood polished smooth as glass. Wide-shouldered, slim, every muscle well-developed yet lean. He shone in the icon of his body, which had the form of both fighter and dancer. On his chest the two jewels of his nipples, themselves erect, were the colour of the purest beer. At his groin the short black pelt resembled, in its silkenness, the thick silk hair upon his head. And from his groin also rose his succulent phallus, blushing and firm as the most edible fruit. He had no flaw. And his face too was a marvel. Where his brother Copper was transcendently lovely, Leopard was incandescently handsome. And while his parted lips – he was breathless with terror and lust – revealed the whiteness of his teeth, his large dark eyes revealed the flames of longing, and perhaps some aspect of his soul.

The Woman regarded him with care. Then she pushed herself off her seat and puttered all around him. She observed him front, sidelong and back, scarcely blinking. Were her own eyes pitiless? Like a reptile's? Surely merely a trick of westering light.

She was not tall, The Woman.

The top of her blue-wigged head was level only with Leopard's ribcage.

Behind him still, she grunted.

He was afraid to turn, in case this sound of hers indicated some annoyance – or disappointment – *dismissal.*

He trembled.

Out of one of his luminous eyes a single tear dropped like silvery jasper. Yet even now his eloquent phallic erection stood its ground. His brain and heart might quake; this rose-gold warrior, primed with battle-juice, was too forthright and too wise yet to surrender.

Perhaps – could it be? – *its* instinct, if not the man's, had picked up from the short round woman who patrolled the vicinity of Leopard's splendour, some secret scent of answering desire...?

"Oh," eventually said The Woman, at Leopard's back, "very well, then. Over there. The room behind the lacquer doors."

"Lady – do you mean...?"

"I mean we'll go to the couch and do what's to be done."

And then The Woman turned and waddled away, and Leopard, dipped in fires, followed her.

Among his self-educations, which as an adult had come to include singing, fighting, drama and philosophy, Leopard had not neglected to add the arts of love. He had learned these, as with the others, from the best teachers, who taught him everything at one remove. And he had then practiced all alone, over and over.

"Beware," they had told him. "If *ever* you should enact these things with a real subject – that is with a *woman* – it will be as it is also when you fight. For in love too your lover, male or female, is unwittingly your opponent, striving to overthrow you. But you must subdue your ardour and yourself remain the master. And, whereas in battle you must kill with force and pain, in sex you must kill with delight. *That* death's a very different matter."

And Leopard, his goal – her – had fully learned and then practiced with total dedication.

Now therefore, even as he saw The Woman take off her clothes, even her wig so her hair fell forth, he kept the confidence of a great mage, whose power sweeps in on him at his instruction. The more mighty the odds against self-control, the more mightily controlled now might Leopard be.

So at last, assured, he went to her, and leaning over her, measured and gauged her with his learned hands and fiery eyes.

Three hours was the time Copper had quoted for his companion, Prince Nine.

But Leopard and The Woman entered a timeless zone. Which

in fact lasted the rest of the day, all one night, and some space of the subsequent morning.

Leopard coaxed and seduced and adored and magnified The Woman. With acts not words he laved her body with caresses, used on her a musician's hands, a poet's mouth like velvet, a tongue like streams and feathers and bees, a sexual organ like a magician's tireless and world-ordering wand. Again and again he brought her to the prolonged spasm of ecstasy.

Sometimes even she might emit a squeak of pleasure, though generally she was noiseless in culmination, only the ripples of her loins and belly giving evidence of achievement.

How he loved her.

Her fat, barrel-shaped form with its sallow, coarse, slightly blotchy carapace of skin. Her shapeless breasts. The thin hair that meagrely clad both her head and the heavenly, wide gate between her short legs. He loved her spatulate hands and ridged nails, and the nails of her toes from which the paint had worn, leaving them like ten square and striated rocks. He loved her teeth, which were so charmingly discoloured, and her sugar-sour breath. The ordinary non-profundity of her face. Her arrogance and indifference he loved too, though they lashed him with tragic fear of failure. And her gelid eyes. Even these – though they condemned him, surely.

Ah gods, even in victory over the reluctant, grudging climaxes of her body, Leopard at last heard the lament of approaching defeat.

Long before the night wore out, the red dawn – no longer peach but bloodied wine – he knew in his heart's heart he had not won her. And never could. None could.

None.

3. The Reject

All that day-night-day, Copper paced his apartment.

It comprised three rooms and a private courtyard on the roof. He went from one area to another, climbing up, descending, walking, turning. Now and then he touched something. A small statue of a dancing lion, a cup of black onyx, a little dagger of twisted wood Leopard had carved and given him when Copper was only five years old.

Copper wept. Chided himself and blotted up his tears. Cursed Fate and The Woman, cursed life and the world. Flung himself in a chair, wrote down his thoughts without coherence, got up and

344

paced again, wept again, chided and blotted and cursed – again. Again.

Gods knew, if only Leopard had loved only men. There were male men who did so. Some of Copper's nicest 'lads' were like that, and those like Copper, if not pretty enough to make their way, came to such gallants for solace. One indeed had married a male man from Copper's wine-house, and they had lived happy now three whole years.

But Leopard was only Man.

So many men, despite dalliances with their own gender, were only – Men.

And so: The Woman of the Crimson City.

Copper knew, despite his hopes and wishes, and Leopard's glamour and virtue, that The Woman would not want him for long. She had never wanted any of the ones who devoted their dreams to her and then passed all the required examinations but one. For to meet and make love with The Woman was the Ultimate Test. No man had ever passed it. Evidently. Or she would not be there still, hung like an over-ripe yellow fruit, cruel and evil with her thorns, on the tree of human longing.

How the gods must hate mankind, to do this to them.

The hours ground away under Copper's pacing, weeping and cursing.

About sun fall, the man he had sent to watch the Palace's Lower Gate bounded up Copper's stair and beat on the door.

"What's happened, Heron?"

But Heron was crying. His tears spoke loudly, in an uncouth bellow.

"So, then," said Copper, gripping in his own emotion, "did he emerge from the Gate?"

"Yes, oh yes – oh gods, I've seen old gentlemen whose white beards brushed the earth, whose backs were humped with age like a camel's – and they walked more sprightly than your brother, lovely Leopard."

"Where did he take himself?"

"Towards the bank of the river…"

"And…?"

"And my companion, Lamplit, our best runner as you know, sped after and caught him. Then Tomorrow, my other friend from next door, ran up too. They took hold of him and are bringing him here now. But slowly. He can barely move, Copper Coin."

Copper whispered a curse then that curled up the air of the apartment. The sun too seemed to wither in it and threw herself off over the precipice of the horizon. Dusk veiled everything. Nightingales and tweet-birds sang from the tall scent tree outside.

One more hour later, when the sky was black and the bright windows and rosy lanterns of the city showed the path, Lamplit and Tomorrow helped Leopard into Copper's reception chamber.

"Drink this."

"Nothing. Please. Give me nothing."

"Darling Leopard. It's myself offers the drink. Look. Do you see me? Your brother. "

"I see you, dear. But take the cup away. The dead need no food, no water."

Finally, persuaded to one sip, the kindly soporific in the drink took its effect.

Leopard was laid on the second bed, his head on pillows of silk.

But even sleeping, his face was old, and ruinous. He looked like a man who must soon die.

The physician came. This doctor was of high quality and learning, but once Copper told him why Leopard was distressed and ill the physician bowed his head. "I shall do whatever I am able. But I also had a brother once. This was thirteen years ago.

He too went after The Woman and won through to her. When she cast him out he lived only two months. We watched him night and day in case he tried to poison or hang himself. But in the end, without assistance of bane or rope or blade, he simply died. It was through his death I set myself to learn medicine, to understand the windings of the human intellect. But I doubt I can help you, or your brother."

"She's vilely wicked," said Copper, "The Woman. A demoness sent up from the hells to destroy us."

"Perhaps," said the physician.

Then Leopard woke up and the physician set to work on him. Seven days, and the nights between them, trudged by.

Then seven more.

Copper went on with his usual duties but refused all those clients he normally had pleasure with. He explained to them privately that he could experience no pleasure at this time. Only

Prince Nine was permitted to arrive frequently, and he simply to talk with Copper, gratis, to steady him and try to ease his sorrow.

In the end Leopard began to be seen. He would walk in the courtyard or sit there quietly on his own. At evening, sometimes, he would dine at the communal table of the wine-house, if not in Copper's apartment.

Regular customers treated him with care, and with respect and sympathy. If they were jealous of his having been a finalist, and briefly winning The Woman and lying with her, they curbed themselves. Decidedly, they could see where his moment of success had afterwards dragged and abandoned him. He seemed quite soulless. He seemed part dead.

One evening a newcomer entered the wine-house and sat down at the main table. He was an older man, of fine physical appearance, and perhaps a philosopher.

He spoke directly to Leopard, in an actor's clear voice. "So, you are the unlucky fellow who fucked the great bitch in the Palace?" he said.

Instantly silence deafened the room.

Heron, who had been eating, got up without a word and went straight to knock at Copper's door, despite the fact Copper was just then entertaining a prince of the High Family of the Ninety-Two.

Leopard however raised his head and looked at the newcomer. "I am he. But she is not a bitch. She is beautiful, and by me beloved, and will be so until the day of my ending."

"Very well," agreed the philosopher, if so he was. "Very well. Maybe she is a bitch since only circumstances have made her one. As also time has made her older and fatter. But I think a snake gave her such cold eyes."

Leopard lowered his gaze. He did not reply.

The philosopher went on, in his clear and reasonable voice, "Surely you, or some of you here at the very least, must understand why men venerate and think such a creature wonderful?"

A man cried out: "Because she is *The Woman.*"

"Just so," said the philosopher. "The *only* woman. That is," he amended, "the only known woman yet living in our city, or in the existing world, who has not yet died of the excessive bearing of male children or grown into an ancient hag."

A vast sigh, nearly a groan, curdled from the room-full of men. It passed on into the courtyard, where the other men had, many of

them, risen and come to see who spoke such words. It drifted up
to balconies of the wine-house and surrounding buildings and was
echoed back from them. It fled along the white streets and found
some kind of other echo always there, in every masculine throat, in
every masculine mind. For there were only men in the Crimson
City, as the philosopher had stated. Men who were feminine or men
who were male, and some who were gifted with both states, and
those who were young or old. Or there were a few old, old women
who had somehow survived relentless decades of child-bearing,
scorned and sworn at on every occasion, which had been by now
every occasion without exception, that they had produced, rather
than a daughter, yet another son.

Beyond the Crimson City, did the curdling echo of the groan
strike out even there, like a cold fist beating on the surface of a cold
metal gong, and the reverberation unfurling, on and on? Probably
so. For in all the land about, in the towns and villages, in the farthest
places, still there were only the differing types of men, male men
and female men, or men of both persuasions, and young men, and
old men, and dead men in graves with death-stones over them like
white fallen pieces of the lonely masculine moon.

And even the hags maybe heard the sigh, the groan. Even the
dead women in their own graves that bore each the symbol of the
barren blazing sun, the dead women burned away by bearing only
men.

While outside the borders of this land, the other lands. All the
same. All, all, the same.

For some years ago, about the time that the mother of Leopard
and Copper Coin had herself died, the very last of all the women
yet able to conceive a child, had perished.

With the last of such deaths, all chance of change died too.

And now there were only the men and the hags. And the female
sun. And She. The Woman in the Palace.

When Copper tore down the stair, Prince Ninety-Two deserted
above in the upper rooms, it was Tomorrow who ran quickly and
caught hold of him.

"Stay, Copper – stay, stay – look there. Do you see?"

And Copper halted, and his pale face went more pale and his
eyes widened.

For there Leopard was, held in the arms of an unknown

348

newcomer to the house, a man neither old nor young, but handsome and well-dressed, perhaps a philosopher, and with an actor's voice. Leopard was weeping his heart out as since returning here he had not wept.

And the philosopher raised his face and glancing at Copper said, softly, "Don't fear it. I am his brother too, his brother in this most bleak of miseries. For I also, long before, was a finalist in the Crimson City. I also won The Woman, lay with her, lost her, failed at the Ultimate Test. A man who wandered in an earthly hell some while. But sense came back to me, and that hell faded. I lived. As Leopard may live. There is more to life than love. I am the proof, am I not, that not all men die who fail with her."

Copper felt his heart clutch, as if a dagger had gone into it. For he sensed that here at last might be the single other man in all the world who could give back to Leopard a reason for existence. And passionate hope had stabbed at Copper's heart, and bitter envy had cloven it.

"Do what you must," said Copper. And offered the stranger his most beautiful and generous smile.

Then he kissed his brother on one temple and left him in the keeping of the unknown man. And in the hands of the gods too, where all things may lie, whether they wish it or not.

4. *The Woman*

High above the terraced streets, the squares and courtyards and gardens, The Woman stood in a long room without a single window, lit only by tall lamps in the shape of flowers. She wore a plain garment, her hair tied back in a knot. She was barefoot on the cool painted floor. Once pink birds had sung here. But one day she had opened a door and let them go free. They had never entirely forsaken her. They still flew about the upper arches and nested in the roofs. How wonderful, she had always thought, The Woman, their magical power of flight.

How old was she when first they brought her here? Quite young, she believed. Five, seven?

She had never been certain of her age.

She was the first and last daughter of a peasant woman called This Fern.

This Fern had birthed The Woman, and been made the heroine of her village, for only recently that year the otherwise last known female child, a girl of eleven years, had died in the far north, of stomach trouble.

But This Fern also soon died, after a bear attacked her at the edge of the forest. Everyone hunted the bear, to kill it, but it was gone, and so of course was This Fern. The Woman had only been two years old then. She could not remember her mother, though they had given her her mother's possessions, her festival robe and her festival shoes, her wooden comb and earrings of tin, and one of her teeth, which had been knocked from her mouth ages before and preserved in a small black box.

These artifacts The Woman still possessed. Now she kept them in a chest of carved and perfumed cedar-wood inlaid with silver, and with a ruby on its clasp.

Men in authority had brought The Woman to the Crimson City. In the Palace she was trained, vigorously and often unkindly, to be a woman. That is, an important woman. That is, The Only Woman.

When, at the age of fifteen, she had fallen in love, or fancied she had done so, with one of her malely inclined tutors, he was beaten almost to death and exiled from the city.

His own feelings she never learned.

Probably he was as crazily infatuated as she.

But she was never sure, nor if he recovered from the beating and the exile.

At sixteen she began to be shown in the city.

Then, seeing young men sometimes of extraordinary attractions, gazing at, or fainting at the sight of her, she herself often lost her heart.

But she had been thoroughly lessoned by then in her role, and theirs. Since seemingly – and soon irrevocably and definitely – she was the last young human of her gender – only those with the highest qualities of looks and skills would ever be allowed to approach her.

During this era, The Woman still had one female attendant, a hag who had been almost seventy when The Woman first met her.

The hag, Ochre, was never very polite and never pleasant to her charge, let alone affectionate. The Woman supposed Ochre had been selected for her unappealing acidity because, after all, Ochre was ancient, all of her kind were by then, and must soon die. Bereavement of her would therefore be less distressing.

But the hag was presently caught anyway mixing ground glass into The Woman's food.

Taken off to be stoned somewhere or other below the Palace, Ochre screeched that The Woman was a demoness, a curse not a blessing on the city. After this, inevitably, no further hags served in the Palace.

Later, when the first waves of lovers, having passed spectacularly well in the examinations, began to approach The Woman and she, as instructed, made love with them – initially loathing the act, which hurt her and also seemed grotesque – another unfortunate thing was discovered. The Woman did not ever conceive. Since tests had been made as well on the semen of all the young male lovers, and it was both wholesome and fertile, the fault must lie with The Woman's body. But as she was The Woman, and the last woman of all women, it was concluded it could not be her fault, even after several quite horrible procedures to which she was subjected in order to 'awake' her womb, proved useless. A general decision asserted that the wicked hag Ochre, prior to the episode with the glass, had already succeeded in somehow poisoning The Woman and so negating her reproductive knack.

With maturity The Woman learned to enjoy the sexual act.

In the beginning, she herself read manuals of love she had been taught to read – and practiced such arts with the waves of lovers. But their frenzies of joy and gratitude frightened her.

She ceased to be active during sex, even restricting her cries at climax, for a similar reason.

At the start she had continued to fall in love and to wish to make a permanent union with this man or that.

But in the Palace the men in authority, who by that time grew old themselves, male hags who frequently went absent in death, had told her she might *never* choose any man above another. To choose one over all the rest would doubtless see him murdered. At best the city would riot and lose its collective mind.

Originally it seemed, the rite of the examinations to find the best, and the making of love between that best and herself, had been organised in the hope of children. Some of which, if the gods were tender, might be daughters.

But of course Ochre, or something or other, had forestalled that plan.

Now therefore the Woman's only value was in her female presence, which must at intervals be revealed, offered and *given* to occasional males.

Until her own demise, this was all The Woman was to be for.

A vision, a goal, a sop. And a method of the most vicious rejection.

Partly she was to represent hope, still, and partly she was to teach that all women were worthless, evil, thus unregrettable. While the dying out of the human race, which now almost without a doubt was unavoidable, could be blamed on the female kind. Also too, perhaps, she was to demonstrate that death, and the death of humanity, might be no bad thing.

In these elements she was like a goddess.

For gods were cruel. They made hells as well as heavens, and all the earthly ills.

Having walked about for a while in the restful windowless room, The Woman sat down on an ivory bench.

She drank a little apricot wine.

She ate a sugar biscuit.

The enormous and never-ending depression that now informed most of her days, and usually sleepless nights, came crouching up the floor and rubbed its flank against her consciousness.

Listlessly, resistlessly, she greeted it.

She did not want the riches of the Palace, nor the extreme – unreal – power she had been given. She did not really even want sex any more, let alone the intermittent torrents of young men who came to her, singing poetry, caressing and coaxing, their delicious kisses less than the momentary sweetness of a biscuit.

She might love none. She loved none.

She might choose none. She chose none.

She sent them away, and they threw themselves in the river and drowned, or slit open their veins or swallowed venom.

Oh, she did not *dare* give her heart now to any man. She would be loving a ghost. A thousand ghosts. Death itself.

So. The Woman did not want wealth or sex or ecstasy or worship or love.

Was there anything then that she wanted, longed for?
Yes. Yes.

The Woman wanted her mother. Sometimes even The Woman would daydream that This Fern, fresh up from her grave, would walk into the room. She would not be phantom, nor skeleton. She would not even be old. No, no, This Fern would be about The Woman's own age. Whatever age that was.

But it was more than that, of course. Not only that she wanted the mother she had never known. It was *women* – Woman – The Woman wanted. Not for sexual love, never that. But ... to talk to. To laugh with. To be with. Oh gods, women about her, easy and familiar, different and the same. Desire? Entirely. The desire of the lonely one for its other self. Here in the Palace high above the Crimson City and the world, The Woman sat on her bench of bone, pining, lamenting, slowly dying – for her own kind.

Gods who see me
When her I see,
See I have become
As a seeing god.

Translated from the poem
by Leopard

353

About the Author

Tanith Lee (1947-2015) was born in London. Because her parents were professional dancers (ballroom, Latin American) and had to live where the work was, she attended a number of truly terrible schools, and didn't learn to read – she was also dyslectic – until almost age 8. And then only because her father taught her. This opened the world of books to her, and by 9 she was writing. After much better education at a grammar school, she went on to work in a library. This was followed by various other jobs – shop assistant, waitress, clerk – plus a year at art college when she was 25-26. In 1974, her career as a writer was launched, when DAW Books of America, under the leadership of Donald A. Wollheim, bought and published *The Birthgrave*, and thereafter 26 of her novels and collections.

Tanith was presented with a Lifetime Achievement Award in 2013, at World Fantasycon in Brighton. During her lifetime, she also received the World Horror Convention Grand Master Award, as well as the August Derleth Award and the World Fantasy Award for short fiction (twice).

In 1992, she married the writer-artist-photographer John Kaiine, her partner since 1987. They lived on the Sussex Weald, near the sea, in a house full of books and plants, and never without feline companions. She died at home in May 2015, after a long illness, continuing to work until a couple of weeks before her death.

Throughout her life, Tanith wrote around 100 books, and over 300 short stories. 4 of her radio plays were broadcast by the BBC; she also wrote 2 episodes (*Sarcophagus* and *Sand*) for the TV series *Blake's 7*. Her stories were read regularly on Radio 4 Extra. She was an inspiration to a generation of writers and her work was enormously influential within genre fiction – as it continues to be. She wrote in many styles, within and across many genres, including Horror, SF and Fantasy, Historical, Detective, Contemporary-Psychological, Children and Young Adult. Her preoccupation, though, was always people.

Publishing History of the Stories

(from printed publications in the English language)

Strindberg's Ghost Sonata – *The Ghost Quartet*, ed. by Marvin Kaye, TOR, 2008

Among the Leaves so Green – *The Green Man: Tales from the Mythic Forest*, ed. by Ellen Datlow & Terri Windling, Viking, 2002

Beauty is the Beast – *American Fantasy. Vol 2 No 1*, Fall 1986; *The Year's Best Fantasy Stories: 13*, ed. by Arthur W. Saha, 1987

Ceres Passing – *Hidden Turnings: A Collection of Stories Through Time and Space*, ed. by Dianna Wynne Jones, Methuen Children's Books, 1989

Cold Spell – *Young Winter's Tales 7*, ed. by Marni Hodgkin, Macmillan, 1976

Elvenbrood – *The Faery Reel: Tales from The Twilight Realm*, ed. by Ellen Datlow & Terri Windling, Viking, 2004; *The Year's Best Fantasy 5*, ed. by David G. Hartwell & Kathryn Cramer, 2005

Felidis – *Under My Hat: Tales from The Cauldron*, ed. by Jonathan Strahan, Random House, 2012

Goldenhair – *Fantasy Macabre, No 1*, September 1980

Herowhine – *Anduril. No 7*, February 1979

In the Balance – *Swords Against Darkness III*, ed. by Andrew J. Offutt, Zebra Books, 1978; *The Year's Best Fantasy Stories: 5*, ed by Lin Carter, DAW Books, 1980

Iron City – original to this collection, written in 1987.

Last Drink Bird Head – *Ministry of Whimsy*, ed. by Ann and Jeff Vandermeer 2009

The Origin of Snow (A Story of the Flat Earth) – this story appeared on Tanith Lee's now defunct web site in 2002

The Pain of Glass (A Story of the Flat Earth) – *Clockwork Phoenix 2: More Tales of Beauty and Strangeness*, ed. by Mike Allen, Norilana Books, 2009

Persian Eyes – *DAW 30th Anniversary: Fantasy*, ed. by Elizabeth R. Wollheim and Sheila E. Gilbertby, DAW Books, 2002; *The Year's Best Fantasy 3*, ed. by David G. Hartwell and Katharine Cramer Eos, 2003

Question a Stone – *The Feathered Edge: Tales of Magic, Love and Daring*, ed. by Deborah J. Ross, Sky Warrior Book Publishing, 2012

A Tower of Arkrondurl – *Legends: Stories in Honour of David Gemmell*, ed. by Ian Whates, NewCon Press, 2013

Two Lions, a Witch and the War-Robe – *Swords and Dark Magic: The New Sword and Sorcery*, ed. by Jonathan Strahan & Lou Anders, Harper Collins, 2010

The Three Brides of Hamid-Dar – *Arabesques 2*, ed. by Susan Schwarz, Avon, 1989

The Woman – *Clockwork Phoenix: Tales of Beauty and Strangeness*, ed. by Mike Allen, Norilana Books, 2008

Books by Tanith Lee

Series

The Birthgrave Trilogy (The Birthgrave; Vazkor, son of Vazkor [published as Shadowfire in the UK], Quest for the White Witch)

The Blood Opera Sequence (Dark Dance; Personal Darkness; Darkness, I)

The Flat Earth Opus (Night's Master; Death's Master; Delusion's Master; Delirium's Mistress; Night's Sorceries)

The Lionwolf Trilogy (Cast a Bright Shadow; Here in Cold Hell; No Flame But Mine)

The Paradys Quartet (The Book of the Damned; The Book of the Beast; The Book of the Dead; The Book of the Mad)

The Venus Quartet (Faces Under Water; Saint Fire; A Bed of Earth; Venus Preserved)

The Vis Trilogy (The Storm Lord; Anackire; The White Serpent)

The FOUR-Bee Series (Don't Bite the Sun; Drinking Sapphire Wine)

The S.I.L.V.E.R. Series (Silver Metal Lover; Metallic Love)

Novels and Novellas

34

The Blood of Roses

Companions on the Road

Days of Grass

Death of the Day

Electric Forest

Elephantasm

Eva Fairdeath

The Gods Are Thirsty

Kill the Dead

Heart-Beast

A Heroine of the World

Louisa the Poisoner

Lycanthia

Madame Two Swords

Mortal Suns

Reigning Cats and Dogs

Sabella

Sung in Shadow

Vivia

Volkhavaar

When the Lights Go Out
White as Snow
The Winter Players

Young Adult and Children's Fiction

Animal Castle (picture book)
The Castle of Dark
The Claidi Journals (Law of the Wolf Tower; Wolf Star Rise,
Queen of the Wolves, Wolf Wing)
The Dragon Hoard
East of Midnight
The Piratica Novels (Piratica 1; Piratica 2; Piratica 3)
Prince on a White Horse
Princess Hynchatti and Other Surprises
Shon the Taken
The Unicorn Trilogy (Black Unicorn; Gold Unicorn; Red Unicorn)
The Voyage of the Bassett: Islands in the Sky

Story Collections

Blood 20
Cold Grey Stones
Colder Greyer Stones
Cyrion
Dancing in the Fire
Disturbed by Her Song
Dreams of Dark and Light
Fatal Women
Forests of the Night
The Gorgon
Hunting the Shadows
Nightshades
Phantasya
Red as Blood – Tales from the Sisters Grimmer
Redder Than Blood
Sounds and Furies
Tamastara, or the Indian Nights
Space is Just a Starry Night
Tempting the Gods
Unsilent Night
Women as Demons

Tanith Lee Titles Published by Immanion Press

The Colouring Book Series

Cruel Pink
Greyglass
To Indigo
Ivoria
Killing Violets
L'Amber
Turquoiselle

The Blood Opera Sequence

Dark Dance
Personal Darkness
Darkness, I

Novels and Novellas

34
Ghosteria Volume 2: The Novel: Zircons May Be Mistaken
Madame Two Swords

Vivia

Collections

Animate Objects
A Different City
Ghosteria Volume 1: The Stories
Legenda Maris
The Weird Tales of Tanith Lee
Venus Burning: Realms: Collected Short Stories from 'Realms of Fantasy'

Of Interest to Tanith Lee Enthusiasts…

Night's Nieces

This anthology is a tribute to Tanith Lee, comprising short stories written shortly after her death by some of her writer friends to whom Tanith was a profound influence and inspiration: Storm Constantine, Cecilia Dart-Thornton, Vera Nazarian, Sarah Singleton, Kari Sperring, Sam Stone, Freda Warrington and Liz Williams. With an introduction by Tanith's husband, the artist John Käine. Illustrated throughout by the contributors and with photographs from Tanith Lee's personal collection.

IMMANION PRESS
Purveyors of Speculative Fiction

Venus Burning: Realms by Tanith Lee

Tanith Lee wrote 15 stories for the acclaimed *Realms of Fantasy* magazine. This book collects all the stories in one volume for the first time, some of which only ever appeared in the magazine so will be new to some of Tanith's fans. These tales are among her best work, in which she takes myth and fairy tale tropes and turns them on their heads. Lush and lyrical, deep and literary, Tanith Lee created fresh poignant tales from familiar archetypes.
ISBN 978-1-907737-88-6, £11.99, $17.50 pbk

A Raven Bound with Lilies by Storm Constantine

The Wraeththu have captivated readers for three decades. This anthology of 15 tales collects all the published Wraeththu short stories into one volume, and also includes extra material, including the author's first explorations of the androgynous race. The tales range from the 'creation story' *Paragenesis*, through the bloody, brutal rise of the earliest tribes, and on into a future, where strange mutations are starting to emerge from hidden corners of the earth.
ISBN: 978-1-907737-80-0 £11.99, $15.50 pbk

Voices of the Silicon Beyond by E. S. Wynn

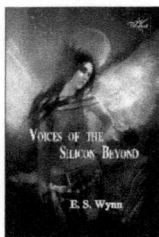

Vaetta is not human, but far more than a mere robot. Her world is overcrowded, it resources at breaking point. The humans who govern this parallel Earth need a solution to these problems. Then a strange, androgynous visitor appears from an inexplicable portal to another world, also seeking help. His world is sparsely populated, following the demise of humankind and the rise of a civilization known as Wraeththu. Vaetta is chosen to scout this new world and begin preparations for invasion, but what waits for her on the other side of the portal doesn't make sense to her, until a fatal meeting through which she discovers a history with far-reaching implications covering all realities. (A novel set in Storm Constantine's Wraeththu Mythos.)
ISBN: 978-1-907737-97-8, £9.99, $14.99 pbk

http://www.immanion-press.com
info@immanion-press.com

TANITH LEE FROM IMMANION PRESS

We are committed to republishing Tanith Lee's long out of print or rare to find novels. The *Blood Opera Sequence* is Tanith's unique take on the vampire myth. If the Scarabae family are indeed vampires – and no one knows for sure – you'll find no others like them in literature or on film.

Dark Dance

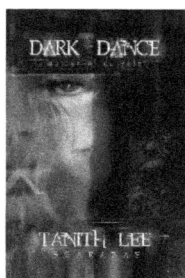

After her mother's death, Rachaela is stalked by agents of the mysterious Scarabae family. Despite her instincts to keep away from the Scarabae, she ultimately relents and is taken to the rambling, isolated house near the sea, where they live in baroque seclusion. The fading splendour of the house closes around Rachaela like a stifling womb, and she's given no explanation for the ménage of bizarre oldsters, who are like creatures from an earlier age, and certainly not normal. Is there something supernatural to the Scarabae, or are they merely lost in delusion? ISBN 978-1-907737-85-5 pbk £12.99

Personal Darkness

The Scarabae, an unconventional and eccentric family, who might not be entirely human, have been forced to leave their reclusive home in a remote part of England. Some are dead at the hands of a child created through incest with the purpose of repopulating this ageing branch of the family. Rachaela trails listlessly with the survivors of the Scarabae. She is one of them but still can't feel that she is. The Scarabae relocate to London, and roost within a baroque old mansion. Here, they lick their wounds, but bizarrely appear to be growing younger and mysterious deaths begin to mount up in the city. ISBN 978-1-907737-86-2 pbk £12.99

Darkness I

Anna is no ordinary girl. Her parents and the other Scarabae don't know that another member of the family has become aware of her – the father of them all, the almost mythical Cain, who lives apart from the world in a frozen wasteland, where's he's constructed a bizarre reproduction of Ancient Egypt within a pyramid of ice. He wants not only Anna, but other children he believes are reincarnations of people from the past – the earliest times of the family. But what does he want them for? Soon, the kidnappings begin... ISBN 978-1-907737-95-4 pbk £12.99

http://www.immanion-press.com

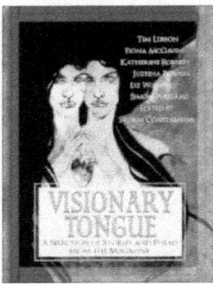

CPSIA information can be obtained
at www.ICGtesting.com
Printed in the USA
BVHW030912180419
545898BV00001B/120/P